head over wheels

Also by Leonie Mack

My Christmas Number One
Italy Ever After
A Match Made In Venice
We'll Always Have Venice
Twenty-One Nights in Paris
Snow Days With You
A Taste of Italian Sunshine
A Wedding in the Sun
In Italy For Love

Writing as Lilo Moore

Beer Fest
Berlin Calling

head over wheels

LEONIE MACK

Bedford Square
Publishers

First published in the United Kingdom in 2025 by
Bedford Square Publishers Ltd,
London, UK

bedfordsquarepublishers.co.uk
@bedsqpublishers

ISBN
978-1-83501-242-0 (Paperback)
978-1-83501-243-7 (eBook)

2 4 6 8 10 9 7 5 3 1

Typeset by Palimpsest Book Production Limited, Falkirk, Stirlingshire

Printed in Great Britain by CPI Group (UK) Ltd, Croydon CR0 4YY

The manufacturer's authorised representative in the EU for product safety is Easy
Access System Europe, Mustamäe tee 50, 10621 Tallinn, Estonia
gpsr.requests@easproject.com

For all women and girls who participate in sport in any form, at any level, especially those women who join in despite personal and societal obstacles. We can be strong.

LoonieDunes: I'm going to do some intervals. You around?

Folklore99: Just having breakfast, but make it a time trial and I'll consider it.

LoonieDunes: You just want to beat me, now you're back to full strength. I didn't know how good you were when we first started.

Folklore99: It's not my fault you're shit at time trials.

LoonieDunes: I've been neglecting my intervals, actually. They're more fun with you.

Folklore99: Misery loves company? If we listen to Taylor Swift, I'll consider intervals. If you make me listen to any more Muse, I'm going to get depressed.

LoonieDunes: It's not depressing, just a little dystopian.

Folklore99: You secretly love Taylor.

LoonieDunes: Whatever you want to tell yourself. See you in a few minutes?

Folklore99: Give me half an hour to get rid of my mum. I don't know why she's suddenly so curious about Zpeed.

LoonieDunes: Maybe she wants to start training ;-)

07:31

LoonieDunes: Ready to bring it? I'm just connecting my headset.

07:33

LoonieDunes: You there?

07:48

LoonieDunes: Folklore?

The user you are trying to contact does not exist. Please check the username and try again.

Chapter 1

Lori

I could pinpoint the exact moment my luck turned.

It was a morning at the end of November, in the hills around Girona, the first day of pre-season training camp – my first day back in Europe after three long months of recovery. There wasn't a cloud in the sky, the crisp autumn air was the perfect temperature for cycling and I was back on the road, not the smallest suspicion of what was about to hit me.

Hurtling down my favourite set of wild hairpins in the high, scrubby hills, I hunched into position for the next sharp curve with a grin twisting my lips. I leaned in and took the corner at speed but, before I could straighten up, something flew in my face – something big and bulging and made of plastic. Panicking and flinging it away with both hands, I lost balance and skidded into the dirt.

I came down – hard – gravel gouging my hip and tearing up my shorts. With a crunch I came to a stop in the rocks by the side of the track.

'Fuck!' emerged from my mouth on my next heavy breath, as I blinked back shock. Pain burned up my back and flared out, followed by stinging at my hip and an ache in my knee. But, instead of swelling to a throb that suggested something was very wrong with my body – a feeling I knew well – the discomfort ebbed and I stared up at the wispy sky framed by dark evergreen oaks.

Lifting my head gingerly, I tugged off my protective sunglasses and peered to my left, glimpsing the prone form of another cyclist, tangled up in his bike. Yep, I hadn't imagined it. It appeared we'd been taken out by a blow-up doll.

It was all her fault, the empty-eyed, pouty-lipped caricature of a woman bobbing rather pitifully in the breeze.

If this had been the Giro d'Italia or the Tour de France, it might not have been surprising. I'd seen everything along the side of the course, from fans in gorilla suits to someone dressed as the Grim Reaper, complete with a rubber scythe he'd held out in front of the peloton.

But we weren't on the Alpe d'Huez and the only spectators were the birds of prey playing in the updraught – and the blow-up doll that some idiot had filled with helium and attached to the other guy's bike, along with a bunch of balloons.

Seeing the familiar blue and orange of the other guy's jersey, I suspected I knew the idiot in question.

My knee twinged when I hauled myself to my feet. I'd ripped a hole in my shorts and could look forward to picking some gravel out of my skin when we got back but I was still in one piece. I'd had injuries like this a hundred times in my career – along with knocked-out teeth and assorted broken bones. But the stab of fear was new, as was the urge to clutch my back even though the action didn't have the slightest effect on my lingering nerve pain – the pain that the physio assured me was only in my head, although it still fucking hurt.

Pain, fear… I couldn't afford either of them.

Propping my hands on my thighs and slowing my breathing, I imagined the headlines: *Lori Gallagher's return to road racing after catastrophic injury scuppered during training by a rogue sex doll*. But my body held and I stomped over to check on my fellow victim, giving the doll a punch in the face that relieved a good portion of my frustration.

'Are you alive?'

'That depends on whether you're the angel of death,' the other rider groaned in response.

A ripple of awareness tingled across my skin. *That voice*. A gamut of emotions clamoured for my attention and it took me a second to whack them all back in their holes. I couldn't afford guilt either – or that warm, fuzzy thing that felt like a pleasant version of indigestion, both of which I associated with my online friend – my *former* online friend.

I obviously didn't have my head in the game if a hint of a French accent – not exactly unusual for a World Team cyclist – took me right back to my parents' basement gym in Melbourne, where I'd tried to rebuild myself, forcing my body to heal before my career fell off a cliff the way my mum always warned me it would if I didn't focus.

I'd heard a similar accent over my headset nearly every day for weeks, making life bearable as I got back in shape on the home trainer, as a blessedly anonymous user of the Zpeed multiplayer simulation game. The voice had belonged to an equally anonymous training partner, who called himself LoonieDunes – presumably something to do with the 'Loonie', the Canadian dollar – and made poor-taste jokes remarkably like the one I'd just heard.

'I'm not any kind of angel,' I snapped. 'Are you hurt?'

He rubbed a gloved hand over his face and extricated his legs from his sleek carbon-fibre bike – the same model as mine, but with a larger frame. 'Just my pride,' he muttered, rising gingerly into a sitting position. His winter training jersey was covered in dust, but couldn't hide the breadth of a nice pair of shoulders, all muscle and sinew, and the lean, tight torso of a pro cyclist. Catching sight of the floating blow-up doll, his Adam's apple bobbed in a gulp as he tugged off his helmet. 'Yes, my pride is… in need of reanimation.'

Damn it, even his choice of words reminded me of LoonieDunes and his penchant for sci-fi films. I'd eventually decided he was either a gangly teenager or a 50-year-old man with six fingers and too many teeth. Either could well have been true as he was only ever an avatar to me.

An avatar I'd left behind, along with my own injury-plagued online persona, Folklore99. When I'd needed to be Lori 'Top Gun' Gallagher, Australian champion, again, I'd killed her off – and when Mum had started asking me too many questions about my recovery and why I was using Zpeed so much. She'd pressed me for answers one morning at breakfast and I'd panicked and shut it all down. She would have freaked if she'd seen my chat history with LoonieDunes – the doubts and the questioning.

This guy, evidently a new recruit in the men's team, was neither a teenager nor an old man. It was difficult to judge his age, with his pink cheeks and bright eyes, but he was cute. He had thick, brown hair that was a touch too long, with a sweaty tuft sweeping his high forehead. They were nice eyes, currently trying not to look at me for too long – the colour of meadow honey.

I was used to those furtive glances. A female athlete was some kind of holy grail for a lot of men and I even had slightly too much in the boob department to be aerodynamic – a fact that bothered me every time I tried to find a comfortable sports bra that didn't require double-jointed elbows to get into.

'Did my brother do this?' I flicked at the strings holding the blow-up doll and the balloons onto the seat tube of his bike. His wary look was all the answer I needed. 'Farking idiot,' I mumbled.

Colin Gallagher, lead rider with the men's team, joker, backslapper, all-round big guy – and my younger brother by 21 months and a shit-ton of maturity – pulled stunts like this every year and, for reasons that remained mysterious to me, no one ever stood up to him.

'Why did you ride off like this? Why didn't you just release her back into the wild? Is this the reason you're so far behind the men's bunch?'

He swallowed, now watching me with his mouth open. I nearly blushed, damn it. I was built to win races, not deprive men of speech, but that side-effect felt kind of good that day. His gaze darting to my mouth felt good.

Clearing his throat, he said, 'I took a shortcut. I thought it would be better to let Colin have his fun, but arrive back at the hotel at the same time.'

I was impressed by his attitude. Since I didn't recognise his face, I assumed he was a domestique, a support rider, and not a big name, but he had some spirit – and a really nice, strong jaw. And those eyes... Crap, I was not here for nice eyes.

'Besides,' he continued, 'I felt sorry for her.' He reached one lean arm up to give the doll a pat on the bum.

With a huff, I studied the vacant expression on the doll's face, the exaggerated lips that reminded me of a vacuum cleaner. Surprisingly, I felt sorry for her as well – not for her, exactly, but for the tangled mess of desire and ego and vulnerability that was sex. 'You bonded with her?'

He choked out an inarticulate response. With a beleaguered sigh, I held out my gloved hand to him and, after a moment's hesitation, he grasped it and allowed me to help him up.

'Do you think your bike's okay? Are the men coming down from la Mare de Déu?'

He nodded as he picked up his bike and inspected it

carefully, hefting the frame with one arm and spinning the wheels. 'Looks okay.'

'Good, then let's go!' Grabbing my bike, I threw my leg over the seat and looked back just in time to catch him staring at my butt.

'What was that?' he asked, his eyes whipping back to mine and blinking rapidly.

'I said, let's go! Let's get down and I'll draft you back to the others.'

'You will?' His voice was high and breathy and boy, it reminded me of the few times I'd given poor Loonie a compliment and he'd reacted as though I'd offered him a medal.

I didn't miss my online training partner – I couldn't. We'd only known each other about ten weeks and he was nothing more than a voice in my ear. It was just that I'd been in a weakened state after all the surgery and he'd always been there and it was a good thing I'd severed that connection, if I was still thinking about him so much.

'I don't know you from a bar of French soap, but I'll help you get one up over my brother.'

'Soap?' Even the doubtful version of his smile was electric.

'Do you want my help or not?'

'Yes, absolutely.'

'Then hop on your bike and let's go, French soap.'

'Yes, sir,' he muttered, grasping his handlebars to follow me, a small smile on his lips. 'But it's Belgian soap,' he continued drily as we pushed off and headed for the next curve.

I snorted a laugh. Thank fuck it wasn't Canadian soap.

'Are you all right?' he asked. 'You're bleeding.'

'Are you offering first aid?' I called back. 'I've had worse. Let's just get back down to the hotel.'

'What are you doing up here alone anyway?'

Setting my jaw, I just said, 'I prefer to warm up on my own.' So I didn't show weakness in front of the rest of the team. 'Lucky for you!'

He remained mercifully silent while we negotiated the gravel and the hairpins. When we returned to the road, I gripped the drop bars and set a high pace, ignoring the sting of the grazes on my thigh. 'See if you can keep up!'

When I glanced back, he had a wide grin on his face, with long dimples above that square jaw, looking cute and utterly ridiculous, with a blow-up doll and a bunch of balloons whipping in his slipstream.

I'd forgotten to ask his name. It was too late now. I'd got him mixed up with LoonieDunes in my mind – although I didn't know *his* name, either.

As we rejoined the road, I glimpsed the men's team ahead – a flash of blue and orange in the colours of our current sponsors – riding in a bunch. Standing up in the saddle, I pushed ahead.

'Still there?' I asked over my shoulder. 'How's the dust taste?'

'Your dust, Lori Gallagher?' he called back. 'Like gold.'

The cadence of my pedalling faltered. 'You idiot,' I grunted, a piss-poor comeback. 'You can't eat gold!'

'You can!' he insisted. 'There's a European food standard for it!'

Damn it, I wasn't supposed to laugh while my muscles were pushing these power levels. 'You Belgians and your food standards! Less talk, more effort!' I shouted, reminding myself as much as him.

We reached a gentle descent and flew. I was made of air, a master of gravity, as all my molecules vibrated with speed and power and force and it was all somehow more exhilarating because I was lending my magic dust to a guy with a nice smile and a comforting voice. For a moment, I was *me* again on the bike.

Throwing all my strength into my legs, I slipped alongside the men's peloton, waiting for Colin to notice me. When he did, his double take was an adrenaline rush all of its own.

'I found something you lost,' I called out, jerking my head in the direction of the new guy, whose chest was heaving with effort from the drag on his bike. He tucked in behind the men's group to a chorus of snickers that he didn't seem to notice. He had his nose up, as though appreciating the hint of thyme in the cold air.

Colin flashed me a cranky look as I joined the bunch as well, but I just lifted my chin pointedly at him. We both knew I got better results than he did and if I wanted to join the men for a day, the team manager – our dad – wouldn't stop me.

We reached the rendered houses and apartment blocks on the outskirts of Girona, sprayed liberally with graffiti, and then the old town swallowed us up: stone churches and tree-lined streets, warm colours and pedestrians to dodge. Ten minutes later, we arrived outside the team hotel.

Watching the new guy pull up, unclipping casually, propping himself up on the handlebars, I had to blink away a fresh tingle of recognition. Colin strode up to him, holding out his hand for one of those macho clasps, since handshakes were apparently for wimps.

'Fair play, mate,' my brother said. 'It's good to see you can take a joke.'

'A hazing, you mean,' I said, showing Colin my teeth.

'Are you defending him?' Colin asked, giving me an affectionate shove. Sending the new guy a sidelong glance, he said, 'Don't get any ideas about my sister.'

'I wouldn't dream of it,' he muttered. 'I've got Matilda now anyway,' he continued, jerking a thumb over his shoulder at the blow-up doll, who bobbed with excitement at his words.

'Matilda?' Colin said with a snort-laugh.

'In honour of my new team. She can sit in the bus with the blow-up boxing kangaroo. I'd offer to let her share my room, but she might miss yours, Gallagher.'

So much for the new guy needing me to defend him.

'You're welcome to her,' Colin said with a chuckle.

'Can Matilda and I go?' he continued. 'Or do I need to get naked and eat worms so we can become "mates"?'

'What you do with Matilda is up to you,' Colin said emphatically, raising his arms in mock horror.

Untying the ribbons from the seat tube of his bike, the guy glanced up and caught me watching him. The doll was losing puff, because she bumped against his head as he freed her from her bonds. He approached me haltingly, biting his lip.

'Thank you,' he said softly, 'for pacing me down.'

I gulped, unable to form a smart response while my mind was still replaying the view of his teeth sinking into his soft lip.

'Matilda says thank you, too.' Gripping the doll's neck, he made her nod, folding over the drooping plastic until her wide-open mouth contorted. I was about to roll my eyes at his silly sense of humour, when he continued, 'I hope you… find someone to get that gravel out of your butt.'

The tingles rushed back as I imagined *him* gently tending my wounds. Was he flirting with me? I felt scrambled up, when I was supposed to be steeling myself for the World Tour racing season. This breathless tingling was too much like weakness.

'Bye, Belgian soap,' I called after him as he handed his bike over to the mechanics in the car park and headed for the hotel. He gave me a wave over his shoulder.

Colin was watching me with an odd look.

'Thank you for ruining my morning,' I said grimly, before my brother could say anything.

'Was he bothering you? Do I need to run him off?'

'No!'

'I should have run off Gaetano last year,' he grumbled.

Lucky it had been months since my ex had dumped me or I might not have been able to put Colin off with a dark laugh. 'He ran off himself, so it's all good.' The only positive about the end of that relationship was that he'd dumped me at the end of his contract and then changed teams. 'But don't worry. I can take the new guy. Maybe I don't want to run him off.'

'What? He's a domestique, Lore. Dad brought him in at the last minute after his old team let him go. He's never going to win anything. He's in the team to bring me and Lars our water bottles.' Unlike Colin and me. Gallaghers were here to win.

'You have no idea how different that word sounds to a woman. You think being a support rider is somehow less masculine, whereas I think it sounds like the perfect man. You'll learn one day.' I patted him on the cheek.

'Knock it off!' Colin batted my hand away and gave me the same peeved look he'd been giving me since he was ten and I was twelve.

'What's his name, the new guy?' I asked as casually as I could. 'He only introduced Matilda,' I added when Colin gave me a curious look.

'Sébastien Franck,' Colin said.

I'd heard the name, but he definitely wasn't a lead rider. *Sébastien...*

He couldn't be LoonieDunes. I was imagining things. Besides, I was certain my Loonie was from Canada – except the argument for that felt weaker the more I thought about it. Maybe he just loved Bugs Bunny.

Colin turned me to face him. 'But you're not really interested in— Ah,' he interrupted himself with a chuckle. 'You're
screwing with me,' he accused with a smile and I allowed
him to think it. 'Just... after Gaetano... no one on the team,
hey?'

'Don't worry. I learned my lesson. There won't be *anyone*
this year.'

Chapter 2

Lori

As I poured my coffee at breakfast the next morning, I couldn't shake the feeling that everyone was watching me. *Poor Lori, that must have* hurt! *Is she ever going to get back to her best? What about her nerves on descents? Surely, after a crash like that, you've gotta feel scared.*

Pre-crash Lori would have eyeballed them right back and invited a fight, but I couldn't quite find her yet. I would, at some point during training camp. I'd be back to my best — *the* best — and my teammates would win with me.

But that morning, the lingering worry that they were right wouldn't leave me alone, even though no one was actually looking at me.

I turned the filter in the coffee machine with a yank that was harder than necessary and pressed the button for the water to run through. I only managed a shit coffee: slightly overbrewed, crema wonky and disturbed, but that was me today.

Not sure where to sit, I dawdled serving my porridge and listened to my teammates laugh and chat as they caught up after the couple of months' break. Bonnie snorted her coffee as Doortje related a story about the Dutch National Team post-Worlds party. Leesa had been gravel racing again back home in the US – in between study for her fancy degree.

When I glanced over my shoulder at them, they were all smiles and friendly squeezes with each other, happy to be back together again.

What amusing anecdotes did I have? That I'd babbled some nonsense about hot Olympic swimmers while the anaesthetic was kicking in during my second round of surgery? I imagined bringing my tray to their table and attempting a smile – which, in my current mood, would look like a creepy viral hoax – and killing all of the team spirit while they avoided the topic of my fitness.

The men's team had similarly formed good-humoured groups at various tables – my Italian ex thankfully no longer among them. Although there were a few new faces, I knew most of the guys well after a few years of these training camps: Lars, the Swedish lead rider who was getting on a bit now; Nelson, a support rider who was getting married this year even though he was only my age; and Amir from Algeria, the only rider in the World Tour peloton with Arabic roots.

These guys would rally around Colin this year, now my brother was 23 and maturing – in the saddle. He was *not* mature in any other context and I doubted he ever would be.

Neither my brother nor my dad had appeared in the breakfast room yet, but I decided I could grab a table and wait for them to avoid vacant conversation and overthinking. Turning warily, I scanned the room for a free table – and discovered someone *was* actually watching me.

Him.

I did not need that zing up my spine.

He seemed as surprised as I was when our gazes clashed, although *he'd* started it. For a heartbeat too long, we just looked at each other across the tables. I *really* didn't need my lungs to seize up and the room to grow fuzzy in the background. He was far too cute, with that swirl of hair I could run my fingers through.

But it wasn't only that. It was the way he gazed at me, his brow askew, as though he couldn't quite believe he could see me, as though I were a ghost or… Taylor Swift or something. Or a puzzle. The thought didn't help the fizz in my veins as the moment stretched much longer than I should have let it.

The doors slid open and Dad appeared – just in time to let me breathe again. Gritting my teeth, I swallowed the stupid tingles of attraction before Dad could notice anything. He'd hugged me while I cried the most pitiful tears over my useless boyfriend – as much as a gold medallist and national champion could be useless – last year and I didn't want him thinking it could happen again.

Dad had thankfully never found out about LoonieDunes, although I'd had a few close calls with Mum. I hated to think of the lecture I'd receive about taking my training seriously if he'd worked out why I was online so much – and hopefully he would *never* discover that I'd let that online friendship drift into murky personal territory. I didn't want to admit that to myself.

That part of my life was over – my injury, the conversations with LoonieDunes. I would be 'Top Gun' again in no time and shake off this panicky version of myself, who got squishy over an online friend and projected the image of him onto the first new guy she met.

I'd hoped ruthlessly ghosting him would get rid of the weakness, but my brain was apparently more stubborn than that.

'Molly, my girl!'

The short, wiry form of the 'Irish bullet', team manager and former national road-race champion – my dad, Tony Gallagher – whooshed into the room with his usual gusto.

'Morning, Dad.'

Taking a seat at a spare table with my back to Sébastien Franck, I waited for Dad to join me, sipping my coffee.

'Sleep well?'

I nodded, even though I'd rolled around a bit, as I often did these days, when my muscles stiffened up.

'Back on the road with the girls today!'

I forced a smile in response, hating that the prospect filled me with dread. 'Oh, I got a message from Mum,' I said, changing the subject. 'She told me to ask you about that quote for garden work at home?'

The message had been a little strange, but I knew Dad got

so deep into his strategising as he planned the season that I hadn't been completely surprised he'd forgotten something. But his expression when I mentioned it was weak and uncertain.

'All right, love. I'll get back to her,' he mumbled.

That feeling of everyone watching me returned in force, but this time I recognised the anxiety for what it was: the feeling that nothing had returned to normal and this year would not run as smoothly as I needed it to.

As I was quietly *not* panicking, Dad glanced up suddenly and raised his hand. 'Frankie! You done already? Come and sit down, son.'

Goosebumps swept up my forehead and I was afraid I was blushing – for no reason, I tried to remind myself.

It didn't help that he seemed equally hesitant. 'Euh…'

Keeping my eyes trained on my porridge, I ignored him – really quite rudely – as Dad insisted he join us. But the hairs on my arms stood up when he took the chair next to mine.

'Settling in okay? I hear Amir snores. If you need some ear plugs, we've got plenty.'

'Thanks,' he replied, with a hint of a chuckle that I wished I could un-hear. Everything he did reminded me of soft words in my headset, breaths, panting jokes as we pushed each other on the stationary bike, separated by the distance of half a world.

It was a good thing I'd ghosted him or I'd be even more distracted from the only goal that counted this year: winning.

In an awkward pause, I caught him glancing at me again and looked down at my outfit to check there wasn't anything off. But no, I had on my usual baggy T-shirt and tracksuit bottoms, no make-up to smear.

'You won't take Colin's stunt too much to heart, I hope? He only meant it in fun,' Dad was saying.

'I know,' Sébastien replied. 'I understand Australians have a... unique sense of humour.'

'Good man!' Dad said, clapping him on the shoulder.

'You could have just taken the doll off your bike,' I added. 'You don't need to let Colin pick on you. It was childish and unfair of him.'

He gave an eloquent nod that had its own French accent. 'He's not going to win the *Miss Congeniality* award, but it's not the worst welcome I've had into a new team.' He was still speaking, but I stopped listening when he mentioned *Miss Congeniality*. A coincidence? At least this one wasn't the fault of my overactive brain. He'd actually said it – mentioned a movie I'd watched with LoonieDunes, before I'd dropped him like a hot coal. I wasn't making it up this time.

But LoonieDunes was Canadian. He was a long way away, somewhere in the depths of the internet, not sitting right next to me, giving me goosebumps and looking at me with wide, honey eyes.

Wasn't he?

'Have you... seen that movie?' I had to ask.

'It's a classic,' he said, his tone oddly halting. 'You probably... don't like romcoms.'

'I didn't until recently.' I wanted to curl the words back in as soon as I uttered them. 'You like romcoms?'

'Euh—'

'You chatting up my sister again, Frankie?'

I'd rarely been happier to hear one of my brother's stupid jokes.

The new guy leaped to his feet as though someone had just ripped hot wax off his legs – and, given he was a pro cyclist, he would know what that felt like. 'I need to...' He didn't even bother finishing the sentence. He just took off like the Road Runner – another *Looney Tunes* reference, damn it.

'You scare him off?' Colin asked, as he set his breakfast tray down and collapsed onto the chair Sébastien had just vacated. 'Good girl.'

'Fuck off' was the best rejoinder I could muster with such a fried brain. Colin knew saying 'good girl' was the surest way to piss me off.

He slouched over his coffee. 'Did he take it okay or do I have to apologise for yesterday?'

Downing the last sip of my double espresso, I hauled myself to my feet. 'How should I know? Fix your own problems.' Without looking back, I headed for the sliding doors of the breakfast room.

Behind me, I heard my dad's Irish-Australian brogue. 'That's my girl. She's back.'

Lucky he didn't know the truth.

Seb

Too much philosophy was more a weakness than a strength in the competitive world of pro cycling. Psychology was useful, sure, although you had to believe it and I'd never quite managed that part. As I stood in the cool morning sunshine outside our hotel in Girona, gazing at the wisps of cloud and the distant belltower of a historic church, I was deeply philosophising, even though I should have been getting in the zone for our next training ride.

This season was my last, one long goodbye to my top-level career, such as it was. I might never get another chance to saddle up in the greatest races on the continent, against the best of the best in European and world cycling – a chance I'd never thought I'd have.

In all my years on the World Team circuit, I'd never attended a training camp quite like this one. I'd been to Girona – of course I'd been to Girona. Every cyclist has been to Girona at least once. I'd never been on a camp where the women's team trained at the same time in the same place. Some of my previous teams hadn't even had a women's division, the short-sighted idiots. But even that wasn't the biggest difference.

The difference was *me*.

It was refreshing to have nothing to lose. Last year, my previous contract hadn't been renewed – not exactly unexpected, but still not my choice. Then Tony Gallagher had come along and given me this one last hurrah with the Harper-Stacked team.

I would turn 35 this year and bow out with grace, knowing the decision had been mine.

If I was completely honest, *that* wasn't the biggest difference either. Lori Gallagher stood 5 m away and my nervous system was firing like an animal shape shifter sensing its mate – which felt as ridiculous as it sounded.

She was hot – that wasn't in question. Her lower lip alone was enough to give me daydreams for years to come. Add in the dips and swells of her body, all strength and resilience wrapped in winter-weight skintight cycling gear, and I saw stars every time I glanced at her.

I'd never lost my shit over a beautiful woman, but the effect of Lori Gallagher defied all expectations of myself, even though there was a simple explanation – an explanation that made it all the more imperative not to get carried away thinking about her.

She reminded me unexpectedly of Folklore. Every time that word rose in my thoughts, my chest squeezed and my thoughts tangled and I was back in November, waiting impatiently for her to join the server, my heart already racing, even though we hadn't started training.

My feelings had nothing to do with Lori Gallagher, but telling myself so wasn't enough for my heart. I needed to keep away from her, or I'd make an even bigger fool of myself – if that were possible.

I couldn't decide what was more embarrassing: being found by Lori Gallagher in the forest with a sex doll or the way I'd lost all ability to speak when she'd leaned over me with a frown, all freckled cheeks and enormous eyes – to say nothing of the awful conversation in the breakfast room this morning. Hopefully, she merely thought I was a huge fan, which was also true.

She was one of the most successful female cyclists of the past five years. I'd watched her bash her way through Paris-Roubaix last year for third place, covered head to toe in mud, except for the bit of her thigh where the skin had been scraped open in a crash. She'd got back on the bike after that crash and almost knocked over Gosia Zielinski in her fight to break away from the peloton.

Actually, that did sound a bit like Folklore99. But my virtual training partner had been... normal. Lori Gallagher had a reputation as a cutthroat competitor, right down to her choice of boyfriend the previous year – Gaetano Maggioli, Olympic time trial champion. And she was firmly ignoring me now.

I was projecting. I'd just got my heart broken by a person who didn't even exist the way I thought she did. It was a sad indication of the state of my heart, if I'd handed it over to an avatar of a cyclist who could have been anyone. I missed her more than was healthy and my synapses had connected the wrong ends until it was my new teammate inciting rushing blood and a racing heartbeat.

She couldn't actually *be* my online friend, even if her name sort of sounded like Folklore and she said 'fuck' a lot in that broad Australian accent. Maybe everyone in Australia said 'fuck' a lot.

I was so distracted I didn't notice what was going on with

the rest of the men's team until the pointed snickering made me turn to find every last gaze trained on me. Perhaps I'd find Matilda's twin sister ready for me today. I had a three-some joke ready to go.

But there was no shrivelled sex doll attached to my bike this time. Instead, pastel spoke beads clinked gently as Colin pushed it towards me and colourful streamers fluttered in the breeze below the handlebars. He'd turned my sexy aero bike into a ride for a five-year-old.

Not wanting to encourage the cocky kid, I stifled my smile. 'We're Barbie and Ken today, yes? You know Ken is French slang for fucking?'

As I clapped Colin on the arm, a prickle on the back of my neck made me peer over my shoulder. Lori Gallagher was staring at me as though she'd recently made plans to watch the *Barbie* film with an online friend, but had never got there because she'd ghosted him.

Seb, you imbecile. It's just a coincidence.

I blinked back the strange feeling, like a premonition, although I'd never been superstitious — well, aside from the usual ones about winning socks and lucky oatmeal.

I let Colin have his fun again that day, ignoring the clink of the beads as we suffered up the epic Rocacorba climb, trying not to dwell on how young my new lead rider must be — and definitely not wondering what age that made his sister.

But the little poop could have helped me get the things off again after the ride. We had to clean our own bikes and my gnawing stomach was terrified I'd miss lunch as I snapped those suckers off the spokes.

Then I almost forgave him – far too quickly – because Lori appeared, a deep gouge between her brows. Dropping to her haunches, she wordlessly set to work helping me. She'd showered already and had her hair in a ponytail that tickled her jaw and I couldn't concentrate on anything except brushing my fingers over that bit of skin until she shivered.

'Thank you,' I managed to say despite my dry tongue.

'I should have got Colin to clean up after himself.'

'He wouldn't have looked so pretty while he did it.' I clamped my mouth shut ten words too late.

The look she gave me could have cut steel.

'Sorry. I mean, you're clearly the capable sibling.'

'Come on, let's put them on his bike.'

I hoped she didn't realise that the idea appealed to me mainly because I'd get another few minutes of admiring her strong jaw.

After finding his bike in the trailer, we squeezed in to complete the prank, making me wonder if the temperature had risen, even though it was the end of November. I kept picturing her making combative jokes on the Zpeed voice call server, the fantasy more compelling than it had any right to be.

But it wasn't a helpful fantasy. When I unwittingly skimmed my fingers over hers through the spokes, I had to suck in a harsh breath. I met her gaze more often than I should have. She had flecked blue irises with a dark ring at the edge and an intent way of looking at me that made me wonder if she could see through my clothes. I really liked it.

As we dawdled back to the hotel in charged silence, the back of my hand brushed hers and I waited, barely breathing, for her to flinch away. She didn't, but she didn't acknowledge me either.

Arriving in the foyer, I made a wild gesture in the direction of my room. 'I'd better... go get some Belgian soap on me.'

The doubtful look she sent me would have had more impact if she hadn't simultaneously chewed on her lip, frying my brain.

'As long as you don't stop to play Ken with Matilda, you should still catch the lunch buffet.' She gave a stilted chuckle and then appeared to choke on her own quip.

'If the music's playing loudly, Amir knows not to come in.' I'd intended to lighten the moment with that one — and remind her of the close quarters we all lived in on camp and during competition — but her expression of mild horror proved I'd missed the mark. 'I'm joking.'

'So was I,' she snapped, visibly pulling herself together. 'I'm sorry for my brother. He's a dick to all the new guys.'

'Don't worry. I can shake it off.'

Her gaze swerved right back to mine and it took me a moment to realise I'd quoted Taylor Swift in her infinite wisdom. Lori took a step back as though I'd pushed her. 'Er, see you later.'

Bolting for the dining room, she disappeared through the doors faster than I could say 'Wildest Dreams'.

Chapter 3

Seb

My agent would have been horrified to hear that I'd spent more time over the first three days of training camp thinking with the contents of my very tight shorts than concentrating on my fitness and my place in the new team. He would have told me about the importance of getting sufficient rest – I was certain of that early in the morning of the fourth day, when I was rolling around in bed, worrying about waking my roommate Amir.

I placated my agent – without him even having to get out of my own head – by making for the hotel gym at six to do some extra core training on the mats, scooping up Matilda at the last minute, taking her with me and setting her on the chest press while I warmed up. Anything for the running joke.

When I put my Bluetooth headphones in and scrolled through my favourites playlist for the song I was looking for, a kernel of self-reflection made me face up to the real reason

I'd got out of bed this morning: I'd heard the Gallaghers were still jetlagged, as well as utterly obsessed with being the best, and they often trained early.

I also had to own up to the fact that I was listening to Taylor Swift, hoping I might catch a short glimpse of Lori Gallagher – if I was lucky, in a situation that wasn't embarrassing for once. I had a terrible history of relationships ending before they'd really begun, but this was a new low: crushing on an entirely unattainable woman because she reminded me of another woman who'd already ghosted me.

Grumbling to myself as I stretched out on the mat and lifted my body into a hollow-hold, I realised I wasn't even sure she knew my name, which was a blessing at this point. When she found out, she might remember stage three of the Vuelta a España last year, when I'd flown off the road into spiky bushes and limped to the finish line, my shorts held together with medical tape. Or maybe the time I was startled by a black cat at the side of the road during the Gent-Wevelgem and crashed.

It was a miracle her eccentric Australia-based team Harper-Stacked had offered me a one-year contract when my agent had given up hope. A miracle I was here at all to embarrass myself as she studied me with her intent gaze, the one that sent heat shooting to my toes.

I *really* had to stop thinking about her. In a second, my heart rate would flip out and I wouldn't be able to hold the position long enough.

Too late. My abs buckled and my legs hit the floor. Taking

a moment to catch my breath, I lay on my back, staring at the ceiling. So much for training hard. I couldn't even keep up a hollow-hold for a minute.

It wasn't only because I'd embarrassed myself in front of Lori that my thoughts seemed to settle on her and then hang like an overtaxed computer. I had great form in making an ass of myself in front of beautiful women who were out of my league.

No, it was the way my brain had mixed up Lori with Folklore – only because she'd seen *Miss Congeniality* recently!

That film had come out when Lori was just a baby (yes, I'd googled her unrepentantly yesterday afternoon and discovered she was all of 25 years old – *25!* How was the film that old?) It had to be a coincidence, along with the similarity between her name and 'Folklore'. My online training partner had chosen the handle because of Taylor Swift. It wasn't anything to do with Lori's full first name, Loredana – given by her Italian triathlete mother.

I grabbed a dumbbell and began a set of lunges, trying to screw my head on straight and not think about my banter with Folklore – and definitely not the way Lori's fingers had brushed mine through the spokes of Colin's bike. Under no circumstances could I start blending the two women in my feverish mind.

If she *were* Folklore, at least I could stop worrying that she was bleeding out in a ditch somewhere – not that bleeding victims with their lives draining away usually took the time to delete their Zpeed accounts. No, she just hadn't been into me and, while she could have been an adult and told me before bugging out, that was fair enough. She didn't want a dork who was afraid of winning, whose best friend on training camp was a sex doll called Matilda – any more than Lori Gallagher would want me. I always gravitated towards unattainable relationships.

Another thing to add to the long list of reasons Lori Gallagher must think I was a loser: I was, in reality, a loser. My entire career was built around being a loser. I was a domestique – or équipier, the slightly less insulting term we used in French – the guy who paced the others, who helped the winners to save their strength for the final burst before caving and dropping back. My palmarès, my (very short) list of wins, was the result of chance and not strategy. I was a team guy and the Gallaghers were... not.

Had I really spent ten weeks training – way more than I usually did, I might add – with Lori Gallagher? She'd been funny and... nice to me. If I'd known it was her—

It couldn't have been her. Christ, what was I thinking?

'Morning, Frankie!'

I whirled so quickly I nearly clocked Colin Gallagher in the privates with the dumbbell. I'd never been called Frankie before, but I'd learned nicknames were a fact of life for Australians and, after the joke with Matilda, mine could definitely have been something worse.

'Gallagher,' I acknowledged, popping out my earbuds and summoning all my cool to cover the fact that I'd just been obsessing about his sister. He bypassed the chest press, giving

Matilda a pat on the cheek, and settled at one of the leg-press machines.

My thoughts swerved back to the first day of camp, shooting down the mountain in Lori's dust. When she'd attacked, she'd come alive, her plait swinging over her shoulder and her whole body rocking from side to side with the bike as she pedalled up out of the saddle. I could have waxed lyrical about that hole in her shorts and the ideas it gave me – some of them simply involving gentle antiseptic and my fingers. She'd knocked me sideways.

I hoped she won – everything she ever attempted.

'What's your strategy?' Colin asked between leg presses.

'Oh, I'm sure she doesn't—' I cut myself off with a gulp. Of course, Colin hadn't meant my strategy for dealing with Lori and Folklore and my confused crush. I covered my faux pas with a grunt of effort during the next lunge. 'Erm, I haven't met with the directeur sportif. I don't know which races we're aiming for.'

'What about your coach?'

The doors swished open again and of course it was her, just in time to hear the sorry truth. I forced my eyes off her, especially when I noticed she was wearing a crop top and her hair was in another high ponytail, brushing the back of her neck. It helped that she ignored me – well, it didn't help my ego.

Colin Gallagher prompted me with a look.

'I don't have my own coach.' I just muddled through following orders.

I remembered with a start that Lori and Colin's coach was Tony Gallagher, their father, the Irish-Australian sprinter who'd dominated at the Olympics 30 years ago. Those were the genes – and discipline – passed down to the power siblings of Australian cycling, while I had only learned the discipline to get up and milk the goats every day and I hadn't seen my own father in nearly 25 years.

Too self-conscious to move into the crunches that were next in my floor workout, I went down into a set of mountain climbers, feeling like an idiot for running on the floor, wondering if Lori was watching.

When she dropped down next to me, I nearly reared back like a cat faced with a cucumber. She was so close I could map the constellation of freckles on her arm and I swear I stopped breathing.

'Out of shape from the off-season, Belgian soap?' she asked conversationally as she held her body effortlessly in an elbow plank.

Actually, I'm in the shape of my life from training with someone an awful lot like you. 'I'm working on not peaking too early,' I said instead, my mouth dry.

'Is that what Matilda is for?' she quipped through gritted teeth.

I nearly swallowed my tongue. Between laughing at her joke and the inability of my lungs to function when she was this close, the noise I made was more distressed donkey than articulate human.

'No, I just,' I began with a cough, 'thought she'd be lonely.'

'Has anyone ever told you, you have a weird sense of humour?'

Folklore had...

She pushed up into a high plank, her hair tumbling over her shoulder, her body taut and strong and so beautiful my eyes hurt. 'Have you forgotten how to do mountain climbers?' she asked, her tone irritated.

I knew that tone. I'd heard it so often through my headphones as she baited me and teased me and made me fight. Holy shit, *could she* be Folklore in more than just my imagination?

I scrambled to get going again, my head spinning and my eyes drawn down her body, as though looking could give me answers to the desperate questions swimming in my mind.

Lori moved seamlessly back onto her elbows and my gaze snagged on her lower back, to the jagged, puckered scar tissue, and I froze in alarm. Folklore had occasionally been in pain while we trained, but she hadn't talked in detail about her injury. It hit me then that Lori had broken her back – I'd seen that crash on replay.

Rocketing down a mountain like a bullet, she must have hit a hidden seam, because one minute she'd been coolly burning the competition, and the next she'd sailed over her handlebars, her bike flipping and flying after her as she landed heavily on her helmet and skidded over the edge.

She was lucky she could walk – lucky to be alive. If something like that had happened to Folklore...

My arms crumpled and I hit the mat with an 'oof', my heart pounding. How much pain did she still have?

Glancing at me uneasily, Lori relaxed her body and sat up. 'Do you want to do burpees? See who can do the most in three minutes?'

'For fuck's sake, Lori!' Colin called out. 'You always have to play with the boys.'

'Sure,' I answered her, ignoring Colin. 'I know you're in great shape— Erm...' I sucked in a panicky breath through my nose as I felt Colin's eyes burning the back of my neck. 'I mean, you're... competitive. It's a compliment!'

Competitive like Folklore – impulsive *like Folklore*. 'Okay,' she said doubtfully. 'Were you listening to music?' she asked, gesturing to where I'd set my phone down. 'Let's use a song as the timer.'

I was such a mess of shock and excitement that my brain froze and I couldn't work out whether I should hide the music I'd been listening to and just put on David Guetta or something. The decision was taken out of my hands when I disconnected the Bluetooth and Taylor's 'Paper Rings' rang out suddenly in the quiet room.

Fumbling with my phone, I tapped the screen to move onto the next song in the queue, but it wasn't any better: 'Hysteria' by Muse – decidedly dystopian. I couldn't bring myself to meet her gaze, afraid to see if she'd put the two songs together and get FolkyDunes – my imaginary friendship that obviously hadn't meant as much to Folklore as it had to me. Even worse, she might not react at all and the similarities really were all in my head.

She said nothing until the moment felt like a rubber band

pulled taut. Then it pinged back and she dropped to the floor as the dirty bass at the beginning of the song got going. 'One!' she barked at me as she completed her first burpee and I lurched into action.

I waited until she started to puff, the skin under her freckles glowing pink, before I slowed down. I *was* struggling – burpees were right up there with cleaning the toilet or waiting for the bus, in my books – but not quite as much as I led her to believe. She was intense – energetic and strong – but I had the completely unfair advantage of being male.

When the guitar solo at the end of the song finished with a crash of cymbals, I sat back on my haunches, heaving in deep breaths. She'd completed eight more than I had.

Colin clapped slowly from behind us. 'Beaten by a girl, Frankie?'

'Not just any girl,' I muttered, hauling myself to my feet. 'I... thanks for the contest.' Holding a hand out to her, I wasn't sure if I wanted to shake hers or help her up. I would have told her what an honour it was to meet her in burpee battle if I hadn't known it was coming on far too strong and I would have sounded like the idiot I was.

But she batted away my hand, eyes blazing. 'You let me win!' she accused icily.

'It was a lot of burpees. I hate burpees,' I insisted.

Shaking her head, she seethed, 'There's no point in winning unless I earned it. And why are you trying to be nice to me anyway?' Her eyes narrowed.

Because if you are *Folklore, talking to you online was the highlight of my off-season. Because I know what your voice sounds like when you're in pain, but still pushing yourself. I know that beneath the surface, you have feelings like everyone else.*

I said nothing out loud. She didn't want those words. I didn't know if I could handle the truth, whichever way it went.

But in true Folklore style, she faced the issue head-on. Dropping her chin, she groaned, long and loud. 'It's from "Walloon", isn't it?' she said under her breath. 'The French-speaking people from Belgium. I should have realised.'

Chapter 4

Lori

'Which one is Franck's room?' I asked Colin when I reached the corridor on the third floor of the hotel after the day's training ride was over. It was the late afternoon rest hour, the most important part of the day, according to my dad. But I couldn't rest until I'd seen LoonieDunes – *Sébastien Franck* – and talked through the situation that was rubbing at the back of my mind like the worst itch and stopping me from focusing.

'Number 315,' my brother replied. 'But, ah, I wouldn't go in there right now, if I were you.' He pouted his lips, looking more like a fish than a blow-up doll, but I understood his meaning even before he added the crude hand gesture. My gaze flew to the ceiling.

But the running gag with Matilda was exactly the kind of thing LoonieDunes would do. He'd had a joke for every occasion, including one time he'd spent an entire time trial on Zpeed telling me *Star Wars* jokes about Luke driving a

Toy-Yoda and the Jedi rock star Bon Jovi-Wan Kenobi until I was so out of breath from groaning I could barely pedal. Thinking of being out of breath reminded me of the burpees and then I was angry again. Good. Anger was something I could use.

I turned the handle of room 315 and pushed, expecting resistance – and hoping to freak him out with a horror-movie doorknob rattle – but the door flew open and I realised it might not have been such a good idea to burst in on him after all.

Matilda was on one of the twin beds, staring at the ceiling and thinking of England as my online training partner groaned and gasped and grunted, all of this to a soundtrack of dramatic instrumental music. I froze, telling myself to look away, but also brutally curious.

'Too hard. *Too hard!*' he howled to the swannie giving his legs a thorough massage after the day's longer ride and gruelling interval training.

'I'd say someone's too soft,' I commented, cocking my head to observe his reaction.

He shot up from the massage table that had been set up in the corner of the room, the little towel slipping precariously. I needed to look away. He might not like me skimming my eyes down his taut, broad chest to his packed thighs and the curve of his muscular butt – which I could see a bit more of than he was probably comfortable with.

Except, he didn't seem uncomfortable. I even had time to catalogue a few tattoos: a band around his upper arm, near the faded tan line. The backs of his muscular calves were decorated with thick patterns that must have hurt – not that pain was unfamiliar to an endurance athlete.

'Uh,' was all he said. I waited for him to finish, noticing he had a tell-tale crick in his collarbone from a crash. A stylised gear sprocket with a pattern of flourishes was inked just below, stark against his pale skin. Just like this morning in the gym, my brain slowed right down until the only thought left in it was how fine LoonieDunes looked in real life. 'I thought... you wouldn't want to see me,' he finally managed.

I do...

That was part of the reason I'd ghosted him in the first place, if I was honest with myself. I'd started to want the laughter in my ear, to need the encouragement that was more than just sports psychology – the little bit of living that I'd unexpectedly found while stuck at my parents' place, in pain and endlessly frustrated.

But I'd left that frustration in my parents' basement, as my mum had told me to, and I was back, ready to focus on racing. The sensation of acids and adrenaline surging and reacting in my blood was part of who I was. I had to focus on those feelings and nothing too... soft.

Winning was part of who I was as well – earning the win, not some guy letting me win.

'Should I come back later?' I asked without taking a step in the direction of the door. The swannie was Chris, an old hand I'd known for years, and he was studiously ignoring me and probably wondering whether to tell Dad I'd burst in on a naked teammate who was only covered by a titchy towel.

'All done,' Chris said, scurrying for the door without even closing the lid on the ointment on the bedside table.

'Amir will be coming back soon,' Sébastien said, referring to his roommate. Road cyclists might have a reputation as divas, but the reality of close team quarters and a gruelling endurance sport was less than glamorous.

He sat up, rearranging the towel as he reached down to turn off whatever he'd been watching on his phone. It had probably been some concept-heavy sci-fi, the weirdo. He'd tried to make me watch some tense deep-space horror crap, but I would have preferred to train alone than put myself through that and it turned out he liked classic romcoms almost as much.

'It's fine if you don't want to see me,' he continued mildly – too mildly for my taste. With the sight of him leaning his elbows on his knees, his posture completely relaxed and vast amounts of skin on show, I struggled to organise my scrambled thoughts. But I did not want him to put a shirt on. I flung myself onto the bed with a dramatic sigh, jumping in surprise when Matilda bounced. 'Aren't you angry with me? I deleted my account without saying goodbye.'

He froze and the emotions churning in his stormy eyes made me feel marginally better for ditching him in a panic. 'Maybe you could have let me down a little more gently.'

I opened my mouth to defend myself, but I got caught up on his word choice and my brain glitched. He thought this had been some kind of break-up? I suppose it had been, even though our friendship had never crossed any lines.

'But I get it now. You had to drop me and move on. I missed you – I mean, I missed Folklore – but I get it. I'm not Gaetano Maggioli. My dad isn't Tony Gallagher. I've won only two stages of the Tour de France in the space of nearly fifteen years on the circuit.'

You missed me? I managed not to voice that one. 'You've won stages?'

The smirk he gave me sparkled with amusement. 'Yeah. Does that make me sexy?'

'I've seen you naked on a massage table, squealing like a girl with one butt cheek on show. Do you think that's sexy?'

He laughed, and I hated that I recognised the sound in my blood, that it made me want to be Folklore99 instead of 'Top Gun' Gallagher, the ridiculous nickname my dad had insisted I get called in the press.

'What do we do now?' I whined.

'What do you mean?'

'Do we know each other or not?'

'Lore,' he began, but stopped suddenly. 'Should I still call you that?'

'This is the weirdest thing ever,' I groaned. 'I thought you were…' Luckily, I stopped myself before I said what I'd been thinking.

'What? Old?' he prompted.

'Too young, more likely. What thirty-year-old man likes *Star Wars*?'

'Ahem, I'm 34. And lots of us. If you thought I was a teenager, you shouldn't have flirted with me.'

'I did not flirt with you!' I had totally flirted with him. The way he'd reacted, as though praise from me was the moon and the stars, had made me think I was doing a victimless good deed.

'What did you think was wrong with me, then?' His mouth moved thoughtfully. When he narrowed his eyes at me, a tingle zipped up my spine. 'Ugly. That's it, right? You thought I was ugly. I suppose I should be thankful it's not true.' His cocky grin was way too cute, but he still needed to wipe it off his face.

'What did you think was wrong with *me*?' I asked.

'Not much. I knew you were back living with your parents, so you couldn't be too old.'

I resisted a wince at his choice of words. I wasn't 'back' with my parents. I'd never moved out. Since Dad was my coach, it had never made sense.

He continued, oblivious. 'I tried to tell myself I had no way of knowing if you were married with kids, but... I imagined you might be pretty. I mean, not as pretty as you—' He cut himself off.

I sank a tooth into my lip so I wouldn't smile. 'Why did you have to add the kids? It could have been you with the kids, but it wouldn't be such a big deal because you're a man and you don't have to sacrifice a quarter of your metabolism for nearly a year for the furtherment of humankind.'

'Yep, you're definitely Folklore,' he murmured. The tinge of wonder in his voice was great for my ego.

'That makes you Loonie. Can I still call you that? And why the dunes?

'You don't know the coast of Belgium? I thought it was a good joke.'

'I know it's cold on the coast of Belgium. I'm now assuming there are dunes.'

He nodded. 'It's not Australia, but we have a lot of sand.'

'I like Loonie more than Frankie, though. I might have to pass it on to Colin.'

He grumbled, but I wasn't sure if it was because of the nickname or the mention of my brother. 'I'd prefer Seb.'

Seb. Three letters that somehow dragged a virtual friendship out into the light. He shifted on the table, running a hand through his thick hair and bringing into sharp focus all the tight lines of bone and muscle in his arm.

'I *never* thought, when you complained about your brother, that you meant *Colin Gallagher*,' he muttered.

Glancing at Matilda, I said, 'He's a bit of a dick, but he's not bad on the inside.'

He started to rise, then froze, his gaze whipping to mine as he clutched the tiny towel in his fist.

I turned around pointedly, coming face-to-face with Matilda again, imagining she shared my withering sigh at the amount of nudity in this sport. I probably should stop assigning feelings to a blow-up doll, especially because I sensed the danger of becoming jealous of her lifeless body.

But why did Seb have to be so cute? My experience with Gaetano last year should have cured me of all this fluttery nonsense my mum constantly warned me against. She'd even suggested I'd lost concentration before the crash because I was worried he was about to break up with me. The fact that he had indeed broken up with me when I woke up from surgery made me more than a little concerned she was right.

'You can turn around now.'

He was still slipping a T-shirt over his head when I caught sight of him. I was used to seeing guys in bib shorts, padded at the crotch, and still somehow finding them attractive, but in a soft pair of tracksuit bottoms and a plain T-shirt, stretching out after the massage, my eyes wanted to soak him up like a sponge – and my hands itched to touch.

But I knew what my mum would say even without her knowing anything about what I was feeling – thank fuck. She'd tell me the only thing I should be thinking about touching was the gold-plated surface of a trophy – many trophies. If I didn't want it more than anyone else, I wouldn't get it.

Seb kept talking in that frustratingly mild tone. 'Look, if you'd rather act like we don't know each other, that's fine. I understand.'

'What do you understand?' I asked.

'Uhm, you—Well, if we're friends… Or flirting—I know I'm not your type in real life and that's okay.'

'Who is my type, then?' I asked with a dark laugh.

'People who… win. I wouldn't want to disappoint you.'

'Gee, thanks. You think I'd only date someone with a few medals around their neck?'

The troubled look he gave me was even more attractive, with his twisted brow and a muscle moving in his sharp jaw. 'It's not the winning. It's the fighting. This is my last year. If I hadn't done all that training with you, last season would have been the end of my career. I work for the team and I love it and I get rewarded for it, but… my contract wasn't renewed. I hit my peak four years ago riding with Arjan Hoogenboezem. I never had what it takes to lead and now I'm only going to keep getting dropped. I'm ready to let it all go.'

I froze, gaping at him. His voice was even, as though he was talking about what we'd had for lunch that day and not the end of his racing career.

If he gave up this easily, perhaps he was right, I didn't want to hang out with him.

'You didn't tell me you were quitting, when we were training together on Zpeed.'

'I didn't tell you I'd been a World Team cyclist at all – and you didn't tell me, either.'

'You *are* a World Team cyclist, you idiot! I can't believe this!'

He gave half a shrug. 'I keep forgetting. When I started training with you, I was out of contract. Maybe I should have given up then, rather than get to know a new team.'

Rather than get to know me flashed unexpectedly through my mind and I shuddered inwardly in horror at my own negative thoughts. I was over Gaetano – at least, I didn't want to get back together with him. But it was frustrating to realise the psychological effects of being dumped had lingered. I couldn't afford to doubt myself right now, when every twinge of my muscles and creak of my bones shot residual alarm through my nerves.

'You were a fighter online,' I pointed out to him. 'You wouldn't have let me win, like you did this morning. It's only your head that's messed up, not your body.' I made my point by running my gaze down and then up again, pausing to lick my lips.

He cleared his throat and shifted on his feet, giving a huff that suggested he'd worked out I was using the attraction between us to make a point. 'I was a fighter online because that's what you needed. And if my head's messed up then... so be it. I've spent 20 years on the bike. I'd like to actually see some of the places we go every year and not be in pain half my life. I'd like to spend time with my niece and nephew, help my grandma, maybe run a little bed and breakfast or something, eat cheese whenever I want.'

My head spun. Thinking about the end of my career was something I avoided at all costs. I hadn't even reached my best years yet – at least that's what I had to tell myself, when I lined up at the first race start at the beginning of the season. I had been right to think Seb would be terrible for my focus.

'You want to retire so you can *eat cheese*? You're on our team now. If you're going to ride with my brother, you'd better stuff this shit down a hole and bury it until the actual end of your contract. My dad built this team. You got selected.

You trained with *me*. Those are the things you need to be thinking about, not a bed and fucking breakfast!'

His lips wobbled and I wasn't sure if I should be offended that I'd amused him when I'd been trying to give him a pep talk. I should have considered his wonky sense of humour and my reputation as a hard arse, which probably wasn't attractive.

'Okay,' he said, his voice quiet but firm. 'You're right. I'm in contract. I'm not retiring.'

'Good,' I said on a long breath. 'And... we don't have to pretend we don't know each other. It doesn't have to be a secret that we made friends on Zpeed. But we both have to focus. No movies, no music, no stupid jokes. No chatting online.' *Made friends...* Was that what had happened?

His gaze darted to my mouth, not quite the action of a mere friend. 'Focus, right. And no letting you win.'

'Definitely not,' I grumbled, wondering why he was still looking at me with that glint in his eye. I licked my suddenly dry lips.

'I probably shouldn't tell you how sexy it was when you said, "Bed and fucking breakfast".'

'Seb!' I told him off through my thick throat, his nickname already familiar on my lips. He couldn't say stuff like that, keep implying I was pretty and desirable, if we were to resist this pull. Teammates weren't supposed to gaze at each other like expensive desserts in a French patisserie. 'If we've... worked everything out, I'm going to go.' Before anything happened.

'Right, okay.' He leaned close and it took me a moment too long to realise he was going in for a peck on the cheek. Every year I forgot the Francophones did this and I squirmed and fidgeted, half expecting to kiss someone on the mouth by accident. That day my hair stood on end at the prospect.

But the soft kiss touched down harmlessly on my cheek as I stared wildly at him, and then he pulled back. But he didn't quite pull back far enough and – oops. We locked eyes. And then a second later, with a groan from him and a huff from me, we locked lips.

Big oops. No longer harmless.

He tasted like summer days and lazy mornings, with a shot of adrenaline, like my first coffee of the day. It was a rush of longing, his mouth open and hot on mine, with shots of fear and vulnerability and so many emotions I didn't want to think about, but revelled in nonetheless. I wrapped my arms around his neck and tipped my head and let him devour me.

His hand snaked around the back of my neck, sending shivers down my spine as he hauled me against him with his other arm. He was so much *body*, with the tough sinew in his chest and arms pressed right up against me. The way he held me still, his thumb brushing my ear, sucked all reason from my brain until I felt molten and gooey.

As my fingers tangled in his hair, it must have been the unexpected feeling of *knowing* him that made me sink my teeth into his bottom lip and then scrape my tongue over it.

The noise he made, between a groan and a whimper, was

the hottest thing I'd ever heard. His hand slid lower and—

There was a knock at the door. Seb sprang away with a jolt, his breath fitful and rasping. With a troubled glance at me, he called out a wobbly 'Yes?'

I recognised the strident voice calling through the door after the first word. 'Are you decent, Franck? I need to talk to you for a sec.'

My mind blanked in panic. I was supposed to be resting right now. Even if by some miracle we didn't look as though we'd just been necking, it was very bad to be found alone in Seb's room by the team manager, otherwise known as Tony Gallagher — my dad.

28 September 06:28
zpeed.com/chatserver/channels/@
    LoonieDunes/22683644572

LoonieDunes: Are you logging on soon, @Folklore99?

Folklore99: Now you decide to message me.

LoonieDunes: Sorry, I was away for a few days with my mum.

Folklore99: Your mum?

LoonieDunes: My dad isn't in the picture and Maman doesn't go on holiday much because of all the animals.

Folklore99: Okay, you're excused – for the sake of those goats.

06.43

Folklore99: I was being a dickhead, sorry. It's nice that you go on holiday with your mum. I just…

06.46

LoonieDunes: Just?

Folklore: I can't concentrate on this stupid indoor bike when you're not there. *My* mum has noticed and I really don't want her opinion right now. I'm not her favourite daughter and she only has one. Out on the road I'm fine because that's my hyperfocus happy place, but here on my own…

LoonieDunes: It doesn't work. Okay, I get it. I'll tell you next time I'm going away so you can find someone else to train with. God protect us if you're left to your own devices.

Folklore99: Oh, shut up.

LoonieDunes: Wanna watch a film and train?

Folklore99: Do I ever. I'll get my headset so we can chat.

Chapter 5

Seb

I made my mind up then and there: I was quitting cycling.

Sure, I'd made that decision a few times before, but this time I meant it. No one should have to discuss their performance on a bike with the father of the woman they'd just kissed.

Holy shit, I'd kissed Lori Gallagher. I'd had my tongue in her mouth and my hands on her butt and I wasn't sure how I was supposed to recover from that. She'd let me lose it with her and it might have been the best kiss of my life.

It was hard to listen to Tony Gallagher when half of my brain was stuck on the feel of Lori's skin under my fingertips. I wanted to kiss her ear, near the little studs leading to small hoops in her lobes. I wanted to scrape my teeth on her neck. It felt as though all those online conversations had snowballed into that moment, that touching her was the final piece of a puzzle.

Thank God I wasn't wearing bib shorts. I needed to adjust my boxers, but now really wasn't the time, so I tried to ignore the way the cotton pinched. I still couldn't breathe properly. I might never breathe again, after Lori's tongue had swiped over my lip.

It didn't help that she was a bare few metres away, behind the bathroom door, occasionally failing to stifle a snicker.

'I realise we haven't got a good indication of your form yet,' Tony continued. 'I'm not going to be a hard arse about the rides we've done so far.'

'Not a… eh, thanks.'

'In fact,' the general manager continued, clapping me on the shoulder, 'you've proven you can take a joke, which is a key skill on this team.'

'I noticed.'

'But we need to develop a strategy for you as well as a plan for the events our leaders are starting this year. At this point I want you fit and ready to support Colin for the entire Tour. But what about the Spring Classics? Do you want to give some of them a burl?'

I gulped, wondering if I needed Lori to come out and translate. I'd learned a few phrases from her on Zpeed, but 'give something a burl' was not one of them. 'Yes?' I guessed. 'The Tour of Flanders is my lucky race.'

'A lucky man! Always happy to have some extra luck in the team. What about Paris-Roubaix? Have you got the balls for that?'

There was a titter from behind the bathroom door. 'Well, I've started it every year for the past twelve years.' I hadn't always finished it.

'Ah, so you don't have any balls left!' Tony said with a snort.

Lori didn't make a noise, but I could *feel* her laughing. At least the crass joke got rid of the last traces of an erection. Even *thinking* that word in front of Tony Gallagher made me want to dematerialise.

'Look, Colin is starting the Paris-Roubaix, so we'll plan to get you in at this stage. You never know what'll happen in that race, so your experience will be valuable. And if the Tour of Flanders is your lucky one, how about we try and win it! All in, show us what you're made of!'

'Eh, what I'm... Win it?'

'Yes, you drongo! Winning!'

I mustered enough enthusiasm somehow, because he made some more mumbling exclamations I didn't quite understand and clapped me on the shoulder some more. He wasn't serious about the winning. It was mind games that I was getting too old – and too jaded – to play.

But for all I'd said about cheese and a fucking B&B, I couldn't truly picture what came next, either. I wasn't rich; I'd had my team salary and a trickle of prize money over the years, not a deluge. It was more about what I was running away from, rather than towards.

'Regarding that, ah, stunt with the doll, Colin's just testing you, son. Don't let him get to you, ay?' Tony said as he turned to go, sending a ripple of surprise and something warm and sharp through me when he called me 'son'.

I had no idea how to respond. 'Ay?' I repeated, adding a

panicked, 'okay,' onto the end when he shot me a confused look. 'A-okay,' I repeated brightly, choking off the urge to add a 'sir' before I embarrassed myself completely.

Tony's fingers were on the door handle and I was looking forward to getting back to Lori – to *talking* to her – when the tinkle of a cell phone sounded through the bathroom door, followed by a bump and a bang before the room fell silent again. Because I'm an idiot, my knee-jerk reaction was to glance at my own phone, sitting on the desk behind me. Tony blinked and his brow dropped.

'Er, Amir must be—'

'I saw him in the dining room on my way up.'

Zut, now I was in the poop. 'Oh, um, I must have—'

'I know it's none of my business, boy, but it's supposed to be rest time—'

The bathroom door swung open and Tony's theatrical gasp would have been funny in any other situation. 'It's just me, Dad. Don't chuck a wobbly.'

Were they even speaking English?

'What are you—'

'Seb is a friend of mine. I didn't know he was joining the team. We… met last year.' She mumbled the last bit after a moment's hesitation. Tony looked doubtfully from Lori back to me. 'You caught me. I sneaked into his room so we could make out like teenagers,' she said, deadpan. Any words I might have uttered died in my throat.

But Tony grinned and patted her shoulder. 'Always the joker, like your old man. Maybe you can talk some sense into your friend. I'm not so sure his head's screwed on right, this one.'

'That's what I thought,' she agreed.

'You need to prioritise your rest, though, especially after last year,' Tony said.

'I'm just about to,' she assured him, although the look that passed between them suggested that wouldn't be the end of the discussion.

I studied Tony, thinking of all the things Folklore had told me about her cheerleading dad and hard-arse mum and, if I'd grown up with these expectations, I would be at home feeding goats right now. She was a tough one. Tough and really very sexy.

With one more perplexed glance, Tony left us alone. When the door swung closed behind him, we both slumped in relief.

'I hope I didn't get you into trouble,' I blurted out.

'If anything, *I* got *you* into trouble.' She laughed then, her body shaking. Grasping my upper arms, her forehead brushed my shoulder as she doubled over with it and I got those full-body tingles again, as though she really was my friend, my… mine. My entire skin bloomed at the light touch and I was getting into trouble again in my boxers.

'Did you really say "a-okay" to my dad?'

'I was terrified he'd hear you. I knew you were laughing in there. And *you* told him we'd been making out like teenagers. It's not funny,' I insisted when she snorted with renewed laughter. 'Your family will want to kill me.'

She looked up and grinned at me and it took all my restraint not to kiss her again. 'It was pretty funny. "You don't have any balls left."' she quoted with a snort.

I had unfortunately chosen that moment for my desperate attempt to rearrange the seam of my boxers to ease the pressure.

'Seb, do you have a hard-on?' she asked, her mouth swinging open.

'Not any more,' I said emphatically.

'Did you have one while you were talking to my dad?'

'Only… half. And not for long.'

Clapping a hand over her mouth, she shook with laughter. 'You seriously had to talk to my dad at half-mast?'

Throwing up my hands, I said through gritted teeth, 'I didn't choose to! After a kiss like that, I can't just say, "Down boy, no more of that." My mind was blown!'

Leaving Lori speechless was my new favourite feeling.

But she pulled herself together disappointingly quickly. She raised her eyebrows and asked, 'Have you really raced the Paris-Roubaix twelve times?' changing the subject abruptly.

'Four times I didn't finish,' I explained.

'You mean, "I finished the Hell of the North eight times,"' she prompted, giving me a shove. 'I have no idea how you got this far with that attitude.'

'Not to the podium, that's for sure,' I quipped.

'I love the Paris-Roubaix,' she said wistfully, the way normal people talk about their beach holiday. Her hair was swept off her face in a no-nonsense ponytail and she wasn't wearing any make-up, showing all of the pale freckles that dotted her nose and cheeks, but she had such a sweet face when she smiled like that. Her blue eyes glinted with silver. She had a generous bottom lip that would star in my fantasies for years to come. An angular face with a strong, elegant jaw.

It struck me again that this was Folklore standing in front of me, my eyes tracing her cheekbones. Her throat bobbed and my lungs started playing up again.

'I saw you— your finish,' I said, clearing my throat, 'last year.'

'When I came third?' she clarified with a huff.

I crossed my arms and drew myself up. I would never be a big brutish type, even if I were allowed to eat cheese and pizza all the time, but I'd caught her checking me out and I could hit some serious functional threshold power stats with these muscles.

'Tell me that wasn't the best third place of your life, though. I saw the highlights, how you pushed through the mud and carried your bike past the melee after that crash. It was lucky I didn't know who you were on Zpeed or I would have been too much of a fanboy and you would have dropped me faster.'

She glanced away with a smile. 'It was my best result in that race, but I still didn't win it.'

'Why do you like it so much? I already know you're a masochist on the training bike but who actually likes the torture of the cobblestones?'

'I do,' she said lightly. 'It's do or die. Nothing else exists for those three-and-a-half hours except me and the road and the fight. It's where I belong.'

'The opposite of the training bike,' I murmured as flashes of our conversations came back to me: when she'd casually explained that she had ADHD, how her mum had always expected more than Lori could deliver – both in the classroom and in sport.

She nodded her agreement, then froze and her gaze flew to mine. 'You won't tell anyone, will you? The stuff we... talked about?'

'Of course not!' I grumbled, snatching my arm away when she clutched at it. 'You trusted LoonieDunes and you can trust me.' For a second, the quiver of her brow made me wonder if I should have been more gentle with her, but then she lifted her chin, pride restored. Lori didn't want gentle.

'Okay, I'm sorry, fanboy. But even the girls on the team don't know about... you know. They only joke about how I lose everything all the time. If you find a pair of socks somewhere, they're probably mine.'

My skin felt tight again and this time it had nothing to do with the embarrassing situation in my underwear. This was the Folklore I remembered: a big mouth and a soft heart – and a broken body. I wanted to grab her and give her a hug.

'I've got to go,' she said suddenly and, for a second, I was worried I'd spoken my thoughts aloud.

'Okay, sure. I'll... see you round then.'

She glanced at me doubtfully. 'You do realise the kiss shouldn't have happened?'

'Ehm, I hadn't quite finished rationalising it actually.'

'Seb, I'm not—' She met my gaze. 'I'm not supposed to get distracted this year. I worked too hard in recovery.'

I tucked my tongue between my back teeth so I didn't say anything and just nodded.

'Plus we're on the same team. It could get... awkward. I learned that the hard way.'

It took me a second to realise she meant when we broke up. I definitely hadn't thought that far ahead, but I also hadn't dated a teammate before. Folklore had spoken about her injury on Zpeed, but she'd never mentioned the ex. There was a lot she hadn't mentioned, while I'd gleefully gone on about my grandma and relaxed days cycling along the river, which must have sounded incredibly dull.

'I didn't realise the men's and women's teams would see so much of each other,' I managed to reply, stumbling over my disappointment. But she was right. We would never work in real life, even as close friends. 'I haven't been on a team where they share resources like this,' I managed. It said a lot about my previous teams that they hadn't bothered.

'Don't worry, we're separate enough that you can still walk around naked – and don't you dare ask if we do the same.'

'If the women's team walks around naked, it's none of my business,' I confirmed gravely.

She paused, her hand on the doorframe and a smile on her lips. 'I forgot you have a whole family of women – and a grandma who taught you manners. I'm... glad you're on the team, LoonieDunes.'

'Me too,' I replied, my reservations about one last season,

about getting used to a new team, new directors, gone up in smoke at her words.

'But I'd better give you some alone time with Matilda.' She laughed, but cut herself off with a strangled choke, her eyes darting to mine. 'I didn't mean anything by that— I didn't think it through. I'm going and I *won't* be thinking about you... Gah!'

I swaggered to the door of my room, grinning at her. 'Bye, Lore. I won't be thinking about you... either.' I wondered if she could tell I was lying. 'See you at breakfast,' I added with a wink.

Chapter 6

Lori

I had to have a discussion with my dad about what I'd really been doing in Seb's room, which was as awkward as I'd expected.

'No, Dad, there's nothing going on. I know him from an online thing and I just wanted to check that he was settling in okay despite Colin's welcome. Now can you please go and ask Colin about *his* love life?'

'All right, all right, Molly,' he said in a tone that was gratingly patronising – even for an actual father.

But I loved that he called me Molly, my Irish middle name. He was the only person who did – except occasionally Colin, when he wasn't calling me monster – and it was a magic word for that safe place he'd always been. He pushed me, but he also caught me, no matter how far I fell.

Racing had always felt like flying for me and that's the thing about flying: sometimes you fall.

Dad liked to say I was born on a bike. That was typical,

and a little insulting to my mum, who'd gone through preg-
nancy hell and major surgery to bring me into the world,
but that was my larger-than-life dad. I owed him everything
and it was the least I could do to forget about romance for
a few more years – ten at least, if I avoided another injury.
At least on the topic of my non-existent personal life my
parents were in agreement.

I hated to think what Mum would have had to say if she'd
been the one to walk in on Seb and me but, lucky for me,
she didn't travel with the team any more. She had her work
with the triathlon club in Melbourne and Dad had his career
and they barely saw each other these days. That they seemed
happy about that fact was something I'd been shutting out
since before I got hurt.

'How's the war wound?' It was just like Dad not to dance
around the issue – and to avoid talking about anything to do
with romance for long.

'Great,' I said, a study in subtlety. 'No pain – at least not
related to my back. I don't think I'm at full fitness yet, but
I'll be good by Nationals.'

He gave me a rough squeeze and a pat that would have
hurt like hell four months ago. 'That's my girl. Your watts are
looking good. We'll do your VO2 and lactate tomorrow, so
save your strength.'

Great. I'd be strapped up to a bunch of machines and spend
a gruelling couple of hours pushing my body to the limit so
someone could stab my finger and scientifically prove where
that limit was.

I sounded jaded like Seb, but at least I was nowhere near giving all of this up for cheese.

After the initial hiccough on the hill with Seb and Matilda, my training camp progressed well. I had as many doctor's appointments as I did training rides, but I was back in the bunch. I could almost feel the old me, the woman who broke records and made history. For the first two weeks, I even managed to push away the suspicion that I'd stumbled into a spate of rotten luck.

Sure, I had a slipped gear and screwed up a finish, snapped a chain halfway up a tough climb and knocked a wheel out of shape, but I figured I was getting all my mechanicals out of the way before the real racing season started.

I would get all the intrusive thoughts, all the uncertainty out of my system before the Australian Nationals in January. By then, I was determined to have banished the recurring thoughts and questions about Seb too.

Although one time I accidentally googled him instead of being sensible and zoning out in front of the telly during rest time – actually, a couple of times. It was bad that there were so many photos of him on the internet for me to study, from the old ones where he was baby-faced and red-cheeked in the colours of teams that now had different names to action shots of him dripping with sweat as he clutched the drop bars of his bike, his jersey flapping open to reveal the heart-rate monitor strapped around his chest – and some skin that I would never admit I'd studied in detail.

A particularly compelling photo of him hefting a bike over a muddy ditch revealed he'd been a cyclocross competitor as well as road racing in his early career. That explained the shoulders.

I read about his Tour de France stage wins, the most recent of which was six years ago, powering into Limoges after unexpectedly dropping the others in the breakaway on the last climb. We all had those special days where it felt as though someone had replaced our blood with pure electricity and we pedalled with fire instead of mortal muscles. I lived for those days, even though I knew there was never any guarantee that I would get one.

But I had to believe I would, so it didn't make sense that I was staring longingly at photos of a guy instead of resting and focusing on my fitness – no matter how delicious that guy looked in skintight Lycra.

Or soft-looking hoodies in the breakfast room. Even the jersey that Colin snuck into his things that read: 'Never underestimate an old man on a bicycle' looked hot on Seb because of the cocky smile on his lips when he strode out wearing it.

I was walking a dangerous line cataloguing those smiles. He caught me a few times and those were my favourite, the smiles that said, '*I see you, Folklore.*' Even more dangerous was the chance that my brother would catch me and I'd never hear the end of it. He hadn't grown out of the 'kid brother' thing with me, despite turning 23 and starting to take on the lead rider position more often – a position I wasn't entirely sure he was ready for, given the way he was acting out under pressure.

The training camp was carefully devised to combine intensifying endurance rides, recovery days and various core fitness activities that often doubled as team building – which wasn't my favourite. I'd done a decent job of hiding my turmoil – all of it – from my roommate Doortje and the others on the women's team, but it was kind of hard to be best buddies when most of them were employed to help me win.

Doortje was seven years older than me, Moroccan-Dutch and blunt to the point of rudeness, and she was one of my favourite people in the world – although I'd never say it to her face. As the daughter of the manager and the lead rider in the team, I didn't expect hugs and tears from my teammates and I appreciated Doortje's straightforwardness, where some of the other girls tied me in knots with comparisons and fear of resentment. All that stuff was in high definition in my thoughts after the months of reflection while I recovered. I kind of wished I could discuss it all with LoonieDunes, but there was no opportunity for that, even if it had been a good idea.

Doortje and I arrived at the fitness studio in the basement together at the end of the second week, grumbling as usual that the men got out of doing Zumba because their masculinity was so fragile, to find Seb there chatting to the instructor, who was definitely making heart eyes at him. She was a curvy little woman, who could shake her hips, so I could understand the appeal. My booty was entirely muscle and refused to move independently of my torso or my legs. When I did Zumba, I usually looked like one of those inflatable tube guys with the generator on the blink.

My brain worked through all of this before noticing that Seb was warming up to do Zumba with us, even though the rest of the men's team was somewhere else doing testosterone yoga or something.

'Did Colin tell you that today was Zumba day?' I asked with a withering sigh.

He wrenched his gaze from our cute instructor – okay, he actually didn't have any trouble looking away from the instructor, but I was oversensitive – and turned to me in dismay. 'Yes. Does that mean the room is booby-trapped?'

'No,' I said curtly. 'It means you're the only guy here to dance.'

'Ohhhh,' he said stiltedly, with a desperate look through the glass panels, as though he could find the men's team just outside and escape his fate.

But he bucked up quickly, even accepting that his fate was in the front row as the rest of us filled up the back. If you ask me, he accepted his fate a little too eagerly once the music started.

He looked more like Mr Bean than Shakira, but it turned out he could do a mean body roll. He copied the moves with such intensity, that Doortje stopped dancing entirely and feetched her phone to film him.

He was definitely a goof, but he was a sexy goof I could picture pressing up against on the dance floor. He noticed what Doortje was doing, but he just winked at her, which summoned that ball of jealousy in my stomach again. God, it was annoying.

At the end of the session, his hair was drenched with sweat and he rubbed a towel over his head, emerging with a grin that he directed at me. 'I'll have to thank Colin,' he said. 'He doesn't know what he's missing.' Leaning closer, he said softly, 'You're my preferred Gallagher anyway.'

Before I could reply, Leesa Kubicka joined us. 'That was awesome!' she gushed with a smile that my jealousy interpreted as proprietary and my intellect interpreted as me being a chump over a guy and sensitive as usual about my American teammate, who was pretty and poised and apparently Mensa-worthy intelligent. '*None* of the other guys would have stayed – except maybe Lars, but he wouldn't have done it with so much style.'

One morning at the beginning of the third week, Seb didn't show up for breakfast and I spent the entire time it took me to knock back my espresso and pancake with fruit (yes, the diet was weird and we were allowed pancakes but no cheese) wondering if Colin had finally broken him. But when we headed out of the dining room, I caught a glimpse of him across the lobby in the conference room, in the corner that had been set up as a photo studio.

Doortje, Bonnie and Leesa must have noticed me looking, because they stopped and peered through the door.

'Now, hands on your hips. We'll try that,' said the photographer as an uneasy-looking Seb stood in front of the lights in his full team kit. Orange wasn't a great colour on everyone, but it worked for him, with his smooth brown eyes and thick hair. That and his shoulders looked impossibly broad, his corded arms lean and tough. Twenty years he said he'd been in the saddle. His body looked it: every inch built for power and resilience.

But in that moment I wasn't thinking about his performance on the bike. My mouth was dry, my gaze glued to the bumps and furrows of muscle and bone.

Damn it, LoonieDunes was *hot* and I'd kissed him and I didn't have time to lose my shit over a guy right now.

He rocked back on his heels, a smile pasted onto his face, as the photographer snapped away, murmuring approvingly. The movement pushed his hips out and I heard Bonnie titter beside me.

'Who's got the ruler?' she whispered, holding a hand out in front of her and squinting to measure—

'Bonnie!' I hissed.

'Come on,' Leesa said, turning to me with an eye-roll. 'The guys make twice as much money as we do, are able to pee over the side of their bikes without even stopping and you want to take away our one remaining joy: that their dicks don't fit in bike shorts?'

I resented her even more when she had a point.

'I bet he's got a big one,' Doortje said with a speculative nod. I had *not* been thinking the same thing.

The photographer spoke before I finished my inarticulate humph. 'Try a few poses. Have you seen the website? All the guys are doing something different.'

'Poses?' Seb repeated, his voice high. 'What, like this?' He raised his fists and eyeballed the camera as though 'Chariots of Fire' was playing in the background.

'That's great!' the photographer gushed.

'Really?' Seb said with a chuckle. He puffed up his shoulders and crossed his arms in front of him, every ripple of muscle visible through his skintight jersey. But he ruined the effect with a wry smile.

'Hold up an arm like a bodybuilder,' the photographer suggested and I stifled a snort, wondering how mortified Seb would be later when he saw his portrait on the team website.

'Pull down the zip of your jersey a little – a bit more,' said the photographer and my hair stood on end. He stared into the camera, intense and a little uncertain. Tugging on the zip, I could imagine he was undressing for me, peeling off the layers so I could run my tongue—

He looked up, his gaze snagging on mine and he froze for a heartbeat. Or maybe I froze and my heart stopped beating. His mouth kicked up on one side and I was back in his hotel room, his hands on me, wishing my dad hadn't interrupted.

I couldn't afford another season like last year's, full of setbacks and distractions and a giant, public break-up with a teammate, even before I crashed out of my life for three months. I *had* to get Seb out of my system.

As I watched him intently, my skin blooming with goosebumps and my heart trying out a Zumba beat, I wondered whether there might be a better way to do it.

Chapter 7

Seb

It made no sense that something that hurt this much could be so wonderful.

I was broken; my lungs hurt, my *blood* hurt. I was so far past muscle pain that my legs had transcended physical matter. My head pounded and my stomach roiled and *nothing* would stop me on this last ride of the camp.

Perhaps something should have stopped me, but I'd switched off the cautious part of my brain at the first winding descent, high on gravity and adrenaline and the ragged peaks of the Girona Pyrenees. Grassy alpine pastures with patches of snow spread out before me and in the distance, the figures of endless summits rose white and grey and blurred with mist.

It was freezing cold – actually below zero up here, while Girona enjoyed a civilised 11° Celsius – but I didn't notice. My metabolism was on fire, and I didn't care what happened to me afterwards, as long as I reached the little flag Colin had programmed into my phone.

I didn't know where the others were but somehow my motivation was always better on a solo breakaway, the gruelling doomed act of a racer who doesn't know any other way to win against better competition.

Perhaps that's why I kept going, when I really should have known — when part of me *did* know — that something wasn't right. This stuff would be great fun to unravel with a therapist when I quit riding pro.

The climb finally levelled out and after a few more metres of pedalling like a maniac, I shot past the virtual flag like a sprinter on the Champs-Élysées. The entirety of Catalonia opened up before me — big hills followed by little hills and the haze of the sea, lost on the horizon — and I was the winner of my own perverse race against myself. It was my favourite kind of race.

I decelerated slowly, making wide loops and drunken figure eights on the lonely road as my legs gradually released the tension. The cocktail of acids and adrenaline in my blood receded a little, allowing rational thought to interfere — or rather, to regain control of my body.

I quickly realised that Colin had finally got the better of me. I laughed and gave him a two-fingered salute with my stiff hand, even though he must have been miles away.

'Well played, bastard,' I muttered. Either he was very clever and had planned to use my own unhelpful psychology against me, or he'd got lucky, but Colin's last prank had hit the jackpot.

There was no one there, on that lonely pass. No team car. No backslapping trainers – not even any side-eye from Tony Gallagher. When I'd unexpectedly dropped them back in Ripoll, my teammates must have turned off and headed to the real meeting point, while Colin had programmed somewhere different into my phone, leaving me stranded on the Coll de la Creueta, a windswept mountain pass, where I couldn't climb into the team coach and head back to Girona in time for a late lunch. It would only have been chicken, vegetables and rice – as always – but I couldn't hold back a helpless whimper when I realised I wasn't getting any soon.

With a deep sigh that only dragged the icy air into my body, I checked the map, plotted a route and set off again, one leg dangling limply as I headed down the mountain. I had no food and not much water with me, only the payment app on my phone, if anyone up here in the mountains accepted that. If Colin had been a real dick about it, there might be a miserable 120 km in front of me. I could call someone, but my pride stopped me, imagining them all gathering around waiting for the ring and guffawing as I babbled in a panic.

As I zipped down the other side of the pass, I mused that I'd been waiting for something like this to happen. I couldn't decide whether it had been the most hellish training camp of my life or the highlight of my career. Matilda had slowly deflated over the past two-and-a-half weeks – a warning that I had perhaps peaked too early?

I was in the form of my life. Despite the side-eye, I'd impressed Tony Gallagher and the men's directeur sportif,

Alan Hargreaves. My legs had been so good, I hadn't recognised myself and I'd tried hard not to grow too confident in them. Anything could happen in this sport and it usually happened to me.

I had earned the trust of Tony Gallagher and – I hoped – the respect of Colin. He was the lead rider and even though I would only be drafting him towards the finish line until my legs gave out, helping him to save energy, the domestique to a leader was still recognised as a damn good rider themselves. I would most likely start the Tour de France one last time.

But every time I looked at Colin, I saw Lori and my thoughts scrambled. It had been maddening trying to avoid her, when I saw her every morning at breakfast and every evening at dinner – and every night in my inappropriate dreams.

It wasn't only me she kept at arm's length; she'd often sat alone before a ride and even when she sat with her teammates, there had been a pride, an intensity to her that discouraged intimacy.

She was right that we should leave things between us. She was too young for me, too ambitious. That was the simple explanation anyway – more than enough to convince me to keep my distance before I even considered how quickly all my other attempts at intimacy had gone down the toilet.

I dropped a couple of hundred metres of altitude quickly as the rocks and meadows flew past and little stone villages appeared and disappeared in the distance. Could I retire here and run a training camp for amateurs? I knew a couple of guys who'd done that, but they'd had families to support the endeavour and I'd never managed to make anyone stay in a relationship – let alone move somewhere for me.

My phone vibrated as I whipped around a hairpin bend, the landscape growing forested, with a pink stone chapel built on a crag among the hills to my left. I gave myself a mental pat on the back for making Colin text me first, but the menacing clouds to the east meant I felt relief as well.

When I pulled over to check the message, it wasn't Colin. It was an unknown number, but when I saw the words, anticipation rushed through my worn-out body.

Hey, it's Lori.

She was typing more and I shivered as I waited for her next message to drop in, taking a moment to save her number in my phone as 'Folklore'.

The guys just got back and told me what Colin did. Can you text me where you are? Weather forecast doesn't look good.

There wasn't anything much in the message, but I still grinned like an idiot as I fumbled to send my current location with frigid fingertips. A sudden Pyrenean gust confirmed her concerns about the weather. Her reply came quickly.

I can't believe he did this to you – or that you fell for it! Get your arse indoors! It'll take a while to get a car to you, but stay put. Get a hotel and have a shower before you cool down too much. I mean it, Seb. Look after yourself.

My head spun at the idea of Lori feeling concerned for me – and the prospect of standing under the warm spray, which gave me an inkling of just how dead I was on the bike. Checking the map again, I sent her a pin on the next town.

I'll hole up here. Can you get a team car to pick me up?

Tucking my phone back into the holder and clipping one shoe into the pedal, I wobbled around the curve, the air cutting into my face and peeling a layer off my arse. Taking a turn-off onto a narrow lane, the town appeared below, a cluster of terracotta roofs and grey stone buildings clutching the slope, facing sheer rock and a steep valley on the other side.

Ten minutes later, I'd pulled up at a charming house with faded wooden shutters and Catalan flags and the sign I'd been looking for: a hand-painted one bearing the word 'fonda' – an inn.

The receptionist hadn't blinked at my request to pay with an app and even offered to store my bike in the garage, as though bedraggled cyclists with no money limped into the hotel every day. Standing under a hot shower in the cramped bathroom, I thought Colin might have been a genius.

It was uncomfortable to put my jersey and bibs back on, but that was a small price to pay for the black bean stew and a salad with enormous hunks of crumbly goat's-milk cheese. Fuck chicken and rice. Like the last day of the Tour de France, I ate and savoured and rewarded my wrecked body with calories, salt and protein while my brain indulged in memories of Lori Gallagher sitting across the dining room at the team hotel.

My phone rang as soon as I returned to the room, where I would happily have stayed a few hours longer. Snatching it up with a sigh, I blinked back a giddy smile to see the name 'Folklore' flash up.

'Hey,' I answered, hoping she didn't hear the eagerness in my voice. 'I thought you were the team car, come to get me. I quite like it here. Do you realise that now I have your number, I might text you sometimes?'

Her laugh was a rueful huff. 'You're allowed to text me congratulations when I win.'

'Do you mean that? I might be texting you all the time, then.' I stretched out on the bed with my arm above my head. 'Give you something to look forward to.'

'Ha ha. Yes, I mean it, but that's *all* you're allowed to say in the text. I am the team car, though,' she said drily. 'At least, I'm driving it.'

It took me a moment to swallow the ball of delight in my throat and convince myself to stay cool. She wasn't here because she wanted… me.

'Oh, you——Yourself——That was quick. Did you leave right after your ride? Have you eaten? There's a really nice restaurant here. If you're hungry, we could…' So much for staying cool.

She paused for a long moment – torturously long, since I couldn't breathe properly. 'Want to text me exactly where you are?' she asked. 'I'll be there in a minute.'

Chapter 8

Lori

When I'd briefly considered the possibility of catching Seb alone to see where things led, I had not imagined the opportunity would fall into my lap. I'd thought about cornering him in a cupboard and getting hot and heavy for a dirty orgasm and then – done. I certainly hadn't pictured the most romantic hotel in the world, floating over dramatic rock faces in the impossibly beautiful Pyrenees.

I was still in my jersey and shorts, now caked with dried sweat. My hair hung in salty strands around my face and a fuzzy plait past my shoulders. I was no one's idea of a well-turned-out date, but none of that mattered when I saw Seb waiting for me outside, holding onto the low lintel of the doorway and stretching.

I'd established he looked great in Lycra: powerful leg muscles, a labyrinth of angles and ripples in his arms and a lean, ridged torso. But it was his smile that made my insides twist with longing – as though I was the only person in the world he wanted to see in that moment, sweat and all.

A sense of inevitability hit me like déjà vu. I'd fought the attraction for too long. I had to let this happen. Once. We could do this once and it would be all right. No one from the team was anywhere nearby. Camp finished in two days and then I was heading back to Australia for Nationals. Once wouldn't hurt.

His smile dimmed as I came closer and he reached for me. I held out my hand automatically before I'd worked out what he wanted and he dragged me close with a kick of a smile that made me light-headed. He smelled like a strange mix of soap and sweat and I couldn't think properly, waiting for him to kiss me, my whole body on fire for it.

But he didn't kiss me. 'Hey,' he said, his voice low and rough. 'You came all the way here for me?' The wonder in his voice showered tingles over my skin and he punctuated his words with a squeeze of my hand.

'I couldn't make one of the support staff drive all the way here again because my brother is a little shit. He said he didn't expect you to actually make it up here alone.'

He tipped his head eloquently in response, a fleeting grimace crossing his lips. I suspected Colin wasn't the only one who'd underestimated him.

He gestured through the doors. 'Come inside. You told me to stay warm and then you came all this way dressed like that!' With a gentle tug, he pulled me into the tiny reception area and closed the door. There was no one at the desk and in the confined space, all I could think about was touching him and my skin lit up in anticipation. 'Did you eat before you came?'

The aromas of paprika and garlic, with hints of beef and fish and everything wonderful in life, wafted from the restaurant, but I only wanted him. Perhaps that should have scared me.

'Mmmhmm,' I assured him. Some energy bars and a sandwich counted. 'But did you get a room? I could do with a shower.' *And maybe* you *in the shower.*

'That's the least I can offer, although I don't mind if you want to head back straight away.'

No, I didn't want to head back. I wanted to get naked and under the spray and then get him naked too. Goosebumps blossomed and if my nipples hadn't already been so hard from the cold, they might have given away my intentions. As I followed him up the steps, the muscles in his back and the curve of his butt right in front of my eyes, I developed some mighty big intentions, most of them involving my hands and tongue and teeth.

We shared a chuckle at the tiny bathroom, but I squeezed in, hesitating before deciding to shut the door. I probably couldn't just strip off in front of him without talking about this first – or could I? Ditching my hoodie and unzipping my winter jersey, I shoved the doubts away and turned on the spray.

A drawn-out moan escaped my lips as the hot water ran over my head, sluicing down my body. I'd made it through training camp. I was tired and mixed up and turned on and

I felt a little dangerous. Warm and clean, I patted myself dry, wrapping the towel around me afterwards.

Flinging open the door before I had time to overthink this, I stepped into the room in my towel and two things struck me at once: first, the room was tiny and the door to the bathroom struck the bed with a little thwack; and second, if I was noticing random details like that, then my bravado was a cover for the prick of anxiety I'd been pretending not to feel.

Seb stood with his back turned, holding his phone, and doubts crowded my mind. Did he even want this? Sure, I'd done a few ads for the women's deodorant that sponsored me, but they'd been posed and airbrushed and not really me. I was a sportswoman. I didn't have much fat on me – just enough to stay healthy – but my leg muscles had their own muscles, I had surgery scars down my back and up one forearm and three of my teeth were implants after they'd been knocked out in a crash six years ago. Maybe he was just a friendly, touchy-feely guy and didn't actually want to do me.

'My phone is dead,' he muttered, still not looking at me. 'Do you have a charge— Hunh.' His tight exhale when he saw me was something between a sigh and a wheeze and it was all it took for me to get out of my own head and back in the game. His eyes were bright as he stared at me, his mouth hanging open. 'Did you… forget to get dressed?'

I was tempted to just rush at him, letting the towel drop to the floor, but I was a sensible adult and we needed to talk about this – about the 'once' thing, at least. So I lifted my chin and sat on the bed, patting the space beside me, where he dropped to join me gratifyingly quickly.

'Okay, so hear me out,' I began. 'It's been kind of hard to ignore each other and my focus has been off.'

He winced. 'Focus. Right.'

'I thought, if we let this… happen. If we…' Now I'd got to the business end of this discussion, it was surprisingly difficult to come out with the words. 'We have sex,' I blurted out as dispassionately as I could. 'Once,' I added – my mantra for today.

'We have sex. Once,' he repeated, his jaw working. 'And that will help how?'

'It'll be d-done,' I stuttered. 'Everything sorted. We… bang it all out and when I get back from Australia in spring, we'll be back to… friends or whatever.' Okay, that sounded unhinged, but I couldn't take the words back now. 'Maybe you don't want to,' I added quietly.

'Lori,' he began emphatically, turning to face me and swallowing, 'You had me semi-hard at, "Okay." I'm struggling to think straight because your collarbone is right there and…'

'My collarbone?'

'Yeah,' he rasped, rubbing the back of his neck as his gaze slipped down my throat. 'I keep wondering what your skin there tastes like.'

With a whump, I had full-on goosebumps, tingles and nerves standing to attention in every part of my body – *every* part. The pull of attraction became a throb and the guy had done nothing except make a comment about tasting my collarbone.

'Well, you can find that out and I can get past this.'

His gaze snapped up to mine and away again. 'I hope you can. I really do. If you think sleeping together once will get your focus back, then... let's do it.'

'Good,' I said with a haggard exhale. 'Once,' I repeated.

He hesitated, glancing at the ceiling, before he murmured, 'Once,' in quiet agreement. 'Hum, do we need to talk about contraception?' he asked, turning to me.

'I'm on contraception and we're both squeaky clean, or we wouldn't be here,' I pointed out.

'Yeah,' he said, tapping his fingers on his thigh.

I turned to him until my knees nudged his and peered into his face. 'Are you nervous?'

He was still staring at the ceiling. 'A woman I've been fantasising about for two weeks – or four months, depending on how you look at it – wants to have sex with me and you think I wouldn't be nervous?'

My brain was in a fog and I needed him to touch me already – before this conversation reminded me too much of those cosy moments hearing his voice in my ear.

'Lore,' he said softly, his palm snaking around the back of my neck and his forehead dropping to mine. Longing flared up inside me – but for what? His warm hand was unbearable and necessary on my skin, but a deep restlessness rose up inside me as well. 'We stay friends, yes?' It was a condition, not a question.

'Yes.'

'I look after you, you look after me. Friends,' he repeated, this time tilting his head and drawing close enough that his breath feathered my lips. I would have said just about anything to get him to kiss me.

'Yes!'

His hand slid from my neck to my face, his other hand coming up to my jaw and I had a moment of fear that everything was about to change and any promises we made could end up dust. But he came solemnly nearer, holding me still and, with a slow, purposeful movement, his mouth tasted mine.

I was making a mistake. The ache that started up inside me should have warned me off, but the soothing brush of his lips, the relief that swept through me when he increased the pressure and teased me with the tip of his tongue, pushed out my concerns in a heartbeat.

It might be a mistake later, but right now, the kiss was everything.

Chapter 9

Seb

The moment was a little *too* real. That instinctive, unpremeditated kiss we'd shared in my room had been fun — an adrenaline rush, a rollercoaster of discovery — but this kiss was soft and scared and achingly slow.

A light tremor rippled through her, scattering my thoughts. I needed air, but I needed her mouth more, so I stayed where I was, my consciousness gradually overtaken by sensations: heat, pressure, tenderness, the tug of her lips and the first brushes of her tongue against mine.

Fisting my hands in the thick towel at her waist, I pulled her towards me and she came with a ragged exhale, one hand sliding into my hair as her knees landed on either side of me and then my mind blanked again when she kissed me — hard and deep this time.

My blood rushed and time elapsed too quickly as she pulled my bib straps off my shoulders and trailed her hands down my chest, her mouth hot and inevitable on mine. Panting, my vision losing focus, I dropped my head to her collarbone. The freckles weren't as dense on her body as on her face, but they were my new favourite thing and I breathed her in, teasing her skin with my lips and tongue until she clutched my head and arched against me.

Spring sunshine — that's what her skin tasted like.

I brushed my lips and teeth at her jaw, over the cartilage of her ear, and she lifted her chin and whimpered — the most wonderful sound I'd heard in my life.

Her towel loosened, slipping to reveal the most beautiful, freckled curves and I pressed soft kisses to her chest while I tugged at the material, chafing gently over her breasts until she was panting too.

'Fuck,' she groaned with a shaky gasp, making me smile into her skin. Slipping my hands under the towel, my mouth dried and my heart hammered and the feel of her was so much that I nearly lost it, as her arms came around my neck and she gave an inarticulate moan, her eyes closed.

'This is already the best sex of my life,' I muttered in wonder, almost to myself.

'Don't stop now,' she grumbled in reply, drawing another smile to my lips. Coming down hard on my cock, she moved against me, sending white-hot need crackling up my spine.

'Steady on,' I choked.

'Hurry up,' she replied, reaching for the hem of my base layer and peeling it over my head. Her mouth was hot on my chest and my fingers dug into her thighs as I fought to hold back.

My palms drifting to the curve of her butt, over her hips and into the crease along the top of her thigh, where I suddenly, desperately wanted my tongue, I held her still and teased her with another tug of the towel.

'If this is the only time I get to enjoy your body, I'm not going to hurry,' I said in a low voice.

She wanted to make a smart comeback – I could see it in her eye – but my palm skimmed her rib cage and she arched up with a gasp. Lifting my hand higher, I loosened the towel right to the brink, but I didn't touch her nipples, enjoying the way her breath hitched and caught.

'You are so beautiful,' I groaned, swiping her wet hair from her face with one hand, as the other one slowly pulled back the towel to reveal her freckled breasts, her tough, taut body, heaving with need, her skin flushed pink.

'Shut up,' she whispered, grabbing my forearms to steady herself. 'I don't believe you anyway.'

'If you don't believe me, then it doesn't matter if I say you're gorgeous when you want me so bad like this.'

She gave me a shove and opened her mouth to say something, but all I had to do was brush my thumb over her nipple and her protest became a strangled moan.

'I want to suck your nipples until they're pink and puffed up, but I also want to keep watching you lose your mind,' I continued, now firmly addicted to the spark in her eye when I babbled nonsense like that out of the depths of my complicated ego.

Plucking her nipple and soothing it gently, I was endlessly

gratified when her eyes slammed closed and she lifted her chin — in submission? Desperation? Invitation? I accepted, dragging my lips up her neck as I teased her breasts, ragged, inarticulate sounds emerging from her throat.

I eased a finger between her legs, gently, carefully, finding her hot and swollen and worthy of my filthiest dreams.

'Yesssss, you're so wet,' I hissed as I let her grind a few times, snagging a nipple and flicking it with my tongue. 'Gonna make you come hard,' I promised. 'But you've got to work for it.'

'You have a big mouth,' she grunted. 'Less talking and more doing.'

Stilling her with a tight grip on her hips, I said, 'Talking and teasing, Folklore. That's what we do.'

She was frowning, her eyes shining and her chest heaving and maybe she had a point. Maybe we should just fuck and finish, because I was worried I would never forget the way she looked at me just then: wary and vulnerable and a little helpless.

'That's what we did online,' she reminded me, swallowing hard. 'This is not...'

I tried to pull myself together. This was a fuck to resolve the tension, not the once-in-a-lifetime opportunity to make love to a woman I could never keep. I was just a sucker like that.

'Okay,' I said with a firm kiss to her lips. Tipping her off my lap and onto the bed, I dropped down on top of her, my face in her breasts. 'It's just a fuck.'

I yanked at my shorts, peeling them off eagerly. Sucking a nipple into my mouth and scraping my tongue around it, I revelled in the sounds she made, the way she clutched my head and dropped her legs open. It was too easy to lose my mind when she smelled like everything I'd ever wanted and the knowledge that I might only get to do this once kept rising in my throat.

'With some heavy foreplay first,' I added with a twitch of a smile, pressing kisses down her stomach. 'We can fuck soon.' My hand on her knee, the pad of my thumb brushing over the patchwork of puckered scars there, I made progress steadily downwards and my mouth watered. I glanced up for permission, finding her eyes glazed. 'Entrée first?'

'Did you just use a stupid food metaphor?' Her voice wavered and she was breathing hard.

'Sorry,' I said, clearing my throat. 'May I perform oral sex on you?'

'Fine, you idiot,' she panted through a laugh, reaching one hand up to the headboard. 'Do it.'

I gazed at her soft, wet centre and whispered, 'How the fuck did I deserve this?' before I took the first, teasing taste that only whetted my appetite for more. She even tasted right and I could have explored that oversensitive, swollen bud and the slick furrows all afternoon.

She whimpered and panted for more and I had to hold her still with a gentle grip on her thigh. With the slightly detached thought that I was the luckiest man in the world, I set to work on her.

Lori

Holy crap, Seb had me so strung out I was about to break. It was supposed to be a quick bang, but instead he had two fingers easing inside me and I was crawling out of my skin with each swipe of his tongue. I was riding the edge and I didn't want it to end, but at the same time, I was desperate to come.

'You want to come now or when I fuck you?' he asked, his voice unexpectedly steady when his words twisted me into a pretzel. I tried to reply, but nothing came out.

He gentled his touch and glanced up at me. 'Now *and* when I fuck you?'

I didn't know how he knew, but he slowed the movement of his fingers to a torturous slide and I was a mess in an instant. I gasped, my grip on the headboard tightening as my vision blurred.

'I love how close you are, Lore,' he muttered. 'You're like my favourite book. It's going to be hell to only read you once.'

'Just... fuck me, Seb,' I whined.

His head came up and he gave me a slow smile that flared over my skin as his dimples deepened. 'What was that?'

'You heard me.'

'I know,' he said, his smile growing sheepish. 'I just... want to hear you say it again. I want to hear you say my name like that again.' His voice trailed off to gusts of breath and his smile faded and I was trapped and squirming, his gaze so hot and my breath so tight.

Taking a shuddering breath, I gave him what he wanted. 'Please, Seb.'

The way he groaned and bit his lip and curled his hand around my thigh turned my spine to liquid and I'd never wanted anything more in my life when he shifted over me again, pressing a soft kiss to my mouth.

So much for that quick bang. I was drunk, dazed, in pieces. And that was before he gently grasped the back of my knee, holding me open, and pushed his tip inside me. The pressure washed over me, tight and sharp and perfect as he went deeper until the whole thick length of him was seated.

Incapable of speech, I mumbled something inarticulate and shifted, my fingers digging into his butt.

'It's— Wow. Lore— Goood,' he choked out, panting.

'I— Ohhhh fuck. I know,' I managed, trailing off to a gasp when he thrust.

Clutching at his shoulders, I hung on as he pumped, his breath hitched and his expression wild. He pushed deep, frantic and rough, but he nuzzled my jaw with such tenderness.

It wasn't supposed to be this good. I definitely shouldn't have been thinking about LoonieDunes and the jokes and easy conversation and the way he'd patiently let me put my life back together around our training rides.

We were supposed to do the animal thing and then get over it, but I snaked my arm around his neck and pulled him close. His ragged breath in my ear was my new favourite sound, even better than his voice in my headphones, dragging me up out of a low moment by telling me how his grandma knitted him leg warmers for cycling in winter that looked like something Cyndi Lauper would have worn.

He pushed me higher and higher, bucking and losing it as though he couldn't contain himself. My thoughts blurred, prickles of something joyful rippling over my skin, my body growing light.

He hiked up my leg, going deeper. 'Ohhh, the way you take it, Lore,' he groaned. 'The way you take my cock.'

'Need it,' I mumbled, long past coherent thought.

'Yeah?' he panted. 'You need this?'

My eyes rolled back and I arched off the mattress, whispering my answer between thrusts. 'Yes. *Yes.*'

'I've got you,' he crooned, dropping his body close to mine, which dragged the base of his cock against my clit, making me whimper and moan. Two more thrusts and I splintered, the orgasm looming. 'That's it, Lori,' he choked out. 'Come for me. You're so beautiful.'

With a flash of heat through my body and light behind my eyes, I tumbled over, hiding my face in his shoulder as I gasped for breath, as my molecules separated and re-formed, sensation ripping through me, leaving me moaning and gasping, not a bone left.

With a huff and a groan and a frantic thrust, Seb joined me, shuddering through his own orgasm as his cock jerked inside me. Coming down slowly, the spots gradually receded from my vision and I felt his deep sigh through my own body.

As awareness returned, so did my concerns. What did we do now? I was just wondering whether I should give him a push so I could get up, swipe my hair over my shoulder and march out of there, when he rolled off, collapsing onto his back next to me.

I met his gaze, which turned out to be a *bad* idea. The light in his eyes, the lopsided smile he gave me, burned somewhere in my chest and that burn could torch my entire career, everything I'd worked for.

His smile faded and he sat up, stilling me with a hand on my shoulder when I tried to do the same.

'Just a minute,' he said softly. 'Let me clean you up and then we can go.'

I froze, coolness spreading over my skin at the awkwardness of his words – at least I thought it was the awkwardness and definitely not the tenderness.

He returned with a face cloth from the bathroom. 'Or do you want to have another shower?'

'Let's just go,' I said hurriedly, making to get up, but he stopped me again.

'Hold on,' he said firmly. 'This will only take a second.'

I looked anywhere but at him while he pressed the warm, damp cloth between my legs.

'What's the matter? No one ever cleaned up their mess with you before?'

I slapped one hand over my eyes, even as I began to relax into his ministrations. 'No,' I admitted quietly.

'Well, I didn't want you driving home with…'

I peeked through my fingers. 'With your come dripping into my shorts?'

He choked and I sat up to wallop him on the back until he laughed and fended off my arm. He grasped my chin and my heart rate kicked up again, wondering if he was going to kiss me and a bit concerned by how much I wanted that.

But instead, he just said, 'Friends, right? Always?'

I nodded eagerly, the promise of that statement wrapping around me like a cosy blanket in that odd moment. 'Friends.'

Perhaps I should have taken the time to ask myself why he'd needed confirmation, his tone a little desperate. If I had, I might have realised exactly how much trouble we could end up in later, when it all came back to bite me.

6 January, 03:15
Seb: *Message deleted*

Chapter 10

Seb

Perhaps it was a sign of ageing – or too long in the bike saddle – that I was struggling to stay awake at 11 o'clock in the evening on a Saturday night. Not that there was any activity on a cold January night in my tiny hometown where the only streets were called 'High Road', 'Low Road' and 'Church Road'. We didn't even qualify for a Rue de la Liberté in this rural idyll, where there were more pigs than people, and an honest-to-God brotherhood of monks who lived in personal poverty and spent every generation trying to turn the locals from lapsed Catholics back into practising ones. As a teenager, I'd always been disappointed that they weren't the useful kind of Belgian monks who brewed beer.

My mum and my grandma – farming people from generations of farming people – had long since gone to bed, which didn't help me stay awake, but it did help me feel less sheepish about my reason for doing so. To make sure they didn't see or hear anything, I'd shut myself in my sparse bedroom – sparse because I'd moved in and out of there so many times, rationalising my belongings each time I left for a short, pointless stint in my own apartment somewhere, before remembering how much time I spent travelling and moved home again.

That night I felt sheepish about a lot of things, including being 34 and still technically living with my mum and grandma – about to hide in my bedroom to watch a race where I hoped to catch a glimpse of the woman who'd slept with me to get rid of me. Some days I was even quite okay with that. At least we'd got to do it.

I'd been surprised to wake up to a message from her two weeks ago, wishing me a merry Christmas with a picture of a spindly eucalyptus branch decorated with tinsel. I'd replied with a picture of my favourite tree ornament – a Death Star bauble – expecting her to tease me, but she hadn't replied.

She must have been busy. While I was trying my best to train in the frost and bitter cold of the windswept roads of the Ardennes in southern Belgium (or more often on my indoor set-up), she had been gearing up for the Australian Nationals in sweltering heat.

After narrowly missing out on bronze in the time trials on Thursday while I slept, she was lining up for the road race right then, Sunday morning already in Australia, and I wasn't going to miss it this time. Powering up my computer, I found the YouTube channel broadcasting the races and turned the volume right down. Mamie, my grandmother, was asleep in the next room and her hearing wasn't as bad as the stereotypes would have you believe.

'... and *we're all looking forward to Lori Gallagher's return to the road today. The climbs on this route are just long enough to give her a chance to outclass the rest of the peloton, if she's back in form. Barring a stroke of bad luck, I think we'll see her back on the podium today.*'

A little shiver of excitement zipped through me at those words and I could picture it clearly: Lori holding her gold medal and a bunch of flowers with a huge smile. I would pump my fist and shout, 'That's my—'

I choked off a grim laugh at myself. My unattainable crush? My secret bang buddy?

The camera cut to the racers, gathering in rows behind the starting line, with Lori up front, tugging on the strap of her helmet. She didn't glance at the camera, even though it must have been practically shoved in her face. She just slipped her wide reflective sunglasses out of her helmet and put them on, chin up, face forward. She was 100 per cent focused – the way I knew she wanted to be.

Forcing out a breath full of nerves, I hunched over my laptop screen as the official triggered his little gun and the bunch lurched into movement.

She didn't push to the front, as I knew she wouldn't. Road cycling was about endurance and it paid to save your strength and choose the right moment for an attack. As the riders raced ahead, packed close together and picking up speed, I realised it was going to be a long, hard couple of hours – for me. Lori would ace it, but I would be a wreck of nerves by the time she crossed the finish line.

They kept moving the camera away from her, which was endlessly frustrating. Bonnie Tham from our team was racing too, currently out in front, and while I was inwardly cheering her on, team spirit wasn't quite my motivation for tuning in, so I just got restless.

The course didn't help my nerves, consisting of nine laps of the same circuit, rather than the long routes I was used to but Lori was cool and effortless, holding a perfect position behind the front riders. After the first few laps, I recognised the bottleneck curves, the climbs and what would be the sprint finish.

'... *she's looking almost clinical, Gallagher, but I think we all know she'll attack with spirit at some point. She's not known as "Top Gun" for nothing...*'

I was glued to every glimpse of her as the race progressed, trying to guess whether she was as tired as she looked, but suspecting she was putting on a show to force the other competitors to overshoot. It looked brutally hot in the Australian bush, where they were racing. Lori was drenched with sweat and even the commentators were starting to wonder if she was suffering, now three rows back and hemmed in by riders from a different team.

'*It's going to come down to the last lap. On the climb, I reckon we'll see Burgess, Lutkins and Gallagher all have a go — if they've got enough left.*'

I frowned, knowing Lori was better than this, wondering if it was just a bad day for her. We all had those inexplicable times when our legs just belonged to someone else. At least, that happened to me a lot – and I knew it wasn't my legs that gave up, but my mind. I didn't like to think of Lori having my weakness.

But in the long, winding section of the second-last lap, when the bunch spread out to alternate sharp turns and bursts of speed, she did it. Whipping out from behind Bonnie, she accelerated to the next curve, zipping out wide to lean into the hairpin, and pedalling fiercely out again.

'*If anyone wanted a lesson on cornering, just watch that!*' the commentator said, her voice rising with excitement.

Lori swung through the curves, her legs and body in concert, tilting and straightening and *flying* ahead of the others. She was a genius and my heart was pumping and my breath caught watching her. The corners were utter perfection: fearless, elegant and fast – *so* fast. *Too* fast, I thought for a moment, when her back wheel appeared to slip.

Everything in me froze, my throat closing painfully, as I gazed at the screen, willing her to straighten up, to do anything except go sliding across the tarmac.

She overcorrected a little but, with only the slightest wobble, she was back on the line, sailing out in front of the rest with no one daring to follow her. Coming into the final lap, she'd opened up a lead of more than 30 seconds.

'Ouah! Holy shit,' I muttered, completely in awe.

My blunt fingernails dug into my palms and I was up on my haunches watching, unable to sit still while she made the challenging circuit look like one of the gentle routes my grandma's Sunday seniors group liked to ride.

'... *an intelligent rider — strategic. She has been almost flawless in this race. We were convinced she had nothing left and—— Look at that!*'

Her plait bobbing against her back, she shot up the climb. Her fatigue had clearly been feigned to put the others off. I wanted to see her face — to see the heat in her eyes. At least the camera would catch every detail of her when she won. I imagined her, arms high above her head, an enormous smile on her gorgeous face.

Legs pumping, she glanced quickly behind her to judge how much breathing space she had and flew through the wide turn with 3 km to go — and suddenly jerked to the side, her bike sliding out from under her.

'*Something's happened to Gallagher,*' the commentator said unhelpfully. '*A mechanical? You've got to hope for her sake it's not a puncture.*'

She swerved again, ducking her head, one hand clutching her helmet. The camera closed in on her flummoxed expression as she glanced up, her mouth hanging open. And then it happened again, the camera this time catching a flash of black-and-white and Lori's frantic hand in front of her face as she ducked.

'*I don't believe this,*' the commentator continued, her voice high. '*She's being swooped by a magpie. In January. That has got to be the unluckiest thing I have ever seen.*'

The internet watched as she swivelled to eyeball the bird and yell, 'Fuck off!' clearly enough to be lip-read. Unfortunately, that only further enraged the creature.

She tried to keep riding, but the innocuous-looking bird flew at her helmet and her bike tipped, forcing her to unclip her shoe and put a foot down and that was that: the peloton roared by, whipping past on either side of her – and apparently scaring off the magpie.

I could feel the burn of disappointment in my chest as she pushed off, frantically pumping the pedals to keep up with the others, but she was still dropped, falling behind before she could find her rhythm. I didn't need the camera on her to taste the bitterness in my own mouth.

Because she was Lori Gallagher, it wasn't long until she caught up, careening down those curves again at speed and slipping into the peloton. But it wasn't enough. When the final sprint stretched before her, she weaved to the front, but she couldn't maintain enough power to contest the sprint, and she flew over the line in fifth, her head hanging and her chest heaving, looking as though she wanted to throw something.

'Godverdomme!' I said, because there was nothing else I could do except swear in Flemish, as Walloons did in extreme situations where French would not do. 'Fuck that!'

'Sebi?'

I whirled around to find my grandma, standing in the door without her glasses on, peering at me. A quick glance at my laptop revealed it was past two o'clock in the morning.

I leaped to my feet and took her arm. 'Mamie, go back to sleep. I'm sorry to wake you.'

'What are you upset about, mon chou? I haven't heard

such language since Denise was in labour.' She shuffled towards the bed in her felt slippers and squinted at the screen.

'I was watching my teammates,' I said weakly. 'These are professional cyclists I was watching… professionally.'

'I can see that, but I also know you don't usually watch women's cycling.' She didn't say it, but I could see the words, 'In the middle of the night,' in her expression.

'They're just as exciting as the men.'

'I'm sure that's true,' Mamie said sagely, 'but I'm not letting you off so easily. I knew there was something different about you since you came home at Christmas. Which one is your girlfriend?'

The hairs on the back of my neck lifted. 'There's nothing different. I don't have a girlfriend.'

She studied me, which, without her glasses, felt as though she was probing my mind with telepathic powers. 'I see,' she said gravely.

In the quiet pause after her words, I heard the commentator say, '*Poor Lori Gallagher. Today was not her day for gold. I've never seen an out-of-season magpie attack in the Nationals in my entire career and it had to be her, it had to be today. Wow, you can see the disappointment on those shoulders. I'd be crying too, Lori.*'

Stricken, I rushed back to the laptop to see her, chest heaving, swiping roughly at her eyes as tears made trails in the sweat and grime on her face and the enormity of her disappointment was broadcast to the entire world. I couldn't look away, but I also wished the camera would move off her, give her a chance to grieve in private.

'Her?' Mamie asked me, her brow low.

'She's a friend. A good friend,' I added when my grandma kept looking at me.

Grasping my arm, she said, 'Looks like she needs a hug.'

All I could do was stare at the image of Lori on the screen and wholeheartedly agree. I snatched up my phone to text her but, as soon as I opened our chat, I remembered my deleted message and my stomach dropped.

Ouch. She couldn't have seen it before I deleted it. I'd realised too late that it was the middle of the night in Australia when I sent it and she probably wouldn't want my poorly worded best wishes for the race – which was why I'd deleted them. Now I was mortified.

The commentator's words looped in my mind: *the unluckiest thing I have ever seen*. I was such an idiot. She'd wanted to focus. I wasn't supposed to be in her head and she'd told me straight up I wasn't allowed to text her except to congratulate her on winning. I should never have sent it.

Chapter 11

Lori

After the magpie incident at Nationals, my season went downhill — and not downhill in a fun way. The first race on the World Tour calendar, the three-day Tour Down Under, was a rain-soaked disaster, where we all slipped and slid our way through the stages, collecting cuts and bruises. After a big crash before the final sprint on the second day, I was out of the running for the general classification victory.

I began to suspect I'd committed an offence against the animal kingdom a few days later, when I upset a redback spider under the sun lounger, and 48 hours later I had World War Three on the back of my thigh. Dad ruled me out of racing the next one so I could have treatment without worrying about failing a drug test, leaving me lying around in the dark at home, feeling sorry for myself, while he and Colin prepared for the Great Ocean Road Race.

I'd shut myself in my bedroom again, crying silently so Mum wouldn't hear me, and let the cortisone shot and antibiotics do their thing. Even if I had been able to pass a drug test right now, I was in too much pain to race. The burn in my muscles, aches in my back and hands – those I was used to ignoring, pushing through. But this constant stab in my thigh tore through my concentration.

I had the women's race running live on my computer, but I was only half-watching – I couldn't face it when I wasn't there myself. Bonnie and Doortje started. They would have been there to support me but, instead, the directeur sportif had given Leesa a chance to be lead rider and she was having the race of her life. Swiping at my stupid tears, I closed the browser and rolled away, tired and hurting, restless – and useless.

After Dad had told me my entire life that there were no limits to what I could achieve if I worked hard, making me believe in the power of mind over matter, it turned out there were limits after all and maybe sports psychology was a crock of shit.

My gaze fell on my mobile, sending another shudder of emotion down my spine. *Seb…*

Sure, my form had tanked since the moment I'd met him but, if I couldn't race anyway, I might as well think about the feel of his skin under my hands and the way his mouth had grazed my ear as though he wanted every inch of me.

Turning back to the laptop, I opened the team website and pulled up the men's listing. It wasn't the first time I'd indulged myself by looking at his photo and every time I felt like a chump – instead of a champ – but it didn't stop me.

The photographer had chosen well. He was looking at the camera with his head tilted, eyebrows raised and a lopsided grin on his face. One hand grasped the zip of his jersey and he was tugging it halfway down, revealing a glimpse of his smooth chest. The picture made my mouth water and my hair stand on end and I kicked myself for the months I'd spent with this guy's voice in my ear, not knowing he looked like this.

And now I was staring at a picture like a lovesick teenager, dreaming about sex instead of winning races. Thank God Dad couldn't read minds.

My bedroom door flew open and I was blinded by the sudden light.

'Mum!' I cried, scrambling to shut down the browser window a moment too late and wondering if I could blame the spider bite for my flushed skin.

'Loredana Gallagher, I hate to see you like this!' she said emphatically. After 30 years with my dad, most of them lived in Australia, Mum spoke with less of a real Italian accent and more Italian-Australian inflection from Melbourne. 'Stop lying around in the dark. Up you get. We'll go for a walk and get some coffee.'

Triggering my caffeine response was an effective tactic, especially because getting coffee in Melbourne was like drinking champagne in Reims or eating chocolate in Brussels. Mmm, chocolate in Brussels, kissing Seb in Brussels – feeding Seb chocolate and then kissing him.

'What's the matter with you?' Mum asked me, snapping

me out of that immersive fantasy. Wow, I'd never had pizza or tiramisu fantasies about Gaetano, but suddenly chocolate and waffles and beer were off limits too. Oh God, chocolate, waffles and beer. I would kill for any combination of those right now.

I rose warily to follow her, hoping she might hold her peace about whatever she'd seen on my laptop screen – and in my facial expression.

'My leg hurts,' I grumbled as I slipped into my sloppy old trainers and shuffled to the door.

The stark summer sunshine mocked me as we walked the 15 minutes to our local quinoa-salad-and-smashed-avocado café with famous street murals copied on the walls and elaborate latte art. My leg throbbed in the heat and I wished I'd put more aloe vera on it before we left the house, but I knew Mum was trying to distract me from the pain, so I ignored it. After my turbulent teenage years, I'd learned it was better to roll with Mum's expectations and not upset them.

Paola Gallagher – née Martinelli, former champion triathlete – was taller than my dad, straight-haired and slim, and I would never be even half as elegant. She was almost always emotionally unavailable and a raging Italian coffee snob to boot.

After we took our seats, I eyed off the uni students who were drinking cold-brew coffee with icebergs of handmade ice cream bobbing on top. It wasn't quite a waffle, but I craved it nonetheless. Feeling Mum's eyes on me, I ordered a long black, while she had her customary espresso. Dairy was an inflammatory food and best avoided during training and competing, a fact that was trying to remind me of Seb again and his desire to eat cheese.

And then I was staring down the thought of quitting the World Tour some time in the future and I swallowed a lump of panic. I'd only just fought my way back.

'You might think you're hiding it, but I know what you're thinking about,' Mum said softly – dangerously softly.

I choked on my first sip of coffee. 'Do they always make it so hot?' I muttered, fetching a napkin from the bar and mopping up my saucer. I hadn't spilled much but I suspected, even if I'd doused my head with it, Mum wouldn't have been put off. She was a dog with a bone when she smelled weakness.

'You're thinking about the things you're missing out on to race, wondering if it's all worth it.'

'No!' I insisted, although perhaps she meant all these thoughts of food that had taunted me recently. That might be a safer topic of conversation – which was saying something, given her violent disapproval of most foods. I schooled my features, hoping the tic in my jaw wasn't visible. 'Racing is what I want to do. I don't need to eat cheese.'

'Cheese?'

'Or ice cream or waffles.' When she eyed me, I realised I'd gone in the wrong direction with the food. 'Seriously, don't worry. I'm feeling a bit sorry for myself, but it won't last. I'm sure I just need a bit of good luck and I'll be back to my normal self.'

I swallowed a grimace when my words reminded me of that text from Seb. He obviously hadn't realised it was the middle of the night when he sent me good luck for the race and he wouldn't have imagined it would wake me up, either. And then he'd followed it up with: *You're amazing.* I'd tried to roll over and go back to sleep, but my stomach had done a few loop-the-loops first. He meant an amazing cyclist. Of course I was an amazing cyclist.

But he'd deleted the message before I got up the next morning, leaving me wondering what exactly he'd regretted about sending it.

'I'm not talking about your diet,' Mum explained, giving me a meaningful look.

For a long moment I just blinked, not sure what she meant, but afraid nonetheless.

She took my hand, which alarmed me further. 'Lolly,' she said gently, which made me squirm in a way 'Molly' never did, 'I know you were talking to someone online last year and I saw your computer screen just now. 25 is still so young. I know I'd already met your dad by that age, but those last few years of competing kept my spirits up after I quit and I'm so glad I didn't give up when my family suggested I should.'

'What?'

'Trust me, you're not ready for love right now.'

'I'm not—' The urge to contradict her was hard-wired into me after years of experiencing her 'care' for me only in criticism. I took a deep breath before continuing. 'I'm not looking for love – truly. But if one day I did want... nothing would make me quit!'

Her mouth pinched into a doubtful frown. 'I do remember what it was like at your age and I wish someone had told me this: in a relationship, someone always loses.'

I clutched my coffee cup, annoyed I felt so fragile that the urge to cry rose behind my eyes. I didn't know what to say – what to think. I didn't like to sympathise or agree with Mum, but her words – her *tone* – struck a chord. I didn't lose – I couldn't, after everything I'd sacrificed.

Squeezing my hand as though I were actually the daughter she wanted and not the one she'd got, Mum said, 'Just make sure it's not you that loses. Please yourself, make your own goals and reach them. No man is worth compromising for. I wanted to tell you this all last year. I was so worried Gaetano would affect your performance and I regretted not picking up the phone and trying to warn you, but your father...'

That was familiar: everything was Dad's fault. I remembered the unexpected texts during the training camp, as though Mum didn't want to contact Dad herself. They shared a bed, but what if that was only out of stubbornness – which ran in the family?

'We don't need to talk about last year—'

'I know, bella. I don't want to go over it again either, but I'm so worried someone will break your heart again, or at least distract you, especially after I saw you looking—'

'It's nothing,' I tried to assure her. 'I don't have a boyfriend. I'm not going to get a boyfriend. I exist on this planet to pilot a bike and win some trophies while I'm doing it. I am a cycling nun with a vow of chastity. So I might have slept with a guy on training camp, but it was just sex and it won't happen again because now I'm focused on the season – if I can just get to the starting line next time. Okay?'

She gulped and I sipped as calmly as I could while she processed my overshare. Yep, I didn't have my mum's poise. Sometimes I thought she used it on purpose to make me squirm.

'Just… be careful. I don't want to see you give up everything you've worked so hard for.'

'I *am* being careful and nobody's giving up. Give me some credit. I'm not going to find a guy and quit like you did.' Ouch. So much for the mother-daughter bonding of a coffee date.

'I didn't have much of a choice, especially after you came along. You wouldn't have your team today if I hadn't. You can't have it all – especially not as a woman. Before you throw away all the time and effort your father and I have put into your training and career, at least make sure you've chosen the right person. At your age, it's difficult.'

Even at 25, she treated me like a mixed-up teenager, but today I didn't feel far off. Worse, I had to admit she had a point and now I was thinking about how much Colin and I – and maybe even Dad – had cost her.

'All right, Mum,' I mumbled. 'Point taken. There's only one thing I really want and that's my career back.'

I usually managed not to begrudge my brother his victories, but this one stung. Since I'd already been bitten and stung,

Colin's triumphal return on Sunday night with the trophy from the Great Ocean Road Race was difficult to swallow. Even worse, Leesa had taken home the women's trophy the day before, making her journey out from the US unfortunately worthwhile.

Not many riders travelled to Australia for the Tour Down Under and the Great Ocean Road Race. It was expensive and tiring for two races without much cachet, but it made them easier to win, being our home competition – at least that's what I told myself when Colin kept parading his trophy around. It was a wonder he didn't poke himself with the pointy bit.

'You've got a break until the Strade Bianche now, ay?' Dad said, slapping Colin on the shoulder. 'I think we should crack open the champagne!'

I accepted a glass with a false smile and raised it in Colin's direction. The way he dipped his head and studied me with his brow low was enough for me to realise he knew I wasn't so calm on the inside. Surprisingly, he didn't say anything or even rub my face in it when no one was looking. I must have looked a sad wreck indeed. Dad wrapped an arm around him and shook him hard enough to slosh the champagne.

'Silver at Nationals, winner today!'

My phone buzzed in my pocket and I snatched it out with relief that I had something to do other than pull a muscle in my face. When I saw it was a message from Seb, my nose stung with more stifled tears and that was a weird Seb side-effect I was not on board with. But when I saw the message, I snorted a laugh, glad I hadn't been mid-sip.

I know I'm only supposed to text you if you win, but is Colin's trophy actually a shark fin? I didn't think it was legal to hunt sharks for their fins.

Studying Colin's prize, I could see his point. I checked online and it was supposed to be a wave. The resemblance seemed unintentional, but now I couldn't unsee it.

It might be because there are seven different species of shark around here.

He replied immediately: *Just when I thought it was safe to go back in the water...*

I should have predicted that response.

You're not selling me on Australia: spiders, sharks, magpies. Oops, shouldn't mention the magpies.

His teasing pricked me with indignation *and* relief and it took a moment for me to gather a smart response.

Yeah, well, life's not all chocolate and waffles.

Dad approached and I hurriedly stuffed my phone away, the conversation with Mum still too fresh in my mind. I probably shouldn't have told her I'd slept with someone on the team. If it got back to Dad... Oops. I'd have to make sure he didn't guess it was Seb.

He clapped his arm around me, giving me a gentler version of the shakedown he'd given Colin. 'How's my Molly? Ready for the next one, ay? Good on ya.'

Actually, no. I didn't feel ready for the next race. I felt adrift – on the brink of failure. I was already the sister, the daughter, with half the prize money potential of my brother simply because of the lack of a warped Y chromosome. If I stopped bringing home the trophies...

It didn't bear thinking about. I had to get back my form – and my luck. And I *really* had to stop wasting time thinking about Seb.

15 October 06:17

zpeed.com/voicechannels/@LoonieDunes/7493376900111

Folklore99: Have you ever been... really bad at something?

LoonieDunes: Lots of things.

Folklore99: How do you sound so chilled about that? I hate the feeling. I have a family of overachievers and I suck at everything except riding a bike. I hate it sometimes.

LoonieDunes: My family is the opposite. They don't expect me to be good at anything, which is maybe why you train more than me despite your injury.

Folklore99: At least you know they'll love you no matter how much you screw up.

LoonieDunes: Lore...

Folklore99: I'm just feeling sorry for myself. Forget I said anything.

LoonieDunes: Did something happen?

Folklore99: Nothing out of the ordinary. I was supposed to

meet my mum yesterday and I forgot and she hates anything that reminds her I'm not perfect. She doesn't blame me openly, she just... I dunno. She can't deal with the fact that I'm not like her – or like my brother, whose flaws she cannot see. But seriously, can we talk about something else?

LoonieDunes: You want to watch a film? Take your mind off it? I'll let you tell me everything that's wrong with the film.

Folklore99: You can't stop me anyway.

LoonieDunes: You're lucky I'm stuck on the stationary bike – and I kind of like your whingeing.

Folklore99: I don't whinge!

LoonieDunes: You get this buzz in your voice and it goes all high-pitched—

Folklore99: Shut up and pick a movie!

Chapter 12

Seb

If the Tour of Flanders was my lucky race, then the one that reliably deflated my ego every year, right at the beginning of the season in Europe, was the Omloop Het Nieuwsblad. Even worse than the late winter weather was the team introduction beforehand in the Ghent velodrome, where we were paraded before a crowd of fans in strobe lighting and manufactured smoke to make the whole thing artificially dramatic. One year I'd even slipped on the blue-carpeted circuit and fallen off my bike and that clip had been played more often than any other footage of me.

In the packed backstage area where the team buses were parked, milling with riders and officials and team staff, there were a lot of familiar faces – too many. The Belgians turned out in force for the opening of the Classics season, the one-day races that dotted the calendar between the longer Grand Tours, and every team I'd ever raced with was in attendance, including the second-tier Walloon outfit where I'd got my start. But I was the only Belgian signed to Harper-Stacked, making me feel even more out-of-place than usual.

Our lead riders Colin and Lars Fiske got to stay home instead of competing in the bitter February cold and Lori was similarly absent from the women's race that started two hours later, although that hadn't stopped me daydreaming about what it would have been like to meet her gaze across the breakfast room of our hotel once more.

I was still low in the pecking order, rolling onto the stage behind my teammates to wave awkwardly to the crowd, wondering how my new kit would look in photos. There had been some unfortunate design flaws over the years that had drawn too much attention to the crotch.

At least I was deep inside the bunch staying warm at the starting line. By the end of the race I was always certain I would lose two fingers and my little toe to frostbite. But the local crowd was enthusiastic despite the weather – or perhaps there was something stronger than coffee in their insulated flasks – and my teammate Derek Sabel, an Australian youngster on his first year in Europe, glanced around him in awe as he shivered. We'd practised parts of the route and the climbs yesterday and I'd kind of enjoyed feeling useful, introducing the kid to the tortures of the Cobbled Classics.

My job that day was to lead the young hot-shot out, ride in front of him to save his strength and help him get into position to attack at the right moment – and hope he didn't lose any skin on his hands as the bike shook him to his bones on the brutal surface.

'Coucou! Sebi Franck!' I heard from the crowd. Turning to smile and wave, I hoped they'd leave it at that. 'How's your new team? Have you settled in?' the fan continued in French.

'Très bien,' I called back. 'G'day mate! She'll be right!' I caught sight of a phone trained on me and gave the person a wink.

'What do you have drawn on your arm today?'

That one surprised me. I hadn't expected anyone to remember I'd used to draw symbols on my arm for luck before every race. I'd stopped after one time I drew a picture that was supposed to be my niece but everyone had thought was Ed Sheeran and the team had taunted me by singing 'The Shape of You' endlessly until I wanted to cut my ears off like a Belgian van Gogh.

'I haven't done that in years!' I called back. That was all I had to say to get a permanent marker flung at my face. I fumbled to catch it and then studied it thoughtfully.

With a self-conscious glance at the fan standing behind the barrier, I pulled up my right sleeve and tugged off the lid of the marker. Once I'd thought of something to draw, I couldn't not draw it, so I scrawled the little picture quickly, capped the pen and tossed it back into the crowd.

'What is it?' the fan asked.

I held up my arm to show him the little black creature, eight legs splayed threateningly. 'In honour of my team.'

'That's cool, man!' Derek said, beckoning to the fan to throw back the marker. Before I had a chance to regret what I'd started, the entire Harper-Stacked team for the race had drawn the little critters on their wrists and I would have to live with what I'd done.

Five hours and 200 km later, I couldn't feel my extremities and black spots hovered at the edge of my vision, but my blood was fizzing with adrenaline despite the exhaustion. I'd done my job. Derek attacked, heading for the breakaway at the front of the race with plenty left in the tank after staying behind me for most of the course. I could listen to my screaming muscles and slow down before I hit the wall.

But I didn't. I kept going. I got in behind Derek and kept up and, with a rush of disbelief and elation, I crossed the finish line half a length behind the kid, as he secured second place in his first Spring Classic.

Meaning I came in third. I was on the *podium*. I was usually ecstatic about a top-ten finish in my lucky race. But third in the Omloop? No, not me.

My thoughts were as foggy as the horizon as I followed Derek to the team bus, wobbling and stumbling as the directors and staff cheered and grabbed at me and then Derek wrapped his long arms around me and squeezed and I had to accept it was real. I'd had *legs* today.

'Frankie!' he hollered. 'I should have been drafting *you* out there today!'

I extricated myself gently and patted him on the shoulder. 'You did great.'

'Yeah, but you kept up, even when we attacked!'

'So I didn't imagine that?'

Derek laughed, as if I were joking.

I must have had a sixth sense for Gallaghers, because I looked up to find Tony emerging from the back door of the bus, a calculating expression on his face as he studied me.

Clapping his hands above his head, he called out to Derek, 'An Australian on the podium at the Omloop! Tell me when that last happened! Well done, son! You're going places!'

Tony swaggered down the steps slowly, maintaining eye contact with me as he approached.

'Great race, Frankie,' he said. 'Why didn't you tell me you felt good today? I would have got the other guys to help you out. Could have been you in second – or even first.'

With a gulp around a lump of nerves, I tried to find an answer that would satisfy him. Me in first – it had never happened and I doubted it would. 'I didn't know I... felt *that* good.' I scratched the back of my neck, hoping he'd take his attention off me soon.

'I'm impressed with what you did for Derek today, but I'll be impressed if you go out firing for yourself some time too, ay?'

I managed an inarticulate response, something like 'Glmph-kay.'

'What's that on your arm?' he asked suddenly and I yanked my hand down again in a pointless attempt to hide it. 'Looks like the fucking spider that bit my daughter!' Tony joked.

'Yep, it's a redback!' Derek added eagerly, showing the boss his own rudimentary spider drawing. 'All the guys did them.'

I bit back a groan.

Tony chuckled and slapped me on the back again. 'Just don't let Lori see that!'

That grew less likely when Derek followed me onto the podium later, brandishing his redback spider in front of the cameras as he shook his champagne bottle with a wild spark in his eye. The winner, a Fleming from another team, popped his bottle first, but then Derek was spraying me full in the face until I had bubbles up my nose, in my ears and drenching the fresh jersey I'd pulled on over my festering body.

'You're a legend, Frankie! I love the cobbles! This is the best day of my liiiiife!'

Lori

To me, Siena was the most beautiful city in the world: terra-cotta roofs snaking out along the hills, ancient brickwork, the striped white tower of the duomo, leafy squares hidden around corners, olive trees, window shutters in shades of green, and everything surrounded by the undulating Tuscan countryside.

And the legendary sterrati, the gravel roads through the arid hills to the south – they were my natural habitat. The Strade Bianche – Italian for white roads – had been my first European race seven years ago and I still felt a touch of wonder every year in March, when I climbed out of the taxi in front of our team hotel, set right on the city walls with a view out into the hills, where we would do battle on Saturday.

The racing season would get hectic later in the year – and

the hotels worse – but arriving at our usual family-run palazzo that was just big enough to house the team and support staff, to the faint scent of pine and sage, felt a little like coming home. I'd told Mum that once on the phone and we'd shared a 'moment' before swiftly dropping the subject.

Ever since I was 18, Dad and I (and Colin, when he was old enough) had lived for six months of the year in an apartment in Lourdes in the south of France – whether because of the proximity to the Pyrenees for training rides or to an airport served by low-cost carriers, I wasn't sure. Dad knew all about the bottom line after all and cycling was not a sport soaked in cash. Although I continually lost my stuff between the two homes, I enjoyed my time in Europe, where I could just be a cyclist and not live in the shadow of Mum's expectations.

Lourdes was our base, but Siena was my happy place. Surely my favourite white roads would turn my fortunes around – and help me snatch back my life. Even if bad luck and the image of a fucking redback spider were haunting me, it couldn't last forever – like these pesky emotional shenanigans about a certain member of the men's team.

He'd been racing while I'd been in the air a week ago and I'd checked the results of the Omloop as soon as we landed, holding my breath while the website loaded too slowly.

I'd seen his grinning face on the podium and I'd felt so light in the chest, like a helium balloon, puffing up with something very much like pride. But at the same time, I'd cracked and broken, my own failure stark in comparison to his success.

But I had also been weirdly angry with him. How could he think of quitting when another race like that could be in his future? Then I'd seen the spider drawn on his arm and the anger had mixed with something tight and worrying. If he'd done it for me, he was in the shit.

Sharing a smile with Colin as we fetched our bags out of the taxi, I made for the doors — and stopped short as soon as I walked inside. Coming down the travertine steps into the lobby, holding a bunch of wilted flowers, was the person I was trying very hard not to feel anything about. I failed — miserably — as I caught sight of him in person for the first time in ten weeks. I remembered — way too much. Each memory was in my skin and in my chest and in my tight throat. He froze mid-step, meeting my gaze.

Damn it, I'd forgotten how hard it was to breathe when Seb looked at me. He was wearing a sports turtleneck that should have looked preppy, but it emphasised his tough, lean torso and reminded me of the feel of him under my fingertips.

He needed a haircut and a shave. The little fluff of beard was a bit ridiculous on him. But I was far too happy to see him, beard or not — redback spider or not. This was *bad*.

I must have stopped suddenly, because Colin ran into me with an 'Oof.' To round off the uneasy moment, Dad appeared with his usual boundless energy. I tore my eyes from Seb's wary face and greeted Dad with a hug, letting him steer me towards the reception desk, where someone had hung a poster with our sponsor logos — and a big, stylised redback spider.

It appeared the team had embraced Seb's little stunt in the face of my misery.

Giving an involuntary shudder, I peered at him again in time to see him wince.

'Get yourselves settled and have a rest. We can catch up at dinner,' Dad said. 'Oh, hi, Frankie. What are you doing with those?'

Seb froze, glancing at the flowers as though he'd forgotten he was holding them and was thinking about shoving them behind his back. 'They're too big for the trash bin in my room,' he said stiltedly.

'They're your flowers from the Omloop!' Dad said in horror. 'You can't throw them away. They'll give you good luck on Saturday. Why else did you bring them?'

'Oh, hum, you're right.' He glanced at me and quickly away again. 'Oops.'

'Go on, son. You'll do fine on Saturday,' Dad assured him. Tony called everyone 'son' but that one got me in the guts.

'I… want to ask the receptionist something, but you go first,' Seb said, standing back and gesturing to Colin. My brother gave him a doubtful look, but approached the desk to fill out his forms.

Colin finished his barely legible contribution to Italian bureaucracy and hotel paperwork before I'd even managed to remember my name. I couldn't think with Seb… existing.

With a quick 'See you at dinner,' and half a hug, Colin left me alone with him. I needed to stop pretending I hadn't known that was Seb's plan all along.

But I hadn't expected him to rush at me and say, 'You have to take the flowers,' in an urgent voice.

I was so nonplussed I didn't even ask him to clarify. 'Look, I know you want to give up and eat cheese, but sabotaging yourself is going a bit far. And if you think I'd want some wilted second-hand flowers from you — *any* flowers from you,' I belatedly corrected, 'then you've forgotten what we agreed before Christmas.'

'I haven't forgotten,' he grumbled. 'But I realised… I've stolen your luck. I have to give it back.'

Okay, that one needed clarification. 'What are you talking about?'

'The Omloop,' he said earnestly. 'Nothing like that's ever happened to me before. I know it looked like I drafted Derek for half the race, but I managed to get in behind other people most of the time. The positioning just happened perfectly for me. It was *luck*.'

'I hate to break it to you, but it was fitness, drive and a good attitude. Maybe 10 per cent luck. No more.'

'Even that's luck you could use,' he insisted, shaking the flowers at me. They smelled stale and a little slimy.

'You have to keep them,' I said firmly. 'You raced a scorcher, Seb. You gave Derek the start of a lifetime. He's never going to forget that race and neither should you.'

'He's a nice kid—'

I wasn't finished. I tamped down that hot spike of pride and continued, 'But you should have ditched him for the chance to win. You know you could have won it, right? You're there to support the team, but you have to grab the opportunities when they come.'

When he shook his head, I couldn't hold in all the things I'd felt reading the race report on Saturday – especially when I'd read about that blasted spider.

'If you're so serious about quitting, you should be putting everything into your last season!'

'I have been putting everything in! You know that – or Folklore did.'

'I don't mean hours in the saddle training. You were the stronger rider that day. You should have gone for the win. If that redback was for me, then it didn't work. I would have told you to ditch him and go for it.'

His gaze clouded. 'There's no guarantee that I would have won. We had two riders on the podium. I'm sorry if third place wasn't quite good enough.'

I resisted defending myself, kept silent about that pride that had swollen in my chest seeing the photo of him with that stupid bouquet.

'Keep the flowers,' I repeated. 'And if you're still feeling lucky, then give it everything this Saturday, knowing that you might do it.'

'I can't,' he said and I wanted to clench my fists and shake him. 'Because it's not my luck anyway. It's yours.'

I crossed my arms and stared at the ceiling. 'You think having sex was some supernatural ritual where all my luck transferred to you? Was that why you started the thing with the spider? Am I some kind of lucky charm?'

'No, no! I'm sorry about the spider. I shouldn't have... I was thinking of you, that's all. I wish Derek hadn't copied me, blown it all out of proportion.'

I wished he hadn't admitted he'd been thinking of me, with that soft hitch in his voice. Now I couldn't even be mad about that.

He sighed. 'I hate to see all this stuff happening to you. It should be you up on the podium.'

I scowled, hoping to hide the pricking behind my eyes. It was as if he could tell a little bit of me had resented his success while I'd seen nothing but failure for months. I'd been sick and in pain and there he was standing on a podium. Reason told me the two facts were entirely unrelated, but I'd still resented him, feeling like a horrible person as I did so.

'It *will* be me up on the podium soon enough – especially if you can't get your head in the game. You'll see on Saturday. It's not my luck or your luck. It's just luck – and skill and focus. I love this race and I'm going to attack it.'

He watched me silently for a long moment, a not-quite smile on his face and a light in his eyes. I realised with a start what he was thinking: *Good luck for the race. You're amazing.*

If he said it, he couldn't delete it again, the way he'd deleted that message. If he said it, I was going to kiss him. I wouldn't be able to stop myself.

131

Chapter 13

Lori

He didn't say it, the bastard – the wise, sensible bastard. He let me walk away without kissing him.

To make matters worse, he then showed his face at dinner – and breakfast the following day, as well as lunch and dinner. And he looked cute while he did it. Derek Sabel followed him around like a disciple and they joked and shoved each other and behaved like puppies instead of grown men – and it was unbearably sweet.

He kept meeting my eye – and then looking away and shaking himself as though he was trying not to.

The utter bastard. I couldn't hate him. I couldn't tune him out. By Saturday morning I was annoyed as hell – well, 'annoyed' was one way to describe it.

I waited for him to text me on Friday night before the race, but – nothing. The last thing I did before rolling over and forcing myself to go to sleep was send him a *Star Trek* gif with something about good luck, which was a low blow since he'd spent so long on Zpeed explaining to me that the fandoms were entirely separate and he was more into Chewbacca than Spock.

In addition to having no reply from Seb when I woke up, I looked in the mirror while brushing my teeth to see that one of my earrings had fallen out. You might not have expected that I wore earrings during races. I had never been a girly girl, or at all precious about my appearance – I couldn't afford to be when I lived my life with helmet hair and sweated off all my make-up. In the second hole in my earlobe I wore lightning strikes. But I'd learned when I was 14 and one hole had closed up that I needed to keep something in. Mum had bought me a pair of platinum hoops that were small enough to wear all the time and I never took them out.

And now I'd lost one on the morning of a race.

It didn't matter. Sure, I always put my right shoe on before my left on race day. I had my favourite socks and a lucky bra from a small Australian label, which was so difficult to replace in Europe that I kept a pristine spare in case I damaged one.

These were crutches to keep my head in the game and wouldn't actually affect my race. But the earring freaked me out. After searching through my sheets and under the bed and examining the pillow with no results, I had to accept it was gone and decide whether to take out the other earring.

Assuming that wearing a single earring might bother me on the road, I slipped it out and placed it warily in my toiletry bag.

I was nearly too late for the early pre-race breakfast and, when I rushed into the dining room, it was to find Seb there, a bunch of women fawning over him. Stopping to stare in bewilderment, I realised he wasn't signing autographs for simpering fans, but drawing little spiders on the wrists of my teammates. At least he blushed fiercely when he saw me.

'Lori! Come and get your redback from Sebi!' Leesa called out.

Sebi? 'Um, no thanks. I've seen enough redbacks.' I stomped to the coffee machine and tried to ignore them. Jealousy before a race might just be worse for my state of mind than losing an earring.

He approached me with an apologetic wince after the other women had left to get ready for our 9:30 start, but I shook my head, silently putting him off.

'See you on the podium,' he said, backing off with a nod and giving me a casual salute.

As he left the dining room without looking back, I stupidly wondered whether he meant I'd be on the podium or he would.

Viewed from the helicopter thumping overhead, the peloton would have looked like a mythical snake, emerging from the dust to weave its way across the clay hills, contorting itself through curves — a giant organism of many parts, not all of them organic. Racing inside the bunch felt more like being in a spaceship, hurtling ahead with perpetual motion, breathing recycled air, listening to the clicks and whirs of the machinery and hoping no one would make a false move and upset the delicate balance.

My front wheel was almost touching Doortje's rear one. My longtime nemesis Laura Colombini was pumping the pedals next to me, her jersey in the colours of the Italian flag reminding me that she was a national champion this year and I was not. I was probably imagining it, but she seemed to glance at me more often than necessary.

She was psyching me out, but knowing that didn't stop me falling into the trap. I started to wonder if I had something on my face, when I should have been thinking about my position, planning a possible attack.

'*Approaching the climb in 500 m. Five in the breakaway, but they're losing steam already. Wait for your moment and go, Lori — even solo if you have to,*' I heard through the team radio. Alf Londis, the women's directeur sportif, was watching the coverage from the team car. We'd learned through bitter experience that Dad needed to stay off the radio when I was racing. I couldn't manage his emotions as well as my own.

Laura glanced at me again and this time I responded with a punchy look of my own. 'What?' As soon as the word was out of my mouth, I realised I shouldn't have said anything.

'*200 m,*' Alf updated me.

'You didn't see him, did you?' she said quietly, sounding alarm bells in my skull.

Keep your mouth shut, Loredana Molly Gallagher. My self-discipline was obviously shot. 'Who?'

'*100 m!*'

I suspected what she was talking about a second before she confirmed it, but not early enough to stop my stomach from plummeting to my toes. 'Gaetano,' she said. 'He said you look different these days. Between you and me, it was probably just his ego talking. You know what I mean.'

She lifted a hand long enough to make a wilting gesture with one finger that made me want to laugh, while my insides twisted tight.

'Lori! Go! What are you waiting for? Go!'

Ahhh, shit, score one: Laura Colombini. She shot ahead of me, stealing the gap that Doortje and Bonnie had worked so hard to set up for me. Shouting an expletive that was sure to have been caught on the motorcycle-mounted camera beside us, I took off after Laura, cursing myself for letting my team down – letting everyone down.

'There's been a crash in the breakaway. Go for it, Lori! Now's your chance!'

Thinking for a moment that perhaps my luck had changed, I pushed hard up the gravel hill, tyres protesting as loudly as my lungs. The landscape disappeared. The only things I could feel were gravity, breath and the bunch-and-release of the muscles in my legs. My vision narrowed to Laura up ahead and two other cyclists who were blurry adversaries.

But I caught up. I was right on Laura's wheel, basking in her slipstream as we pushed it up the rest of the climb and over the other side. I finally registered that my back ached. Everything ached and I couldn't tell if it was the remaining damage from the crash and surgery or if it was the usual pain, the stuff we all pushed through.

'Are we sticking together for a while?' Laura called behind her.

'If you shut up about Gaetano,' I shot back, which made her laugh. I caught myself wondering if we could be friends, if we ever had time or energy. The best cyclists knew how to cooperate and earn the respect of the peloton – and strategically drop them at the right moment. I'd always been better at the latter than the former.

'You shouldn't be so sensitive about him. You weren't married.'

'I said you should shut up about him.' It was unfortunately clear who had been the loser in that relationship.

'Okay, but you take a turn in the lead. There's a headwind.'

Giving her a wary look as I overtook, I pictured the route in my mind, wondering where she would try to drop me, trying to remember everything I knew about her style and strengths, reminding myself I was *good* at this stuff. Giving my naked earlobe a quick tug, I wondered whether losing that earring had been a sign of good luck and not bad.

But it was not a good moment to take my hand off the drop bars. Was that—? It couldn't be. I must have been seeing things. In the middle of the— *Ohhhh, fuck!*

Seb

I had never been happier to see the finish line in my life – and there had been plenty of times when I'd limped to the end, a physical and emotional wreck after a gruelling race.

As I threw my bike forward the last metre with a grunt that would shame a tennis player, I thought I might just have made it — and beaten that great fool.

Decelerating after the finish line, I steered wildly in the direction of the orange Harper-Stacked bus, stumbling short of the support team and teetering to the ground. My blood bubbled and my vision blurred as I stuck my head between my knees and just breathed. Disembodied hands clapped me on the back and I heard Colin's voice as though through a tunnel.

Then I threw up right on the cobblestones of the beautiful Piazza in Siena, with cameras broadcasting my vomit to all corners of the internet. Somewhere inside I was deeply embarrassed, but I had more on my mind.

'Did I...' I couldn't finish my question until I'd heaved in a few more breaths. There were tears on my face. Wow, I was real crash-hot that day. 'Did I beat him?'

'You did, son!' There was no mistaking Tony Gallagher's voice — or the violent clap on the back that brought another glob of vomit up my throat. With a whimper of relief that it hadn't all been for nothing, I spat as discreetly as I could, hoping Lori was far, far away. 'I don't know where you got it from, but that was a real fight today! Where have you been hiding those legs?' Tony asked while I prayed that he refrained from any more backslapping.

Despite the lapsed status of my religion, someone heard me and Tony left me to shudder and sway and grimace at the sour taste in my mouth all by myself.

I'd started out distracted, wishing I could ask over the team radio how the women's race was progressing. I'd seen Lori make a good start, protected by her teammates and cruising comfortably to save energy for the end.

Then I'd recognised Gaetano Maggioli in the peloton and been even more distracted with thoughts of how he'd broken up with Lori in *hospital*, the heartless bastard.

It was silly – completely immature – but the race had become personal.

I'd launched Colin into an attack on the breakaway group 10 km from the end and then I'd fought Gaetano with everything I had left – which hadn't been much – for the dubious honour of sixth place.

With that thought, another wash of nausea rose up and I retched again, bringing up nothing. Swiping a dribble of spit off my lower lip, I painstakingly lifted my heavy head – and found Lori standing by the bus, her gaze trained on me.

Ah, *shit*.

Looking away, I flagged down one of the swannies, waving my hand to make sure he didn't wander away again after handing me a ketone drink.

'The women,' I began, guzzling half of the drink because fluids were life itself to me in that moment. 'How did our women go?'

His frown made my chest heavy. 'Lori was in the breakaway with 30 K to go, and you'll never believe what happened.'

Another wave of nausea. 'What happened?'

'A horse ran onto the road! A fecking horse! She came off

the bike and when she got back on, the thing ran after her. I've never seen anything like it. Once they got the animal off the road, she only managed tenth.'

Tenth would still have been a dream result for me last year, but I understood that for Lori it was heart-breaking. She was talking to Colin, her expression twitchy, and I wished I could give her a hug – if I hadn't stunk of sweat and sticky glucose gels and vomit and wasn't expected in the drug testing tent to take my turn peeing in a cup.

I was a real catch. She must have been relieved we'd agreed sex would be a one-time thing.

Which was why I was so shocked back in my room a few hours later when I opened the door after my shower to find Lori there, chewing on her bottom lip. Stepping inside, she closed the door behind her and said, 'I hope you've recovered. You were right. I need my luck back, so drop the towel. We're doing this again.'

The race wiped from my brain, I'd never got turned on so quickly in my life. But with those motives, I couldn't go through with this – could I?

10 September 15:23
zpeed.com/voicechannels/@Folklore99/7493376900111

Folklore99: Are you trying to tell me she ends up falling in love with him? Urgh.

LoonieDunes: You can stop gagging now. It's not that bad. She's only five years older and he does grow up in the next film.

Folklore99: I bet you have an enormous crush on Natalie Portman.

LoonieDunes: Uh… Humm. Not— Maybe? Is this warm-down harder than usual? What did you set? Do you have the normal view of the ride up on screen? Did you see the guy at the front of the bunch in the pink jersey? Do you think he's real or a bot?

Folklore99: … Did I say something wrong? Do you have a girlfriend or are you married or something? Does she… know about— Not that we do anything except talk and even if we— I mean, I might as well be Natalie Portman, since we live across the world from each other and will never meet.

LoonieDunes: Urgh, please shut up. Now I have the mental image of you as Natalie Portman and it's not helping. I don't have a girlfriend so you don't have to get worried. Would you want to imagine me as a Star Wars character?

Folklore99: As long as it's not Anakin.

LoonieDunes: I would *not* be Anakin. Maybe I'd be Qui-Gon Jinn.

Folklore99: Except he fucking *died*. I can't believe you made me watch this schmaltzy thing.

LoonieDunes: We don't have to watch episode two. Maybe I should have made you watch them in the original order. You can really ship Harrison Ford and Carrie Fisher and blame the... what did you call it? Schmaltzy? You can blame it on the seventies.

Folklore99: I had no idea you liked Star Wars for the romance... Ahhh *hiss* Shit my back didn't like sitting up.

LoonieDunes: You okay?

Folklore99: Yeah...

LoonieDunes: Ehm... Folklore?

Folklore99: What?

LoonieDunes: Do *you* have a boyfriend? I know we just train together on screen and watch films. I can understand why it wouldn't come up. We don't have to get personal.

Folklore99: Keep your pants on, I don't have a— Ahem. *cough*. Fucking allergies. Damn it. *rustle, swipe* No boyfriend – not that it matters. That guy in front is totally not a bot. His cadence is too bad. He's probably just an introvert. I never used to talk to anyone else on Zpeed before. I had an actual life and this was just a place for occasional training.

LoonieDunes: Well, you know, harsh winters.

Folklore99: Not really… *cough* I have two summers every year.

LoonieDunes: Ouch, and two springs with those allergies must be hell.

Folklore99: …yeah. I didn't mean to imply you have no life by the way.

LoonieDunes: I know. But do you ever think about how much time we spend staring at fake people's arses on a screen?

Folklore99: Gngh. Sometimes I think about how much of my life I waste listening to your voice over my headphones.

Chapter 14

Lori

It was the worst moment of my life.

Okay, maybe not the worst. I'd had a lot of worst moments over the past year. But as my skin prickled cold with the realisation that Seb was going to turn me down – LoonieDunes, who I kind of knew had had a puppy-dog crush on me, was turning me down – mortification sluiced over me like sweat.

I hoofed it for the door, turning away with a cry of 'Forget it! Of course it's a bad idea!' and hoping he didn't hear the stifled choke as my throat closed. I hated that I was upset – about something so stupid. I'd just lost a race because of a horse! It didn't matter if some guy didn't want to sleep with me. 'You've just heaved your guts up anyway. I shouldn't have asked.'

Ouch, taking it out on him was petulant and unfair and I regretted my words as soon as they were out of my mouth.

'Forget I said that too,' I muttered over my shoulder. 'You busted your butt today and I have nothing but respect and... well done.'

Ohhhh, shit. I was going to cry.

I'd always thought that one of the best reasons to watch road cycling was the opportunity to see grown men cry. We put ourselves through hell, sacrificed the good things in life — a lot more than just cheese — for shit days like this and tears weren't uncommon. But I was supposed to be tough. I'd been *brought up* to be resilient.

That day I burst into tears like a 7-year-old who'd skinned their knee at the park. To make everything worse, Seb's posture softened immediately and that place on his shoulder, right near the crooked collarbone, looked more inviting than a comfy bed with a laptop for Netflix.

'Don't touch me!' I said when he took a single step in my direction. 'I'll go as soon as—' *Hiccough*.

'What did you do with Amir?' he asked, glancing down the hall behind me before closing the door.

It took me a second to clock the subject change. 'You think I lured your roommate out so I could have my wicked way with you? I just saw he was settled downstairs. It was opportunistic, not planned. And I just needed to get out of my—' Damn it, thinking of my own roommate and the team I'd let down made my eyes sting afresh.

'If you want to... sit down—'

I just glared at him in response. But instead of looking away from the awkward display of emotion, he studied me — too closely.

'Just to be clear,' he began, in a tone that gave me goose-bumps and reminded me of isolated Spanish B&Bs with tiny showers. 'I would love nothing more than to tackle you onto the bed and touch you until you definitely get lucky again.'

The tingles whooshed to my hairline and, as much as my pride protested, the weakness in my legs was louder. I groped for the armchair by the desk and sank into it.

'But not for superstition.'

'You're the superstitious one!' I insisted. 'I'm just desperate.'

'Exactly,' he said with a wince.

'Not that—' I released a frustrated breath. 'Desperate for something to go right – not so desperate that I'm settling for you. God, have some self-respect! I thought everyone in this sport was supposed to be on an ego trip.'

'Not farm boy Walloons, I'm afraid,' he deadpanned, but I was so all over the place that I didn't laugh. 'I have enough self-respect that we can't do the thing right now unless you want a very unimpressive performance and too much Vaseline.'

He dropped earnestly down in front of me and my throat was tight again – my stomach was tight, *everything* was suddenly tied up in knots. For a guy who warned me he might be shit in bed right now, he had no right to have such warm eyes under those lashes.

'But I want to help you get your luck back and I have an idea. Can you walk?'

'If you can.'

'Just let me get dressed and we can go,' he said, clutching the towel and flashing a muscular thigh as he stood up.

I shouldn't have made a habit of ogling him while he

dressed, but the chair was comfortable and he didn't ask me to leave, so I dipped my head and watched out of the corner of my eye as he tugged on a pair of snug boxers, jeans and a soft T-shirt, tossing a hoodie on the bed as he sat to pull on his socks.

'Can I borrow that?' I asked, making him look up from his task, his tongue tucked between his teeth. The ripple of something warm and dangerous through me was alarming. It was a goofy action, poking his tongue out when he concentrated, but that didn't stop me staring as he licked his lip before answering.

'My sweatshirt?' he asked with a frown.

I didn't want to admit how reluctant I was to go back to my room and see Doortje. But I was only wearing a light shirt and it was March outside.

'Sure,' he said before I had finished overthinking. He handed me the black hoodie and rummaged for something else in his suitcase, coming away with an old canvas jacket. But as I slipped the hoodie over my head, catching the light scent of his deodorant and unfamiliar washing powder, my skin was oversensitive to the fact that it was Seb who'd softened this material with his body.

And as he shrugged into his jacket and flicked up the collar, he looked edgy and fashionable, while I was wearing a tracksuit, with my hair not properly brushed after washing it. My Italian heritage was screaming in dismay and my libido was screaming something else entirely.

When he shot me a brief smile before heading for the

door, I suspected everything I did at the moment was doomed to backfire — but I wouldn't be doomed alone.

I should have been resting — my brain and my body — but instead I was outside, breathing in the tangy air, running my fingers along the irregular brickwork of the old city wall, with its niches and slits and little tufts of hardy grass growing in the cracks. Silvery olive trees grew down into the valley, with a few stone pines, tall and dark in the distance.

Keeping the ancient terracotta bricks under my fingertips, I was less tempted to snatch Seb's hand. I wanted to say something about the sensation of the sharp air in my over-worked lungs, the curl of exhaustion in my spine, the strange feeling of walking companionably in silence.

'I don't like surprises,' I said softly instead.

'We're going up there,' he said, gesturing to the brick edifice at the top of a cliff ahead of us, flanked by cypress trees. Low rays from the afternoon sun hit it from one side, making the enormous church glow orange.

It wasn't the Duomo di Siena, the cathedral, which I'd visited a handful of times to gawk at its striped façade and gilded interior. This church was blocky and dark and almost forbidding, the way it perched on the hill looking down on the common folk. The crumbling houses of the historic centre of Siena tumbled down the hill before it, clustered as though huddling against the evil eye. Perhaps I had the evil eye, the malocchio my mum had never satisfactorily explained to me, since it didn't make actual sense, but every Italian respected it anyway.

'Are you going to make it up the hill?' I asked.

'You might have to drag me,' he rasped. 'But, if I lay down right now, I think I'd turn to stone, so I need to keep moving.'

'Wouldn't want you to become a Sienese gargoyle when you've only just signed on,' I quipped. 'Dare I ask what we're going to find up there?'

'Your luck!' he said pointedly and maybe he was even more eccentric than the Italians. 'Here's the first stop,' he continued, gesturing to a squat brick construction with three pointed arches.

I peered doubtfully at the old building as he strutted to the archways and beckoned for me.

'Have you got a coin? Come on!'

As I came closer, I saw still water shimmering in a pool through the arches, reflecting the vaulted ceiling. 'What is this place?' As many times as I'd been to Siena, I'd never stopped to look under this crumbling arcade. The water was clear and tinged blue. A flash of movement drew my eye – fish meandering beneath the surface.

'A water source for the town from mediaeval times. Here, if you don't have your purse, let me find one.' He pulled his wallet out of his pocket.

'I don't see any other coins in there,' I said doubtfully. 'It's not exactly the Trevi Fountain. Maybe we're not allowed.'

'Since when do you care about rules when winning is on the line?'

I scowled at him, but he had a point. 'Okay, give it here.' Holding out my hand, I waited while he rummaged in his beat-up leather wallet.

'Ehm, I don't have any,' he said flatly. 'Except—' Opening a zip at the back, he retrieved a tiny brass coin. 'This is perfect. It's my lucky one cent.'

'I can't take your lucky one cent.'

'It's exactly what you need to do! And don't worry, I definitely found it with the heads up for good luck and not the tails for bad luck.' He pressed it into my hand and peered urgently at me.

With a sigh, I closed my hand around the coin. 'Do I have to throw it over my shoulder?'

'No idea. You're not wishing to come back to Siena – although maybe you are, next year for the Strade Bianche, where you'll win!'

Giving him a shove with my closed fist, I turned away and hurled the coin over my shoulder, squeezing my eyes shut. I heard a ping, but no splash. 'Did it go in?'

'Ehm,' he hesitated, 'not quite. Hold on. I'll get it.'

With a groan, I watched him hop up the steps and press himself into the ancient brick wall. 'Seb, no!' I cried as he stretched out a foot and wobbled onto a moss-covered stone sticking out of the wall. Balancing precariously, he reached out for the next stone with a grunt of effort. 'Stop! You're going to—'

I buried my face in my hands as his foot slipped into the water with a splash.

'For crying out loud,' I muttered, but he turned to me with a triumphant smile, holding up the tiny coin, before sloshing back to the steps through the water. Luckily it wasn't deep, but he'd soaked his trainers and socks and the bottoms of his jeans. 'Next time we just beg a cent from a stranger,' I mumbled.

'Next time?' he repeated slowly. With a swallow and a measured nod, he continued, 'We'll get your luck back and then there doesn't have to be a next time, hmm?'

Why I experienced a sinking feeling at his words, I didn't want to know. Watching carefully this time, I threw the coin gently into the old water source, letting it plop without fanfare.

'How do you even know what's heads and tails with euro coins? There are no people on them.' I asked suddenly.

'I think it's the side with the map of Europe,' he replied, tugging off his shoes and squeezing out his socks.

'You *think*?'

His frown didn't exactly inspire confidence. 'I *hope*? But we still have the next stop on Lori's lucky tour of Siena.' He grinned up at me, all dimples and gut-punching brightness, and I gulped.

'Do you need to go back and change your shoes?' I asked warily.

He shook his head, tying up his laces again. 'Let's just go up to the church. It's not far now.'

'Why this particular one? The cathedral is prettier.'

'Don't judge a church by its façade. It's not the basilica we're visiting, but what's inside. Come on!'

Chapter 15

Seb

Maybe I really was a bad luck charm, because I screwed up again at the San Domenico Basilica.

We arrived before closing time, which felt like a miracle, given how much my legs screamed in pain as I hobbled up, squelching with every step. When we reached the top of the hill, the last of the day's sunlight brushed the rooftops gold and a few lights had flickered on in the clustered houses of the city.

She wanted to stop and look at the view, but I tugged her up to the old brass portal of the church, swallowing an idiotic comment about how the door looked like Han Solo frozen in carbonite – even though it totally did. We'd never made it to episode five.

Once inside the cavernous nave, I located our destination quickly from the clutch of tourists ooh-ing and ahh-ing at the railing in front of a grand marble side-chapel.

'Do I have to pray for an explanation?' Lori asked. I glanced at her and that pang returned, the pleasant ache that had throbbed to life in my room when I'd been privileged enough to see her cry.

I suspected it might never go away again.

She wasn't happy to have had a witness and I wouldn't bring up the subject to save my life, knowing she could push me away just as easily as she could come along on this hare-brained pilgrimage to the relics of a saint. Perhaps this had been a crappy idea. How would lighting a candle in front of a sliver of a discoloured fingernail actually help? I hoped the relic wasn't actually a fingernail. My stomach was still a little sensitive.

But we were here now and she'd asked for an explanation. We had to try something – other than sleeping together again, which I was pretty sure would only make things worse. 'This church holds the relics of Saint Catherine.'

Lori didn't immediately react, despite my dramatic tone. 'I know I'm Irish and Italian, but I'm mostly Australian and… saints aren't really my special subject.'

'Saint Catherine is the patron saint of *wheels*. It's a great coincidence. You can light a candle here, make a gesture and reset your thinking.'

'Isn't the patron saint of cycling the Madonna del Ghisallo, that chapel in northern Italy? Dad took us there a few years ago.'

'I know the one, but that's too far away, so I figured wheels might do.'

'I suppose it can't hurt,' she said glumly.

I didn't really believe the saint would grant Lori good luck for her next race. Although I wasn't very religious, I did understand that saints weren't genies. But there could be meaning for her in the gesture, even if I couldn't describe what — at least not sufficiently for Lori to unfold her sceptical frown.

As we waited our turn to peer at the relics, she rummaged in the front pocket of my hoodie, which only reminded me how good she looked in it, how watching her pull on my clothing made me feel like the possessive jock who got the cheerleader — except for the fact that Lori was a more famous athlete than I was and not a cheerleader. I just wished I had something with my name on it for her to slip into.

'Damn it, I left my phone in your room,' she muttered. 'Can I have yours?'

I handed it over without questioning her. 'The code is 6920. It's the postcode of my family's place.'

She eyed me as though I'd given her my PIN number, although to be honest, I probably would have done that if she'd asked to borrow my card.

'What? You're not going to turn up and murder us all in our sleep,' I said defensively.

'I thought you'd be more worried about me going through your camera roll and posting everything on Instagram, but if you're concerned you're hanging out with a murderer, you don't need to be.'

'Ehhhh, maybe don't look at my—'

'Don't worry!' she said, giving me a pat on the cheek that should have felt teasing but still shivered through me. 'I'm just looking up Saint Catherine. I know every cyclist has photos of their shaved, muscly legs on their phones. I won't even risk seeing that.'

I had a few weird selfies I'd sent to my sister and her kids in my gallery, but what really worried me was Lori finding the couple of photos of *her* I'd saved off the internet.

'And nobody wants to see me on Instagram, least of all me! I haven't posted on there in years and I haven't missed anything.'

'Just put up your team portrait and you'll get a few followers,' she said without looking at me, which was helpful because heat spread right up my throat to my cheeks.

She tapped at the phone screen, then scrolled slowly, reading and humphing every few moments. It seemed she really was just reading about Saint Catherine.

'It's pretty awful that she's the patron saint of wheels and wheelwrights because they tried to kill her with one,' she commented eventually.

'They did? Ouch.' Further suspicions that this had been a bad idea rippled through me as we shuffled forward in the queue.

'Wait a second,' she said, her frown deepening. 'It said she was born in Egypt. What's the connection with Siena?'

'To be honest? No idea. I'm not a very good Catholic either, but don't tell my grandma.'

'I won't tell her if you agree to ask her to knit me a pair of leg warmers,' she said with a twitching smile as she peered at the screen.

'They're really not that fash—'

'Ah!' she said with a grimace, glancing at the marble embellishments on the chapel we were shuffling towards. 'Seb, this is the wrong Catherine.'

'The wrong…' I couldn't finish my sentence because she clutched my arm and squeezed as she continued reading and my brain froze, wondering if the casual touch was affectionate. Of course it wasn't. I was the idiot who'd stolen her luck, fallen into a fountain and brought her to see the wrong saint. An orgasm and a pair of my grandma's leg warmers wouldn't make up for that.

'These are the relics of Catherine of Siena, not Catherine of Alexandria! There's no connection to wheels at all, although I'm personally relieved this Catherine wasn't tortured, to be honest. Did you ever realise how much violence against women is internalised into western culture?'

'No, I—'

'I like this story much better. She refused to marry and then became a powerful political adviser. Except she got sick and died at 33 and then—' Her eyes widened and she looked up at the chapel in alarm. Only four tourists separated us from the railing. 'Do you know what this relic is?'

'No. What?' I asked urgently. I'd only seen the name 'Saint Catherine' before dragging her on this wild goose chase and when would I learn my lesson about leaping before I looked? It was probably a whole pile of fingernails and a pair of underwear.

I stepped up to the railing with dread and slowly lifted my

gaze. Lori's hand on my forearm clutched more tightly and I needed that painful squeeze when I saw the object enshrined in a little reliquary of gold and brass and gemstones. My stomach protested and I swayed on my feet.

It was a severed head, withered and leathery, with a toothy gap for a mouth, a grizzly, noseless, partly-mummified capitulum that had – rather violently, I assumed – been separated from the corpus.

Okay, Lori's hand wasn't enough for me to hold it together. I made an unattractive choke and grappled for the railing as my knees gave out. 'I think I'm going to be sick – again.'

Deep breaths. In… Out…

With Lori tugging my jacket as we dodged the pews, I made it outside and plonked my bottom onto the concrete steps, dropping my head between my knees. My face was hot and I almost wished Lori hadn't been there to witness this – except I couldn't imagine wishing Lori wasn't there, ever.

She wasn't the touchy-feely type and I didn't expect a back rub, but she sat next to me – almost touching! – and I peered at her out of the corner of my eye as the nausea passed. Her expression was pensive and the image of her swiping away tears came back to me.

'Did you eat?' she asked. 'After the race?'

'Yeah… something? I think.'

'Do you chuck up a lot after races?'

I shook my head. 'I just went too hard today.' She would know what I meant. Cycling was called an endurance sport for a reason. We trained to operate beyond the sustainable capacity of our metabolisms on race day – and ignore the physical warnings telling us to stop. Although I wasn't usually so good at ignoring those.

'Are you going to try to tell me your result was also down to luck?'

'Partly,' I insisted. 'I've rarely had better legs. I didn't even fall for Gaetano's mind games.' I stifled a sneer, which probably looked like an impression of Sylvester Stallone, given the doubtful glance Lori gave me.

'What mind games?'

Oops, perhaps I shouldn't have given that away. Now my cheeks were radiating heat into the dusk air.

'The usual, talking shit. I should have retired last year; I'm the 110th best Belgian cyclist; does my girlfriend even remember my name? He was more creative than most. I think he wanted me to drop back just so I didn't have to hear the insults. It's a cheap trick.'

Lori was silent for longer than I would have expected, but when she did speak, the words exploded from between her clenched teeth. 'He's a fucking wanker.'

The heat spread from my face to my chest as she vibrated with indignation, her knees bumping mine. I nudged her back. 'That's a mental image I didn't need. I'm just glad I had it in me to beat him where it counts.'

'I wish I could hit him where it counts. I couldn't even *gallop* over the finish line today.' The look she gave me was tinged with hurt and I hated that my good performance went hand-in-hand with bad luck for her.

'I know you're good, Lori, but surely you've had difficult finishes before. What happened today wasn't your fault. You haven't let anyone down.'

She flashed me a stubborn look. 'I've let *everyone* down — for months. I bet you can still remember your worst losses.'

All I could do in reply was wince at exactly how well she'd hit the nail on the head.

'You know everything Gaetano said shows more about him than it does about you?' She tucked her knees up, propping her elbows on top.

'I know. Big talk, small penis.'

Peering at me from where she rested her head on her arms, she asked, 'Do you think if he has a small penis there is some justice in the world?'

'I wouldn't want to be him anyway, regardless of... size.'

It was a relief when her shoulders shook with a chuckle. 'You're disappointingly mature sometimes, Franck.' Muffling her next words in her sleeves, I nonetheless understood when she continued, 'And you've got a really nice cock.'

I had no hope of formulating a response to that when my skin was burning with juvenile pride and a big dose of embarrassment. 'Uh, thanks,' I gulped, staring helplessly as she threw me a smirk.

But her next words made me cold again. 'Gaetano didn't say anything about me, then?'

'Did you want him to say something about you?' It was hell not touching her, but she was wrapped so tightly in on herself I knew she wouldn't accept it.

'No...' she replied eventually. 'How much of a relationship is ego and how much is actually a relationship? The way I see Gaetano now, I don't know if I'll ever be able to tell.'

... or if I'll ever be able to embark on a relationship. That's what she was saying. I wanted to press a kiss to the pinch between her brows. I couldn't take my eyes off her but I also had no idea what to do with all these cords of emotion. I just wanted her to feel safe with me.

'You don't... It wasn't allergies, was it? On Zpeed?' I ventured quietly.

At first she shot me a peeved look but she pressed the back of her hand to her face, rubbing her nose vigorously. 'Of course it wasn't allergies. I was just an emotional idiot on Zpeed and my back hurt like hell.'

'I liked that emotional idiot— Not that I'm agreeing with your choice of—'

'You liked me because you imagined I looked like Natalie Portman,' she accused with a snort.

At least I managed not to blurt out that I thought she was just as beautiful. She didn't have the flawless features of an actress, but her snub nose, her freckles, her top lip that was thicker than the bottom one and often betrayed her feelings— I gulped as the memory of kissing her washed over me. No, I liked her face just the way it was.

'I kind of miss our chats on Zpeed,' I said haltingly, the words entirely inadequate, but I didn't want her to bolt. 'Not that you're not... lovely... in person? I like this too! But things... complicated... Did I always say the wrong thing online too?' I asked, rubbing a hand over my face.

'No,' she said with a smile I didn't expect. 'You usually said the right thing, Loonie.'

'Star Wars and melodramatic rock?'

'Yes, and you didn't judge me, because you didn't know who I was.'

'I won't judge you now—' One look from her and I had to admit to myself that I had judged her after meeting her in person. Her reputation preceded her and I'd only seen one side of her online – the vulnerable bit she pretended didn't exist. Which was why she liked to pretend I didn't exist. I should probably try to remember that.

'Top Gun' was still in there somewhere, even if I kept getting caught up with Folklore.

'I googled Leesa Kubicka once,' she said, her voice thin. 'She's been studying part-time at a top university. Apparently, she got the highest mark possible at high school and loads of scholarship opportunities.'

I knew better than to try to convince her it didn't matter that her teammate was academically gifted. 'It's never a good idea to google other people,' I said instead. 'Except me? You can google me.'

She gave me a shove with her shoulder, but it lingered – unless I imagined that prolonged press of her side to mine because of the ripple of gratification it sent through me. 'I did google you,' she said with a provoking smile.

'What did you find out?' I asked, my voice rough.

'I got a bit distracted with the pictures.' Her smile grew and I couldn't have replied if my life depended on it. 'They held my attention more than your palmarès anyway. It's shorter than your—' Her gaze dipped and I snapped my knees together, shoving her with my elbow.

'Shut up,' I grumbled through gritted teeth as heat blossomed in my cheeks again. 'Hoogenboezem won the polka-dot jersey because of me!' I insisted.

'Reverse psychology works so well on you.'

'I'm a simple man,' I mumbled, giving a shrug that brought my arm against hers again. Did she feel the same deep shudder inside, the same pull, at every light touch?

'You know I thought you were Canadian. I assumed you must be some rich Québécois who'd got into cycling from your posh social circle.'

'Huh. Why?'

'You used to go on about winter and cycling is such a middle-class sport in North America. And the Loonie, of course. Apparently, that's what they call a Canadian dollar. I thought it was a jokey nickname like Fifty Cent.'

'You thought I was a rich guy named after a rapper?'

'Instead, you're a farm boy with an inferiority complex,' she said with a sigh.

'That could describe the entire population of Wallonia. Cycling in Belgium isn't the upper-class sport it is in some countries – and it's crazy competitive. But I'm sorry I turned out not to be rich.'

She wisely ignored me. 'How did you get into cycling? Pro, I mean? Obviously in Belgium you probably started riding a bike before you could walk.'

'We did a try-out in school. A guy came and tested us all for aptitude for different sports and I was told to join the cycling club.'

She stared as though that was not the answer she'd been expecting. 'No strike of lightning? Deep inspiration or love of the sport?'

'It was physical aptitude, not psychological,' I added, which only made her laugh. 'Apparently I have a big heart.'

The quick smile that crossed her lips before she hid it behind the sleeves of her – my – sweatshirt gave me a burn that should probably have been indigestion but was definitely emotional.

'What about your stomach?' she asked. 'Do you have a big, empty stomach?'

'Ehm…'

'Well, I do,' she said, hauling herself up with her hand supporting her back. 'I saw a restaurant over there and I bet we can even spring for cheese, since we raced today.' She stifled a yawn that made me want to observe every one of her facial expressions and keep them in a little log book.

I unfolded myself slowly too, my muscles already growing stiff. 'Lore, is this… a date?' I asked, trying to inject lightness into my tone for plausible deniability.

'Nope,' she said immediately and that put me in my place. 'I hate dating. I'm not dating this year.'

Dragging my steps behind her, I turned her words over in my mind, watching her ponytail swing as she walked. 'So this is just dinner,' I clarified. 'Between…?'

'Us!' she called over her shoulder.

And I'd be damned if that didn't sound better than any date I'd ever been on.

Chapter 16

Lori

'Maybe I should move here,' I mused with a sigh.

It was full dark, now, the wooden shutters of the old brick houses drawn. I usually craved pizza after a race, which was convenient when I was in Italy. We'd shared two perfect pizzas – a classic salami and a garlicky white one with fresh yellow tomatoes and olives – washed down with a glass of sangiovese that had felt like a good idea at the time.

Now I was a little too loose and the alcohol added another layer of complexity to the mix of natural chemicals building up in my body. Passing under a stone archway illuminated by the soft light of the wrought-iron lamps, I was certain now that we were lost, but I wouldn't be the one to mention it. I needed to rest, was about to shut down, but I was too stubborn to succumb.

'There are fewer aggressive creatures in Siena than Australia,' Seb agreed and I had that urge to touch my shoulder to his again. He was so… nudgeable. But I wasn't supposed to be *nudging* anyone. Plus, he'd already turned me down once today.

Unfortunately, it hadn't stopped the tightness in my chest, the thump of fresh adrenaline fizzing in my blood as my skin tingled with memories and possibilities every time I looked at him.

'I have an Italian passport you know,' I commented absently.

'Ah, so you only date compatriots?' Seb teased. 'You're lucky that gives you three countries in your pool of candidates. I would be stuck with Belgians.'

'How awful!' I gave a mock shudder. 'How come you speak such good English? I didn't find a mention of your qualifications on the internet – or maybe I was just distracted by the mud-spattered cyclocross photos.'

His grin gave me that little heart-flip again. He had more pride than he realised and I kind of liked stoking it. 'I learned English, but not very well – not at my technical school. But I've been in international teams for a long time. Even in a Belgian team – I speak better English than Flemish, so... Except the swear words. I'm good at those.'

'Do you realise you talk about Belgium like you're apologising for its existence? But I suspect you wouldn't want to live anywhere else.'

'Well, my mum and my grandma... and my sister.'

'What do they think about your career?'

'They don't know what to think,' he said with a far-off smile. 'They often come to watch if it's not too far. They drive up in the old truck and stand by the barriers in their rubber boots. I don't think they really understand what's going on.'

He painted a vivid picture and it was striking how much I wanted to meet them in real life. 'Not quite like my dad, then,' was all I said. And unlike my mum, his family seemed to value him just the way he was, regardless of his achievements.

'No, not like your dad,' he agreed emphatically.

The lane opened out up ahead and we emerged onto the Piazza del Campo, the scene of our ignominious race finishes today. Seb stopped so suddenly I walked into him – a rather soft landing against his pliant, tired body. He turned to me, standing close, and I wouldn't have moved for the world.

The crescent of warm stone buildings with wrought-iron balconies and the crenellated town hall looked different at night from this afternoon, when the square had been filled with barriers and marquees and officials with lanyards. Staring at the stunning white loggia at the top of the tower, while Seb did the same, I thought that this quiet moment in a place I loved would surely turn my luck around.

His fingers brushed mine and I froze, my heart pounding. I was tense, mixed up, with no idea what I wanted from him – except definitely more touching. The world seemed different when we were together. But I wasn't supposed to be indulging in *romance*.

He swept past without taking my hand. 'I'd rather not look too closely at the piazza,' he called over his shoulder. 'I hope someone's cleaned up after me at least.'

I caught up to him quickly and we dawdled together, the cold air swirling around us while heat gathered between. It had been a hellish day with a fruitless, painful race and tears – far too many tears.

More of them gathered as my thoughts flitted aimlessly over the events of the day. Laura and Gaetano, the armchair in Seb's room, his dimpled cheeks and my cute mental image of his mother and grandmother in rain gear, failure, rejection, a saint's severed head and this overwhelming feeling that I would do it all again if it meant we got here. I didn't even know where 'here' was and he wasn't even holding my hand.

A car clattered past on the flagstones and we veered off onto a little piazza to make room. It was ridiculous that cars were allowed to drive these narrow lanes but I didn't mind squeezing off the road because it brought me back into a full-body nudge against Seb, his arm slipping around me.

Nudging. That seemed to be where we were at.

I recognised the drinking fountain with the brass statue of a panther and realised we weren't far from the hotel now.

He saw me looking at the fountain. 'Maybe we were on the wrong track with the coin and Saint Catherine.'

'You think?' At least the weird, romantic mood hadn't killed my sarcasm yet.

'Since your bad luck has been distinctly zoological, we should have been visiting all these animals around Siena and rubbing the statues for luck. How's your calendar looking for tomorrow?' he asked with a little huff.

My throat was thick. 'I'm leaving tomorrow.'

His gaze shot to mine. 'You should at least rub this one. The bones of Saint Francis are too far away, in Assisi. He's the patron saint of animals.'

'I think we established that looking at bits of dead bodies isn't the right way to turn my luck around,' I muttered as I ran my hand over the cool brass. Seb did the same and when our fingertips brushed, we both paused, but he didn't look up. His throat bobbed and, after a long hesitation, he drew his fingers back.

'That will— Ehm… Surely the panther is a good-luck animal,' he said softly, taking a step back. When he glanced at me, the wariness in his gaze sucked me in. *He feels all this too.*

As we set off again in the direction of the hotel, I scuffed my feet, my mind racing. Digging my hand out of the pocket of the hoodie, I let it hang, my knuckles grazing his while I tried to decide if I wanted to take his hand and ridiculing myself for agonising about something so simple, given the places on me he'd already had his fingertips.

He could make a move, although I wasn't usually one to stand around waiting. But maybe he didn't want to. Hand-holding was some whole different shit to banging the tension out of our systems and that's all we'd done – as well as spend a couple of hours together trying to shed my bad luck while nudging each other.

We passed under another brick archway near the hotel and I wondered with some detachment whether I was going to hyperventilate, my body was so wound up. About nudging and hand-holding! What was wrong with me?

Although we were walking more slowly than a nonna with a Zimmer frame, it was only when we reached the stone porch that my thoughts progressed to goodbye kisses and that dilemma landed on me with a whump to my stomach.

He paused by the first step, opening and closing his hand. 'I— Erm… You—' He rubbed the back of his neck, glancing at me and away again as though there was something painful about the action. 'What time are you leaving tomorrow?'

I gulped, trying to switch off the prickle of awareness of everything he did, but he drifted closer and, instead of turning off, I zoned right in. As though I was on the bike, every fibre of my being trembled into focus.

His gaze rose warily to mine, all warm amber and confusion. I wanted to rub my thumbs in the hollows of his cheeks, kiss his angular jaw. I forgot everything except how the air buzzed when he was this close and how it had felt to kiss him – like letting go.

His nostrils flared and his chest rose sharply on a ragged breath. We stood so close the steam clouds of our breath dissipated as one.

'You…' he tried again.

His brow dipped as a sigh escaped his lips and he studied me, my mouth. He'd done nothing, but I still felt the look in my spine.

'You left your phone in my room. Do you want me to get it for you?'

Only when I stumbled back onto my heels did I realise

how close I'd swayed to him and with the crash of my feet came the tumble of my pride.

'I'll just come and get it,' I mumbled, gritting my teeth.

I turned away, but his hand shot out and closed in the soft fabric of the hoodie, at my waist.

'Okay, maybe I don't even care if you only want me when you lose,' he murmured. Before I'd had a chance to process those words, his hands plunged into my hair, he tilted his head and then everything flipped upside down again as he pressed a hard kiss to my mouth.

What began as firm pressure, the scrape of his bottom lip over mine, quickly turned deep as I fumbled for him, for something to hold onto. My mouth fell open and I needed to get closer, even closer, clawing at him as his tongue swept through my mouth.

Maybe I did want him because I'd lost, because that evening had been wonderful, when I could have been wallowing in my own failure. Maybe if I lost again, he'd be there for me.

He broke away with a heavy breath, his eyes still closed. That upside-down floating sensation was still interfering with my balance when I stared at his face, his dark eyelashes, sharp cheekbones. I blossomed into a different person when I looked at him – someone protective and soft and chaotic. That person didn't win races, but I didn't mind her that night.

Turning his head so his cheek was on my forehead, his breath tickled my hair as he said, 'I don't want you to think I'm rejecting you.'

I stilled, the words sharp inside me. The blossom shrivelled like the weak thing it was. I didn't like flowers anyway.

'You're a winner, Lori. No matter how much you add to your palmarès this year, even if a thousand horses cross your path, you're a winner. I wanted to help you see that tonight, but it all went wrong.'

All wrong was a good way to describe that day, but I still struggled to regret it.

'Go and fight. You deserve it – everything. I'd love to be your consolation prize, but you have to go for your main prize – right? Look to the future? You didn't want any distractions this year and this… whatever we're doing…'

'Nudging each other,' I muttered. 'That's all we were doing.'

His lips twitched and he smoothed a strand of my hair between his thumb and forefinger, making me shudder at the tenderness I didn't know how to bear. 'Nudging,' he repeated with a wobbly smile. 'It was nice nudging you, but… I don't want to bring you down. You should be… up.'

He drew away and headed for the door to the lobby, leaving me to stumble after him, dazed, mixed up. Thankfully the hallways were empty as most of the team were sensibly flopped on their beds, groaning.

Seb knocked on his door briefly before opening up to retrieve my phone, while I hopped from foot to foot in the corridor. He greeted his roommate quietly and reappeared at the door with my phone and an earnest look.

'See you…' I wouldn't have known how to finish that sentence either.

I was about to have a go at saying something — probably choked and stupid — when a loud voice from down the hall made us both jump. 'Lori! What the fuck? Dad's been calling you for hours!'

Hearing Colin was enough to banish the last of that soft, weak version of me. Gallaghers had steel instead of vertebrae, so I turned to my brother with a shrug, flapping my phone nonchalantly. 'I forgot it in Seb's room,' I said, offering no further explanation. 'Don't worry. I'll let Dad know I'm not dead. But now I'm going to bed.'

I turned away from both of them, heading for my door at the other end of the hall. I'd never been so relieved to have remembered my keycard, retrieving it out of the pocket of my tracksuit bottoms. Slipping into the dark room silently, I leaned back against the door while I got my breath under control.

Seb was right. I should be looking at the next race. Moonlight and romantic cities were for losers, even if that thought made my nose sting at the sudden image of him holding someone else's hand while they meandered through the narrow lanes.

God, even when I'd been spending all my spare time with Gaetano, I'd never been so far off the map as this. Thoughts of luck were counterproductive. Seb had told me to fight, so I'd fight.

I heard a rustling in the corner as my roommate rolled over. 'Are you okay, Lore?' Doortje asked groggily.

'Yeah, I'm fine,' I lied. 'But don't wake me for breakfast in the morning.'

Forceful claps on my back from my dad and Colin's annoyingly self-satisfied posture helped me shed the remaining hints of my wobble from the night before as we piled into a taxi to take us to the airport an hour away in Florence.

'Leave it all behind, hey, Molly?' Dad said.

I nodded wordlessly, definitely *not* sad about everything else I would leave behind in Siena.

As Dad went back to retrieve a final suitcase from the lobby, Colin loped up to me, dipping his head to say quietly, 'I found this outside your door this morning before you got up and I thought I should look after it for you in case Dad saw it.' He slipped a paper bag into my hands, giving me an assessing look. 'Seb wasn't at breakfast either. Do I have to beat someone up?'

Swallowing a fresh surge of those pesky feelings from last night – embarrassment, shame and a prick of longing – I snatched the bag, crinkling it a little in my fist. 'No common assault required, Brothernator. But watch your own nose if you stick it too far into my business.'

His pained look wasn't what I was expecting. Perhaps my attempt at banter had sounded as weak as it had felt. 'I'm here for you, monster. I'm trying to be here for you.'

'And I'm your big sister and always will be,' I retorted. 'I was injured, not quitting!'

'That's the spirit,' Dad said with a grin as he emerged from the lobby.

Hurriedly concealing the paper bag behind my back, I had to admit – only to myself – that I appreciated what Colin had done for me in picking it up.

Strapped into the back of the cab, I waited for Colin to predictably fall asleep and Dad to be deep in conversation with the cabbie, and then dived for the mysterious gift. Peering into the packet, I found a clear plastic box with gold writing on the outside and a velvet pillow. Jimmying it open as quietly as possible, I tugged out a fine gold chain with two medallions hanging off it. The first bore a relief image of a woman in mediaeval armour holding a sword, with the words 'Jeanne d'Arc' around the edge. And the second showed a monk feeding a wolf, surrounded by other animals, with two birds flying overhead. I didn't need to read the 'San Francesco' on the side to know this was the patron saint of animals.

With a wobbly smile, I dropped the necklace back into the box and shoved it into my backpack.

18 March 20:56

Folklore: Colin looked ready to die on the Poggio today. I bet Dad's happy you got him up and over. Bad luck on the sprint.

20:59

Folklore: But I hope you're celebrating. Seventh is amazing.

22 March 18:42

Folklore: Congrats on fifth. Awful conditions. Hope the scrape isn't too painful.

26 March 17:13

Folklore: Holy shit that was close. Colin should have won it. *You* should have won it.

2 April 19:26

Folklore: I hate to say I told you so... I bet the champagne tasted amazing, even without alcohol. You deserved that podium place today.

19:48

Folklore: This is really childish, Seb. You're the one who said we should stay friends. We're finally in the same city again. Are you going to keep pretending I don't exist at dinner tonight?

19:59

LoonieDunes: You told me I was only allowed to text you to congratulate you when you win. It didn't go so well last time I wished you luck. Bon appétit.

Folklore: Don't be so superstitious.

LoonieDunes: I hate to say I told you so...

Folklore: What are you talking about? I just dropped my fork. I can get another one.

LoonieDunes: Dropping a fork is bad luck. It means an unwanted visitor is on their way.

Folklore: Stop texting me from across the room or *you'll* get an unwanted visitor.

LoonieDunes: Oh look, here comes your dad.

Folklore: I was right. You should only text me to congratulate me when I win.

Chapter 17

Seb

It always rained in France when I was here.

That morning in early April, though, I knew exactly why it was raining: because of my stupid bad luck that Lori was still battling. So far in the Spring Classics, she'd come 20th at Lake Maggiore after a peloton crash that took out both Doortje and Bonnie and left her needing to swap bikes. She'd got caught by a brand-new pothole opening up in heavy rain during the Brugge-De Panne and crossed the line 15th in the Gent-Wevelgem after sneezing through most of the race. Then she'd crashed out of the Tour of Flanders with a sprained wrist last week, at pretty much the exact moment I was crossing the line in second place in the men's race.

Today was the Paris-Roubaix Femmes, one of the most prestigious one-day races in the calendar. Lori would be waking up in her team hotel at a town further north, the start for the women, and I was here in a place called

Compiègne, which I only knew was not quite Paris, even though it was the start for the men's race tomorrow.

I was awake early, as I often was when Lori was racing. She hadn't had any further altercations with animals since the Strade Bianche, but she certainly still had my bad luck. I hoped she hadn't worn the necklace.

What had I been thinking giving it to her? She'd cried in front of me and tried to get me out of her system. A trinket from me was like a blessing from the Jamaican bobsled team, even though it seemed I had the spirit of John Candy as my coach at the moment, rest his soul.

I wondered if she'd seen that film and fumbled for my phone to write her a message – as I had a hundred times over the past four weeks, but put it down again when I remembered that disaster struck – her – every time I reached out.

'What fucking time is it? Go back to sleep, Frankie.'

That was another development I wanted to talk to Lori about. Since Amir was competing mostly in the Continental circuit, I was now not only racing with Lori's brother, I was sleeping with him too – in the sense of actual sleeping.

It was… strange, to say the least.

Rolling over, I tried to go back to sleep, but I knew it wouldn't work, so I pulled on a tracksuit and jogged down to the breakfast room of our crappy hotel with furry brown carpet and a signed portrait of Gérard Depardieu on the wall in the corridor.

It wasn't long before Colin joined me, collapsing groggily into the chair across from where I was nursing my black coffee.

'Do you want to head out early to check out the course? Alan wants to talk to us after lunch.'

'Sure,' I replied listlessly. I should be more excited about discussing tactics with our directeur sportif for the race tomorrow — my 13th Paris-Roubaix, well didn't that sound lucky? — but all I could think about was Lori out on the cobbles in the rain.

But the women didn't start until later, so I got out in the crisp spring air for a short practice ride with Colin. I was so used to having him on my wheel, swearing and spitting, but everything he said reminded me of Lori. Everything I *did* reminded me of Lori. She would hate knowing that, instead of fighting through my final year of professional racing, I was mooning over her and waiting for every little glimpse of the back of her neck in the breakfast room when we happened to be in the same hotel — which had only happened twice since Siena.

Back at the hotel for lunch, Colin and I both looked incessantly at our watches as we shovelled in the chicken and rice without tasting anything. When the time ticked over to a quarter to two, I was tapping my fingers manically on the table, picturing Lori's tough, streamlined — sexy — body in her tight orange-and-blue jersey, a scowl on her freckled — gorgeous — face.

'Dad will text me if something happens,' Colin said casually, setting his phone down next to his plate.

My gaze snapped up.

'Do you think you're being subtle? Whatever's going on

180

with my sister, just be aware that the only reason I'm not on your case is because she told me to back off — and maybe because I still feel bad you actually made it up the Coll de la Creueta on training camp.' The last part was mumbled; a poor excuse for an apology if you ask me.

'There's nothing going on.'

Colin's only response was a doubtful glance that also reminded me of her.

'Just because we share resources with the women's team doesn't mean we can all just hook up.'

'I know, mate,' I assured him hurriedly.

'I'm not your mate.' His tone made me look up again and study him. There was a crease on his forehead I hadn't noticed before, shadows in his eyes that both reminded me of how young he was and made him look so much older.

'Fair enough,' I agreed. 'But I only want what's best for her too, you know. And I'm well aware that I'm not it.'

I might have given too much away, because his brow lifted. 'Good, because I regret not running Gaetano off sooner last year. I thought it was just some fun. She hasn't... she was never the type to go after guys. She was never... you know, that into anyone before. But he got into her head.'

The cold down my spine had nothing to do with the weather. I wasn't sure what upset me more: that she'd felt something — real — for Maggioli or that he'd hurt her because of it. I'd unfortunately got into her head too, without anything much romantic between us. I needed to keep staying away from her — not even any messaging banter.

Colin's phone beeped and he snatched it up.

'What's happened?'

He released a breath on a sigh and I tried to calm myself down too. 'Nothing much. Early breakaway, but it probably won't last. She's well-positioned in the peloton with Doortje.'

Colin gave another humph and then tapped at his phone until he brought up the coverage on the sports channel that showed most of the races. Propping it up with a glass on one side of the table, we ate in silence, glued to the little screen, until Alan Hargreaves, the DS, found us half an hour later.

The peloton had just reached the first section of cobblestones when Colin shut the phone down as reluctantly as I would have. Slouched in our chairs in the conference room listening to the spindly director, I was distracted and in no way expecting the shock that came at me.

'Right, chaps, we're shaking things up a bit tomorrow, as you'll see, because we've called Nellie away from his wedding plans.'

Nellie was actually called Jarin Nelson, another Australian from somewhere called Adelaide. He didn't look old enough to be getting married, but he'd barely spoken about anything else on training camp back in December.

'I'm not going to talk at you too long because some of you know this route verrrry well.' Alan gave me a wink. 'Today's rain is going to make the course entirely unpredictable tomorrow, so we're making a two-pronged attack. Two leaders, two primary domestiques, three floating support riders. We make a break with three guys early on – chance it and see what happens. The second leader and whoever's left stays in the peloton and makes a break at Pont-Thibault, just before the pavé. We want to be ready before the Carrefour de l'Arbre.'

Even hearing those place names made me shudder. How many times had I come off on that single stretch of cobbled road? The surface was torture on a road bike. Not water-boarding or the rack or the iron chair, but *bone-shaking*. I'd finished the race with bleeding hands more than once. Only the French could be *proud* of the terrible state of their roads. Our Belgian cobbles were more civilised.

Lori was speeding in that direction right now.

'… and Frankie!' Alan said with a flourish, making me sit up straight so quickly I nearly came out of my chair.

'What?'

'He'll miss me, DS,' Colin drawled. 'He's used to cleaning up after me in his apron with a broom.'

The DS eyeballed me with a twinkle I hadn't seen before. 'It's your chance, Frankie. Show us what you're made of.'

'Eh——' I was pretty sure my brain was made of biscuits and goat's cheese as my thoughts struggled to catch up.

'You lead tomorrow and next year it could be a few stages of the Tour.'

Next year?!

I must have looked as stunned as I felt, because the room erupted into laughter.

'Pull yourself together, boy,' Alan said, his grizzled hands on his hips. 'We're taking a chance on you. You go out early tomorrow. If you only break up the peloton and then run out of steam, then fine, but you need to be ready for anything – you need to be ready to win.'

That *might* be a problem, but I wasn't going to put my hand up and say so.

Stumbling out of the room, shell-shocked, I nearly fell when Colin thumped me on the back and said, 'Weren't expecting that, were you?'

I didn't answer him. 'What's happening with Lori?' I asked, not even bothering to conceal my interest.

'Nothing from Dad. Let's keep watching upstairs.'

It was an odd sort of daytime sleepover, sitting on our beds with Colin's laptop on the desk, showing the women's race. I perched at the foot of the bed cross-legged, dragging my hands through my hair as we waited for the first glimpse of her.

'Why do you care so much?' Colin asked, his tone deceptively light. 'You barely know my sister.'

The camera panned along the peloton and I strained my eyes to find her, looking for that pink helmet over the orange jersey. 'I've known her longer than you realise. We trained together on Zpeed when she was injured.'

Colin turned to me and laughed, full and deep. 'You're shitting me. *You're* the guy who watched *Miss Congeniality* with her? Makes sense.'

'She told you about that?' I asked.

'No, but the walls are thin and I was home. Does Dad know?'

I shook my head, still scanning the footage. 'There she is! Phew! On the edge, getting ready for the pavé right? What's the plan, do you know? Break on the cobbles? She might be better at a bottleneck.'

The side-eye Colin gave me then was subtly different from the sort I'd got used to since training camp. 'You're her coach now?'

'No, I—'

'There she goes!' Colin called out suddenly.

I hopped up on my knees, peering at the screen like a meerkat. She'd made a break, head down, arse up, her plait over her shoulder – and a glint of gold swinging against her chest. My throat closed and my heart clobbered my ribs.

The necklace. She was wearing my necklace. No, she'd lose, but... holy hell, she liked it. Maybe she liked *me*. I couldn't cope.

She attacked with the grace and ferocity of Joan of Arc as the commentators got excited too and I couldn't have torn my eyes off the screen for anything. Mud spattered her face, but she swiped a hand over her mouth and kept pushing.

There were other riders up ahead, but they had to be growing fatigued. Light rain started up and the cameras caught her again, droplets cutting through the dirt on her cheeks to drip onto her wet jersey, plastered to her chest.

I wanted her to win. I also wanted her to stop and let me wrap her in a towel and usher her into a steamy shower with scented soap and clean up every inch of her. As she juddered over the cobbles, her expression twisted, I wished I could create some kind of telepathic bond using chunky metallic props where I could take the pain from her.

But she could handle the pain. She was tough, and had I ever seen anything so beautiful in my life? I certainly had never looked at someone and *wanted* so much. What if I hadn't turned her down in Siena? She would probably hate me by now, she'd had such continuing rotten luck.

But as the gold chain glinted in a weak flash of sunlight, my skin felt too tight as I imagined her hanging it around her neck and thinking of me, of that evening in Siena.

She would tease me so badly if I ever told her what I was thinking. But maybe she'd kiss me afterwards – or maybe I was dreaming. I felt Colin's gaze on me and, when I risked a quick glance at him, I suspected I wouldn't even need Lori to tease me because her brother was about to take on the task – with relish.

But before Colin could say anything, the commentator cut in with a cry. '*Oh! What is going on here?*'

Chapter 18

Seb

'*She's slipped! Is it a loose stone? No, she's dropped her chain.*' My heart in my throat, I watched her leap off the bike, leaning over the frame to grab the slipped chain. '*That's poor timing, but we've seen it again and again on these surfaces. Gallagher isn't even today's first victim of the cobbles.*'

It was helicopter footage now, hovering over her as she wrestled with the pedals but, because she was capable and hot and utterly amazing, she got the chain back on in a few seconds. Just as the peloton swooped past, she threw her leg over the saddle and set off again, Doortje hanging back to help her get up to speed.

Watching her standing on the pedals, my eyes wandering the lines and curves of her body and remembering her skin under my fingertips, my mouth, I had to have a firm word with myself to settle down, especially given that Colin was in the room.

'Come on, Lore,' I couldn't help muttering. I needed her

to put me out of my misery. It was so much worse than racing myself, which made me uneasy.

She and Doortje weaved their way painstakingly through the pack while I tugged at my hair. The breakaway had lost time against the peloton. She could still do it. She was wearing my necklace; she *had* to succeed.

Colin was mercifully silent. But when the commentator grew animated again, we both shot off the beds to peer more closely at the screen.

'*There's a ruckus in the peloton! Someone's gone down — more than one. They don't call the Paris-Roubaix the Hell of the North for nothing. The peloton has ground to a halt, but Laura Colombini has escaped — there she goes. Given Gallagher's luck this season, I'm expecting—— Yep, there she is, off to the side. What is——?*'

'Fuck!' Colin bit out.

If she'd moved off the road, that wasn't good. It might mean medical intervention. I couldn't breathe. What if her back injury caused more problems? I saw flashes of her skin behind my eyes again, but in a different context: the puckered slash of scars on her arm and her back.

The camera zoomed in on her as the nearest team support car pulled up and one of the assistants jumped out. The next minute, I had to flinch and cover my eyes as she yanked her arm at a strange angle.

'*Dislocated shoulder,*' the commentator confirmed — unnecessarily for me. '*If she can get it popped back in, she might still finish, but I think this is the end of Gallagher's chances of winning this one. Bitterly disappointing.*'

'You can look now. She got it back in,' Colin said flatly.

'Putain de merde,' I cursed under my breath, watching her climb back on and start pedalling. I'd had my share of dislocated shoulders – enough to know it hurt like hell. To finish another five sections of cobbles with her hip scraped and her shoulder throbbing, she'd have to be superhuman.

Colin's phone vibrated and he glanced at the message. 'The DS is telling her to DNF.'

I nodded, awash with relief, even as I knew she'd hate to abandon the race. On the screen, she rolled to a stop, her head hanging. Then, because Lori never did anything by halves, she ripped her earpiece out and flung the cable to the side of the road with an angry flourish.

Covered head to toe in mud, she let her bike clatter to the ground, giving it a swift kick, and then another when that obviously wasn't enough. When an assistant went to her, she shoved him away before grabbing her shoulder with a howl of pain.

'Ah, fuck, it's popped out again,' Colin said grimly.

Pressing the balls of my hands into my forehead, I wanted to get on my bike and race to Roubaix right then. She turned to me when she lost and that didn't feel like such a bad thing if she'd let me wrap my arms around her as she yelled and cried and let it all out.

I glanced at my phone, wondering if she'd believe me if I told her I was so impressed with her fight today and that meant I was allowed to text her.

'Dad's not going to be happy,' Colin mumbled and I turned,

realising only then that I was leaning over the laptop, propping myself up on my knees. 'She's supposed to race the Amstel Gold in a week.'

'She can't stop a peloton crash.'

'No, but she's stubborn – and got stuck in her own head. She lashes out when she's down. She'll regret it tomorrow.'

That sounded familiar.

'She's a wounded bear,' Colin continued, eyeballing me. 'You might have seen the wounded bit, but don't forget about the bear.'

I stepped back from the laptop with a slow sigh. The camera had moved away from Lori anyway. I'd known I was an idiot for making so much of my interactions with her, but those few hours in Siena, watching her come back to life, and every message she'd sent since then, even though I'd been disciplined and hadn't replied – mostly – had made me forget I was an obstacle in the way of her goals.

My phone remained untouched on the bedside table for the rest of the evening. I left it in the room when we went down to our dinner of – you guessed it – rice. Tony Gallagher arrived halfway through the meal, looking windswept and haggard. He exchanged a few words with Colin, but quickly disappeared again. I wondered whether Lori was relieved her dad had left Roubaix, could barely stand the curiosity about her mental state.

I jogged up the stairs to our room after dinner, Colin dragging his feet behind me. But when I looked at my phone, the only message I had was from my mum, confirming she and Mamie would make the two-hour drive to Roubaix to watch me finish at the velodrome, since there were no signs of labour among the pregnant goats.

Imagining them clapping enthusiastically regardless of what position I rolled in made my chest uncoil a little – a very little. I managed to settle myself down with a hot shower, until Colin banged on the door with an impatient demand that I let him have his turn.

Lying in bed staring at the wall and listening to him tune-lessly hum in the bathroom, the awkwardness of the situation struck me again. I was lying there ruminating obsessively about my roommate's sister, but kind of enjoying it because if I couldn't be in the same room as her, I might as well be hanging out with her sibling.

I remembered her calling him a bit of a dick and she was right, but the bond between them was obvious and I suspected Colin would turn into a defender of her interests if necessary – when he grew up a bit.

He came out of the shower and threw himself onto his bed, his arm flung over his eyes.

'Stop thinking and go to sleep,' he muttered. 'I've seen enough of your arse to last a lifetime.'

I tucked my arse under the blankets, annoyed to acknow-ledge the wisdom of one so young. 'You'll only see it from a distance tomorrow,' I quipped.

To my surprise, he erupted into laughter, his chest jerking with it. 'Good. And I'm betting you'll be in a hurry to get to Roubaix.' He met my gaze from under his elbow.

Turning off the light, I tried to settle, but my legs were restless. Just as my roommate's breathing was beginning to even out, my phone buzzed, lighting up the room.

Jerking upright and snatching the device, I already knew from the twist in my chest who the message was from.

I heard the plan for tomorrow. Don't screw up.

My thumb hovered over the keypad, but my mind blanked in the onslaught of the thousands of things I wanted to say to her. *You were beautiful today; I hated to see you hurt; I wish I could make it all better.* I went with something that felt safe.

How bad is the pain?

Her response was predictable: *The only thing you're allowed to type is 'congratulations on winning'.*

I saw she was typing again and held my breath. But what she wrote made me exhale on a cough.

I'm on painkillers and one side-effect seems to be to make me horny — and overshare.

Turning away so Colin didn't see the grin I couldn't stifle, I replied: *How am I supposed to not respond to that?*

Wow, I wished I could see her — tuck her into bed and stroke her hair until she fell asleep. Yeah, those were some sad fantasies when she'd just admitted to being horny and I knew how amazing she tasted.

She kept typing and I bit my lip, waiting to see what she'd say.

You know what? If you win tomorrow, I'm going to kiss you.

My hair stood on end and my throat wouldn't clear, no matter how many times I spluttered. She wasn't serious — or if she was, then she surely realised she wouldn't need to make good on her promise – or threat or whatever. She couldn't know how much I'd thought about her mouth since Siena – since training camp in December.

Shit, now I was never going to get any sleep. Another message lit up my phone screen.

Do you think I'm not serious?

I sent back a zipped-lip emoji, my heart looping somewhere up near my ears.

You'd better win, Seb. I'm really fucking horny.

My tongue felt like the Goodyear Blimp inside my mouth. She wasn't typing and my mind got a bit feverish under the pressure to reply.

Congratulations on winning – as many kisses as you want.

That was more than your word allowance.

I groaned – thankfully under my breath – hoping Colin was very asleep. But her next message caught me in the ribs.

I think you can win, Seb. If I can't, then you do it.

She had me – mind, body. I wanted to get to Roubaix tomorrow and I wanted to do it faster than anyone else. With a gulp, I typed a message, letting my fingers loose on the keypad because I wasn't allowed to send it. My thumb hovered, but I wouldn't do it.

If it wasn't luck, then it was psychology. She made me want to win, but I made her think of her own weakness. I was reminded of what Colin had said about Maggioli. There was no way I'd hurt her or take advantage of her when she was down. I had to keep my stupid infatuation to myself.

'Are you texting my sister?' came Colin's gravelly, disapproving voice.

Quickly shutting down the phone, I set it back on the bedside table and took a deep breath. 'She's just messing with me,' I insisted.

Chapter 19

Lori

Waking up after the painkillers had worn off was a hundred times worse than waking up with a hangover. I couldn't decide what hurt the most: my shoulder, my hands, my hip or my pride.

Doortje was still asleep, so I bit back my groan as I shifted on the bed. I didn't want to face her yet. I didn't want to face anyone. I'd basically told Dad to go to hell last night on the way to the hospital to have my shoulder scanned.

If I'd been back in Melbourne, I'd be hiding in the basement again – which triggered a vague memory from last night, some time after I'd told Dad to go to hell but before I'd been swallowed by drugged sleep.

Groping for my phone, I woke up the screen and the app was still open to the scene of the flaying of my pride. Damn it, I really had texted Seb, as though I were a needy barnacle when I lost, instead of the professional I was supposed to be.

Eek, looking back over last night's messages, I had been a

long way from professional. Woozy memories returned with force: the relief as the painkillers started to kick in; how my body had relaxed into syrup and I'd found myself suddenly thinking about Seb's hands, about the way he'd teased me with the towel and casually talked about fucking me.

Then I'd remembered his knees nudging mine as the sun set over Siena and I'd grabbed my phone to make a fool of myself. I'd apparently conditioned myself to want him whenever I hit bottom and there was nothing good about that — well, except when he smiled, and wrote things like: *Congratulations on winning — as many kisses as you want.*

My throat was thick as I reread his message. He *really* wasn't supposed to say stuff like that, making me imagine him watching my race, maybe checking me out. But then I shouldn't have threatened to kiss him and goaded him to win.

It was thoughts of today's race that dragged me upright to take some more ibuprofen and smear on the analgesic gel. Since I wouldn't race for at least ten days, I could have taken something stronger, but after my recovery, I didn't want to go anywhere near opioids again unless I was screaming.

Contorting myself into Seb's baggy hoodie and strapping on my sling, I slipped down to breakfast, staring at the carpet and refusing to meet anyone's eye. As I shovelled muesli into my mouth — making a mess because I'd unfortunately popped my right shoulder — I scoured the cycling news for mentions of Seb.

There was almost nothing. Nobody had guessed that he would be a lead rider for the day. I was desperate to know how he felt, but that was exactly why I'd told him not to message me. I needed to be strong in my thoughts as well as my body if I was going to make it back from the miserable place I'd found myself in – far too low in the World Tour rankings.

But I was so sick of keeping my distance. There was nothing I could do about my shitty luck. The season was already a disaster. The way I'd manhandled the bike yesterday, I was restless and needed to shake things up. I recognised the feeling and it usually meant nothing good, but I felt it nonetheless.

Ignoring Doortje's concerned look, I grabbed my shoulder bag and left the hotel. I might have told myself I was wandering aimlessly, but my feet took the quickest route to the velo-drome. Bypassing the concrete entrance to the spectator stands that looked like a brutalist municipal swimming pool, I skirted the fence and slipped through the back gate to where the team bus was still parked from yesterday.

Swallowing bitter memories, I climbed the steps to join the support team, thankful I didn't have to explain myself as they all assumed I was supporting Colin and not fawning foolishly over Seb. They spoke to me sparingly, as though my emotions were still close to the surface, but that was just one more frustration encouraging me to blow a fuse.

He had better win. I'd never looked forward to doing something stupid more than in that moment.

When one of the assistants turned on the TV and tuned into the online channel with English commentary, I plonked my butt in front of it, trying to resist the urge to tap my fingernails on the armrest of the seat.

Aiden, the middle-aged driver who'd worked for the team for years, placed a coffee and a banana in front of me and I somehow managed to spare him a moment to say 'Thank you.'

As the race got under way, my stomach twisted in knots. The start was slow, the peloton wary and sedate as clouds billowed overhead, threatening rain.

The glimpses of Seb were frustratingly quick – a flash of his face, his sharp cheekbones. I wondered if he had a redback drawn on his wrist, what other rituals he had for luck. I sat on my hand to keep it still, desperate for something to happen to end the waiting, but knowing a break this early was usually suicidal.

I couldn't help thinking that was the DS's strategy. He wanted to see where Seb would break. Usually, a domestique would have broken already, every time, dropping back for self-preservation after delivering the leader to the head of the race. But Seb was riding a wave of luck and good form and I couldn't help wondering if it had something to do with me.

'Come on, Loonie,' I muttered through my teeth.

The commentator and the DS saw the break at the same time.

'*It's Andreu! Francesc Andreu is going to have a go early and that's quite a pace he's set!*'

Alan's voice was much more sedate over the team radio. 'On the right, Frankie, Nellie. Off you go.'

Less than a second after the Spanish rider pushed ahead of the peloton, another five riders broke out and pumped the pedals in a burst of speed, attempting to follow. Watching Seb on the screen made me wish we were on Zpeed and I could chat to him directly, or at least hear his grunts and heavy breathing. I couldn't gauge how much he was struggling, how long he could keep up the blistering pace.

When he stood out of the saddle, my stomach coiled and I couldn't swallow. He was using too much power and no one could sustain that for long. He might exhaust himself and not even manage to stay with the lead group. The camera followed him for several breathless seconds, catching the clench of his jaw, the muscles standing out in his thighs and the tattoos glistening damp on his calves.

He was tense, his face strained with focus and his body taut and rippling, and I had to swipe a hand over my mouth because I was too strung out to be able to swallow my own drool. Even when Seb settled into the breakaway behind Nellie and I could take a shaky breath, I didn't know how I'd get through another four hours of this. And he had the hell of all the cobbles still to come.

'*The only team with a pair in the breakaway is Harper-Stacked,*' one of the commentators said, his tone intrigued. '*Do you think they forgot Gallagher?*'

The other commentator laughed. '*The only other explanation is that they're letting Franck out to play. I think we're all interested to see what happens here, after some surprising performances from the domestique this season. He's got form. But to hold onto an early breakaway will take some serious nerve.*'

The commentators had hit the nail on the head. I wouldn't

have said that nerve was Seb's strong point, but he couldn't *not* win, not with my sanity riding on it.

The door of the bus banged open and I jerked back from the screen, crossing my legs in an attempt to look casual, as Dad emerged up the steps. His strained face crinkled into a smile when he saw me and I thought I might have got away with it.

'What are you doing here, Molly?' he asked as he pressed a kiss to the top of my head.

'I just... wanted to watch the race and it's better from here. One of the Gallaghers needs to do well, at least.'

He muttered something that sounded like 'Tell me about it', which made my stomach clench. I knew he was in discussions with sponsors at the moment – he always seemed to be in discussions with sponsors. Dad hustled for the money to keep the team afloat, while everyone else hustled for contracts – and that was before anyone had clipped a foot into the pedal. It reminded me of Seb's confession about retiring.

Lunchtime came and went, but eating was out of the question and I managed to put Dad off with a lie about a big breakfast. If my shoulder throbbed as the ibuprofen wore off, I didn't notice as the breakaway sped inexorably towards the cobbles.

Dad muttered about Colin and occasionally called through to the assistant in the team car. He wasn't allowed to talk to the DS during a race, after bitter experience. I was glad he was distracted with Colin that day and didn't question me.

The comments over the radio were clipped. Seb asked for a Coke — even holding down the button of the microphone while he said please, the idiot.

A light shower of rain misted the landscape and as the breakaway ploughed into the first cobbled section, conditions promised a mud-bath.

A crash narrowly missed taking out Colin, making Dad leap up and tear out more of his thinning hair, but I wanted the camera back on the breakaway as they juddered past the quaint windmill in sector eight, kicking up mud. The speed and conditions whittled the group down to four, then three, when Nelson finally had to drop back.

With 50 km to go, more chasers took their shot and another team was pushing the speed of the peloton, narrowing the gap to the lead group. Colin bided his time while Seb looked ragged out front, mud spattered up his back and smeared on his face.

Now he'd lost Nelson, Seb cooperated with the others in the breakaway group, sharing the lead to make the pace more sustainable. I knew he would be past thinking by now, running on instinct and years of training, losing nutrients and fluids faster than he could replenish them, but there was no time to stop.

'*Lead is fifteen seconds,*' came Alan's voice over the radio. The peloton was advancing, the mother ship approaching to sweep up all loose riders — and I truly was a mess if I was making a space joke. Seb would have a field day.

What would he think if he could see me hunched in front of the screen, biting my fingernails for him?

Picking up speed, the three-man breakaway hurtled onto the notorious Carrefour de l'Arbre. Fifteen seconds later, all hell broke loose. A group made a break to chase the leaders, while another rider hit a poorly placed stone and bounced off the barrier, careening back into the peloton. Bikes tumbled and flipped, riders landing spread-eagled, and a typical mud-soaked Paris-Roubaix melee filled the screen.

'We're just trying to see who's down. There's Janssen and Hurley — and Gallagher? Is that Colin Gallagher signalling to the team car? It is! His bike looks like another victim of the Carrefour de l'Arbre!'

'Bleedin' 'eck! Just one year I'd like to not wreck a bike here!' Dad cried.

The team cars were caught behind each other on the narrow lane and Colin had to sprint back on foot to change bikes, dropping more than two minutes behind the leaders before he started off again. I felt faintly guilty to be relieved when Dad stomped back out of the bus in frustration, but I definitely didn't want to explain why my nerves were likely to get worse from here.

A group of chasers caught Seb and the breakaway just before the turn and I held my breath, picturing the many disasters I'd lived through myself on that single curve. The new lead group was restless and too big and travelling at speeds that made crashing on the cobbles likely, rather than just possible. Seb was hemmed in by other teams, riding a dangerous line between tumbling on the stones and running into a competitor.

Clenching his teeth, he pulled to the side to make space and promptly clipped the barrier with his pedal. He went down hard, his body bouncing on the stones.

I was going to be sick. The commentators' voices were only gibberish in my ears and I couldn't even make sense of Alan's calm inquiries over the radio. I could only see the heave of Seb's chest as his breath came back, the smear of red down his arm when he sat up and then hauled himself to his feet.

Hobbling to his bike, he fished it out of the mud, threw his leg over the frame with a grimace and took off again, wobbling a little before he picked up speed.

The voice of the commentator rushed back in my ears as the panic receded.

'*All is not quite lost for Harper-Stacked today, but Franck appears to be the last man standing and I'd say he has a hell of a task in front of him — assuming the bike isn't damaged.*'

The camera zoomed in on his face as he pumped it, dancing his bike over the bumps, his brow low and lopsided and his breath coming in gusts. His jersey was ripped at the side, showing his pale rib cage with a nasty gash.

'*Is anyone... there?*' came his voice over the radio, punctuated by a grunt of effort. '*I'm chasse-patate here. Could do with some help.*' I knew the French expression — 'potato chase', when a rider is a sitting duck between the peloton and the breakaway — but my thought in that moment was how rarely I'd heard him speak French. I kind of wanted to hear more.

'*Sorry, Frankie, the boys are stuck. You're on your own*,' Alan replied.

The camera caught him lifting his head as though measuring the task ahead. '*Okay*,' came his muffled reply, on a pent-up kind of sigh. '*See you at the end*.'

The hairs on the back of my neck lifted as I wondered if he knew I was here listening, if he was talking to me. He couldn't be, but the idea of him racing to the finish to see me grabbed me around the ribs and squeezed.

He'd had a roaring race and he was nearly home. It would kill me if I couldn't kiss him when he rolled in. I'd been an idiot to make that stupid promise.

12 September 22:15

zpeed.com/voicechannels/@Folklore99/7493376900111

LoonieDunes: You… you're okay, right? You said you were injured. I don't have to press the emergency button or anything?

Folklore99: I just have to get better. There's no button for that. I'm just gonna get better again.

LoonieDunes: …If I say I'm sorry, will that help?

Folklore99: No. Say 'faster' instead. Make me want to beat you.

LoonieDunes: Ah, well, in that case, if I win, we watch more Star Wars. If you win…

Folklore99: *grunt* We listen to Taylor Swift for an entire week.

LoonieDunes: Really? I didn't pick you for a fan of T Swizzle. Isn't she a bit… harmless for you?

Folklore99: I'm harmless! And I like pop music. Deal with it.

Chapter 20

Seb

I felt like a zombie, my flesh necrotising in real time as the world passed by in a smudge – with the occasional blinding yellow of a field of rapeseed. The sensation was probably just mud drying in my cuts but, despite the scream of resistance in my blood, I was oddly calm as I inched closer to the breakaway after the crash.

As though I could suddenly tell the future, I knew I'd catch them at the last stretch of cobbles – or perhaps it was more the clarity of knowing that if I didn't, it'd all be over for me. No win, no kiss.

The rational part of me had dismissed her promise as big talk – unorthodox sports psychology to support her team – but that rational part had clocked out after the first 100 km, and the animal part of me was focusing on surviving and procreating in a heady mix that had me tapping into my last reserves.

But those reserves got me there. With sweat and rain

dripping into my eyes, unimpeded now I'd lost my glasses, I found myself on the wheel of the last guy in the breakaway and I hadn't died yet.

That was when a win started to feel like a real possibility and my cadence stalled. I survived the stress of this wild sport by being the underdog. Yeah, I'd stood on the podium twice already this season – which still didn't feel real – but that had been a fluke. I wasn't that guy – the guy who won things.

But I wanted to win today.

Everything inside me seized up at the thought and I nearly lost the wheel of the guy in front before I pulled myself together. I only had to survive another ten minutes of questioning all of my life choices.

The brown fields gave way to houses and light industrial properties as we were swallowed up into the outskirts of Roubaix, one of an agglomeration of towns that sat tucked into a curve of the French border with Belgium. The cold rain was falling more steadily now. I knew the route better than I knew myself in that moment, knew exactly where I would push forward. I hated the chaos of a sprint finish, but with five riders still left in the lead, it was going to get scrappy.

In silent agreement, we picked up speed through the streets lined with fans waving banners and shouting. One guy – I was too tired to even note who – pushed ahead and I swallowed a groan as I forced even more out of myself to follow.

I flew into the velodrome on his wheel, no idea if anyone was behind me or how much the other guy had left to give.

As we whipped around the first curve, he tried to drop me, sticking to the edge of the track, but I held on in his slip-stream. I'd never manage a whole lap performing so far over my threshold and, even at the last minute, conserving my strength was a necessary strategy.

Dimly registering the clang of the brass bell announcing the final lap, I held my nerve, bided my time, the effort of waiting and holding on just as difficult as what was to come when I sprinted. I didn't know if we were the first group or not. The words on my radio were gibberish.

The finish line in sight, I threw everything I had at the bike and the track, pushing ahead of the other guy with 100 m to go – and vaguely registering a flash of colour on my left. With a wallop of panic in my chest, I kicked the bike forward with one last push and blacked out for a second or two as I crossed the line.

Still pedalling on muscle memory and conditioning, only half-conscious and covered in mud and blood, I came to enough to decelerate around the velodrome, the crowd in the stands suddenly deafening. The air was cool and sweet and still. The world slowed down around me, winding back – winding down – as I waited to see what shape I'd be in when my body finally stopped.

Skidding off the track and onto the grass in the middle, I wobbled off the bike and let it fall to the ground, the throb in my hands suddenly swelling to a roar. A team assistant grabbed me heavily as I stumbled, my vision tunnelling as the entire race washed through me.

The feeling was awful and wonderful and I wanted to talk about that race for the rest of my life, bore Maman and Mamie at the dinner table as they gave me their bewildered smiles, not a competitive bone in their bodies.

Lori would understand. *Lori*...

At first I thought I was imagining her in front of me and I gave the apparition a cocky, half-drunk smile. But then I imagined her saying my name in a breathless tone that shot straight through my battered body and groped with my left hand – blindly as my vision swam a little from dirt and exposure and exhaustion – and connected with the soft cotton of her – *my* – hoodie.

I wasn't imagining her.

A fresh surge of... *something* rushed in my blood and I swayed towards her. Her palm flattened on the back of my neck and my mind went completely blank as I leaned close and kissed her. Or did she lean and kiss me?

It didn't matter. We were kissing – as though our lives depended on it. Her lips shook against mine, her mouth open and hot. Tilting her head, she tugged me close. I cupped her cheek with my other hand and everything would be right with the world, if I could just kiss her a little longer.

Oh God, I needed her. Thrusting a gloved hand up into her hair and fisting there, I soaked her in, her choked whimper, the eager press of her upper lip, the sweep of her tongue against mine. She tasted like coming back to life – like a shared victory.

A niggling confusion made me break off for a moment,

tugging off my helmet. 'Does this mean I won?' I asked, my voice high.

She pressed another kiss to my mouth and I was just convincing myself I was satisfied with that instead of an answer, when she shook her head and said, 'No, you came second.'

'But I thought—'

She cut me off with her mouth on mine again and I rubbed a thumb over her cheek in clumsy, desperate affection. Kissing her at the finish line was a heady thrill I hadn't felt in... ever?

'It's close enough,' she breathed against my lips.

'Thank God,' I groaned, capturing her mouth again. I was basically mauling her in public and I didn't care a—

The sound of someone clearing their throat made me pull back, noticing with a stab of remorse that I'd smeared her face with mud.

Then the world revved up to full speed as someone shoved a camera in my face and, at the same time, I heard my grandmother say in French, 'It's nice to finally meet your girlfriend!'

Lori

I was deep in the shit now.

Had I planned to publicly declare something that wasn't quite true with a scorching post-race kiss? Not exactly. But did I embrace the chaos when it happened? Absolutely. Seb deserved all the attention today and if I could direct the spotlight a little closer to him, it could only bring good things.

Maybe he'd get his contract renewed – or at least give his ego enough of a boost to enjoy the win.

He'd been dragged away from me for the post-race drugs-testing protocol and to face the crush of international sports media before the podium ceremony. I'd watched from the periphery as he'd given a few comments, mainly in smooth, deep French with a wry smile that made me realise there was a whole language of his that I didn't speak – so many sides to him I'd probably never see.

Now I was busy ducking among the team vehicles trying to avoid Dad and Colin – as well as Seb's mum and his cute little grandma. I should have borrowed the grandma's parka and bucket hat for camouflage.

I would have to face the consequences of my actions at some stage, but I wanted to have a word with Seb before I did so – get our story straight now I'd sufficiently recovered from the kiss to form actual words. Veering away from where Dad was talking to Colin as he warmed down on a stationary bike, I made a dash for the spartan old shower block, where I'd noticed Seb disappearing five minutes ago. Although the team buses had showers these days, the 1940s Roubaix shower block was an institution, with a plaque bearing the name of a past winner on every stall. There was little heating and no privacy, but I could understand that Seb was so old-school that he visited the block as though it were a pilgrimage. Hearing voices, I didn't go into the communal shower room, but waited in the hall, knowing the podium was calling and he wouldn't be long. The door was ajar, releasing the fug of steam and the oceany scent of Seb's shower gel. A tuneless hum reached my ears, followed a moment later by a few snatches of Taylor's 'Wildest Dreams' in a slightly groggy falsetto.

I couldn't help myself. I peeped and I would never regret doing so. His eyes were closed as soap suds slid over his dimples and dripped onto his chest. His arms raised to wash his hair, he was hard and wet and the kiss bubbled in my veins again as my mouth watered.

Stifling a laugh, I enjoyed his gravelly version of Taylor's words about a tall, handsome guy with utter pandemonium in my chest. What was I supposed to do with him? With us?

If he retired at the end of the season to run his fucking B&B, I'd never see him again. That had become an unacceptable outcome. But he wanted out of the sport and I *was* the sport. He might have put up a fight today, but I'd manipulated him into it. Being with me was a challenge I was pretty sure he didn't want, especially since I wouldn't have any space in my life for him when I started winning again, the way I really, really had to.

Shit, post-adrenaline symptoms had made me feel decidedly loopy if my thoughts had drifted into long-term territory. Before I was close to working myself out, Colin clomped into the shower block under a dark cloud, followed shortly after by Dad.

'There she is, my little chaos muppet!' Dad exclaimed.

'I hope you have a decent explanation for why a reporter just asked me what I thought of my sister dating my domestique!'

Seb emerged, his whistle going flat and trailing off, his

presence completing the absurd tableau before I could work out a suitable justification for my behaviour. He'd changed into fresh bib shorts, but he hadn't bothered with a shirt. The gear sprocket tattooed above his right pec was dewy and dark with moisture. The muscle and tendons over his chest and arms bunched as he moved and his skin radiated heat and there went my ability to form sentences again.

By the time I curled my tongue back into my mouth, I noticed the ugly graze on his side that would need to be bandaged before he pulled on a clean jersey.

It was little wonder I was scrambling around for the slightest feeling of control over my own life when I was a wreck just looking at him, torn between the desire to protect him and the insistent firing of all my pheromones in the presence of his battle-hardened body.

He seemed to accept Dad and Colin's presence as the requisite drama of the afternoon, his shoulders jerking with a deep sigh as his gaze switched between us, lingering on me with a hint of a raised eyebrow that shouldn't have been enough to steal my breath, but was anyway.

Then Colin put his foot in it, turning to Seb in indignation. 'You said she was messing with you, not the other way around!'

Seb

I opened my mouth to respond, but froze with the knowledge that anything I said right now would be the wrong thing. Lori was less circumspect.

'I *am* messing with him!' she insisted and although part of me melted at how very *Lori* that blurted statement was, mostly I was scraped raw everywhere and rather put out that she'd reduce the best kiss of my life to messing around. 'He's got such good form, he just needed a… nudge to get a result.'

That kiss had been a hell of a lot more than a nudge and I was *put out* enough to think about walking her back into the shower stalls and proving it.

'You didn't have to *kiss* him to do that, Lori,' Tony Gallagher said, his tone nasal and high with exasperation.

'You were worried about the sponsors, Dad. If I can't win races, at least I can do something to attract attention to the team.'

My head spun with all the subtext in her statement. It had to pinch that she'd had another rotten result yesterday and, if she resented me for having form when she didn't, I wouldn't judge her for it. But using this… chemistry between us for sponsors? That part made me want to barf.

'Lore—' I began, but Colin cut me off.

'Did you hear what those reporters were saying? They're talking about how you have a *type* and it's guys in a Harper-Stacked uniform! They even asked him if you're the reason he got a contract with the team!'

She flinched, a flicker of panic crossing her expression, and our audience started to chafe. I didn't want to make things worse for her, but I also needed to settle my own feelings about the kiss and what it had meant.

'Chill out, little bro,' she responded, and the expression

'Attack is the best defence' crossed my mind as I watched her press Colin's buttons until he inflated like an accordion. 'You document all your pranks on social media. A bit of attention to my love life isn't anything new and I've heard it all before — and worse.'

Her words sent a chill of dismay through me: she was talking about Gaetano. The more I learned about her life, the more complications I saw.

The conversation felt like a tightrope. 'I'm sure no one will—'

'Does that mean he's your boyfriend?' The disbelief in Colin's tone pricked me, even though I understood it was warranted.

'Um' was all I managed, earning a blistering look from Lori. 'No!' I insisted more strongly. 'Of course not. She's completely focused on her training.' When Colin narrowed his eyes at me, I wondered whether I'd come on too strong with that one, even though it was true.

'But there's no harm in a few reporters thinking he is,' Lori said with a jerky shrug. 'People love a romance.' She said 'people' with such a particular tone, I suspected she'd thought about substituting 'suckers'.

Tony reached for her, his wrinkles curled up in concern. 'I know I talk a lot about the sponsors, but it's not your—'

'Don't worry, Dad. I know what I'm doing.'

That one was clearly a lie.

She whirled to face me, her jaw set. 'I really didn't mean anything—'

I cut her off with a shake of my head. She'd made her point as best she could in front of her family and I wanted to wallow in the misery of remembering that kiss on my own from now.

'Enjoy the podium,' she said, her voice unexpectedly heated. 'You bloody deserve it.'

zpeed.com/chatserver/voicechannels/@LoonieDunes/645
  8362946115

Folklore99: One more sprint? Just something quick? I had a nap today and I don't think I'm going to be able to get any sleep.

LoonieDunes: Are you sure your handle shouldn't be Hardcore99?

Folklore99: Are you sure yours shouldn't be LoonieSoftcock?

LoonieDunes: I'm sorry BallBuster99, but I have to go milk the goats anyway.

Folklore99: … Is that some kind of euphemism?

LoonieDunes: *choke, cough* No! There are real goats. If they don't get fed and milked, they eat the shed.

Folklore99: Okay… I hope they're cute at least.

LoonieDunes: They've got sweet little faces, yeah.

Folklore99: Go sort out your girlfriends with their sweet little faces then.

Chapter 21

Lori

Seb held up his little mounted cobblestone to cheers from the spectators. The novelty trophy for such a hellish race usually made me laugh, but I was a jumble of conflicting wants and needs as I stared at him from the back of the crowd. I heard my mum's voice in my head, talking about winners and losers and I had to get back control of my feelings somehow – and find a way out of this mess of my own making. He wasn't my boyfriend – he'd said it himself. I couldn't handle a relationship right now, especially not with someone who could put me in such disarray with just one kiss.

I knew I shouldn't interfere with his career, but threatening to kiss him had worked, damn it! And my cheap fib about making a scene for the media? Actually, that was a great idea.

Scurrying after him into the team bus when the podium ceremony was over, I opened my mouth to say – something, I still didn't know what – but he just grabbed an old duffle bag and squeezed past me again, his mouth set.

Huh, it turned out Seb could sulk. Was he upset I'd kissed him in public? Or that I'd told my family it was only for the cameras?

'Seb?' I called after him.

With a groan of frustration that I would never be able to let those questions go, I went after him, catching up as he stalked to the gate and pushed through without looking at me.

'*Seb!*'

His earnest look from December flashed in my memory: the moment he'd made me promise we'd always be friends. For the first time that day, the consequences of my behaviour scared me.

'Seb! Can we at least talk?' I said, grasping his wrist, which made him hiss in pain. I knew from experience that he hurt *everywhere*. 'I know you don't like the attention, but don't you see——?'

'Is that what you think I'm mad about?' he asked, giving me a sidelong glance – probably because his neck hurt. 'Okay, I am really mad about that. If you're trying to turn me into Gaetano Maggioli, I'll have to disappoint you. But, Lore, you should be focusing on *your* next race, not mine! After this year, I'm gone.'

Confusion rippled over my skin.

'You're more than just some guy's girlfriend,' he said emphatically. 'You don't need to use me to stay in the spotlight.'

'I'm not——' I cut myself off, worried he was right.

Seb's sigh was deep and reminded me of my dad's exasperated tone – Mum's weaponised disappointment. 'If you kiss me, I'd like to think you mean it,' he said tightly.

'I did!' His gaze jerked up to mine with a flash that quickly dimmed to wariness.

'I mean, I wouldn't have kissed you if I hadn't wanted to. And maybe the spotlight thing can work both ways. You could get sponsorship – a contract extension!'

'I'm not looking for a contract extension.' *Of course, I'm not your boyfriend.*

'Why not?' I cried in frustration. 'You just came second in the Paris-Roubaix!'

'It's a pretty good way to go out with a bang,' he insisted. 'I'm your bad-luck charm, Lore – remember? You've got to remember that, otherwise I'll end up kissing you again with everything I've got!'

How much I wanted another kiss was unfortunately the only thing that was clear to me in that moment.

He groaned and rubbed a hand over his eyes. 'When you look at me like that, Lori… it doesn't make it easier to walk away from you like I should.'

'Why should you? We both know this can't work long-term, but it *is* a great story for the media – the team.'

His expression darkened and my heart sank. There was definitely a winner and a loser in this conversation and my streak was obviously continuing.

'It's not in my contract, is it?' he snapped.

'No! I just thought—' I hadn't thought before I acted. 'I

hate feeling useless like this. The team is my family and, if I can do something to help, I will.' And maybe I didn't want him to go, but I wasn't enough of a loser to tell him that when he clearly wanted out.

His hand closed around my upper arm – probably reflexively, but regardless of his motivation, it was lovely to have him touch me again. 'You're going to win again soon. But, even if it takes a while, you don't have to sacrifice yourself—' He cut himself off, his gaze caught on something over my shoulder. I turned to see two older women in matching dull green parkas, standing by a dented little Renault. His grandma peered at me curiously, but both looked ready to murder me in my sleep if I hurt him.

Oops. How much had they heard? It must have been obvious we'd been arguing. He dropped his hand abruptly.

Leaning close with a stormy expression in his gaze, he said the last thing I expected. 'Look, don't get their hopes up too much, eh?'

'Their hopes?'

'I never... bring girlfriends to meet them and we're not... anyway.'

My brain froze on the word 'girlfriends' and that big fat 'never'.

His grandma approached me first, hesitantly. 'You're *Lori*,' she said with meaningful emphasis that gave me goosebumps. 'I didn't know if he would admit the reason he spent so much time in his room in the autumn!' Her accent was detectable, but her English was excellent.

'You know about that?' he spluttered.

'Our boy goes from punishing training alone to talking all night and laughing – of course I know,' she said with a twitch of a smile that caught me in the ribs. She added something under her breath in French that made Seb grit his teeth. 'I'm Albertine,' she said, 'but you can call me Mamie.'

'You don't have to call her Mamie,' Seb interjected.

'You call your grandma "Mummy"?' I asked.

'*Mamie*,' he repeated, correcting my pronunciation. I really hadn't heard him speaking French often enough. The little pout in his lips gave me a whole new set of ideas. 'It's just French for "Grandma". And this is my mum, Rôsine.'

'Don't call me Maman,' she said sharply, extending her arm for a haughty handshake that felt like a test I was destined to fail.

Seb tossed his duffle bag into the back seat of the Renault and I stupidly only then understood why he'd walked out to the car park. If he was going to eat with his family, would I even see him again tonight at the hotel? What about our conversation? I wasn't done here.

Ouch, that word reminded me of December with a wash of something very much like guilt. Nothing between Seb and me was 'done'. Everything I'd said in my fog of emotion had only made things worse.

He'd warned me off meeting his family. I should take the hint. But I couldn't stand him thinking the best kiss of my life had only been for show – which was why, when he climbed into the dinky car, chaos muppet Lori dived in after him.

Seb

I could still feel the rough surface of the cobblestone trophy under my fingers, even though it was in my bag in the boot of the car. The best result of my career – the scrappiest fight with the biggest payoff. But I suspected the elation of hard-won success would always be twisted together with the heart-stopping touch of Lori's lips on mine.

For the cameras. For the team. Maybe because she was attracted to me, but she wouldn't admit it and that didn't remove much of the sting.

She wanted to use me for whatever wild reason she'd come up with and the worst part was, I wanted to let her. She was sitting across the back seat from me, a storm in her eyes. When she lost, she came to me and my heart beat a loopy, syrupy rhythm when that thought curled up in my brain.

But no, the kiss had rattled me. I had a new life to plan – a gaping hole that didn't need the addition of a gaping wound in my chest if I accidentally got attached. She'd ghosted me once and, even though I understood the pressure she was under, I didn't want a repeat of that when her form returned. She'd leave me. Sooner or later – and later would only hurt more. I leaned my head against the window as spatters of rain started up again, consumed by questions about why Lori Gallagher had jumped into the car after me and whether she realised where we were headed. I assumed it had been something of an accident – one of her split-second decisions.

Were we kidnapping her? Taking her out of the country under false pretences? I would have felt more guilty about that, except that after Colin's prank in the Pyrenees, I had no problem making him come and collect his sister from the countryside in Wallonia, damn it.

I could feel the questions from Maman and Mamie – lots of questions – but what was the point in insisting we were only friends when she'd kissed me senseless and was coming home with me? If she really wanted to play out this public romance, we still had to talk. For now, I was perversely enjoying Lori's discomfort.

One of her legs moved restlessly and her arms were crossed as she gazed out of the window at the gathering dusk. As much as I knew we didn't work as a real couple, there was a real tightness in my chest as I looked at her. I'd missed her face – her freckled, angular cheekbones, the firm set of her mouth.

Before the farce with the media and her family, today's race had been the best of my life – not only because of the fight and the result. Because she'd breathed life back into me at the end and reminded me to be proud. I wanted to take her hand and lace my fingers with hers while we both looked out the window, sulking.

Her brow furrowed – not delicately, because nothing about Lori was delicate and I loved that about her. Her gaze snagged on the blue sign at the side of the road setting out the national speed limits with a big 'B' on top. As we cruised past, she kept looking, craning her neck.

'You had a hankering for real Belgian chocolate and waffles?' she asked, turning to me.

'Hmm?'

'You're going to eat somewhere across the border?' she clarified.

'I grabbed a sandwich from the bus and we'll eat later. We always eat Mamie's beef stew when I'm home after a race. You'll love it.'

It was so hard to keep a straight face as her eyes grew bright with alarm. She sent a panicked glance at my mum and grandma in the front.

'It'll be dark by the time we get to the farm, but I'll show you in the morning, *honey*,' I added darkly.

She swallowed. 'It's just a shame you were so reluctant to introduce me to your family before now, *babe*,' she countered. 'They're lovely, as I knew they would be.'

I felt Mamie's indignation, even though she didn't turn around and my mum's surprise was reflected in the slight kick of the car as her foot faltered on the accelerator.

'I didn't think you'd take the time from your busy schedule just for us.' I winced inwardly.

'Are you kidding?' she responded, warming up to the pretence. 'I've been dying to see this place.'

She sounded convincing and I was enough of a dork that my heart went ahead and leaped.

'Don't get your hopes up,' I mumbled. After a few minutes of driving in silence as the tension in the car hovered, I leaned across the seat, my lips near her ear, and whispered, 'You don't have to come. I can explain everything and take you back – or call your dad.'

I lingered, hoping Mamie's sharp ears wouldn't pick up our conversation and that they'd think I was just nuzzling my girlfriend – not that that was something I had ever done in front of my family. As the hairs stood up on the back of my neck, all I could think about was nuzzling. She smelled amazing: heady and vital.

'No,' she said simply, drawing in an unsteady breath.

'No?' I repeated groggily. I had to stop thinking about putting my lips on her skin.

'I'm not going to call Dad,' she clarified. I managed to lift my head and meet her gaze questioningly at her firm tone. 'Look out, Seb,' she continued, lifting a hand to my face. 'You're bringing your girlfriend home to the farm.'

Chapter 22

Seb

'Seriously, let me make up the guest room for you,' I said under my breath, rushing in front of Lori to stop her in the hallway. She'd already blown my remaining synapses by eating stew at the kitchen table with a fixed smile while the two women who'd brought me up watched with thinly veiled doubt. Seeing her in my childhood bedroom would finish me off and I'd already died once today on the cobbles.

'Your family isn't offended if we share a room, are they?' she asked. 'I thought when Mamie winked—'

'They're not offended,' I interrupted her. 'But...' I pulled at my hair with a sigh.

'Is there something wrong with your room?'

Other than the fact that I would always think of her in it, once she stepped over the threshold? 'No! I mean the bed's pretty small. I don't want you to be uncomf—'

'Stop arguing,' she said, cutting me off. 'Have you forgotten that we *have* slept together before?'

'I'm not going to forget that for the rest of my *life*,' I grumbled. 'But what about the bad lu—'

'Getting my head in the game is my problem, Seb. I'm out of the next race anyway.' She gestured to her sling. 'Might as well have some fun.'

My skin tingled and my body dragged itself sluggishly to life again at that suggestion.

Then she dropped her chin, eyeballed me and said, 'I'm pretty sure you're just going to fall asleep anyway.'

My thoughts swam, not sure what she wanted from me and willing to give it to her, whatever it was. Grasping her face in both of my hands, I drew her close and said, 'Do you want to? Have sex again? Is that why…'

I could live with it if that was the reason she'd jumped into Maman's car this evening, especially when feeling her skin under my fingertips was such a blessed relief. But I needed her to tell me what she wanted, if she even knew. Tension and frustration flowing through me, I pressed a hard kiss to her forehead because I couldn't *not* do it.

'Do you really think I came all the way here because I'm horny?' The bitterness in her tone was pure Lori.

'I don't see anyone here to take our picture, so I assume it's not part of your "everyone loves a romance" plan.'

'We're friends, right?' Her tone was belligerent, but her wobbly lower lip gave me questions.

'Friends don't usually share a bed – or make out on TV.'

Her cheeks glowed light pink. 'You know it wasn't *only* for the cameras,' she mumbled and everything inside me went quiet as I grasped for the meaning of her admission. 'Maybe I shouldn't have done it, but— you know. Chaos muppet.'

That got me in the stomach again, reminding me of everything we'd shared online. 'Does that mean the thing about pretending to be in a relationship was—?' She cut me off with a shake of her head. 'It's a good idea. But you look like someone used you to mop their floor and you're about to keel over, so we'll talk about it later. Which door is your room?'

I gestured limply to the wood veneer door from the 70s that I'd passed through millions of times in my life. But when I followed Lori Gallagher inside, everything felt different.

Her gaze roamed the room, her fingers brushing items that caught her interest: my first cycling trophy, Under 17s Cyclocross Champion for the province of Namur; a photo of my sister and her kids; my Princess Leia rubber ducky that was too funny to throw away but pretty embarrassing to actually have on display.

A flush spread up my neck as she took in my Zpeed set-up: a racing bike with the rear wheel removed, connected to a drive trainer, facing the wall where I'd hung a flat-screen TV. Lori stepped hesitantly towards the bike, her hand hovering over the saddle.

'So this is where you used to ogle my virtual butt.'

My head spinning a little, I sank onto my bed with a sigh. 'That's it.' Looking up at her, I continued, 'You know what's strange? I never knew what you looked like – back then. But now it's as if my memories have changed. When I think about that time you beat me in the Tourmalet simulation, my memory insists it was you in front of me – in real life. *You* as I know you now. That's weird.'

She glanced at me with a pained look and, yeah, I was probably the only one still stuck in the past, when I'd lived happily in a constant state of anticipation of the next time we could meet up in not-real life.

'Do you have a toothbrush and some clothes I can borrow? Some ibuprofen?'

Right, keep things practical. No gushing about how much those months online had meant to me. 'Sure.'

She looked far too sweet in a pair of my shorts and an ancient sweatshirt, her hair in a high ponytail and her face scrubbed. I'd given her a kiss on the cheek before I realised what I was doing.

'How's your shoulder?' I asked to cover my affectionate slip.

She set the sling onto my desk with her clothes. 'The same as usual after a dislocation. Hurts a bit. You want to show me your hands?'

As she plonked down beside me on the bed, I held out my hands without even questioning what she had planned. Hers were smaller than mine, with freckles spreading like the arm of a galaxy down one side and over her thumb. God, even her hands were unbearably beautiful.

Turning mine over, she pressed her thumb into the palm and I stifled a moan as the firm touch unlocked the muscle after hours of strain. It hurt. When she moved on to the flesh below my thumb I became a groaning mess, my head falling to her shoulder as the pressure drained and revitalised my body all at once.

I wasn't sure when I'd be able to move my arm again after she was done with my right hand and by the time her strong fingers had finished with my left, my tongue was almost lolling out of my mouth.

'Do you want me to do your legs?'

Surely I was imagining Lori offering to massage my poor mistreated legs. I answered her anyway with a shake of the head. 'Hurts too much.' Her fingers in my hair must have been a dream, it felt so good.

'Lie down and close your eyes,' she said into my ear. Despite the distant protests of my brain, insisting we had an argument brewing and we shouldn't get so close, my body dragged me down into peaceful sleep.

Lori

Seb was wrecked, a semi-conscious ragdoll, as I tugged his clothes off, with my thoughts and feelings a dumpster fire.

The muscles in his shoulders were rock-hard with strain. The veins in his arms stood out over lean muscle and bone. The bruising on his side was coming up, an ugly purple patch the size of a dinner plate. I left his shorts on, even though I wasn't sure they were comfortable for sleeping. He wasn't conscious enough to consent to me taking them off when we didn't wear knickers under those things.

I hesitated over his socks, feeling like a weirdo for being curious about his feet, but I left them on in the end, because it seemed Rôsine and Albertine had turned the heating off already. Tugging the blanket out from underneath him, I soothed him with a hand on his back and he purred sleepily, mumbling something incoherent about family.

Thinking of family gave me a twinge of guilt about my impulsive behaviour and I rummaged for my phone in the little pile of clothes I'd left on Seb's desk. I didn't have my charger with me and the device would give out soon, so I quickly shot off a message to Dad and Colin.

You don't need to send a search party. I'm safe with Seb. Be back soon.

Catching sight of the thread of my text conversation with Seb, I thought of the way he'd marvelled softly about the transition of our online relationship into real life. He'd been right. All those months had become something even more now the real Seb had slotted into my memories with his dimples and his sometimes cocky, sometimes goofy grin.

We were *friends*. I was clinging to that now. Except the designation didn't feel the most appropriate after I stowed my phone and crawled into bed. I snuggled in the heady warmth of his blankets and his body, his skin under my fingers and his scent in my nose. Maybe we were a little more than friends.

It was a giddy prospect, that my promise of a kiss might have motivated him in one of the toughest races on the calendar, but he'd been angry with me afterwards.

232

We lived in opposite corners of the planet for half the year and he wanted to open a fucking B&B. He probably wanted seven children and the Belgian equivalent of a white picket fence, but I lived for the bike. He could only ever be a fling and the whole fake-romance thing had been a low attempt to manipulate him into staying. I'd apologise in the morning.

One thing was clear: I was overthinking what was probably nothing more than a friendship with benefits. I wasn't looking for romance anyway – in fact, it was probably a symptom of my undignified break-up with Gaetano that I was reading so much into Seb's behaviour. He hadn't wanted me to meet his family. I couldn't tell if he truly wanted me close or was just tolerating my advances. Maybe he was just a good guy – with really tasty-looking shoulders.

I rolled onto my back with a disgruntled sigh. Life was so much easier when I only wanted to win races.

Chapter 23

Lori

It was so fucking quiet in the Belgian countryside.

Still only two days post-race for me, I would normally have let myself sleep late, maybe even watched a few episodes of something in bed, but I didn't want to wake Seb, haunted by how much pain he'd been in last night.

Trying to be quiet seemed to turn me into a restless troll in bed – a restless, horny troll, if I was completely honest – and I rolled around as best I could with my sore shoulder, trying to keep my hands off him. He didn't help my cause, murmuring in his sleep when I nudged him in the small double and fisting a hand in the shirt he'd given me to wear.

When he mumbled, 'Lori,' so softly my hair stood on end, I was tempted to press my lips to his and not give a damn if he needed his z's.

'Go back to sleep,' I whispered instead.

'But you feel good,' he continued with a sigh. 'You smell good too.'

'I used your soap last night,' I told him with a smile he couldn't see, since his eyes were still shut – swollen from exposure to the wind yesterday after he'd lost his cycling glasses somewhere.

His mouth turned up and he rolled towards me with a sigh that was part groan from stiff muscles. He reached for me, his hand landing first on my hip, giving me a fumbling stroke, and then a smearing caress over my cheek, as though he needed to confirm I was truly there. Then his hand fell back to the sheet between us, where I studied his thick knuckles and weathered skin, wondering what it would feel like to slip my fingers between his and hold on. I needed to get up before I did something weird like kiss his fingertips.

Sneaking out of the bed, I rummaged in his wardrobe drawers until I found a pair of socks – ignoring the deflated form of Matilda staring jealously at me from where she'd been stuffed behind the hangers. Padding into the hallway with its beige tiles and frayed woven rug, I headed in the direction of the dining room where we'd eaten a late dinner last night.

It was empty, so I crossed the little foyer, pausing to peer at an old photo of Seb as a child, blond and with several teeth missing, his arm draped over a slightly smaller girl with glasses.

His sister... I didn't even know her name.

I tried the last door and was welcomed by wafting heat and the smell of coffee. The country-style kitchen was tired but cosy, with a stone feature wall and a cast-iron stove lacquered beige. A solid-wood buffet cabinet stood against one wall, in the place it had probably held since before Seb was born.

Rôsine stood at the stove, dirt already on the seat of her heavy-duty trousers, wearing a thick woollen pullover. She called something over her shoulder without looking, of which all I understood was 'petit'. Turning with a smile, she froze when she saw it was only me.

'Good morning,' she said, her tone more measured. Rôsine was a handsome woman, with Seb's high cheekbones and honey colouring. Her hair was turning grey and tucked underneath a patterned bandana headband, and her thin, straight mouth gave her the look of someone who could deliver a calf – or in this case a goat kid – while also canning vegetables and fixing a fence.

'Good morning,' I mumbled in response. 'Seb's still asleep. I didn't want to disturb him.'

Rôsine glanced down at my bare legs and feet in Seb's socks, her expression barely changing although she must have realised I didn't have any clothes with me.

'You want breakfast?' she asked.

'You don't have to… serve me. I'm sure I could just find something,' I suggested, colour rising to my cheeks.

The look she gave me was quelling. 'You're a guest.'

'Well, I'm sorry I… invited myself then,' I said with a sigh, hoping my dad had accepted my short message and wasn't phoning Europol. I should get back in touch with him before he suspected kidnapping and the cops showed up and scared the goats.

Rôsine was silent for so long I thought perhaps she agreed I shouldn't have come. Taking a heavy kettle from the stove, she poured water into a French press and the blessed smell of coffee reached my nose again. Giving it a stir, she set the plunger on top and placed the coffee on the table, adding two small cups and four spiced biscuits.

She pulled out her chair with a short, pointed glance at me and, hoping that was a subtle invitation, I scrambled to accept, taking the seat opposite. When I found myself fiddling restlessly with the painted china cup, I wrenched my hand back and sat on it.

Rôsine pressed the plunger and wordlessly poured out the coffee.

I lifted the cup to my nose and inhaled, more out of habit – Melbourne habit – than anything else, but a hint of caramel and something like burned toast tickled my nostrils and Rôsine's brow furrowed.

'It's mixed with chicory. That's our way of taking coffee. I hope you don't mind.'

Taking a cautious sip, it was very bitter on the tongue at first, but I suspected I could get used to it.

'Did you argue with Seb?' Rôsine asked, watching me splutter over my hot drink as though she'd orchestrated the timing of that question.

'Um,' I said with a gulp.

'I hope it wasn't about visiting us?'

'No!' I assured her immediately. 'Nothing like that. But I should probably admit that there's… we're not really together or anything.' My words petered out on my tongue when I tried to explain what we *were* if we weren't together, especially since we'd spent the night snuggling.

Rôsine laughed, but there was a bleakness to it. 'I understand. I don't know if he's ever been really together with someone before – only "sort of" or "maybe". I didn't expect anything else.'

If she was attempting to reassure me, it backfired. I'd been one of a few girlfriends – now former girlfriends – of Gaetano, but with Seb I was only one of his 'maybes'. Wow, that hurt. I took another slurp of the scalding, bitter coffee because it fitted my sinking heart.

'It's difficult for him. I suppose that's what happens when your father leaves and never sees you again. I hope one day he can commit, but they'll have to be someone… very special,' she said with an apologetic smile that looked more like a wince.

Before I could decide between a defensive response and an indignant one, the kitchen door banged open, making me jump and scald myself again. 'Il se passe quelque chose avec Seb? Mamie m'a envoyé un message bizarre!'

On a gust of cool, damp air, a tall woman with tight curls and a baby on her hip swept into the room, approaching Rôsine with a kiss, while my brain tried to catch up, managing to understand the final two words of the French and something about Mamie and Seb.

Belatedly catching sight of me, the woman – undoubtedly Seb's sister – performed a double take worthy of a slapstick film. 'C'est vrai?' she cried, close enough to a shriek for the baby to cover its ears with chubby fingers. Collecting herself, she gulped and opened her mouth to say something, although it took several seconds for anything to come out. 'Mamie said Seb brought a pretty Australian girl home to meet the family and I was certain all I'd find was a big plastic kangaroo.'

'We do have a blow-up kanga—' Suddenly I was thinking about Matilda and I probably shouldn't mention that in front of his family. 'I'm Lori,' I said instead, getting to my feet.

Her smile would have been lovely if she'd toned down the glee a notch. 'Denise,' she said, taking my hand and shaking it. 'I've been waiting my whole life to torment him with this!' she said, her voice high with something like wonder.

'They're not *actually* together,' Rôsine added with a twitch of her lips.

'Of course not,' Denise said with a snort. 'She just *accidentally* came home with him!' She burst out laughing and even Rôsine snickered.

'Well,' I began, but quickly gave up. Even *I* struggled to believe the chain of events that had brought me into this kitchen, with these two women.

Denise clasped my arm. 'Sorry, dear, but it's just so… *Seb*. It's a constant mystery to him – and only him – why the women he's interested in always leave. My brother is a disaster.'

'He might be a disaster,' I blurted out before I'd thought

through the end of that sentence. 'But he's...' my *disaster*. 'A good disaster,' I finished weakly, gulping when the two women just blinked at me in surprise.

Oops. So much for not getting their hopes up. Seb would just have to explain to them later and take the blame, since it seemed he had a history and this mess wasn't all my fault after all.

I should have expected the absurdity of Mamie striding in at that moment, but she still surprised me when she peered through the door and said to Denise, 'Oh good, you got my message. Give me the baby.'

She fussed over the child, with its curls and pudgy cheeks, until he – or she, I couldn't be certain – wriggled to be put down. He mustn't have been too young because he toddled confidently around the kitchen.

'I love great-grandchildren,' she said, pointedly *not* looking at me in such a way that she was definitely inwardly winking at me.

'Mamie!' Denise scolded. 'You can't say that – and we should know better!' She turned to me, grasping my arm again as though she was already fond of me. 'We're a whole family of single mothers – and poor Seb!'

'Single or not, women do the work – well!' Mamie said, slapping her thigh for emphasis. 'But why are you standing here talking? There is *shit* to clean!'

Seb

I woke up groggy and befuddled in the mid-morning, as though I'd rattled out part of my brain yesterday on the cobbles. But the lethargy felt deeper, in my bones somehow – a pleasant sort of contentment I couldn't initially identify.

My jersey had disappeared, but I was still in my clean bike shorts from the podium. I had vague recollections of warm touch, hands on my skin and in my hair. I'd never had hallucinations after a tough race before, but would Lori—? *Lori!*

I sat up with a start – and a groan at the loud complaints from my body. Looking around frantically for her, I found I was alone in my room.

Had she left? Already?

That possibility got me out of bed in an instant and I threw on a tracksuit, hopping into the hall while pulling on my socks.

The kitchen was empty, with only the lingering scent of chicory coffee. The dining room was too. Racing for the front door, I noticed her sneakers were gone and my heart rate kicked up again. Shoving my feet into the first pair of my shoes I found, I dashed outside into a crisp, sunny day. I hobbled across the garden like an old man, thinking Lori wouldn't exactly congratulate herself for knowing me just then and perhaps it was for the best if she'd called her father and was already on her way back.

Damn, I was even more of a loser than I'd thought. She'd

come home with me – even if it had been under false pretences – she'd touched me and stretched out next to me and all I'd done was fall asleep! If she was gone—

What could I do? I'd never expected she would stay. It didn't make any sense that my heart was in my throat as I scanned the property for signs of life, ignoring the bright yellow rapeseed field at the back and the rolling hills of home that were usually a comfort, regardless of whether I won or lost.

Hearing voices in the barn – Maman's measured tones with animated replies from Mamie – I shuffled in the direction of the bleating, no idea what I'd say to them if I discovered she'd gone. *She was too good for me anyway…* wouldn't work on my biggest cheerleaders.

I also couldn't admit the embarrassing truth: *We didn't actually have sex.* That wasn't my greatest disappointment either, although I had vivid, physical memories of touching her skin, dewy from exertion, of hearing her hitched breaths as a secret language only I could interpret. I just… didn't know what this was.

With a sigh, I swung open the door of the new barn – Maman's pride and joy – to a sight that was close to the last thing I expected.

Chapter 24

Seb

I was screwed.

I hadn't thought it possible that Lori could get any more beautiful than when she was naked and begging me to touch her, but with hay in her hair, holding a baby goat, she could have come right out of my deepest fantasies – *my downfall*, wherever that melodramatic thought came from.

She was perfect on a bike, her body as powerful as it was beautiful. She was a dream in bed – either blowing my mind or just stroking me to sleep. And now I had to watch her smile brightly at my family as though she belonged in this picture.

I should have told her not to get *my* hopes up. She was in a different place to me – younger, tougher, more motivated and successful. She would be gone from my life even before my retirement. But she wasn't in a different place right now. She was right in front of me and I wanted to take her face in my hands and kiss her the way we'd kissed at the finish line yesterday.

This was bad.

'Bonjour, sleepyhead!'

Still in a daze, I turned to find Denise grinning at me from behind her broom handle. Luckily, I wasn't racing, because my reaction time was atrocious.

'Salut, little sis,' I managed, looping an arm around her neck when she approached to press a kiss to my cheek. 'Where are the petits?' I tried to keep my focus on her, but my gaze kept straying to Lori, as did my feet when I let go of Denise.

'Alice is at school and Maël is… somewhere here.'

'Tonton!' Wobbly steps finally wrenched my attention from Lori and I hefted my nephew into my arms when he threw his little body in my direction. He always felt like the meaning of life and I still wasn't sure if I was pleased or resented my sister for procreating and doing this to me.

'Hé, petit gars,' I murmured into his forehead, giving him a squeeze.

'Nori!' he said earnestly, pointing at Lori, and even the baby was conspiring to bring me to my knees.

'Lori,' I corrected him gently.

Meeting her gaze, a hundred questions seemed to pull tight in the air between us and I still couldn't breathe properly. She wanted different things – from me, in life. She wanted to use me for team PR. Gulping around my tight throat, I raised my eyebrows at her and jerked my head in the direction of the door, setting Maël back on his feet in the hay.

Feeling my family's curious gazes, I led her out of the barn so we could talk in private, fisting my hand to stop it from grabbing hers.

Scratching the back of my neck as my chest burned, all I managed to say was, 'I thought you might have gone already.'

'Nope. Still here.'

God, I wanted to kiss her, but I thought I was supposed to be angry with her. 'I can take you back to Roubaix,' I offered instead.

'I don't really want to see my dad or my brother right now.'

'You want to stay here in the middle of nowhere with goats – and me?'

'I wouldn't have put them in that order.'

I didn't dare react to the joke. 'There's no one here to see us together.'

Her gaze clouded. 'Look, I shouldn't have said we only kissed for the cameras. I panicked in front of Dad and maybe... it was an excuse.'

For what? Before I could voice the question, my phone vibrated insistently in my pocket and I tugged it out with a frown, since I muted most functions entirely. My agent's name flashed up on the screen and my frown deepened. I didn't usually warrant much of Ravi's attention these days, so I connected the call warily.

'Hey! Seb, my man!'

I nearly tugged the device away from my ear to peer at it in incredulity, it had been so long since I'd heard such enthusiasm from him. 'Hi, Ravi.'

'I've had quite a few calls this morning.'

Did that require an apology? 'Yesterday was a big day.' But I'd thought the team PR would handle any extra media inquiries?

'Everyone wants to know what your plans are.'

'My plans?' I glanced uneasily at Lori. 'You know what my plans are.' A peaceful retirement.

He laughed, then the sound petered out to an awkward huff. He dropped his voice. 'I mean with your girlfriend. I don't usually like to pry, but you could have told me you have *Lori Gallagher* in your back pocket! If you're planning to be active on social media, I've already got two inquiries about sponsorship.'

Misgiving skittered over my skin.

'Think about the options it would give you for next year.' Ravi knew my financial situation. 'If it goes well, you could get more sponsorship opportunities even after you retire.'

I couldn't, if they were contingent on a relationship with Lori that would only exist until my – her – luck ran out. My head swam, remembering her agonised tone as she spoke about letting the team down and wanting to do her bit. Were people really so interested in her love life?

'Ehm, thanks Ravi. Can we talk about this later?' *How about never ever again?* 'I'm kind of… busy.'

'Of course, of course. Text me when you're ready. And say hi to Top Gun for me. I'm a big fan and *you're* a dark horse, tiger!'

I blinked at the phone for several vacant seconds after I disconnected.

'Your agent?'

I darted a glance at her. 'He says hi. He's a big fan.'

'Ah, I landed you in the fire?'

'No,' I insisted, but my voice lacked conviction. I drew myself up with a sigh. 'Do you really think pretending we're… in love would help you and the team?' I hoped she couldn't tell that the words stuck in my throat.

A grimace briefly crossed her features. 'Now that we've kissed, it would probably be better than leaving people wondering. And at least they might stop talking to me about Gaetano.'

That flicked a switch inside me. 'Maybe it's a good idea after all. If we do it, am I allowed to text you more than "congratulations"?'

She scrunched her nose at me. 'Yeah, I suppose so.'

'Okay, then. This is it. The most unlikely love story in the peloton. Maybe it'll help with our luck problem too.'

She studied me as though she might question my sudden change of heart, so I rushed on.

'Just use a filter on me, hmm?' I posed with my knuckle and thumb on my chin.

Batting my arm away, she gave me a dry look. 'Use your own filters. I'm pretty real on social media.'

'I know,' I said, pausing when I belatedly thought that through.

'You've looked at my feeds?'

'Not every day.' I inwardly winced. 'I mean, I don't go on there much. I haven't posted anything for three years.'

'That'll have to change,' she said pointedly.

I gave an eloquent shake of my head that wasn't a no or a yes. 'Let's start with yours, hmm?' And never move on to mine.

Ravi might be dreaming of sponsorship dollars, but I'd never see a cent. For me, this would never be about the money. I only hoped Lori didn't realise. She could keep her pride until she was gone.

Lori

Pretending to be romantic was far more nauseating than I'd imagined. First, Seb produced an actual tandem bike, which was sickeningly couple-y, even before he gently explained that I could rest my shoulder in the upright position behind him and still get some light training time in. Then he took me shopping for underwear and earnestly told me I'd look hot in the no-nonsense sports bra I picked out – before scowling at me when I suggested I could post his blush on social media.

I might have been less volatile about it if he hadn't taken to this fake romance thing with gusto, peering at me warmly when I took his photo and asking me if it was okay to touch me in front of the camera. *Yes*, I could have yelled. *Touch me* behind *the camera too! Grab me and don't let go!*

I might have snapped a few more pics than were strictly necessary, just to get him to slip his arm around my waist or dip his face to mine.

He even had such incredible shoulders to admire that I didn't mind relinquishing the steering on the tandem. Seeing him as a doting uncle that morning had ripped me wide open, even though I had zero interest in procreation right now. His 'someone very special' would hit the fucking jackpot, when he decided to settle down – which he would probably do as soon as I let him out of this stupid sort-of-fake arrangement I was beginning to regret.

It wasn't a good idea to wallow in hypothetical jealousy right now. The way he looked at me, the way I felt, we might have ended up in another Paris-Roubaix finish-line moment and, while I was taking pictures in preparation for outing us on social media, I needed a bit more control over my feelings before I kissed him again.

My shoulder throbbed as we made our way back from the leafy town of stone houses and slate roofs nearest to the farm, but I knew he was riding smoothly, neatly avoiding obstacles so I didn't jar my arm. The countryside was restful, bright green with spring growth and quietly alive with people either working the land or enjoying the natural environment – walking, cycling, canoeing.

'How's the pain?' he asked.

'Pfft, it's just the usual now. Riding this thing barely hurts at all.' I studied the slim tandem with white lacquer, buttery leather seats and a gleaming vintage Campagnolo chain drive that was a thing of beauty. 'Where did you even get this bike?

'It was my grandpa's,' he explained casually. 'I found it a few years back and did it up. I used to work for a bike shop.'

'Wait, there is an actual man in your family tree? I thought you were all immaculate conceptions?'

He laughed at my joke, but there was a tightness in him that reminded me that he hadn't invited me here and I had no right to be as burningly curious about his family as I was.

Expecting him to shut down, I was surprised when he explained. 'Grandpa wasn't a great guy. He worked in France most of his life and… Yeah, Maman probably has a few half-siblings she doesn't know.'

'Wow, that's… a lot,' I murmured as my thoughts churned. After Rôsine's comments, I was beginning to understand his complex family legacy. It was no surprise he was wary of relationships, but it didn't explain what I was to him.

'No one's family is perfect, right? Mine is just particularly screwed up,' he said with a huff.

'And I thought it was just me,' I muttered, thinking of the distance between my parents: not only geographical – the grudges held over so many years.

He glanced over his shoulder at me: warm, curious, wary. I could make an entire Instagram feed of that expression and find nuances every time I looked at it.

'Your dad's hard on you,' he commented.

'It's good for me,' I insisted, but I couldn't stop adding, 'most of the time,' to the end. 'Your mum said your dad left and you never saw him again.'

The cadence of his pedalling faltered. 'You guys really had a heart-to-heart.'

'To be honest, I don't think she likes me. She was warning me off, saying you need "someone special".'

A choking splutter reached my ears and he slowed the

bike, putting a foot down and turning to face me. 'She didn't mean you're not special.'

The words sent sparks over my skin and my throat grew thick.

'She just knows you're leaving – I mean, not staying. You know what I mean. She's got a thing about people leaving – her.'

Rôsine wasn't the only one with that 'thing'.

'It's not personal,' he insisted, turning back to the path with finality.

I wanted to keep him talking, but he pushed off and we settled into a rhythm again, which felt strangely like riding together online.

'We'll have to tell her about the fake thing,' I mumbled. 'She won't be happy, right?'

'Nope,' he replied immediately. 'What about your mum? Is she going to ask? Is she even in Europe?'

He couldn't have known that the simple question made my spine freeze up. 'She doesn't come to Europe much these days. I'll put her off somehow. She'll probably be horrified. I promised her I'd focus and not get distracted this year.'

'*Both* of your parents push you?'

'In their different ways,' I said quietly. 'Kind of "good cop, bad cop".' I swallowed heavily, hoping he wouldn't pursue the topic.

'Well, it won't be long and you'll be winning everything again and you won't need me.'

He spoke brightly, but his words dug deep under my skin.

For the briefest second, I wondered what it would be like if my losing streak continued – and so did this romance. This *fake* romance. With a commitment-phobe. No, I didn't belong here on a tandem bike with Seb, no matter how good he looked in a white T-shirt and a pair of supple old jeans.

'It's so… domestic here,' I commented, changing the subject as we meandered along a narrow river.

He paused, as though deciding whether to let the topic drop. 'There's nothing that will kill you in Belgium, unlike in Australia,' he joked lightly. 'We have to make our own excitement.'

His excitement would not include me. Shaking off my stupid thoughts, I pointed out a family wrestling with a temperamental boat that had got stuck in the bushes. 'You might have to learn to canoe after you retire,' I teased, my tone dripping with mocking. 'To guide all the guests at your fucking B&B.'

Chapter 25

Lori

'It's like an arranged marriage, but without the marriage?'

I'd known this odd discussion over dinner with every woman in Seb's family wouldn't be fun, but I was squirming in my seat before we'd even explained ourselves in a way that made sense. I wasn't sure what was worse: Albertine's persistent misunderstanding or the daggers Rôsine was shooting with her gaze. More concerning was Seb's sister, who was still looking at me as though I were joining the family.

His little niece with her messy plaits piped up with something in French, to which Rôsine replied firmly. Denise stifled a smile.

'Alice doesn't speak English, but she understands more than we think,' she said with a chuckle. 'She just asked if Uncle Seb was getting married.'

It was my turn to choke on a roast potato.

The way we were sitting around the big scarred table in the kitchen didn't help either. I was certain my chair was drifting closer to Seb's as we faced the austere features of his mum and grandma, with Denise obviously enjoying herself on one end and her daughter gleefully arranging our marriage on the other.

'It's not anything like a marriage, Mamie,' Seb said through gritted teeth. His elbow brushed my forearm and then stayed there as though for solidarity – or the same pleasant tactile sensations my skin experienced at the touch.

'Nothing good ever came of marriage in this family,' Albertine added emphatically. 'So you're having a fling privately and also having another fling publicly.'

I'd never seen Seb's complexion quite that shade of scarlet. He glanced at me, the pressure of his arm growing, and all I could think about was the private fling. We hadn't discussed that angle of the fake relationship. I held my breath as I met his stormy gaze, suspecting he was thinking about the same thing, but with reservations I wasn't sure I wanted to hear.

'It's less complicated than some of my relationships,' Denise pointed out, shooting us an amused, sympathetic smile.

'How long are you staying?' Rôsine asked, cutting straight to the practical stuff I wasn't ready to deal with.

'Maman, Lori's a guest—'

'It's a fair question,' I said, cutting him off.

Another stormy look. He dropped his arm, but then snaked it along the back of my chair and all my hair stood on end. 'But first we're *friends* – right? You're welcome to stay.'

Albertine humphed. 'Friends who—'

'I'll clean up!' Rôsine interrupted her. Seb mumbled

something about helping her before rising from his chair. His palm touched down between my shoulder blades and the breath left my lungs as though the light caress had been a blow. The stroke of his fingers along the back of my neck as he removed his hand was enough to set my skin on fire, my body growing heavy.

But if Seb noticed, he didn't react, following Rôsine out to help and leaving me alone with my out-of-control libido. When I recovered my breath, I noticed Albertine and Denise eyeing me.

'I don't— I didn't mean to cause any trouble,' I blurted out.

Albertine just blinked at me, but Denise juggled her sleepy son on her lap until she could snake her free hand across the table to squeeze my arm. 'It's okay.'

'What trouble?' Albertine said indignantly. 'You're the best thing that's happened to him in years. You have to feel something in life.'

I froze, needing to contradict her for my peace of mind, but unwilling to. 'But we just explained it's not a real relationship.'

She shrugged. 'The feelings are real.'

My churning stomach proved her point — for attraction, at least. 'It doesn't mean we'll ride off into the sunset one day. I'm— We're—'

'Do you think I don't understand that? A bit of heartbreak might do him good.'

Goosebumps skittered along my skin. I didn't want to be the one to break his heart and I certainly didn't want his grandma inviting me to. Plus, I didn't even know if he wanted to sleep together again.

Denise said something to Albertine in muted French, which made the older woman humph again and stand to clear the remaining plates. A moment later, I was alone with Seb's sister and her children and Denise's quiet contemplation of my expression scared me almost as much as Albertine's predictions of heartbreak.

'Don't worry. I'm not going to give you advice or judgement,' she began. 'But the way he looks at you...'

The way he touches me...

Seb's voice cut through the restless moment. 'I think Lori's had enough guilt-tripping tonight.'

I turned to find him in the doorway, his arms crossed, leaning on the frame and giving his sister a dark, warning look. I'd preferred it when he was defending me to his prickly mother, but that easy posture, his lanky form set off all my endorphins again.

Denise sighed and rose gingerly to her feet, propping up her sleeping son. 'I can take a hint.'

'Don't leave on my—' I tried.

'I'm more than happy to take the kids home and leave you two to... work things out,' she said with a twitch of a smile that Seb either ignored or didn't see.

He sighed. 'Take your progeniture home before they fall asleep. Let me put this one in the car for you.'

She handed over a floppy Maël, who settled onto his shoulder contentedly, pacifier working in his mouth.

'Oh, tu pars?' Rôsine said a quick goodbye to Denise, pressing kisses to her cheeks, Albertine repeating the gesture a moment later, and then I followed her onto the porch to see Seb dropping a soft kiss onto his nephew's head before easing him into a car seat.

'The two men in our family,' Denise said with a soft sigh. 'He never forgave me for having kids that he couldn't help but love.'

That strange statement made a lot more sense to me after our conversations today, but it didn't help me untangle what *I* wanted.

With another squeeze of my arm, Denise pressed a kiss to my cheek, pausing to whisper, 'If anyone can knock some sense into him, it's you.' Without waiting for my reaction, she headed for her car, trailed by the sleepy Alice, who turned back to stare at me as though she were seeing rings and bouquets.

Seb dawdled back from the car, waving with one hand as he kept his other in his pocket. He was wearing his socks and Birkenstocks again, like the dorky European he was, but my eyes enjoyed a long, slow study of his form, from the hint of muscle under his jeans to the hard, lean lines of his torso. I made a show of yawning and stretching as well as I could with my stiff shoulder.

I was relieved his family kept country hours. If we'd been staying with my Italian relatives, we'd never have got to bed before mid-morning the next day and I was hoping we could... clear a few things up tonight.

Rushing my shower because I could barely stand the sensitive state of my skin, I dumped my clothes in Seb's room and then hesitated, the door still open. Could I stay in this bed and not make a move on him, if that's what he wanted?

The light in the little sitting room was on and muted voices reached my ears. I couldn't just pounce on Seb in his bedroom when he emerged semi-naked after his shower.

I grabbed a glass of water from the kitchen and lingered awkwardly in the corridor in indecision, hoping neither his mum nor grandma would appear, because I couldn't come up with a reason why I wasn't sure if I should go into his room.

When he did appear, he was in a comfy pair of tracksuit bottoms and a soft T-shirt and he stopped up short when he saw me. Perhaps my thoughts were visible, because he peered at me quizzically as he approached, taking my chin between his thumb and fingers. For a considerate fake boyfriend, sometimes he touched me in the most divinely assertive way.

'I'm, uh… tired,' was all I managed to say.

His gaze clouded. 'Are you actually tired, or just sick of my family?'

'Bonne nuit, *mon chou*!' I heard from behind us, in a decidedly put-out tone.

Seb bit his lip over a wince and then called out good night to his grandma. When she was gone, he prompted me with a look.

'Er, it's time to lie down kind of tired.'

His small smile was more sympathetic and less sexy and I

258

was obviously failing at this. 'So, guest room and sleep? My room and sleep? My room and film first?' he asked lightly.

After all the little touches, the confusing emotions of the day, it shouldn't have surprised me that I blew a fuse. Stretching up to whisper into his ear, I said, 'Your room and I suck your cock?'

I wished I could have caught and bottled the whimper that emerged from his throat. His breath was hot on my cheek. 'You——We haven't discussed the... boundaries of the arrangement,' he said in a low voice. I was worried for a moment he'd resist, but his hand fisted in the front of the sweatshirt I was wearing – another of his soft ones that I was considering stealing.

'Bonne nuit, tous les deux.'

He snatched his hand away as Rôsine flapped her farming magazine at us and shuffled towards the hall. 'Bonne nuit,' he called back casually, but his eyes didn't leave mine. Waiting until after his mother had disappeared down the hall, he softly rasped, 'Do you mean a fake fuck?'

Watching his lips form those words made my vision blur and my mouth water, hot, syrupy need flooding my body. 'Well, I could give you a fake blow job or a real one,' I murmured in reply. 'Up to you.'

His exhale was so laboured it was almost a whistle. 'You don't have to do anything.'

I licked my lips and enjoyed the sight of his throat bobbing – probably as he swallowed his tongue. 'If you want to keep boundaries, I could just tell you, instead, how I'd put my mouth on your dick. I remember how thick and hard you got last time and I want to see how deep I can take you. I'd be on my knees, pulling down your pants, and then I'd take the head in my—'

With a strangled grunt, he grabbed both of my hands and dragged me down the hall to his room, slamming the door harder than he'd intended, if his grimace was anything to go by. Caging me in against the jamb, he took a deep, unsteady breath.

'Fake relationship, real sex, okay?' He seemed to struggle even to say those few words.

'Okay.'

Chapter 26

Seb

That 'okay' was all I needed to put my mouth on hers like a match to kindling and then I was consumed. All I could feel, could see was Lori, her hair in a messy bun on top of her head, wearing the shorts and sweatshirt I'd given her last night, smelling like my soap and all of my dreams come true.

Sex was fine – it was fun and light-hearted and not serious and definitely wouldn't mess with our heads when we got back to racing.

All that stuff might not have been true, but sex was definitely happening. It was *necessary*.

'It's so hot when you wear my clothes,' I mumbled, my hands finding their way to the skin of her waist.

'That's a simple fantasy,' she replied, smiling against my lips.

'Oh I, eh, have some complex ones if you'd prefer,' I said, my words puttering out as she nudged my chest, making me stumble backwards.

Dropping to her knees, she tugged down my tracksuit bottoms and boxer shorts with an enthusiasm that brought a groan up my chest. Her words were still echoing in my brain and my heart was ready to burst at the proof that she hadn't been bluffing — she really was about to take my cock in her mouth. Thrusting my fingers into her hair for balance, I landed heavily on the edge of the bed as my knees gave out, spreading my legs to encourage her.

I didn't know if I was dragging her to where I wanted her or just hanging on while she came close, but her keen little hum gave me all the encouragement I needed to push my aching cock past her lips.

I hissed as her tongue curled around me and she sucked. 'You've got to tell me,' I said tightly, holding her still as I thrust in. 'Tell me if I go too far.'

Pulling off with a grin that turned me into a puddle of need, she said, 'You haven't got there yet,' and ducked down again.

'Fuck,' I whined, brushing my fingers over her face, cupping her jaw and watching as she let me pump, slow and hard, into her gorgeous mouth, as she invited me to. I couldn't keep the words in. 'How did I ever get so lucky? Nothing is ever going to be as good as this, as your mouth. I don't know if you should let me do this, baby. It's so fucking good.'

She moaned around me and her hand sneaked down her own body to tease herself and a flash of longing of a different sort ripped through me. Pulling out of her mouth, I drew her to standing when she peered questioningly at me.

'Can we fuck? I want to fuck you again.'

'Yes,' she replied, her voice breathy and high.

Kicking off my tracksuit bottoms and underwear, I dragged my T-shirt off in one motion, desperate to feel her skin against me. I stripped off her jeans like a madman, nipping at the swell of one buttock as I came back up, just because I knew she'd squeal and I couldn't resist. Her sweatshirt and her T-shirt followed, although I managed to be gentle as I tugged them over her bad shoulder.

Then she leaned against me, her back flush with my chest, and I wrapped my arms tight around her, one palm sliding up to her breast. Her hair tickled my nose and she arched against me. I wanted to soak her up, drink her in, and I couldn't stop myself from sinking my teeth into the cartilage of her ear.

'Ungh, yes! Ohhh, Seb,' she groaned, going up onto her tip-toes and wriggling until my cock slipped between her thighs, and then releasing a full-throated moan.

I grabbed her hips and stroked against her, panting, moisture coating my cock. It was a perfect notch in her body and I could have fucked her like that, bending my knees until I made contact with her sensitive clit, but she opened her mouth and then it was her words making me pant.

'I want it deep. Need you, Seb.' When she dropped her hand to the bed and gasped, grinding against me, I was so far gone I wasn't sure I was ever coming back.

The scars on her back showed in stark relief in the light of the lamp. Shadows stroked the subtle curve of her hips and the muscles in her shoulders. As I brushed my fingertips over her skin, exploring and admiring the strength of her with my jaw hanging open, the vulnerability of her struck me too.

She might not like showing vulnerability on the road – or even in her own family – but she was bare in front of me, inviting me to take pleasure in her body. I hoped she understood how beautiful she was with her fight on show alongside her softness.

As I pressed my lips to the puckered skin up the middle of her back, she stilled, but I didn't linger long after honouring her scars, crowding her body with mine and nuzzling her neck until she shuddered.

All for me... I knew Lori's life was complex, but all of the obstacles fled to the back of my mind, leaving only this beautiful woman who made my body ache – my chest – with everything she did.

Opening my mouth, I bit down – hard – on her nape, drawing a delicate whine from her lips. As she panted and groaned – or was that me? – I drew up and slipped the first inch of my cock into her slick body.

With an inarticulate sound from her throat, her arm buckled and we tumbled onto the bed. Landing heavily on top of her, I shoved the rest of the way in with a grunt, choked by the flood of sensations rippling through me. Gripped by the need to pump, I tried to slow things down, be gentler with her, but she was a live wire beneath me, pushing back and clawing the sheets and gasping, 'Harder!'

'I should be worshipping you, Lore,' I grunted into her ear with another thrust. 'You are so beautiful right now.'

'I don't want to be worshipped,' she panted as I bottomed out again. Hitching her hips up until she was on her knees, I held onto her thighs as I let loose, thrusting into her over and over again. Dropping one hand, I circled her clit, making her cry out, belatedly muffling the sound in the sheets. 'Don't stop!' she whined.

I soaked up all her frantic cries, her restless squirming.

'Yessss,' she said on a long breath.

'You don't want me to worship you,' I repeated, grasping the last strands of rational thought as I melted further into her, into the heat of this furious coupling. 'You want me to fuck you.'

Lori

Wow, when he'd said 'real sex', he'd meant really *real*. I was raw under his touch – intensely myself and painfully exposed.

'Ye-es,' I managed to answer him. I wanted him to fuck me, to make me feel something – *everything*.

As the sheets upbraided my cheek with every thrust, I struggled to keep a hold of my thoughts, which seemed to detach and float somewhere outside my body. I was consumed by sensation, by the need to follow this frantic act through to its conclusion – both physically and emotionally, whatever that meant.

'I want you to fuck me, to do whatever you want to me,'

I panted, squealing when his teeth found the side of my neck and then he pressed an uncoordinated kiss there, slipping up to my ear. 'I want you to lose control,' I said on a gasp. 'Let everything out on me.'

'Lose control?' he repeated on a huff. 'If I had any control where you're concerned, I would have stayed away on training camp. I'm bad for you, but... fuck this is good.'

My brain had shut down, but the words still flowed out – from somewhere deeper. 'I want you. I want to see you...'

His lips were at my ear. 'You want to see the mess you make of me?'

'Yes!'

He pulled out and hauled me onto my back, tumbling on top of me to kiss me – long and searingly deep. Hitching my leg around his waist, he fumbled to slip his cock back in, but when he was there, he thrust so hard I had to press a hand to my mouth to stifle a shout.

He tugged my hand away and replaced it with his own. 'You've got to be quiet while I fuck you,' he whispered into my ear, punctuating his words with a pump of his hips that made my vision blur and a muffled whine escape my lips. 'Be quiet and see what you wanted to see.'

His mouth feathering my neck, the pace of his thrusts slowed, but the pressure only built. He was thick and hard and mind-altering inside me, taking pleasure and forcing it on me.

'I can't go deep enough,' he mumbled. 'The way you feel around my cock, baby... Your eyes when you look at me... This feels like winning – better than winning.'

The trouble was, I knew what he meant. In that quiet moment late at night, my breath tight and my body clutching him, holding him, feeling him, I had nothing to prove and everything to be joyful in. I was enough.

I was enough to make him shudder as he started to come apart, his chest heaving and his expression turbulent. His fingers dug into my cheeks as his thrusts grew wild and punishing, holding me down. My knees fell, boneless, to the sheets as he plunged deeper, hard and heavy and glorious.

'I'm so crazy for you,' he muttered and along with the relentless pressure, a crack of uneasy wonder opened up inside me. He just meant his body. It was enough that I could make him lose it in bed. 'I'm gonna— Holy shit this feels— Ohhh, fuck!'

I was almost sorry when the rush of sensation zinged up my spine and overwhelmed my senses. The view of him, panting and desperate and pouring out into me, grew fuzzy. Biting down on his hand, I gurgled a cry as the orgasm broke over me, the buzz hanging suspended for a breath before slowly receding. And what flooded in after it was even more concerning than those thoughts about winning I'd had while under the influence of this gorgeous human and his hot body.

Contentment...

There was no need to strive, nothing to aim for. There was only that moment, as Seb collapsed next to me with a wrecked half-smile, his hair in his eyes. Stretching his arm over me, his thumb brushing my nipples and then my stomach, he sighed and said, 'You are the best thing that's ever happened to me, Lore.'

Goosebumps tingled over my skin and I rolled over, hoping he'd just think I wanted to go to sleep and not that his words were burrowing into my chinks and letting that insidious contentment steal the dreams I'd held since I was a teenager. I shouldn't be thinking of staying longer, wondering if Dad would let me train here, but there it was. I couldn't un-think it.

Besides, he'd unconsciously echoed his grandmother's words from earlier that evening – when she'd suggested I could break his heart.

Then Seb continued, mercifully reminding me that we were a long way from having a relationship and I didn't even know what a healthy one of those looked like anyway – and apparently neither did he. He breathed sleepily, 'I'll never forget you.'

Chapter 27

Lori

I awoke restless the following morning to find Seb still passed out next to me and my reservations roaring into overdrive. The only training I'd done for two whole days was a little countryside jaunt on a nostalgic tandem. My shoulder was buggered, but the rest of me needed to stay fit. Slipping out of bed, I pulled on Seb's shorts and my new bra and fiddled with his Zpeed set-up until it came to life, swallowing a grim smile when the message flashed up: *Welcome back, LoonieDunes*. Flicking through the menus, I couldn't help pausing on the chat server, where our last conversation was still the most recent.

The user you are trying to contact does not exist. Please check the username and try again.

I could still feel the panic at the prospect of Mum finding out I'd been anything other than disciplined and ambitious online, but now there was so much added guilt at the way I'd left without saying goodbye.

My skin prickling with misgiving, I selected a threshold workout and pressed 'Start' before I reconsidered and jumped back into bed with Seb, who would be warm and sleepy and soft.

The hour was torturous without music – or a voice in my ear. I kept thinking of all the conversations we'd had during warm-ups and zone two training. He knew me too well.

I must have slipped into my zone eventually, because I didn't notice he'd woken up until his gravelly voice reached me.

'Wow, good morning. I'm going to think about your tits in that bra every time I work out on Zpeed from now on,' he groaned.

My foot slipped and I had to grapple with the handlebars for balance, which made the pain in my shoulder roar to life. 'Fuck! I should never have tried this barefoot!'

He was out of bed in an instant, curling an arm around me in that unbearable way he had of touching me. 'Hey,' he began, but I shook my head.

'I'm fine,' I lied. 'I just hate being injured.'

He looked ready to challenge me, but apparently decided against it. 'It was my fault for distracting you.' He was too good at taking the wind out of me.

Giving him a half-hearted shove, I said, 'You sure did. You should give me a warning before you say the word "tits".'

'Consider yourself warned,' he said, his voice low and smooth, and that was all it took for me to leave the Zpeed simulation to its workout and let Seb show me exactly what he liked about my bra.

When he left to shower, I rolled over and caught sight of my phone, connected to Seb's charger. I'd turned on flight mode yesterday and ignored my real life while snapping photos of Seb and me, but I should probably turn everything back on and see what the damage was with my dad.

I'd expected endless buzzing for a few minutes while the notifications dropped in. But, even when I opened the conversation with Dad, there were no new messages. Was this the long-distance silent treatment?

I thought about checking my Instagram – I had the notifications filtered and switched off for the sake of my focus and mental health – but I decided against it. I'd start posting the fake photos of Seb and me soon enough, but I didn't want to think about that when I was wrapped up in his sheets – in the memories of his body against mine. Chicory coffee was a much better option.

Seb had an appointment with his old cycling club in the early afternoon. I decided to tag along, curious about his professional beginnings and eager to distract myself from the feeling of being a ticking clock, about to blow this thing between us apart.

We were all contractually required to wear our team jersey when we appeared in public. He had to pull a brand-new jersey out of a packet, which reminded me how little time he'd actually been with Harper-Stacked.

But I hadn't forgotten how smooth and toned his body

looked in Lycra. As we cycled the short journey to his appointment, I was thoroughly distracted by the flex of his butt and his glistening tattoos, peeking out of his socks.

The afternoon wasn't quite how I'd imagined. Instead of arriving at a community sports club, he stopped the tandem outside a little white building with a sign that read 'École de la Communauté Française.'

'This is your school?'

He nodded. 'The club organised a trail for the kids in the forest this afternoon to give cyclocross a try.'

'With their famous son to inspire them?'

He peered back at me with a scowl. 'You have no idea how many times I've turned up to this event and none of the kids have recognised me.'

'Well, today they have the runner-up of the Paris-Roubaix,' I pointed out, pressing a quick kiss to his lips and enjoying the dazed look that came over him whenever I did that. 'Here, we should take a photo.'

Raising my phone, I lined up the shot with Seb in the foreground, wearing his helmet and sunglasses, with the school in the background.

'Smile!' Of course he pouted instead, but the result was still unbearably cute. Leaning on my handlebars, I slung an arm over his shoulder and set up a selfie that was mostly helmets – and smiles, I noticed with a start.

My finger hovered for one last shot and he craned his neck at the last minute to press a kiss to my cheek. I shut the phone down quickly, unwilling to check the photo where I probably looked just as dazed as he had.

As he slipped the padlock through the chain around the tandem, a voice reached us from across the road. 'Sebi! Salut, mon garçon! Quel résultat à Roubaix, petit veinard!' A grey-haired man with a prodigious moustache climbed out of a tiny car and approached, enfolding Seb in a hug with so much backslapping I wondered if it had grown aggressive.

Seb replied with more French, sparing me only a single awkward glance. It was unfortunately enough for moustache-man to peer at me and then clap a hand over his chest in melodramatic disbelief. 'Loredana Gallagher! La vache, our boy brought home Loredana Gallagher!'

'Just say hello, JP,' Seb suggested sourly.

'Excusez-moi, mademoiselle. My name is Jean-Philippe Delginiesse and I'm delighted to meet you.'

Although the president of his old club was warm and genuine, the flicker of alarm up my spine didn't go away as we met a young trainer and eventually headed inside to collect the children.

I tugged at Seb's jersey before we entered the gym. 'Maybe it's better if you don't introduce me,' I murmured. This wasn't about me. It was Seb's moment to give back to his community on a day where he deserved every bit of attention and praise. The fleeting fake relationship had no place here.

But it was too late for the club president, who insisted on taking a photo of the two of us in front of the course they'd

273

set up for the kids. I didn't imagine he'd like that photo haunting his retirement.

He didn't seem to pick up on my concerns, smiling at the kids and tapping their helmets in encouragement, before hopping on the bike the trainer had brought for him and showing off. I knew he was good. I'd seen him racing. But seeing him handle a bike over tree roots, slaloming around tight curves and over dips and rolls was a whole other level of skill.

When he finished off with a gratuitous hop and a wheelie, to raucous applause from the children, I couldn't help thinking again that he shouldn't retire, that he was as good as he'd ever been and 34 wasn't even old – or at least not *that* old.

My fingers were restless, holding his phone while he chatted to the kids and the teachers, his hands tucked under his armpits against the chill of the April afternoon. Without really intending to, I used the code he'd given me in Siena and unlocked the device. I knew I should leave it alone, but I noticed the Instagram icon and tapped on it. His last post was nearly two years earlier, which made me inwardly groan. How much sponsorship money had he been missing out on? People loved cycling action shots and training videos and a rider's view of the big races.

He also had hundreds of notifications, many of them from the past two days. I recognised several cycling insider accounts and tapped on one, hoping I might see his finish in Roubaix one more time. But instead, it was a reel with photos of him and me. Words flashed up on the screen: *Lori Gallagher has breathed new life into a tired career.*

No wonder he hadn't wanted the attention. But he had it now, and I had to fix it for him. At least we'd agreed to fake this relationship, so I could make sure he looked good.

Before I could talk myself out of it, I snapped a photo of him smiling at the kids and sent the one I'd taken outside the school to his phone. One post at least would not be about me. Opening the messaging app to download the picture, I saw an unsent text in the box and my breath caught.

No matter what happened today, you were gorgeous on the bike. I couldn't take my eyes off you. You had your heart in it. You're so beautiful and real, whether you win or lose.

Time stopped. Tears had been threatening all morning and I had to pull myself together in the next five seconds or I'd be in trouble. The only good decision I'd made recently was telling him not to text me anything except congratulations, because I was devastated – spilling open and messy and in danger of... believing him.

How could I focus on racing when he kept twisting me up with feelings?

Taking a couple of heaving breaths, I swiped away the messaging app and concentrated on what I'd planned to do: get him the attention he deserved – sponsorship, fans, everything in the sport.

I uploaded both photos with the caption: *la nouvelle génération, and I don't mean* Star Trek. Adding a winky face, I posted the pictures, making sure none of the children were identifiable.

Taking up my own phone, I liked the picture and shared it.

Opening up a new post, I selected the selfie of the two of us smiling and my thumb hovered over the button to post. It was a nice photo and a lot less damning than the make-out session on Sunday, but I still felt raw just looking at it. The next photo, where he'd surprised me with a kiss on the cheek, made me panic. The stars in my eyes were obvious to the naked eye.

But my heart raced and I couldn't post it. The fans wanted to see 'Top Gun' Gallagher and that's not who I was with Seb. Me and my big mouth, suggesting a stupid fake relationship. I shut down my phone before the vulnerability struck me again.

Arriving back at the farm, I tackled him with a hug, making him drop the tandem with a clatter. I belatedly realised we had never hugged before, but that was a detail I was determined to overlook. His arms came around me adorably slowly, one hand clutching the back of my head.

Staring up at him with my chin on his chest, I said, 'You enjoyed that, didn't you?'

'A little,' he admitted playfully. 'It's easy to impress a bunch of kids.'

'You impressed me.'

'Really?' Clearing his throat, he dropped his voice. 'I mean, sure I did, baby.'

'You're only allowed to call me that in bed.'

He chuckled and rested his head on mine. 'You have to stop getting my hopes up. Remember you're not Belgian and I'm not allowed to date you.'

He was joking, but it got to me anyway. 'Yeah, because you want to retire and live in your stone house and take guests at your fucking B&B canoeing instead of racing another season with me.'

His fingers tightened in my hair. 'It's not about you, Lore,' he said gently, but again, his words hurt. 'And you can be certain while I'm dealing with the mess of my retirement next year that I'll be wishing I was still with you – and watching every single one of your races, even though it hurts.'

I froze, horrified that my eyes stung afresh. 'Shut up,' I said, searching for the stubbornness I needed now more than ever. 'I'm still here. Right now, I'm here.'

His hand on my cheek was rough, holding my face up to his. 'I know,' he said, his eyes roaming my face as though my freckles and fake teeth and strong jaw could be exactly what he wanted in a woman. *I couldn't take my eyes off you.* 'You're here, for now.'

When he kissed me, it was unbearably soft – slow and aching and here was LoonieDunes again, my safe space, my *friend*, and the kiss was just as devastating as anything we'd done last night and this morning.

Maybe I'd stay another day. And then another?

Just when I was starting to believe in something other than watts and power-to-weight ratio and gradient, a voice sounded behind us and I wrenched away in shock – and yeah, embarrassment.

'Well, this wasn't what I was expecting to find, Molly!'

My priority became keeping Dad away from Seb for long enough to smooth things over. If I made his place in the team too awkward, I'd never forgive myself, especially because I didn't want him to retire.

But that meant keeping *me* away from Seb too. After an inadequate farewell to Rôsine and Albertine, I'd encouraged Dad to bundle me back into the car and, before I'd forgotten the feeling of Seb's hands on my face, we were heading back to Roubaix as though nothing had happened.

I clutched my phone in my lap, wanting to write a message to Seb, explain something, but I didn't know what I would be apologising for or whether it would make any sense.

'I think I... need an explanation, Moll,' Dad said earnestly as he swerved to change lanes. Years of navigating narrow roads with packs of cyclists had made him a haphazard driver. 'I had hoped after last year—'

'This has nothing to do with last year.'

'Even if you think so, what happened last year is still affecting you,' he said, gently enough that I couldn't ignore it. 'It's only natural. Your body's healed – I can measure that. But your heart?'

'You're giving Gaetano too much credit.' I didn't remember feeling so upside down when I was with my ex, even after he broke it off, but I didn't want to admit that.

'He distracted you and look what happened. When you took off with Seb after the race, I was worried about your training schedule – your focus!'

Ah, so not about my heart after all. 'I worked out this morning. And besides, I dislocated my shoulder, in case you've forgotten.'

'All right, kiddo. I'd just hate to see you hurt by another bloke.' *Winners and losers*... Both of my parents were worried I was a loser in relationships. And they couldn't even see the doubts and fears crowding my mind.

'This has nothing to do with last year,' I assured him, 'because it's fake. Seb and I are just friends, helping each other out.' *With a few orgasms.* 'We're doing this for our careers.'

I let that declaration sink in for a silent moment, staring at the road signs as they whooshed past. In a moment of frustration — at myself, for losing control of the fake relationship situation — I pulled up the selfie from earlier today and posted it. No caption. The pic was so cute it didn't need it and I refused to feel anything.

'Are you sure you know what you're doing?'

I whipped up my gaze, worried Dad could see through me to the churning emotion underneath, but he was watching the road.

'I just don't want to see you reduced to being "someone's girlfriend" again, especially given everything you've achieved in your own right!'

I hadn't achieved much recently.

'You know how it works. Fans support me and I owe them a piece of myself. I bet our coverage and interactions have gone up.'

Dad's grumble proved my point. 'I don't want coverage and sponsorship at your expense.'

'I'm a team asset, Dad,' I reminded him. 'And so is Seb.' For now. 'It's a win-win situation.'

'You looked… well, ahem… Are you sure he hasn't… developed feelings for you? Feelings that might be… a problem later?'

Maybe he had. Maybe *I* had.

Dad gave me a concerned 'dad' look, which coaxed a ridiculous blush up my chest. But my dad knowing I was having casual sex was better than him suspecting the truth: my head was a mess over a guy who was all wrong for my future.

Those moments of weakness where I'd imagined staying in the Belgian countryside for him were exactly that: a weakness. Another few days and I might have imagined crazy things like getting pregnant and having a sweet kid like Maël or Alice.

A sweet kid who would torch my fitness and possibly end my career, as I had done for Mum.

'We've been pretty up-front with each other,' I mumbled.

Dad's breath came out long and deep. 'Good, because I have something I need you to ask him for me.'

20 April 10:42

LoonieDunes: You ruined my phone.

Folklore: You rediscovered Instagram then?

LoonieDunes: Yes, because it buzzed at me 15,000 times. I'm not even joking.

Folklore: Are you… mad? I just thought the world could do with more hot pictures of you. Plus the whole fake relationship thing. But I am sorry I didn't ask first.

LoonieDunes: A fake relationship doesn't give you the right to hack my social media. The adoring public has enough pictures of you and me from your account.

Folklore: You are mad, then.

LoonieDunes: Yes. We need to stage an argument – to cover for the real one.

Folklore: I see you're not mad enough to stop joking around with me.

LoonieDunes: Apparently not.

Folklore: I promise you can tell me off properly at the finish line on Sunday. Dad's letting me race again, so I'll be coming in a few hours before you.

LoonieDunes: I saw the starting list. I hope you've got your luck back.

Folklore: We did fuck again, so maybe.

LoonieDunes: Seriously, we should talk. After the race.

Folklore: I'll kiss you after the race, like a good fake girlfriend, and then you'll have to go stand on the podium to get sprayed with champagne.

LoonieDunes: You have a powerful imagination.

Folklore: Well, you're picturing it too, now.

Chapter 28

Seb

I wanted to be watching the women's start on Sunday at the Liège-Bastogne-Liège, the old lady of the Classics, as the race was known, but I had to line up with the team to be photographed and cheered at. I only had time to quickly check the news ticker on my phone while I warmed up on a stationary bike in front of the team bus, scrolling until I found a photo of her cruising in the peloton. I was even grateful for that glimpse of her freckled cheeks under her sunglasses, her plait over her shoulder and her body primed to fight.

It was screwed up, but I was enjoying being mad at her — something real, despite the elaborate farce we were performing. She'd been drip-feeding the photos she'd taken two weeks ago into her social media and each had more likes than the one before, but I didn't like the way they started to feel fake, when the time had been real. I didn't know what to expect when I saw her.

Colin caught me looking at her photo and said with a snort, 'Are you serious, Frankie?'

'I just want to see if she's got her luck back,' I said defensively. 'You know you should get her a new pair of earrings,' I added.

'What?'

'She lost one of the ones from your mum. They were her lucky earrings.'

'She doesn't need luck. She believes in being the best. That's the way we were trained.'

'Did you forget your lucky bibs today?' I asked.

'Nope, I found them. I'd just put them in the wrong bag.' His words tapered off with a grumble as I laughed at him. I knew for a fact that he was wearing dirty socks, too, and he'd kiss the Southern Cross tattoo on his arm before the start of the race.

'Just buy her some earrings.' My brain added a 'kid' to the end of that sentence because I was incapable of forgetting that Lori's brother was 11 years younger than me.

Hopping off the bike, I headed for the bus to try to clear my thoughts, but Colin's voice stopped me. 'What have you got drawn on your arm today?'

'Nothing I want to show you,' I replied.

'I hope it's nothing to do with my sister this time.'

He would hope in vain. Everything I did came back to Lori, even when I wasn't sure I wanted it to.

In a light drizzle, we lined up for the neutralised start, rolling past the tall brick terraces on the outskirts of Liège. I was a team man that day and much more comfortable than I'd been at the start of the Paris-Roubaix, with the pressure on. I wasn't sure if Lori's promise to kiss me if I won – or at least earned a podium position – still stood if I rolled in exhausted after pulling someone else for three-quarters of the race.

The rain fell in earnest as the kilometres disappeared behind us and the hills of the Ardennes, the forested region of Belgium that was my spiritual cycling home, opened up around us. Colin was coddled in the middle, conserving his strength and hurling the occasional insult, which I'd learned was his way of showing affection. Despite the terrible conditions, we reached the notorious climb of the Côte de la Redoute with 35 km to go and sailed up it together more easily than I'd expected.

Then the director was urging us to go and I accelerated wildly, with Colin on my wheel. We managed a ten-second gap, then twenty seconds.

My chest started to ache. On the final climb, black spots appeared in my vision and there were moments when my legs felt like jelly. Colin powered ahead and relief swept through me: I'd delivered my teammate into a good position for the finish. I could cruise home without pushing my over-taxed body

Except that every kilometre I put behind me was one kilometre closer to Lori. Just a bit further and I could see her, ask how her race had gone, grouch at her for trying to drag me onto social media. Kiss her – for the cameras or not, I didn't care with my thoughts hazy and fevered.

I slipped and slid down the descent back into Liège, barely

conscious of the shouts from the fans as the route took all of my remaining concentration and handling skills to navigate the technical curves.

Imagining Lori watching at the end, I saw another rider ahead of me on the final straight and pushed hard, catching him at the last minute as I plunged over the line.

I nearly ploughed into a TV crew as I struggled to brake, trying to wake up and follow the directions of the race officials to where the team assistants were waiting. More shouts of my name rose up and I waved manically. As my legs finally listened to the command to stop, I skidded to a halt and someone caught me.

Grasping them for stability I pulled back to look, but dropped my hand again when I saw it wasn't Lori. *Idiot.* I didn't know what place I'd rolled in, but I didn't much care. I just scanned the crowds. She'd probably been joking about kissing me, but I had to look.

A strong hand grasped my jersey and I turned, the bike clattering to the ground between my legs. She was there, right there, her hand slipping around the back of my neck below my helmet, and she planted her mouth on mine.

I was alive again. Relief welled up inside me and I hauled her closer, one hand cupping her jaw. She'd landed me in an online mess, but she was here with me, her mouth open and hot and reckless.

Maybe we shouldn't have kissed so wildly in front of the cameras again. Fans couldn't share anything that wasn't entirely safe-for-work. We were supposed to talk about this fake/real relationship, the boundaries and exit strategy. But I didn't care. I hadn't seen her for ten days.

I might have kept my mouth on her – and screw the necessity of oxygen – but she drew away gently, her eyes clouded. As I sucked in several much-needed breaths, I realised this wasn't all about me and something was wrong.

With a wobbly smile, she pulled off my glasses and tucked them into my helmet, pressing another quick kiss on my lips.

'Hey,' I breathed, not capable of a proper greeting.

Her smile was quick and amused. 'Hey.'

'What happened?' I asked quietly. 'Did you finish?'

She nodded and I wrapped her in a hug of relief. I couldn't have lived with it if she'd been injured again. She stilled against me, rigid at first, but slowly relaxing.

'I came twelfth,' she murmured.

'That's great!'

It was her turn to laugh. 'It's not great. I got caught in a crash and then isolated without Doortje and the others. It wasn't disastrous, but I came second last year.'

Tugging off my helmet, I peered earnestly at her and said, 'You'll win it next year.'

'Yeah, without you,' she muttered.

It hurt, but when I noticed the necklace I'd given her around her neck, I didn't blame her for the bitterness. Maybe her luck hadn't been terrible today – perhaps it was still turning. But I was still tangled up with her recovery and not with her future.

I noticed a mark on the inside of her wrist and pulled back her sleeve to see a little faded redback on her skin.

Her blush was obvious on her pale face. 'We all did them this morning. Did you?'

Grasping my arm, she turned my wrist over and peered at the doodle I'd drawn there this morning, now smudged from the rain.

'Is that a redback?' she asked doubtfully.

I shook my head slowly and swallowed the lump in my throat. 'It's an X.'

'Marks the spot?' she asked, adorably confused.

I cleared my throat and mumbled, 'It's a kiss.'

Embarrassment might have swept up my throat, but it made her smile, those gorgeous lips turning up into my favourite shape. She laughed, swallowing a snort, and said, 'You drew a kiss? I thought you were mad at me.'

'I am,' I insisted, grasping her tightly around the waist. 'But I was still thinking about a kiss,' I admitted, making her look away with a scrunch of a smile. 'A lot.'

The rueful look she gave me was enough to tell me I'd been right and we had to talk about our murky motivations and what the future held. I opened my mouth, but nothing came out.

'You should go,' she urged gently. 'Get cleaned up.'

'What for?'

'Seb,' she said, giving me a poke. 'For the podium.'

'Podium?'

'You came third.'

'I... whaaaat?'

288

Chapter 29

Lori

I hitched a lift back to the guys' hotel with the swannies, hating that I was nervous. I wished I was just sneaking in to spend time with him – or even going on some wild scheme to get my luck back.

But no, I was here on behalf of my dad.

I was in full support of Dad's proposal: a contract extension for next year. I might even have suggested it, if Dad hadn't beaten me to it. But the timing was off. Seb was still mad at me, even though he'd kissed me as though his world depended on it. I hadn't had enough time to convince him to stay and he'd sent that ominous: *we have to talk*. I hated to admit how many times that message had caught and hung in my brain during the race today.

He hadn't replied to my 'where are you' message, so I asked one of the guys in the lobby which one was his room and banged on the door. When it flew open to reveal Colin, I took a step back in surprise.

'What are you— Er, hi brotato chip. Nice win today. You finally managed to finish something.'

'You can't fool me, brat. I know you're here looking to…' He gagged before he'd finished his sentence. 'Actually, I don't want to know what you and Frankie get up to.'

I rolled my eyes. 'Are you two roommates?'

'Most of the time,' he said with a shrug. 'For someone you're just messing with, you text him a lot.'

After three months in Northern Europe my tan had faded, meaning Colin must have seen the blush creeping up my neck. 'Maybe there are lots of girls messing with him.'

'With Frankie?' Colin said with an amused grin. 'Nope. Besides, I know when it's you who's texted him because he turns into a puppy and he can't stop smiling.'

My stomach dipped and I kind of wished I hadn't heard that. 'Where is he? I need to… mess with him a little more.'

'Yuck, I said I didn't want to know!'

Stifling a groan, I countered, 'I didn't say I wanted to tie him up and give him a lap dance. Get over it. I need to talk to him about something. That's all.' I was too restless and annoyed even to enjoy the view of Colin gaping, incapable of speech for a moment.

'Is everything all right?' he asked.

'Yes!'

'You're not wearing your earrings,' he commented.

'I lost them back in March,' I said, confused at the change of subject.

'Did Mum give those ones to you?'

'Years ago, but why are you suddenly interested?'

'What about that necklace? I don't remember that either.'

I tucked it self-consciously under my shirt. 'You obviously haven't been paying attention.'

He watched me more closely than I liked. 'Lori,' he began, his tone setting off alarm bells in my mind, 'you know if you need anything—'

'I don't. I'm fine. You never used to ask me if I needed anything before I got pins in my vertebrae!'

'All right. Take it easy. I get the message. Frankie's probably—'

'I'm here. What's up? Lori!'

I turned to find him emerging into the corridor from the lifts, holding a cardboard box.

'I thought the women were staying in Bastogne and I didn't... I wasn't sure I'd see you.'

'She needs to talk to you,' Colin supplied. 'Talk,' he repeated, enunciating clearly. Although I suspected he was trying to deliver a veiled threat, it only made me think about what Colin thought we wanted to do with each other. I kind of wished I'd booked a hotel room to drag him to.

'Come on,' I said, grasping Seb's sleeve and dragging him back into the lift. When the doors finally closed, I sighed deeply – and picked up the most spectacular smell. Straightening, I sniffed curiously. Did the cheap hotel have a signature scent like the Ritz? Or did they pump out something delicious to disguise the odour of old cyclists' socks and sweaty bibs?

'It's this,' Seb said, holding the box under my nose. 'Vanilla.'

'Vanilla what?'

He placed the box in my hands. 'Waffle.'

'God, I love Belgium,' I murmured, enjoying his chuckle as I opened the box to find a rustic-looking waffle, glistening with sugar and doused in vanilla sauce that might be nearly as good as custard, since no one in continental Europe appreciated the magic of custard.

I broke off a piece with the little wooden fork and chewed slowly, not caring if my moan would make the CCTV sound X-rated.

'Good thing I bought it for you,' Seb commented.

'You bought it for me?' I mumbled around another mouthful.

'No. I was joking.'

'You didn't have to share it with me!'

'Sharing? Is that what we're doing?'

Giving him a dirty look, I cut off another piece and shoved it into his mouth, dripping vanilla sauce onto his chin. He swiped it up with his thumb and even that fizzed in places that it shouldn't have.

'Well, this is romantic. How about you take a photo for—' I shoved another piece in to shut him up.

I obviously hadn't had enough to eat after the race – or maybe it was just a really slow lift – because the waffle was almost gone by the time the doors opened three floors below.

Hotels were a constant problem for my dad – well, money was a constant problem. Rooms booked up years in advance and the hiked-up prices for teams around the time of an event meant that the guys were staying in a two-star hotel above a bar, while the mechanics and technical staff struggled to find somewhere to park the bus and the trailer of bikes. But the women were in an equally crappy hotel in the countryside somewhere near Bastogne where there weren't even any waffles, so I suspected the men had the better deal.

Outside the hotel, the evening was dim, despite the longer days of spring. I tugged my jacket around myself as a gust blew through it. The cathedral loomed dark across the square, all turrets and gothic arches, but we wandered in another direction.

He spoke first. 'So we have to talk. I kind of thought we weren't finished when you rushed off today.'

I didn't want to talk. I just wanted to wander aimlessly through the paved streets of Liège – and finally hold his hand.

'What do you need to talk about? I won't touch your social media again. I shouldn't have intruded.'

He swiped his tongue thoughtfully over his lip and I indulged in the spark that went through me at the sight. 'Apology accepted.'

'That's it?'

'Apparently.' He shot me a half-smile that I wanted to catch and bottle.

My heart soared for a moment, imagining we could do the wandering and hand-holding thing now and forget the 'talk'. I could do Dad's bidding another time.

But then he continued. 'I thought we had to talk about... the publicity stunt relationship and when we need a fake break-up.'

That sent my heart plummeting again.

'Ah, that stuff.'

'Did you need to talk to me about something else?'

'How are your Instagram woes? Is that why you want a fake break-up?' I asked, avoiding the topic a little longer.

'I didn't say I wanted to fake break up. I just assumed we'd have to end it as soon as you got back in form.'

'Well, that hasn't happened yet.'

'But if you ever want to fake break up, then just let me know. I can post something for my people and you can post something for your people and our people can talk to other people and we'll get the message out that we're still friends.'

'Still friends,' I said, needing those words more each time we repeated them.

'Oh, look. A waffle shop. We'd better just stop here and buy me another waffle, since my first one got stolen.'

I whacked him on the arm. 'You are such a pushover! Letting strange girls hack your Insta and steal your waffles.'

His side-eye was amusing as he ignored me in favour of the waffle stand. He came away with another of the crispy sort covered in sugar, but this one also had chocolate oozing out of the inside. My mouth watered as he took a bite, licking his finger when the sauce dripped.

I sidled close. 'You know I gave you a few bites of… your waffle.'

'Only two.'

'Well…' I lifted my chin.

'Am I getting you into trouble?' he asked. 'Waffles aren't exactly in the approved diet.'

'First you introduce me to waffles, then it's a slippery slope all the way to cheese.'

He gave me a withering look. 'Something like that. We've established that I'm bad for you.'

'Maybe I want bad. I definitely want a bit of that waffle.'

With a sigh, he held it out for me. Shooting him a sly smile, I opened my mouth wide and took the biggest bite I could manage, chewing and licking my lips until he was staring, slack-jawed, at my mouth.

'Everything you do turns me on,' he said accusingly. 'Especially with your mouth.'

'Mmmm,' I said, wiping a drop of sauce off my lips and sucking on my fingertip. 'The chocolate kind of exploded in my mouth.'

He gave a faint sound like a whimper from deep in his throat. 'You do realise I have to go back to my twin room with your brother,' he said, his voice high.

'Urgh, that is rough luck.'

A few drops of rain landed on his shoulders, then I felt them in my hair and it struck me just how grim the sky looked now and how far from the hotel we'd wandered – without me even broaching the subject of his contract. Maybe we'd find a place in the lobby of the hotel, or the bar down-stairs.

'Shall we head back?' he asked.

He reached back for my hand when I nodded – and then obviously realised what he'd done and snatched it back. My throat was thick with the loss of whatever that moment could have been and maybe it would all be better if neither of us had been pro cyclists, if he'd just been that middle-class Canadian I'd pictured and I'd been...

That was the problem. I didn't know who I was without a bike.

We headed swiftly back through town, but the intensity of the rain increased steadily until I was shivering. We were still across the square from the hotel when the downpour began.

'Over here!' Seb called over the rain and tugged me by the sleeve to the entrance of the cathedral, where we ducked into the stone passageway to the main portal, gazing out into the wet. The rain fell in sheets, but a smile stole over my lips as the back of my hand brushed his.

He glanced at me, catching the smile, and the corners of his eyes crinkled and the bursting sensation in my chest spread again.

The door to the cathedral opened to reveal a middle-aged couple in matching bucket hats – and a hint of warm light from the interior. As the couple exclaimed about the rain in French, I drifted towards the doors, peering in and – wow.

The gothic vaults were illuminated by numerous chandeliers, the sandstone ribs glowing gold. The most astonishing thing was that the vaults were painted with a forest of colours – plants and trees and animals.

Seb folded the cardboard packaging of his waffle and followed me warily inside. 'You don't think there will be any severed heads in here, do you?'

'They're not going to jump out at you. If you get scared, you can hold my hand.' I cringed, but it was too late to call the words back.

I brushed past him into the church, staring up at the vaults and the glowing colours of the stained glass struck by the dim evening light. My gaze was drawn to a bright marble sculpture of a muscular man with lush curls and a pair of articulated bat wings. The crease between his eyebrows reminded me of Seb's wary expression – and his muscles reminded me of the skin and sinew under his clothes that I probably wouldn't get to see tonight, damn it.

'He's a handsome devil,' I commented lightly.

'He's *the* devil, I think. Tempted?'

'Very,' I joked, taking slow steps further along the nave.

Seb fell into step beside me, his throat working. 'I'm kind of glad we don't have to fake break-up today – in case I get scared of the haunted relics. But did you really come back just so I could get mad at you?'

Shit, I couldn't even lie in a church – and I was worried about losing touch with reality anyway, with everything we were faking. With a sigh, I stuffed my hands in my pockets and turned away, gathering my wits to say what I needed to say.

'Actually, there is another reason.' I paused, as though that could make my next comment less bad. 'It's about your retirement. Dad wants you to stay.'

297

Chapter 30

Seb

My steps faltered, the rubber soles of my sneakers squeaking on the marble tiles. Whatever I'd thought she would say... This was worse.

'He asked you to talk to me?'

She nodded, her face expressionless.

'Why? Because we're "together"?'

'No!' she insisted. 'Because he knows we're friends.'

'I meant is that why he wants me to stay in the team.'

'That has nothing to do with me!' She'd raised her voice, attracting a handful of disapproving glances from other visitors. 'You've had a great season. Why would you think there was any other reason?'

'I'm currently helping you draw extra attention to the team for the sponsors. It wasn't much of a leap.'

'Seb,' she said, frustration in her voice, 'retiring now would be such a waste!'

'Of what? One year of thirty-five-year-old fitness?' I

scoffed. 'I've been lucky this year — whether that's down to you or not—'

'It's *not*!' she hissed.

I looked at her askance. 'I've had fifteen years of mediocre results, with the occasional breakthrough. A season like this is... not me. You think I'm affecting your head game. Why is it strange to believe you're affecting mine? If I stayed on next year, it wouldn't be the same.' And who could tell what my 'friendship' with Lori would look like, if she needed me to perform. The thought pricked me.

'What if Dad promised to make you lead rider for some of the Classics? You're good enough for it!'

Rolling my eyes, I countered, 'He wants me as a domestique for Colin in the Tour. I know how this sport works. You don't have to dress it up as something else. I don't crave that recognition anyway — you know that. You just haven't accepted it because winning is all you know.' I hadn't meant that to come out as a criticism, but her flinch suggested she'd taken it that way.

'You give up too easily — on everything!' she accused. 'Even this fake relationship! Two weeks in and you want to plan the break-up.'

'Someone has to think ahead before we get hurt!' Before she moved on with her life without me.

'But your career is now! Take a fucking risk sometimes! There are so many cyclists hitting their prime at your age. Why would you give up now?'

At my age... I didn't often notice how much younger Lori

was, but she couldn't understand. She thought I was some kind of exception, when I was just the rule. I grasped her arm, my thoughts swirling. 'I appreciate that you... want good things for me. And I'm flattered that Tony wants to extend my contract. But it would only be postponing the inevitable and giving me more chances to fail.' *And it would give you the chance to walk away from me.*

She tugged her arm back. 'With thoughts like that, you *will* fail! Urgh!'

'I told you I was bad for you. You're twenty-five. You haven't even hit your physical peak. You can't see it yet, but this season is a tiny blip in an impressive career. I'm ready to retire and eat cheese and I shouldn't be tempting you with waffles!'

'It's not your waffles that tempt me,' she said grumpily.

'What? My *buns*?' I turned on her with a severe look.

She sighed through gritted teeth. 'I knew this wouldn't go well.'

'Then tell Tony to talk to me himself.' Instead of ruining the little time I had with Lori.

'He's going to talk to your agent – soon. He wanted me to... soften you up first.'

I eyed her.

'I know. I'm sorry. But what do you stand to lose?'

'What do you hope to win by making me stay? We can't fake a relationship for a whole off-season and it's difficult enough to find opportunities for actual sex.'

She didn't have an answer for that. Of course she didn't.

'It's not about sex,' she insisted, snapping her mouth shut when the older couple in the next aisle turned to glare at us.

I headed further along the side aisle, gesturing for Lori to follow. 'I didn't want to post anything to my feed because I had no intention of accepting any sponsorship. I went along with this hype for you, so you could get back on your feet without worrying – and maybe kick Gaetano out of your thoughts. But I won't stay another year for you, even if it's the only way we could still see each other.'

Her quick intake of breath sounded tortured and guilt prickled under my skin. She felt something of what I did. I didn't want to hurt her, but I remembered how I'd felt when she'd disappeared from Zpeed back in November. I had to keep some boundaries.

'Will you at least wait until after the Tour to formally refuse the offer – and end the fake stuff?'

'Why? Because you think I'll change my mind?'

'Because I like having you around, you idiot!' She gave me an abortive shove and swiped at her face. 'Because it's an excuse to hang out while we still can!'

She didn't look at me, instead turning to stare into the side-chapel where we'd found ourselves, but I couldn't have said what was in it. I was stuck on her words. *While we still can.* The boundaries could maybe wait until after the Tour.

As I matched her gaze, trying to reason with myself that 'hanging out' with Lori for another few months wouldn't hurt me, the objects in front of me gradually took on form and colour.

I stepped back with a start. 'Wh-what is that?'

She peered at the sign off to the right, reading, but my stomach lurched. A casket of sorts, gold and silver and covered in gemstones, lay on a carved dais and it didn't take a genius to work out what would be inside.

'Let me guess. Bones? Hair?' With a shudder, I remembered the head in Siena with a strange mix of revulsion and fondness for what had happened after that.

'It's bits of his skeleton and a piece of his skull,' she explained out of the side of her mouth. She came in close. 'Are you scared?' she asked softly.

I didn't hesitate. 'Yes.'

When she slipped her hand into mine, I was sure I felt something break. Awareness of her rushed in my veins. She glanced at the floor, but I felt her uncertainty in the light tremor of her hand. Twisting my fingers with hers, I held on, blinking back light-headedness. Her hand in mine shouldn't have felt more intimate than everything we'd done in bed — or the kisses in front of the cameras.

But it was just us. *Us*. FolkyDunes. Standing together in the face of success and failure and weird religious relics. After the argument, it was everything.

And I *wanted* so badly, in a way I hadn't dared to *want* before because built into wanting things was the disappointment of not getting them. Working hard for a race and losing. Waiting for Papa to come home...

But as I brushed my thumb over the back of her hand and soaked up her muted inhale, disappointment didn't exist. She turned to me – slowly, questioningly, her eyes lit with wary anticipation – and I dipped my head. Her breath ghosted over my lips and I could already taste the relief in the impending kiss.

'Lori,' I whispered, just because I liked saying her name.

With deliberate slowness, shared breaths and the history of every moment we'd known each other – both virtually and in real life – our lips met, softly, achingly. This wasn't the desperation of a post-race kiss when I'd been dreaming of her for days, or the need we awoke in each other in the bedroom. It was something else – something that would haunt me in its tenderness.

This was Lori with her armour cracked.

Bringing my other hand up to her face, I kissed her as though nothing else mattered.

The high-pitched sound of shoes scuffing on the tiles echoed suddenly and I pulled back, belatedly remembering where we were. My chest was heaving and the way she sluggishly blinked open her eyes and smiled reordered everything inside me. She was still clutching my hand.

Lori spoke first. 'I suppose we should stop before the bones wake up and get us in trouble for kissing in a church.'

'Don't even—'

She silenced me with another quick, hard kiss that left me off balance. 'Do you still want to hang out with me tonight?'

I couldn't have stopped the words even if I'd wanted to. 'Of course.'

'Good.' She tugged me away from the chapel, heading for the portal. When she wrenched it open, it was dim outside, but the heavy rain had stopped. 'Because I want a beer.'

I was glad I'd stuck with the non-alcoholic version of a golden Belgian brew later that evening when I dragged her back to the hotel, already dreading what Colin and her dad would say. She'd had two — fairly small — beers, but I should have guessed how poorly she'd metabolise the alcohol. Post-racing drinks were always dangerous, especially after a bad result where the crash in adrenaline was immediate.

She hung off me in the lift, her lips at my neck.

'Do you think my brother would clear out so we can get naked?'

My hands tightened on her waist. 'Colin isn't the only problem here,' I muttered, brushing her hair out of her face. She'd tugged it out of her plait during the second beer. She was loose and beautiful and fun — and far too tipsy for anything more than a kiss.

'But I don't know when we'll get another chance,' she pouted. 'Our training schedules are mad.'

'Three weeks at altitude with Colin and without you. And you really think I should do this all again next year?'

'It's better than a fucking B&B — without me.'

'I almost agree with you,' I murmured in dismay. 'But even if I stayed next year, we wouldn't have an excuse to hang out.'

'Just be private fuck buddies,' she mumbled. 'I won't tell

my parents if you won't.' She pulled back with a frown. 'I don't know where the hand-holding fits into that.'

'I don't either,' I whispered, pressing a kiss to her forehead and leaving my cheek there. She felt... heady.

'What about when *I* quit,' she slurred. 'What if I stay really shit and my own dad drops me from the team. We could fuck then.'

I scowled, drawing back to frame her face and stare intently into her clouded eyes. 'Don't even think about that. You are strong and focused – a winner.'

'I could be strong and focused *and* we could fuck?'

The back of my neck tingled. 'That hasn't worked so far.'

'My mum says there's a winner and a loser in every relationship. She's bitter, but I'm scared she's right.'

I thought of Maman and Denise – even Mamie. 'Perhaps your mum is on to something.'

'Or maybe she's wrong and thinking of life in terms of winning and losing isn't helpful. Maybe then she'd see something more in me.'

Words stuck in my throat, wanting to comfort her, but afraid of what might come out of my mouth if I did. She solved my dilemma by leaning heavily on my shoulder and making a sleepy snuffle that suggested she wouldn't hear anything I said right now anyway.

Juggling Lori, I managed to extract my room key from my wallet and shove the door open, stumbling through. At first, I was relieved that the light was on and Colin hadn't already gone to bed, but then I saw the other figure in the room, standing by the desk and flipping through a sheaf of papers, and blushed as red as the rooster on the flag of Wallonia.

I opened my mouth to defend myself, but I couldn't decide where to start. At the bones of the saint? Or the waffles? Or right back to the first time we chatted on Zpeed? Perhaps my contract extension would be in the bin anyway.

'Molly!' Tony Gallagher exclaimed. A deep sigh escaped his chest. 'What have you done now, my girl?'

By the time I'd recovered from my surprise, Lori had pushed away from me. 'One evening, Dad,' she said, holding up a finger and only slurring a little. 'Two beers. That's all I've done now.'

'Besides, she was only doing what you asked her to do,' I added with a dark frown.

Tony turned to me, eyebrows raised. With a bark of laughter, he clapped me on the shoulder. 'She was, was she? I knew if anyone could get you to sign, it would be Molly.'

Mystified about why he kept calling her Molly, I glanced at Colin in confusion, but my roommate only gave me a shrug.

'I haven't agreed to sign,' I said evenly. 'I just said I wouldn't refuse to sign until after the Tour.'

'Good man, good man,' Tony muttered. 'Do what you have to do. Wait for other offers. That's fair. But just know we'd be lucky to have you back next year – happy to have you back. Lori says you're just friends.'

I could almost feel Colin's raised eyebrows at that statement.

After Tony shepherded his daughter out of the room, Lori recovering quickly enough to bicker, I found my roommate watching me speculatively.

'I probably won't sign,' I told him before he asked. 'I'd planned to retire.'

'You're the age for it, I suppose,' he said with a shrug. 'You've lasted longer in the competition than a lot of guys. But what if Lori wants you to stay?'

'She does, but I don't see the point in putting myself through this when my fitness will only—'

'No, I mean what if she wants you to *stay* – with her.'

'I'm not—'

Colin's expression hardened. 'She might be messing with you, but you're messing with her too, you know. She's distracted.'

'I didn't mean to—'

'And she's *happy*.'

'She's not,' I insisted. 'She thinks that getting injured and performing below her potential is failing all of *you*.'

'I know that, but do you think she'll let us take the pressure off her? She only lets *you* do that! And then she comes back happy.'

Any response I might have had died in my throat. I made her *happy*? What miracle caused that? But I also split her focus, when racing was her protection from a chaotic world. She might want me to stay, but for both our sakes I had to go. I didn't have a better solution.

30 April 6:52

Folklore: How's the mountain air?

LoonieDunes: Thin.

Folklore: Ha ha. Did I say anything embarrassing while I was drunk last week?

LoonieDunes: Wouldn't you like to know.

Folklore: I mainly remember trying to work out a way that we could fuck.

LoonieDunes: That was about the extent of it.

7 May 19:48

LoonieDunes: Instagram told me I might want to post something.

Folklore: So post something. Or don't.

LoonieDunes: That photo you posted of us from Liège is nice.

Folklore: …

LoonieDunes: Especially considering that beer knocked you out.

Folklore: I can still tell Dad about the waffles.

LoonieDunes: I knew you were kind of immature, but 'telling on me to Dad'? How old are you?

Folklore: Nine years younger than you.

LoonieDunes: Actually, you're only eight years and nine months younger than me. You obviously haven't googled my birthday.

Folklore: Don't take it personally.

LoonieDunes: …

Folklore: I know you didn't text me just to ask me about Instagram.

LoonieDunes: I've been watching your races. You're so hot on a bike.

Folklore: Yeah, a supersexy fifteenth overall.

LoonieDunes: You finished. And Friday's stage was amazing.

Folklore: Yeah, until I punctured.

LoonieDunes: I was just glad you had a solo attack so the camera stayed on you a lot. I've watched it a few times.

Folklore: …

LoonieDunes: Is that weird? Sorry. The thin air must be getting to me.

19 May 20:46

LoonieDunes: You been busy today?

Folklore: It's nice someone's checking I'm alive.

LoonieDunes: I might panic if I didn't hear from you for a whole day when you're not racing.

Folklore: I've got a fever. Waste of a day at altitude.

LoonieDunes: Have you got tea?

Folklore: Tea?

LoonieDunes: Mamie would give you liquorice tea if she were there. It's pretty disgusting, but it seemed to work when I was a kid. Ginger tea might help if you don't have any liquorice root.

Folklore: I don't have any liquorice root.

LoonieDunes: Call me if you start hallucinating.

Folklore: How will I know it's really you?

LoonieDunes: I'll tease you about it afterwards.

20:55

LoonieDunes: I would give you a hug if I could.

Folklore: I'd give you a fever.

LoonieDunes: I've already considered that possibility.

12 June 21:06

Folklore: Colin said you're more fun when I'm around.

LoonieDunes: He's probably right.

Folklore: I've been watching the Tour de Suisse with Doortje.

LoonieDunes: Please tell me it's because I look hot on a bike and not because you enjoy our pain.

Folklore: Doortje thinks you look hot on a bike.

LoonieDunes: Eh… she has good taste?

18 June 19:57

Folklore: I hope you're celebrating (even if it is without me).

LoonieDunes: Yeah. Having a beer with Colin (even though I always feel like I've got the wrong Gallagher).

Folklore: If you're kissing him, you've got the wrong Gallagher.

LoonieDunes: It's very clear to me that I haven't kissed anyone since 23 April...

Folklore: I saw the 'X' on your arm.

LoonieDunes: I seem to have developed a few superstitions.

Folklore: I'll pray the rosary to Saint Catherine for you. If her severed head appears in your dreams, that means it's working.

22 June 06:03

LoonieDunes: Happy birthday! Did your card arrive?

Folklore: Thanks. It did.

LoonieDunes: You already opened it?

Folklore: Yesterday. I couldn't wait — but now I've had an earworm of gnomes singing 'It's Your Birthday' for sixteen hours and twelve minutes.

LoonieDunes: Welcome to twenty-six.

29 June 16:13

Folklore: T minus one day.

LoonieDunes: Don't you mean two? The Tour starts on the first?

Folklore: One day until you see me. I'm coming to watch the Grand Départ before I head back up for training camp.

LoonieDunes: You tell me that now?

Folklore: It was supposed to be a surprise, but I can't keep a secret.

LoonieDunes: Wow. You do realise I haven't shaved all month for luck?

Folklore: You forget I watched the Tour de Suisse. I have seen that thing growing on your face.

Chapter 31

Lori

Craning my neck over the gathered crowd, I held my breath waiting for my first look at the Harper-Stacked riders for the Tour de France. My heart was looping in my chest, the beat so irregular I'd probably alarm a cardiologist right now and it had nothing to do with the Grand Départ tomorrow from this beautiful city on the Adriatic Sea, or the excitement of the team presentations currently under way.

It wasn't my fitness, either. I'd just come down from three weeks at altitude training as though my career depended on it — and bickering comfortably with Doortje and trying not to resent Leesa Kubicka for being so damn clever and talented. I was in the shape of my life.

But right now, I was about to see Seb again and I suspected it would not be pretty.

I was in Trieste for the first two stages in Italy and Slovenia and I'd follow the team back to France until stage four. In other years, I'd followed the team around and helped Dad and I was almost sorry I couldn't this year, except that I'd never be sorry the organisers had finally introduced a women's event with the same branding, starting when the men's Tour finished, after a century of men-only competition.

The crowd cheered the next team to emerge from the arcade of the historic building across the square and they wheeled their way up onto the stage, their bikes extensions of their bodies. Music played and the announcers spoke a chaotic mix of languages as the riders waved and threw signed caps and water bottles into the crowd. I thought I caught a glimpse of blue and garish orange through the arches of the arcade signalling that Harper-Stacked was up next.

And then I heard a voice, which was definitely not the one I'd been desperate to hear. An arm slipped around my waist to give me a light squeeze.

'Have I missed it? My flight was delayed.'

'Mum?' I said, whirling and stumbling. My heart sank, thoughts about winners and losers shooting through my brain as I imagined my parents fighting – or ganging up on me – or fighting *about* me.

She hesitated, studying me. 'Is everything all right?'

My foot drummed on the floor of its own accord. 'I didn't know you were coming.' I obviously hadn't inherited Mum's ability to keep a secret.

'Colin didn't mention it?'

I shook my head. 'How long are you staying?'

'You could just say "hello", Lori. I was worried you wouldn't be happy to see me. You're so much like your father.'

'Are you here to see Dad?'

She looked away. 'Not exactly. Your brother invited me to come. It's his first tour as lead rider. I'm not sure what your father will say about me turning up, but we'll see.'

'What do you mean you're not sure what Dad will say?'

'I don't think Colin told him I was coming either.' I expected her to look sheepish, but there were tight lines at the corners of her mouth. 'You know your dad and I haven't been…'

She gulped before she could finish the sentence or I could process anything about what she'd said that I wanted to understand. I already knew anyway, somewhere deep and dark inside me where I stuffed things I couldn't deal with.

Over the loudspeaker, the announcer bellowed in French and Italian and although I could get by in both, that day it sounded like a bunch of gibberish, until he said with a flourish, 'Harper-Stacked!'

I made out Colin across the square, doing wheelies, the charming idiot, for the cheering fans. The rest of the team filed out after them: Nellie and Derek, Amir and Lars and the others.

I recognised Seb as soon as he rolled out – last. Despite the helmet and sports sunglasses, the gloves and the team kit, I knew his shoulders, the way he sat effortlessly on the bike, as though he operated it with his thoughts.

Mum continued, oblivious, 'I assume your father's blaming me for everything. I don't expect you'd understand, the way you gravitate to him. I've only ever tried to guide you to what's best for—'

'Mum!' I said through gritted teeth. 'Maybe I wouldn't gravitate to him so much if you gave me the tiniest indication that you *liked* me as a person and not just a winner!' Her jaw dropped, but I didn't waste time enjoying it. I shoved my fingers into my mouth and whistled as loudly as I could. 'Seb Franck is a smoking hottie!'

He looked up and that was all it took. I melted on the spot. The crowd would be picking bits of me off their shoes all evening and I might never reach a solid state again after he'd looked at me as though I was the sight he'd most wanted to see in weeks. I knew the feeling.

Next to me, Mum was gaping, but I ignored her, taking off in the direction of the barriers.

'How can you say that?' she huffed, bustling after me. 'I love you, Lori.'

'You've got a funny way of showing it!'

'I just want you to meet your enormous potential.'

'What about how I am right now? Is that good enough for you?' Recovering from injury, messed up over a guy, restless as usual and belligerent as hell. But a mother should be the one to fucking love me. 'Are you going to watch *my* Tour as lead rider?'

Her hesitation spoke volumes. 'I didn't think you wanted me involved.' She had a point, but I didn't want to concede it. 'I know you're struggling now, but you can be so much more. What is going on with that boy?'

With an indignant snort, I hurried ahead. Nothing would

stop me finding that 'boy' and Mum knew nothing about how I worked inside.

The presentation had wound down, the announcer still speaking over the chaos as the crowd milled at the barriers. I pushed through, not caring what my elbows connected with or whether I should wait until the team arrived back at the crappy hotel.

Finally, I caught sight of him signing a child's autograph book. I leaned over the barrier and, as though he knew I was there, his gaze connected with mine and there was that smile again. As soon as he came close enough, I grabbed at him, my fingers slipping on the Lycra as I wrapped my arms around him.

Thankfully for my dignity, he snaked an arm around me and lifted a hand to my hair. And he kissed me without hesitation as though he'd thought of me as often as I'd thought of him, as though he'd spent the past two months waiting for this, picturing it with a dreamy smile, even though I wasn't sure if we were still just faking it – if we'd ever been faking it.

The gloved hand in my hair tightened and a shiver shot through me. His mouth moving, hot and deep, on mine was *more* than I'd remembered. I brushed my thumbs over his cheeks and noticed he'd trimmed his beard short. Rubbing my thumbs in the bristles, a grin grew on my lips and I planted another kiss on his mouth, a big, wobbly, smiley one.

Tilting his head, his kisses grew softer as well and I was

falling to pieces, right there at the barrier, while the sun set over the Adriatic.

'Hey, you,' I said, with rare eloquence.

'Hey.' His voice was soft, curling around me.

But then I heard my brother calling, 'You can stop now! The camera crew left before their footage could only be shown on adult websites!'

That made Seb pause, his fingers gentling. With a sigh, he stepped back, fumbling under his chin to unclip his helmet and sweep it off. Glancing around, I located the camera crew, chatting as they packed up their equipment. Then my gaze settled on my mother, standing a few metres away, her expression frozen. Ouch, I should have kept a better hold of myself.

'Lori, are you going to introduce me to your—'

Fake boyfriend? Fuck buddy? Casual lover? Text-message bestie? Inappropriate distraction? I took a deep breath and gave the only answer I could.

'No.'

Seb

There was something fraught in Lori's expression as we ate dinner back at the hotel. While I was grateful she hadn't dragged me to a table with her family, there was obviously something she wasn't telling me.

Seeing her after two months had been potent, an unexpected mix of completely normal and desperately wonderful.

Then I'd remembered the camera and with that, the ambiguous nature of our relationship.

She'd kissed me because she wanted to. Even I wasn't stupid enough to think it had only been for show. But the Tour was still supposed to be the end of our performance. Her mum had been watching too and I didn't know what that meant.

Paola Gallagher was still shooting glances in our direction from where she sat with Tony and Colin. Lori ignored her completely and everything she'd ever flippantly mentioned about her former triathlete mother whirled in my mind.

Lori ate quickly and I did the same, wondering, hoping we would get a chance to talk.

'Do you want to… go somewhere?' I ventured as she scooped up the last of her rice.

'Do you need to rest?'

I shook my head with a faint smile. 'There's an easy walk to a little chapel up the hill. That's our vibes.'

'Our vibes are not grizzly relics and religious buildings, Seb,' she said. 'I've got an idea.'

'O-kay,' I replied, struggling to interpret the unexpected intensity in her expression.

Following her out of the dining room, I took her hand, slowing our steps through the lobby. 'Are you in a hurry?'

'Yep. To get out from under all of those eyes. You aren't?'

'I suppose, but I was enjoying… this.' I squeezed her hand, remembering with a warm glow her drunken admissions back in Liège that she'd probably be horrified to remember in detail.

'Don't worry,' she said with a chuckle, drawing me towards the lift. Whispering in my ear, she continued, 'You won't have to take your hands off me for a while yet.'

My mouth went dry. Standing in the mirrored lift, meeting her gaze on several different angles, my mind raced with the sudden change of direction. 'You have a single room,' I guessed.

Her nod was enough to send heat racing up my spine. I could still picture her in high definition, baring her throat as she arched on my small bed at home, awash with need. My cheeks heated and my knees lost strength as I remembered what she'd coaxed out of me the last time we were together like that.

I was a darker ego, a deeper self when she offered me her body and it would have scared me except that she somehow held me together while I let it all out.

But there was still something in her eyes, in the slight wobble of her jaw. I suspected she didn't want me to see it.

Catching her eye in the mirror as the lift ascended, I let her see my thoughts in the rise of my chest, a lick of my lips as my gaze wandered over her soft skin, the curve of her throat. The slow perusal was torture for me too and I had to squeeze her hand hard so I didn't reach for her already in the lift. But as much as I wanted to close the door of her room behind us and reacquaint myself with all my favourite places on her body, I wanted her to tell me what was going on first.

After hurrying down the corridor together, she got the

door open and a moment later she was reaching for me, biting her lip and tugging me against her. Pressing her tight into the door and opening my mouth on her neck until she whimpered, I resisted the urge to devour and instead settled my hands firmly on her hips.

Then I whispered in her ear. 'What's wrong, Lore? Talk to me.'

Chapter 32

Seb

'You're kidding,' she whined, her chest heaving. 'I'm practically begging you to fuck me and you want to talk?' She pushed past me, giving my shoulder a half-hearted shove.

'Talk, then I'll fuck you.'

She whirled to face me. 'You didn't imagine I might want to *stop* thinking about it?'

'*I* want to be the only one in your head when we get there.'

It was a tiny room, so all I had to do was reach out to snag her shirt and haul her to the single bed. I settled next to her, my thigh pressing into hers, and leaned my elbows on my knees as I waited. It took only a few unsteady breaths for her to soften, leaning into me, and I had to swallow around the tenderness that rose in my throat.

'Is it your mum?' I asked quietly.

'No. Yes,' she admitted with a groan. 'I accused her of only loving me when I achieve something.'

I couldn't quite stifle my amused huff. 'Wow. That's wisdom

beyond your years. I bet you gave her something to think about.'

She slapped me on the arm. 'She messes with my head. I don't know if the problem is me or her. She keeps saying I have to reach my potential and I probably wouldn't be here right now if she hadn't been hard on me, but she makes me so scared I'm not good enough.'

Her tone took me back to last year, Lori talking to me in her cracked voice as she battled back to fitness.

'After the season I've had—'

I shook my head to cut her off. 'You showed your greatest strength this year. You kept going. They don't call road cycling an endurance sport for nothing.'

'Because I don't have a choice,' she said, her face curling up with an expression I'd never seen before. Unable to stop myself, I hauled her into my lap and pressed her cheek into my chest, grateful she let me. 'I can't just retire and eat cheese.'

'And you don't have to. You've got your best years ahead of you.'

'It's not that,' she insisted. 'If I give up – even when I lose – then she's right. Mum's *right*, I'm not good enough. If I stop trying... I don't know what else there is. I always just fight. I don't know what to do except fight.'

Leaning my head on hers, I clutched her and just breathed. 'You don't have to fight right now' were the words that eventually tumbled out. 'You can just hurt, if it hurts. Be happy, if I can make you. Regroup today and fight tomorrow.'

'Mum had to quit competing when I came along,' she said, her voice impassive. 'It was a difficult birth – we both nearly died. I suppose she should be happy I only ended her career and not her life.'

Imagining something similar happening to Denise made me nauseous. Adding a spike of anger at Paola Gallagher for making Lori feel guilty for something that wasn't her fault, I was swimming in feelings.

But I managed to speak the most urgent words. 'I'm just… glad *you* survived.'

She was in my arms – unusually motionless for Lori – her forehead nestled against my neck, and I felt as though I'd come to Trieste for this moment. Not tomorrow, when some race was starting. This was bigger.

'I survived to be your fake girlfriend,' she joked, her tone gentle. 'It fits, I suppose. I'm pretty sure my parents are separating. Gallaghers only know how to win and relationships have losers.'

Even those bleak words didn't detract from the power of the moment. It was only a moment, after all. 'I thought you'd started to doubt that?'

She drew back to study me and I regretted saying anything. She'd been drunk and I shouldn't have held onto anything she'd said that night. 'There's no way that both of *us* can win, right?'

'I suppose not.'

Licking her lips, she drifted closer and said, 'Except in bed.'

Except in this room, right now. 'We both win in bed,' I agreed huskily, tipping up her chin. Holding her still, I let the seconds stretch, waiting for my opportunity. I sensed it coming. I would give her everything in me and then hopefully she'd see that she was worth all that and more. It no longer mattered what would be left of me after it all ended.

Perhaps it was a family curse to fall hard – for the wrong person.

Lori

The air was too heavy in the room. I couldn't catch my breath with the way Seb was regarding me so fiercely, his knuckle firm but gentle under my chin.

I'd wanted him to help me forget the turmoil of Mum's arrival and the reopening of a season's worth of wounds, but whatever this was, it was better.

I didn't think I'd ever forget the way he'd said, 'Talk, then I'll fuck you.' The memory of his voice, smooth and a little bit cocky, shivered up my spine and I had to get closer. I dipped my head, my mouth at the base of his throat.

'Did you trim your beard for me?' I mumbled as I kissed his skin.

'Yes,' he admitted through soughing breaths. 'Do you like it?'

'Mmm-hmm,' I said, pressing a soft, teasing kiss to his throat, making him swallow heavily. 'Are we up to the fucking yet?'

He plonked me onto the bed more roughly than I'd expected, settling his hands on either side of me and peering into my face. 'Are we the only two people in the room now? I don't want to share you.'

My hair stood on end. 'Yes,' I managed to answer, but it came out mostly breath.

'You're here with *me* now? Not the team or Instagram or the sponsors?'

'I'm here with you.'

Nuzzling my ear, his voice low and inviting, he said, 'Just one more thing.'

I grasped his shirt as I nodded, drunk on that cocky tone.

'Your tits look spectacular in this shirt.'

Heat blossomed so suddenly I wanted to laugh, my breasts growing heavy. 'Thank you,' I said drily.

Dropping to his knees, he scrunched up my vest top, raking his hands up my sides as he tugged it off. Extricating me from my sports bra a moment later, he clutched me around the ribs and hesitated over my breasts with a lopsided smile.

'I've never spent enough time here,' he murmured, dropping his mouth to the inside curve of one breast. With his hair grazing one nipple and his breath teasing the other, my vision dimmed at the torture of anticipation. He gave the soft flesh a little nip, sending a thrill over my skin, and then closed his mouth over the nipple – slowly, while peering up at me from under his lashes, as though he knew I would splinter.

His mouth over my nipple, his fingers digging into my skin, he wound me up so tight I was wriggling and whimpering,

326

needy and demanding, pushing my breasts into his face, not caring if he knew I was desperate.

'You're so beautiful, Lore,' he hummed. 'You're beautiful when you fight and even more when you let me see you.'

He groaned and took my breasts into his hands, working the nipples with his stiff tongue, and any thought of questioning his words flew from my mind. I had to accept them. My freckly, restless body drew satisfied rumbles and needy moans from deep in his chest.

Pushing me down onto the bed, he grasped the waistband of my pink sweatshorts and peered at me again. 'These are cute. I really like you in summer.' Here was sweet Seb, LoonieDunes, and even though cocky Seb could get straight into my undies any day, sweet Seb was welcome too.

'I dream of this sometimes,' he murmured, before leaning in to press a firm kiss right over my clit, drawing a keening moan from my lungs at the burst of sensation. Slipping a finger inside my underwear to tease me first, he peeled it off, not even bothering to tug the fabric over my other ankle before coming back with a groan.

And then his mouth was there, nipping, sucking, his tongue nudging my clit gently and then swirling around it until I was losing my mind, shaking and throwing my head back. He teased me with one finger and I blurted out some gibberish.

'I can't take it!' I panted. 'I want you inside me.' Next time we had two months apart, we were having phone sex.

He pressed kisses up the centre of my stomach and between my breasts, both blowing my mind with tenderness and mercifully giving me time to recover from the overstimulation. Stripping off his shirt, quickly followed by his shorts and boxers, he came down on top of me, propped up on one elbow, and settled my leg firmly around his hips.

His feet were still on the floor, pressing the hard length of his cock tight between my legs, making my eyes cross and a gasp escape my lips. He soothed me, brushing the strands of hair out of my face as my heart pounded against my ribs.

'I wish I could play more,' he said with a small smile, pressing a kiss to my jaw. 'But you're so sensitive right now.' A slow, drugging kiss to my mouth. 'And I want to be inside you too,' he whispered. 'More than anything.'

Slowly, gently, with building pressure and an expression on his face that made me wonder if he was breaking a little as well, he pushed all the way in, locking his body to mine. We stilled for a moment, panting, staring at each other.

Then I reached for him, needing my fingers on his skin, more points of contact, and the friction broke over us as he gave a tight thrust. The sound that emerged from his lips was tortured with pleasure and would ring in my ears for weeks. His eyes slammed shut and his mouth came down on mine, hungry and clumsy and breathless.

Fumbling for my hand, he tangled his fingers with mine and thrust — again and again.

'There's no one in the world like you, Lori,' he mumbled. 'No one I can fuck like I mean it.'

My skin prickled, adding another layer of sensation to the onslaught from his body over mine. I needed to hold onto something in his words, but my thoughts kept slipping into feelings. The frenzied pump of his body into mine, so hard I had to roll my hips to take it.

'S-s-seb,' I whimpered through the first cracks.

'Yes,' he whispered. 'I feel you. Let go, baby. I'm gonna come so fucking hard.'

Flailing an arm out for him, I found his hair and fisted my hand in it. I had to squeeze my eyes shut as I went under, unable to breathe for a moment, buffeted and thrown and overrun, floating somewhere in sensation. I was only aware of Seb gasping in my ear, his breath flowing out on a rush as his body spent itself with mine.

He was so close I heard him swallow as we tried to calm our breathing. He collapsed onto the bed next to me, our legs hanging over the edge, and rubbed his forehead. When he glanced at me, there was a hint of haunted dismay that he quickly blinked back.

I didn't want to push him – not then. But I knew what he was feeling. We'd gone too far, blown this thing between us way out of proportion. I, for one, didn't want to go back.

Chapter 33

Seb

I'd competed in the Tour de France eight times, but I'd never felt the way I did at the starting line that day.

The air was thick with summer on the piazza in Trieste, the arches on the square bathed in sunlight. But it wasn't the stunning city – one I'd never visited before and wouldn't have time to see now – that was different. I couldn't remember ever having sex the day before a race and it was concerning that I could still feel her in my body. Maybe I'd fail the post-race drug test because they found traces of Lori in my bloodstream – one of the most potent performance-enhancing drugs I could imagine.

'You all right, mate?' Colin asked and I gave him a quick smile, hoping that would satisfy him.

No, I think I'm in love with your sister wasn't an answer for the moments before a race.

I was in a lot of trouble. She'd become so precious to me I was starting to understand that character in *Lord of the Rings* who sacrificed everything, only to become a jealous, shrunken husk of a person because the ring didn't rightly belong to him.

Not that Lori was a ring. She was a person. And people were free to make their own decisions – decisions like when to leave me.

I'd awoken to her pressing kisses all over my face, with my heart ready to explode out of my chest. I'd never been happier about having access to a single room, even if it meant that Colin knew where I'd been last night – and I knew he knew, because of the pointed looks he'd been giving me all morning. I didn't blame him. He was under a lot of pressure and my performance would have a knock-on effect on his.

He leaned towards me and said, 'Are you going to ask me not to say anything?' out of the side of his mouth.

'Hmm?'

'About you sleeping with Lori.'

'I didn't realise I needed to hide it.'

'Dad still thinks it's some misguided stunt for publicity. If he knew you were really together, things would change. And my mum is a whole other problem.'

Glancing at him with a frown, I wondered if he might be trying to help me, rather than warning me off. But that didn't stop his meaning from sinking in: I was a stick in the wheel of Lori's success – of Colin's. I'd been in her room last night instead of resting up for the opening stage of the biggest race on the calendar.

I found her weakness beautiful, but she was stronger by

herself. She didn't need me to convince her. She'd see that soon too – maybe already today, if I screwed up the way I was scared I might.

'We aren't really together,' I insisted. 'It *is* a publicity stunt – at least that's why she keeps kissing me in public.' I couldn't quite stifle my rueful smile at the memories of her flying at me and planting kisses on my mouth and how they'd been the highlights of my season.

'It's not why you weren't in our room last night,' Colin said gruffly.

'Don't worry,' I assured him. 'I'm not coming back next year.' I couldn't, with these feelings choking me. 'She'll be free of me soon enough.'

'Maybe not soon enough,' Colin mumbled. 'If Mum finds out you're sleeping with her – casual or not – she'll make life difficult for Lori. I try to take the pressure off her, but Mum's always been—'

'I know,' I cut him off. Cold was already creeping over my skin despite the warm summer morning and the crowd of cyclists. 'She told me,' I explained when Colin looked at me in confusion.

'She… told you?'

An image of Lori saying goodbye flashed behind my eyelids with the inevitability of a relationship with winners and losers. Except she might not even say goodbye. She'd ghosted me once, after her mum had sent her into a panic.

As I waited in the restless bunch at one of the defining moments of my career, I saw with sudden clarity that it was truly time to give up. For Lori's sake, for the sake of my own fragile emotional state, I had to give *her* up – in four days at the latest, when she left for her own race.

'I understand, okay? I'll stay away from her. She's heading off to train in a few days anyway and I know how important the Tour is to your dad.' It was time anyway – time for this dream season to fizzle out.

'Your… last Tour, then?' Colin asked me quietly.

'I suppose so.'

He extended a hand haltingly to me and I grasped it, letting him give me a slightly aggressive bro handshake. 'We'd better make it a memorable one, then.'

Later that day, after I'd launched him into an attack, my legs screaming from too long at my limit, I dropped back into the peloton to rest with the satisfaction of knowing he had a good chance of finishing well in the first stage.

And then I was free to think of the woman waiting for me at the finish line. Glancing at the 'X' she'd drawn on my forearm herself that morning, I knew she'd be there. What I didn't know was exactly why. I wasn't going to be anyone's hero today. This wasn't a one-day Classic where I could go hell-for-leather and see what happened.

As Tony had said that morning, 'A dead man is no use to anyone.'

I crossed nine minutes after the stage winner in 26th place – a decent result for me, nothing special. But there was Lori standing behind the barriers, her hair in a high ponytail. To look at her face, you would have thought I'd won the thing. I didn't believe I'd stolen her luck any more, but I'd certainly chased away Top Gun Gallagher right when Lori should have been back at full strength. Light-headed – not only from the exertion – I indulged the thing between us even as the clock ticked, letting her kiss me, brushing her cheeks and giddy with the view of her face after too many hours.

Cameras flashed, one close enough to make her flinch. And I couldn't ignore the question that rose in my mind: *how long until you're gone from my life again?*

Tony clapped me on the shoulder when I dragged myself into the team bus. 'Nice work, Frankie. You didn't leave enough for yourself today?'

I ignored the question. 'How did Colin do?'

'Fifth,' Tony told me. 'He's only thirty seconds down. It was a good result – a real team effort and I'm proud of y'guys!'

The Tour was a marathon – a hellish three-week marathon – and wasn't won or lost in a day. We'd stuck to our strategy and brought Colin in with a good time. We'd been saving our strength, not going for a win.

But I couldn't shake the feeling that this was the beginning of the end, perhaps because my agent had the contract from Harper-Stacked sitting on his desk, waiting for me to formally refuse it – along with two other offers I'd never wanted. Or maybe my luck was just running out now.

There were too many eyes on me at dinner, where I sat with Amir and Nelson, keeping my gaze off her. I was only allowed to eat, sleep and race during the Tour. She knew that. I was lucky Colin wouldn't say anything to the DS about last night.

It pricked me to think that the night with her truly had been the beginning of the end.

Discipline was important at the beginning of a stage race, so I summoned all of mine and I didn't even text her when I rolled over to go to sleep that night, Colin and I ignoring each other because we were both struggling in our own heads.

I woke up to a message that read: *Everything okay? I miss you. You're doing great.* I took a second to wonder at the earnest words that didn't sound much like the prickly Folklore I knew, but I didn't have time to answer as we ate an early breakfast and then set off for the starting point of the race, in the Julian Alps in Slovenia.

Conditions were miserable. The climbs needed all of us around Colin to keep the pace, taking turns to punch it at the front. As the day wore on and other teams pushed the pace, the guys gradually had to drop back. I held on as long as I could, but I was dropped eventually, slipping out of the peloton and joining the struggling gruppetto.

Although the sun came out as we crossed back into Italy, the day had taken a lot out of us and we had 19 stages to go. I wouldn't be able to face Lori's pride.

But she could read me too well. Seeing her in the crowd, I glanced around for the cameras as I unclipped a foot and pushed the bike towards her, my back aching – my balls aching, and not in a fun way. I didn't want a congratulatory kiss. I wanted to rest my head on her shoulder and why would she want that?

When I raised my head to kiss her, I wasn't expecting anything, which was why it caught me in the gut when she grasped my face.

'Seb,' she said, her hands torturing my cheeks. 'I have to go the day after tomorrow.'

'I know. You have to focus on your training.' I met her gaze, reading confusion there. God, I was going to miss her eyes, the way she could look at me and strip away the nonsense. Lifting a hand to the back of her neck, I said, 'It's your time, Lore.'

Tony called and I only had time for a quick peck on her lips before I had to get back to the bus. There were eight hours of driving ahead of us before tomorrow's third stage – not quite far enough away to warrant the packing and inconvenience of a flight, but long enough for all the riders to suffer in the coach.

Lori didn't drive with us and her mother was absent too, an observation that made my concerns flare up. She should just go, get away from her mum – away from me.

She sent me another message asking if I was suffering much, but I ignored that one on purpose. I had to let her go.

Stage three was flatter, with the sprint teams vying for position in the peloton. The pace in the final kilometre would likely be too high for the riders aiming for the general classification – the coveted maillot jaune, the yellow jersey. But

I got in a good rhythm, blocking everything out as I pulled Colin with me, even the fuzzy tiredness from sitting in a coach until past midnight.

It was only later in the afternoon that the looming disaster I'd sensed finally struck. At a roundabout on the outskirts of Nice, I was riding on the inside of a curve and clipped a barrier with my foot. A stupid mistake, a split-second lapse in concentration. A moment of weightlessness felt like a year of my life and then the asphalt greeted me with a crunch and a white-hot shock slammed through me.

I couldn't make any sense of the words over my radio for several seconds as only my heartbeat and the blinding throb of pain registered. But the adrenaline in my blood was working hard and I hauled myself up, looking around for my bike in a panic.

Amir was down as well, a graveyard of bikes strewn across the road between us. And up ahead, there was Colin, pushing his bike at a run to try to get started again.

'*If anyone can get to Colin, do it!*' came the DS's voice over the radio and I snapped into action, throwing my leg over my bike and pushing hard to catch up.

By the time I'd paced him back to the peloton, my shoulder was screaming – my legs stung, my eyes were as dry as burned toast, since I'd broken my sunglasses in the crash, and I didn't know how I was supposed to get through another 18 days of this.

It didn't help to tell myself I felt this way every single year I was named in the team for the Tour, or that I'd been expecting this irrational dip in confidence. It was like my relationship with Lori: I'd seen the end coming, but I still didn't know how to stop it hurting.

Luckily, she was leaving tomorrow and wouldn't have to watch me screw up any more.

I limped over the line with a grimace, almost wishing I never had to finish, because Lori would see me like this and any hope I had of going out of her life as some kind of hero had fled.

Flicking sweat out of my eye, I glanced at my fingertips to see a smudge of red and realised it hadn't been sweat at all. *Shit*. If I didn't pass a physical exam, I'd have to pull out of the race and then I wouldn't be of use to anyone any more.

Catching sight of Lori, I pushed over to her with a sigh. Surely she could see this was no victorious finish. She'd pull away, give me a wave instead of a kiss. That would be for the best, even though it meant missing our last kiss.

Our last kiss… With my vision blurring, I imagined I could see those words on the backs of my eyeballs. I'd always known if there was a first kiss, there'd be a last one.

But I couldn't do it. Not like this.

I drew away, hoping it didn't look as much like a flinch as it felt. 'I'm disgusting, Lori,' I muttered. 'We can't do this any more. You should just go.'

She opened her mouth to say something – disagree with me, I could tell – but I shook my head in warning and turned away.

I needed her to get the message that we were doing the fake break-up thing. She could ghost me again if she wanted. The alternative was saying goodbye to her properly tomorrow, and I wasn't sure I could survive it.

Chapter 34

Lori

I stormed through the hotel that evening, full of adrenaline and turbulent energy and frustration. Dad saw me, opening his mouth to say something, but he wisely reconsidered. I didn't know which room was Seb's, but I was prepared to knock on every fucking door until I found him.

He'd stopped believing, I could tell. He'd forgotten what he was capable of and would write his own failure if I couldn't talk some sense into him.

I was annoyed as all hell and he would feel my wrath. It was the only thing I could do to hide how much it had hurt when he'd refused to kiss me.

The pounding of my heart warned me I was acting on impulse – chaos muppet Lori. But I didn't have the luxury of thinking this through – or any idea how long it would take for me to recover from seeing him cruise in, blood trickling down the side of his face.

He was okay. I'd spent the past two hours pausing regularly to tell myself that.

Seeing a swannie with the first-aid case emerging from one of the bedrooms, I took a punt that it was the right one and stomped in before the door could close. It served me right that I was greeted by the sight of my brother's bare arse.

Whirling around with a groan, I covered my eyes as well for good measure. 'Can't you guys ever wear clothes?'

'I could be happily naked if you learned to knock,' he quipped through gritted teeth. 'Did you summon the witch, Frankie?'

'I strongly advise you to get out of my sight as soon as you've covered up your bits, adopted child.'

'With pleasure,' he muttered, brushing past me when he was dressed and pulling the door firmly closed behind him.

'You know, I still can't tell if you two are really close or worst enemies,' Seb said mildly from behind me.

'Both. Always,' I said, hesitating as I gathered my thoughts as best I could – which was more difficult now I'd heard his voice.

Bracing myself, I turned to find him sitting on the massage table that had been shoved into a corner of the room, a T-shirt in his hand. His shoulder was draped in dressings, with a bandage around his elbow. His eyebrow had been patched up with two little butterfly bandages and his eyes were bloodshot.

'What time are you leaving tomorrow?' he asked evenly, throwing me off balance.

'Early.'

His single, curt nod made me feel out of control. 'You'll be able to focus on your training.'

'Why are you so interested in my training?'

'You've been following the men's race for days.' He gave a gruff sigh. 'I hope it won't impact on your performance.'

'I've been on the bike every morning,' I said defensively. 'Not that it's any of your business.'

'But you've had enough setbacks because of me. It's your time now.' He tugged the T-shirt gingerly over his head and manoeuvred his injured arm into the sleeve.

His calmness – his *wrongness* – set me off and I planted my feet in front of him, my hands on my hips.

'You idiot. It's *your* time, Seb. You're the one in the middle of the Tour de fucking France. It's day three. It's way too early to give up. We all make mistakes. I know you crashed today and I know it hurts like hell, but you need to get up again and hit the road! Leave today behind you. You haven't retired yet!'

A crooked smile grew on his face. 'Thanks for the pep talk, Lore. You'll make a great road captain one day.' He blinked something back – it probably even hurt him to smile right now.

'Except you're not listening to me!'

He looked me in the eye, his gaze intense, but dark in a way that was unfamiliar. 'I am listening. I've been listening very closely to you since the first time we chatted on the server. I'm going to get up tomorrow and get Colin over the line – and do that every stage until the Champs-Élysées. But it's the end for you and me. You've worked that out, haven't you?'

My stomach twisted. 'We said after the Tour,' I began, but he shook his head to cut me off.

'There's no time left, Lore. I've been your mistake and it's time for you to leave me behind you.'

My breath spluttered out like the flame of a candle. *You've worked that out, haven't you?* I'd felt something – feared something. But my stubborn heart didn't want to accept it.

'What are you talking about?'

'You're back at your best. You don't need me any more and I won't change my mind about retiring.'

I felt as though he'd physically pushed me. 'Do you think I'm only with you because I *need* you?'

'We created the fake relationship,' he reminded me, in an infuriatingly reasonable tone.

'Yeah, but that was all a load of crap I made up because I wanted to kiss you without freaking out my family – my *coach*!'

If I'd hoped that statement would have an impact, I was disappointed. Alarm rippled across his expression, but then his brow hardened. 'You needed an excuse to kiss me because you knew your "coach" had a point, Lori. It's not the right time for a relationship.' I hated how calm he was. 'I'm maybe not the right person,' he added, his expression drawing tight. 'You have years to live and race and work out what you want. My time is up.'

How could he not be the right person? He was LoonieDunes. He'd been holding all my fears and vulnerabilities for months and I didn't want anyone else. 'You're not *dying*, Seb! You're just quitting. It doesn't have to mean—'

'We both know it means the end of... whatever this is too. You're twenty-six, a world-class cyclist. I can't give you the time you need to think about settling down.'

'You mean you *won't*. Things got real and now you're running away.'

He wrenched his gaze from mine, his chest heaving, but I didn't feel any satisfaction to have made him feel something. 'If I'm running away, it's for both of our sakes!'

He kept talking, part of me wanting to stop him before he ruined all of my memories. 'You don't even know if you want me for real. If not today or at the end of the Tour, one day you'll leave and the longer I'm with you, the harder it will be when you're gone.'

'So you're leaving me first?' I shot back.

'Where could we possibly go?' The strain in his voice cut into me. 'If I stopped you reaching your goals—'

'Cyclists have relationships,' I blurted out but, even as I said it, I shuddered at the memory of trying to make it work with Gaetano: constant travel, compromises, negotiations – and heartbreak at the end. 'Some do anyway,' I qualified in a small voice. Now my nose was stinging and my vision swam. 'What about that night? Didn't it change something?'

He hesitated. I could tell he knew exactly which night I meant, when we'd reunited after two months and discovered our feelings had got stronger, not weaker.

'Didn't it mean anything to you?' I pushed.

'Lore...' he began, staring at the ceiling as though I shouldn't have spoken. 'It meant *too much*. You have to see that.'

I shook my head. 'In that sentence, all I hear is giving up. I've asked you to stay and you're still leaving.'

'Yeah, stay in the team,' he muttered grimly. 'I wanted to stay, Lori. There were moments where I almost thought I would. This season has been the best of my life, and not only because of the results. I had something else to race for. Racing for you was... an honour.'

It was so damn hard to be angry with him when there were tears streaming down my face. 'You have this all wrong.' My voice broke. 'I've been trying to tell you. You want the best for everyone except yourself. You don't believe you could be happy. You have so little self-respect you don't believe *we* could be happy.'

He swallowed heavily. 'I *was* happy with you. On Zpeed. In Girona. It's enough.'

'Siena and Liège,' I added, my lips wobbling. 'On the goat farm. I was happy too, Seb.' My tears fell in earnest and I pressed the heel of my hand to my forehead, as though I could turn them off.

He sighed and hopped off the table to stand in front of me, lifting a hand, but pulling it back again without touching me. Perhaps he knew I'd break. 'We pretended for a while and it was something I'll treasure for the rest of my life.'

I wanted to shove him. 'You're making it worse!'

'You'll see it too, when I'm gone and you've got some perspective. We were always taking time out of reality – time you need to get back into your real life.'

Thinking back to what I'd said in December, in March, the

excuses I'd given so I could reconcile my ambitions with how much I wanted him, I realised I'd been naïve and selfish – and clueless. I'd had no idea what he would mean to me, how much I'd want to fight to make this work.

'I might have said I didn't want any distractions this year, but that didn't mean I couldn't fall in love with you anyway.'

Choking off my speech five words too late, I turned away with a flinch. Was that the truth? Was I already in love with LoonieDunes? I certainly felt like the loser in this relationship and damn Mum for being right again.

'I… I know, Lore. I didn't mean to make this so difficult for—'

He knew? I held up a hand to silence him before I broke in two right before his eyes – a new worst moment in my life. Taking one panicked step in the direction of the door, and then another, the realisation of just how dumb I'd been washed over me.

I'd thought my break-up last year had taught me a lesson, that saying I wasn't in a relationship would be enough to make it true. In my defence, spending time with Seb had felt nothing like my dates with Gaetano. But Seb and I…

Fuck, fuck, fuck, fuck, fuck…

The word looped in my head, because everything else was scrambled. I'd made a huge mess of this. How had I not understood what my feelings meant? I'd pushed him away when he was already so afraid of people he loved leaving him. I'd ruined the best thing that had ever happened to me and all I had left was the chance at a crappy trophy.

I made it to the door, clutching the handle.

'Lori, I'm sorr—'

Shaking my head vigorously, I cut him off. 'You said we'd always be friends, but friends don't give up on each other! Enjoy your cheese and your fucking B&B!'

His flinch was a poor consolation for the wrench of loss inside me. I'd missed a chance. My nose ran and my tears flowed and I managed to force myself through the door somehow, slamming it behind me, but for once, there was no satisfaction in releasing my explosive feelings.

Fumbling behind my neck, I yanked off the necklace with the two medallions, cursing when I used too much force and the clasp broke.

I'd lost him – completely. I'd lost.

Seb

The door slammed like an ice bath over my feelings. It was what I'd wanted: something to make it hurt less when this was over. Except nothing had happened the way I'd expected. I found myself staring at the door, my fist raised as though I were about to knock, when really I wanted to bang it down, go after her and change the way the past five minutes had played out.

I wanted the hurt back, as long as she came with it.

The door flew open and would have caught me in the nose if I hadn't had razor-sharp reflexes, honed by years of high-speed racing. Colin stormed in. I wasn't often struck by the

347

resemblance between the two of them, but the stab of regret that this was the wrong Gallagher and not an opportunity for the do-over I suddenly, desperately wanted, shook me.

But what would I change, if I could?

'What did you do to her?'

'The right thing – I thought.' Except why did I feel as though I'd destroyed something? The precious moments of the past ten months – on- and offline – gaped inside me like a wound.

That didn't mean I couldn't fall in love with you...

Those words were not supposed to emerge from her lips, not in any version of reality I'd prepared myself for. *I* was the one who'd lost my grip on the boundaries and fallen in love. I'd felt certain saying goodbye was the necessary course of action. But if there was a chance she felt a fraction of what I did...

I could still see her face as she blurted it out: reckless Lori. And I'd responded in a panic with, 'I know,' like Harrison Ford in *Star Wars*, so stuck in my own misery of emotions that I hadn't even told her how much it would break me to give her up.

'It had better be the right thing,' Colin growled. 'You look like shit, mate.'

Gulping, I tried to settle my feelings so they weren't written all over my battered body. 'I feel like shit,' I muttered, my voice gravelly.

3 July 16:22

LoonieDunes: I didn't mean to hurt you.

Folklore: But you did.

LoonieDunes: You'll thank me for this when you're my age.

Folklore: Fuck off, Seb. Don't text me unless it's congratulations on winning.

Chapter 35

Seb

After she left, I lined up every morning, more numb than anything else. The sun beat down on the peloton and every day was a battle of attrition that not all of us survived. Although each team was only allowed eight riders, one of our bigger, richer rival teams dominated the bunch, keeping the pace brutally high.

Derek developed saddle sores that looked like World War Three in his shorts, so he was sent home. Lars picked up a stomach bug and, although he battled on, he missed the timecut on a particularly brutal mountain stage and that was it for him this year. Losing two riders increased the surface area of Tony Gallagher's bald spot by at least half and our pool of prize money was also looking sparse, despite Colin picking up a few euros here and there with decent finishes.

If I hadn't been this close to my limit many times before, I might have panicked, but I wasn't going to cave – not on my last Tour. I was just going to suffer, which I had quite an appetite for. Colin maintained a good standing in the general classification rankings, but no one really expected him to win it. Tony talked big on the team bus every morning, but he knew it too.

I couldn't see either Tony or Colin without thinking of Lori. Every evening, I rolled over in bed and my mind played imaginary text-message conversations with her teasing me, until I realised what I was doing and started panicking.

Could people fall in love over text messages and virtual training rides? It was a stupid question. Of course they could. I had the evidence for it every time I looked in the mirror and saw in my expression the part of me that was missing.

I'd loved her – last year on Zpeed, I'd already loved her in an abstract way. Now she'd turned my real life upside down I struggled to imagine it without her.

It had all been real. She'd made excuses because she thought she had to be tough and I'd believed her because the alternative was believing in myself and I'd never been good at that.

Reliving that awful conversation at least twice a day, I couldn't move past her accusation that I'd given up. She was right, I had. But I wasn't sure I could truly believe she'd stay.

In the third week of the Tour, the DS adapted our strategy. Now Colin had settled into a solid position in the general classification, stage wins came into play and that was when the director said just about the only words capable of shocking me back into real life.

'Amir and Nelson will stay with Colin. And Frankie? Are you ready to have a go?'

My gaze snapped up. *Noooooo.* I was happily Colin's support rider, managing the team in the peloton and quietly suffering. But aiming for a stage win that I surely wouldn't achieve? Allowing the others to ride in support of me?

I heard Lori's voice in my head – again – telling me I had nothing to lose, which certainly felt true that day. The chances of winning were low, but... not nothing. Could I believe it? Not for her, but for me?

'Come on, boy. Your legs don't just shut down. It's your head that's the problem. But if you think you can't do it, I'm not—'

The words erupted from deep in my chest. 'I can do it.'

Lori

'That's it, Lori! "Top Gun" strikes back! That's our girl!'

As I crested the hill, even the director's gravelly praise in his ponderous Welsh accent didn't break through the fuzz of detachment in my head.

While my lungs burned, heaving in thin mountain air, and my muscles screamed, I was thinking about how 'Top Gun Strikes Back' sounded like a parody film about X-Wing pilots at the special rebel academy, with Darth Maverick in the central role. Seb would laugh so—

Seb would never hear my stupid joke.

As I came to a stop by the team car, the DS Alf clapped me on the shoulder. 'You're back, as strong as ever! Tony is going to be so happy with everything I've got to tell him.'

I managed a smile, but he thankfully turned away before

he looked close enough to see it hadn't reached my eyes. I was satisfied with my performance, proud of my hard work. But 'happy' looked quite different from my feelings after that epic training ride. I felt as though I'd lost all orientation since coming up to train at altitude. I wanted to win, yes. But that couldn't be *everything*. The goal felt so empty.

But there was nothing else in my life the week before the most prestigious women's stage race in the calendar. Was there ever anything else in my life?

There had been, up until last week...

Doortje eyed me as she tugged off her helmet. One small mercy of this training camp was that I wasn't rooming with my old friend. She'd grill me until I broke down and blubbered about falling in love. Instead, Leesa was in the other bed in my room and I only had to ignore the pinch of jealousy when she effortlessly put on a light brush of make-up and used big words, when I usually poked myself in the eye with the mascara wand and said 'fuck' for all occasions.

'Are you okay?' Doortje asked.

I forced another smile. 'In great shape.'

'I know you are, but that's not what I asked.'

I tried not to be touched by her concern – and failed. 'Seriously, it's fine.'

My phone beeped that night as I turned out the light and I froze, my heart racing. Part of me had been waiting to hear from Seb, remembering those months after December, when he'd obviously wanted to text me and I'd been stupid enough to forbid it.

But the message was from my dad: *Alf says you're in top form. Proud of ya, my Molly.*

I felt nothing but disappointment. Was that my future? Winning some races and losing some races? I'd never allowed myself to look beyond that, too scared of failing – not even sure who I was without racing.

Not sure what else to reply, I tapped out: *Tell Colin he's doing great.* Watching the highlights each day had been torture, catching glimpses of Seb's sharp jaw, his firm mouth, the tattoos on his ripped legs, and never his whole face.

He'd left a giant hole in my life.

I stifled a sigh. Even the day's climbs hadn't been enough to silence the questions running sprints through my brain. Resting had been the gruelling part, trying to concentrate on a film and then force down food – no offence to our artistic and very sensitive chef. I was the problem. Everything I ate tasted like the bones of long-dead saints.

My sigh was echoed from a metre away on the other bed. 'If you're awake anyway, do you want to just get it off your chest?'

'Sorry if I'm stopping you from getting your beauty sleep.'

'I've got used to you moving around in the night,' Leesa replied. Hauling herself into a sitting position, she switched on the lamp and reached for her phone. 'Doortje thought we might need to perform an intervention.'

'You and Doortje were talking about me?'

'Keep your hair on,' Leesa said with a roll of her eyes. 'We weren't planning your downfall. I know you think we all resent you for being Tony's daughter, but not everything is about you.' Her brow pinched, as though she hadn't quite intended to say that. Even with a pinched brow, Leesa Kubicka was delicate and pretty. If I hadn't seen over and over that she was a scrappy fighter on the bike – and one of the few members of the team who told my brother off for his pranks – I would have badly misjudged her.

'I know not everything is about me. I promise I'll have my head in the game for the start of the Tour.'

She gave me a withering look I was sure I'd seen her bestow on Colin numerous times. 'That's not what I mean. We're all behind you 100 per cent. I just haven't told you, yet, that I'm retiring at the end of the season, so you don't have to worry about competition.'

Retiring... The word alone was enough for hundreds of images to burst in my brain: cheese, a fucking B&B, the yawning abyss of nothingness. 'Why?' I blurted out. 'You're not even thirty.'

'I'm finally graduating in December. Apparently, it's time to get a real job.'

Her answer reminded me that I was paid an unusually substantial salary for a woman in cycling, even though mine still wasn't much to write home about. Unless we brought in lots of prize money, Leesa's salary would be a lot less than she could make elsewhere.

I studied her, the years we'd trained and competed together suddenly feeling short. I hadn't even taken the time to work out if we could be friends.

'Are you looking forward to it?'

Before she could answer, Doortje flung the door open. 'You summoned me?' She sat heavily on my bed, bouncing as she did so.

'The DS is going to get us into trouble if he knows we're having an intervention instead of resting,' I grumbled.

'It's for the greater good,' Doortje said far too brightly. 'So, tell us what went wrong with Seb. Did he break your heart or are you just restless now you've lost your favourite hobby?'

'What hobby?'

'Seb,' Leesa said with a chuckle. 'You seemed to enjoy doing him, if the pictures were anything to go by.' She tapped on her phone screen. 'This one was cute.'

To my horror, she flipped the device around to show me the smiling selfie I'd taken that day at his old school. Since I was sticking pins in myself, I fumbled for my own phone and scrolled to the next picture I'd taken that day. My stomach clenched, soaking in the lines of his throat, the way his lips were puckered against my cheek. The soft smile on my face. This wasn't helping.

'I was talking about *texting* Seb, mainly,' Doortje continued, oblivious to my threatening tears. 'Although maybe you had a more energetic hobby you liked to do with him. Ohhh, dear, sweetie,' she said suddenly when she caught sight of the photo on my screen. 'He broke your heart.'

She exchanged a look with Leesa while I sniffed back stupid tears. 'He wasn't a hobby,' I insisted. 'He was... a good friend.'

'And you realised too late that you shouldn't fuck a friend?' Leesa finished with a wince.

'Yeah, maybe we shouldn't have... without talking about...' We shouldn't have slept together while I was trying to convince myself that I could shut down my pesky feelings, that no one could mess with 'Top Gun' Gallagher.

I wasn't sure I wanted to be 'Top Gun' any more. I could be the very human 'Folklore' Gallagher, who laughed at corny jokes and felt pain and enjoyed the anticipation of receiving a text message from a special someone and did some stupid things sometimes – like blurting out that she could fall in love with a person who might not return her feelings.

Why had I ever wanted to forget those few months I'd spent living mostly online? I'd been focused on the difficulties – on the grief, the pain. I never appreciated the freedom to find myself, perhaps for the first time in my life.

He'd found me too – and he wasn't getting rid of me as easily as he might think. Folklore was just as much a fighter. Maybe Folklore would win races too and, if she did, then I could show Seb our relationship was unrelated to my career – and more long-lasting. I could show him that love could be a strength for both of us and not an impediment.

'I think the intervention worked,' Leesa said to Doortje in a stage whisper.

'I didn't realise we'd done the intervention.'

I chuckled, allowing a few damning tears to leak out. 'You guys are the best. I can't believe I'm lucky enough to have you on my team.'

As they cooed and wrapped their arms around me in a three-way hug, I wasn't sure I deserved, my phone screen lit up again.

'Is it him?'

'I'm sure it's—' I frowned when I saw the name pop up. 'Colin?'

Leesa responded with her usual eye-roll. 'What does *he* have to say?'

I read the short text from my brother and froze: *We're aiming for a stage win tomorrow — with Seb. I thought you'd want to know. He's terrible company but refused to text you himself. Maybe he needs a pep talk?*

My hair stood on end, imagining him a wreck of nerves, dealing with the pressure he wasn't used to. I wished I could give him a kiss, poke him in the ribs and say something silly until he smiled — or rolled his eyes. But I wouldn't give him a pep talk.

In Siena, before the Paris-Roubaix, I'd wanted to give him some confidence — some fight — but really, I'd wanted him to like me and I'd been scared there wasn't anything to like outside of my career.

He'd shown me my life had more meaning than winning and losing. It didn't make me any weaker or split my focus. I'd moved a little closer to his point of view, and perhaps he'd moved a little closer to mine. I wished I knew what he was thinking right now, the night before one of the biggest chances of his career. Whether he won or lost, I'd—

Okay, I hadn't developed that much chill overnight. He'd

better win. I wanted to see him wipe the others' faces on the tarmac and then I'd admire his body on the podium.

If he believed in himself enough to go for the win, could he take a chance on me – on us?

Lost in indecision for several minutes, my thumbs hovered over the keypad, my conversation with LoonieDunes on the screen – all eight months of it since the day I collected him from the hills after Colin's prank, all the cross-purposes and misunderstandings, fears and vulnerabilities. I treasured all of it and the main thing I regretted was telling him not to text me.

I tapped out a message and hit 'Send'.

19 July 20:52
Folklore: Live long and may the force be with you, my friend.

Chapter 36

Seb

Overanalysing everything on the morning of my stage, I dressed carefully in the precise order my feverish nerves insisted would be lucky and made sure I took an even number of spoonfuls of oatmeal at breakfast. Spending an age meticulously wiping down my bike in the team area near the start, even though the mechanics had already tuned it, I was a mess of jitters.

When Colin strode up to me with a Sharpie, I stared at it with a gulp. I hadn't drawn anything on my arm since the last 'X'. I didn't know what would be appropriate. Everything I thought of felt juvenile, too earnest or meaningless. Quite a lot of things had felt meaningless since that Tuesday when I'd tried to shove Lori out of my life. Nelson and Amir and the others approached, curious to see what I'd choose.

'Just draw something before I throw the pen at you instead,' Colin grumbled and I snatched it from him.

Not something to remind me of Lori, which was difficult,

when just about everything did. I thought of her message last night, that had made me laugh and tied me up in knots all at once. I'd never shared so much with another person that a simple mangling of two different film catchphrases could blow open our entire relationship.

With a deep breath, I drew the first thing that took shape in my mind: a rudimentary female form with balloons attached. Of course it reminded me of Lori, but it wasn't only about us.

Colin snorted a laugh. 'The blow-up doll?'

'Her name's Matilda,' I scolded, adding 'Matilda' beneath the picture. 'In honour of my first day on the team.'

Nelson snatched the pen and grabbed my arm, holding it still while he scrawled his autograph onto my skin with a cocky grin, adding 'May the force be with you' down my wrist. Amir added some stars. A few minutes later, I had the names of the whole team down my arm and Colin was approaching with a worrying glint in his eye. Working earnestly with the tip of his tongue poking out, he sketched something and then capped the pen with a click.

'You'll need all the balls you can get today,' he said, with not quite a straight face, patting me on the cheek and walking away to fetch his own bike. I glanced down to see he'd graffitied my arm with a cock and balls, complete with pubic hair, and shook my head with a groan.

Those Gallaghers...

When we lined up at the start, even though my heart was in my throat, conviction settled over me. This was a moment to honour my past and define my future. I might be retiring, but I'd always be *the* Seb Franck, who'd come second in the Paris-Roubaix and helped Arjan Hoogenboezem win the polka-dot jersey.

Stranger things had happened at the Tour de France than a domestique winning a stage – maybe even things like Top Gun Gallagher falling in love with her fake boyfriend.

Releasing a heavy breath, eyes forward, battle-ready, I pushed into action, rolling out with the bunch to kilometre zero.

By the time the race director's flag waved, like baiting a whole herd of mechanical bulls, I was positioned well at the edge of the group and picked up speed comfortably.

It was a hilly stage, not flat enough for the sprinters, but not tough enough to be purely the domain of the climbers. I'd studied the route until my vision blurred last night. I was ready to attack, ready to react – ready to make this the race of my career.

Deciding against following the first break, I stayed in the bunch for half the race, the radio in my ear providing regular updates on the position of the breakaway. I would have the element of surprise, because even I hadn't expected to be preparing to attack with all my strength.

The relentless peloton caught and reabsorbed the first breakaway with one of the other teams driving a blistering pace.

My thoughts seemed to speed up – or life slowed down – as I flew around the curves with the pack, aware of the slightest movements of my competitors as the wind created a tunnel around us. My concentration was trance-like and yet—

Movement over my shoulder was enough for me to realise that another rider was attacking. This time, I went. A burst of power, springing into life, I threw everything into speed, quickly outpacing the peloton.

The radio crackled in my ear, but I zoned it out, aware only of the burn in my legs, narrowing all of my focus to the road ahead, the rider I expected to appear at my side – and never did.

'Farking hell, Frankie! What was that? I was certain the peloton was just going to swallow you again. I don't know how you got free!'

I realised with a wince that no one had attacked. I'd been trigger happy – and somehow got away with it for now.

'You've got fifteen seconds, Frankie.' That was a good enough start. It was now a familiar test: mind against body. Only time would tell if I could keep my lead.

Fatigue tugged at my thoughts as the kilometres disappeared beneath my lonely wheels, the stone villages rushing by in a blur while the road filled my vision. I knew my body, recognised the point where my thighs threatened to cramp. I was certain they wouldn't. Pushing on and ignoring the twinge, I proved myself right.

I was out in front, extending my lead, chewing up the distance to the finish line. I was *good* at this – a solo break-away, my signature move.

Of course, the moment I thought that, everything went haywire.

There was a smudge of colour on the road ahead and then, in a mess of braking and swerving, I narrowly avoided taking out whatever it was, but I skidded and clattered to the ground with an 'Oof'.

Dazed, I turned my head and jumped in surprise to see a pair of beady black eyes staring back at me. A stout woman wearing a Cochonou checked bucket hat rushed onto the road to collect the ball of fluff. It was a long-haired chihuahua. At first, I thought I was imagining it, but no, the little dog was actually wearing a tiny yellow jersey.

The familiar crunch and whir heralding the approach of the peloton had me scrambling to my feet and fumbling for my bike. A spectator ran out to give me a push to get going. At any second, I'd be absorbed back into the bunch. But it didn't happen. My blood was rushing in my ears and it was many long moments until I could actually hear the DS over the radio, praising the rest of the team, and I realised they must have taken control and slowed everyone down to give me a chance to get going again.

My chest heaving and swelling and my heart pounding all over the place, I was touched by my teammates' actions – and flummoxed and more than a little amused by the chihuahua mishap that had almost stolen my lead. It appeared I had my own bad luck back.

As I passed through a little town of charming, run-down cottages with coloured shutters and geraniums exploding out of every pot, spectators lined the narrow road thickly, waving French flags and hand-painted signs. I spotted one that said '582km to Paris' which was less than encouraging a moment later on the next lonely climb, when my muscles were on fire and my lungs could explode at any minute.

At the top of the climb a cheer went up, which raised my spirits until someone said, loudly enough that I heard it, 'It's that Dutch rider. What's his name again? Frank somebody?'

There wasn't enough of a descent to recover and I ploughed on towards the next hill. A cluster of people up ahead put me on alert because I couldn't tell what they were holding. It was too narrow to be cardboard signs. I was worried I was about to be buffeted with blow-up hammers or something, but it turned out to be worse.

As I approached, coming into focus in front of me was a little platoon of Napoleonic soldiers in salute formation. But instead of swords, they held baguettes.

'I'm going to take a loaf to the face,' I muttered, the French expression for being punched more apt than any other time I'd used it in my life.

I didn't slow down, even as I hurtled towards the bread-swords, hoping I wasn't meeting my Waterloo. A man dressed as Napoleon himself standing on an upturned bucket barked an order and the 'soldiers' raised their weapons one by one to allow me through. Of course, there was one clumsy hero who didn't quite get there in time and I took some crust to the helmet, but I was through.

After a chihuahua in the yellow jersey and a bread salute

from a Napoleonic guard, it almost didn't surprise me when an inflatable neon pink unicorn stepped out from behind a tree and took a run-up in my direction.

Past a gingerbread man sprinting along the road with me, a guy in a mankini who made me want to poke my eyes out, and at least two pairs of spectators dressed as Astérix and Obélix, I swerved and struggled and kept my eyes ahead, no matter what. This stage had picked the wrong guy to mess with. I'd competed in cyclocross and a few obstacles were nothing but extra fun.

Just as I was beginning to think of taking the pace down a notch to rest on the flat, my radio crackled to life, informing me that a rider was putting in a chase, and I groaned, the sound emerging more like a grunt of pain. I didn't know if I could maintain speed to head them off.

I decided to let the rider catch up. We could cooperate to conserve energy and I would lose him at the last moment. But then I recognised the rider from my previous team – from the *youth* development squad of my previous team. The kid was 21 if he was a day.

'Salut, mon vieux!' the cheeky kid called out, calling me 'old man' as he hopped onto my wheel. 'Are we going to work together?'

'Why, do you need my help?' I called back.

But we were both caught out a moment later, when another rider shot ahead of us with an astonishing burst of power, his taut body dancing over the frame of the bike.

'Farking hell,' I muttered.

367

My stomach sank even further when the team sponsor logos and red, white and green stripes of the Italian champion's jersey revealed exactly who had caught up to me. Well, *shit*.

This race was cursed.

The bizarre obstructions hadn't stopped me, but now I was confronting my two personal demons as we hurtled into the hills near Tours: my age and my inferiority. Defeat seeped up into my throat – or was that just stomach acid? I was so close to my limit I could reach out and touch it.

There were too many kilometres still to go. I'd fought hard, but this was my stop. I'd never keep up.

Then Maggioli called out to me and the kid, 'One of you take the front or we're all dead!' That was when I noticed the lines of strain in his back, the way his sides were heaving. The kid was puffing too. If I could settle them, drop the pace for a rest, I might be able to open things up again once we got through the vine-covered hills.

I recognised my previous thoughts for what they were: giving up – too early. I was running away from success. What did I even have to lose? I'd already lost the one thing that had given me any sort of inspiration over the past year: my relationship with Lori, in all its forms.

Yes, I was 34 years old, would be 35 in another two months, but 'older' wasn't my only attribute, as an athlete or as a person. I might not have been a national champion and a household name, but Lori had said she could fall in love with me and Gaetano Maggioli with his Italy-coloured stripes and ego the size of the Colosseum was all out of luck.

If I was doing this, riding this stage for me and my pride, I had to get past those two little demons. And maybe... Maybe I needed to tell Lori I wanted to be with her – be *hers* – screw the consequences.

I eyeballed Gaetano, risking a long moment to get his attention. 'All right,' I said, my voice low. 'But you know apparently, my cock is bigger.' I stayed a moment to enjoy his flustered outrage and then took my turn at the front of our little row with a wild grin.

My thoughts went fuzzy as adrenaline shunted me into battle mode, my reflexes on high alert, the vineyards dotting the hills little more than a blur. We hurtled down to the Loire river, the spires of the city of Tours beckoning from the other side, the finish line just one bridge away.

In silent agreement, the speed ratcheted up as we pushed each other, a game of chicken to see who would be first to crack.

It was the kid. He broke too early, when we were still on the historic stone bridge. I had a moment of doubt, but didn't chase him and neither did Maggioli. Half a minute later, the kid panting and huffing as he blew up, we caught him again and then dropped him.

Maggioli glanced at me and, even though I couldn't see his eyes behind his reflective glasses, I sensed his uncertainty. He didn't know how tired I was. Hell, *I* didn't know how close I was to hitting the wall. All I knew was that it was too late to worry about it.

I needed nerves and I needed power for as long as I could maintain both.

Navigating corners at speed, jostling for position, I got on his wheel and he tried to shake me. My vision tunnelled, my whole body in flames, and I had the fleeting thought that there might not be much of me left to lie at Lori's feet and tell her how sorry I was that I'd screwed everything up.

God, I missed her. With everything stripped down to the pound of my heart, the clench-and-release of my muscles and the rush of my blood, she was still there, not a dream or a reason or a talisman for luck, but as part of who I was – who I'd become over the past year.

Yes, I was scared – terrified she'd leave one day. And maybe she would. But she was with me now, nestled deep among the things I loved.

Admitting that to myself, letting out the feelings that had eaten away at me for months, was like opening a door to a future where I was allowed to want something for myself – to be proud and maybe a bit arrogant. I was allowed to win. I could retire, if that's what the next stage was – no guilt, only thoughts of making the future work.

And getting over the fucking finish line.

1 September 16:33

zpeed.com/chatserver/channels/pace-a-need-a-training-partner

Folklore99: I don't know what time zone any of you guys are in, but I wanted to try a few climbs with a partner, if anyone's around. Not going too hard today.

LoonieDunes: I can boot up @Folklore99. Haven't seen you around before. Welcome to the server. Jump in my DMs and we can set up a simulation.

16:35

zpeed.com/chatserver/channels/@LoonieDunes/22683644572

LoonieDunes: Do you want to race or just ride?

Folklore99: Just a training ride.

LoonieDunes: Gotcha. Categorised climbs?

Folklore99: Of course. I'm still getting back to fitness so probably just twos today.

LoonieDunes: 'Just' twos??

Folklore99: I thought this was the 'A' pace group.

LoonieDunes: No, I mean yes, it is. Twos are good.

Folklore99: But I want to keep the ride private. No points
or leaderboard.

LoonieDunes: That's fine by me.

Folklore99: And I don't want to talk much.

LoonieDunes: Okay. I'll manage that.

Chapter 37

Lori

My stomach was hollow with nerves and my bed was strewn with strands of hair I'd tugged out over the last unbearable hour.

A solo breakaway? He was an idiot. He was an idiot who'd cost me a year of my life that afternoon – a big-hearted idiot who made me want to yell and cry and jump in a car and drive straight to Tours.

Seb and Gaetano looked well matched in the final sprint, even though poor Seb had been solo for over an hour and Gaetano safe in the peloton. He was up out of the saddle now, duelling my ex with every muscle in his body – and he had some rather lovely ones.

Looking at the two of them, despite the fact that I was supposed to be still hurt and angry, I realised Seb meant so much more to me than Gaetano ever had. I'd been my best self with him. He'd made it all right to be me – *me*, and not just a star cyclist.

I wished, hoped that he'd been his best self too – and not only on the road.

They fought so hard; the bikes see-sawed and Seb's expression contorted, his teeth clenched. As the finish loomed, his hoarse shout of effort came through on the video. Throwing his bike forward as Gaetano did the same, his wheel crossed the line—

. Half a metre behind Gaetano's.

After a heroic effort in a solo breakaway, during his last Tour de France, he'd come second. He wouldn't even stand on the podium, since only the winner got to do that for the individual stages. Taking up the mantle of responsibility for the team, pushing himself out of his comfort zone – he hadn't quite won.

And while I inwardly screamed in aggravation, I was far more frustrated that half of France currently separated us and I couldn't grab him and kiss him and tell him he was a fighter and a keeper and he had to believe that now.

I held my breath, glued to the post-race coverage for his reaction with as much tension as I'd felt in the final kilometre.

Unclipping his foot, he staggered and fought to stay upright, then his bike clattered to the ground and he went down with it. My heart seemed to stop. The coverage moved on to show Gaetano with his smug grin, hands up high as he sailed past the spectators, since Seb had fought too hard to allow him to raise his hands at the finish line.

When the video switched back to Seb, I hopped up on my knees, squinting close to the screen of my laptop as though that would help me gauge his condition. Two of the swannies had reached him, tugging him to a sitting position and helping him to drink. Then Dad appeared, slipping an arm around him to haul him off the road.

I needed him to be okay – not only physically, but to realise the enormity of what he'd achieved. It was suddenly clear to me that we'd both been right and we'd both been so wrong, those times when we'd argued about his retirement, about giving our all for a win.

My expectations had been close to impossible, especially the expectations of my healing body. I'd set myself up for failure instead of redefining success. Seb had never believed in success, so he was never disappointed, but then he'd rarely reached his potential – except today.

I was right to want him to fight and he was right, I was worth more than my palmarès. But maybe if he believed in me and I believed in him, there would be a way forward there somewhere. I didn't want to change anything about him any more, I just wanted him to get up, to smile – preferably at me, one day soon.

Damn it, if the last text I ever wrote him was, '*Live long and may the force be with you*,' I'd kick myself into the next lifetime.

The camera shot changed to pick up the peloton roaring through the streets of Tours, with Colin and Amir and the others comfortably among their number. But all I wanted to see was Seb's face, to gauge how he felt.

Gaetano's handsome smile filled the screen and I jerked

back in disgust, wondering how I'd spent over a year with him when I felt as though I didn't know him at all. Far from being tough, I'd been young and naïve, thinking that an element of emotional distance in a relationship was normal.

I'd never been good at distance with Seb, which was why I'd been so afraid of getting distracted. But fighting my feelings had been a distraction too. Loving him, committing to each other would ground me and not put me off course – I was determined to make that the case.

When the footage showed a top-down view of Seb from within a crowd of journalists, his chest still rising and falling erratically and his hair a sweat-slicked mess, my heart tumbled to my toes. His gloved hands on his hips and his shoulders back, his lean body filled the screen, all ridges of tough muscle. His arm was covered in smudged pen marks. He was alive and breathing and gorgeous and all *mine*!

His head was turned slightly to one side, listening to a reporter's question, but I stared at his mouth as it twitched, holding my breath.

'... *a real Jedi moment for you today, but it wasn't quite enough in that final few metres*,' was all I caught of the reporter's comment.

Bristling fiercely, I closed my hands into fists at the nerve of that guy reducing Seb's achievement to 'not quite enough'. He'd made a solo breakaway and held on until the end. He'd produced the team's best stage result of the Tour. And he was fucking hot in his tight jersey, every defined muscle pumped from long hours of endurance.

Seb's lips broke into a smile – wide and twisted and self-deprecating – and something was overflowing inside me again as I stared at him. If he didn't defend himself, I was going to lose it.

'*Yeah, credit to Maggioli. He made all the clever moves.*'

'*You* fought it, you fucking wonderful idiot!'

Seb continued, '*It would have been great to get in front of him at the end, but I had a cracking day and the team behind me. I suppose I had something to prove and, although I didn't win, I think I proved it. I had some great coaching this year – from all the Gallaghers.*' He glanced at the camera, the briefest of cheeky looks, and my heart flipped. '*As you might know, this is my last Tour, but I hope to be… involved… in the sport… still. You know, I love it.*'

Seb

Maggioli might have won the stage, but I won the combativity award – a nice extra bit of cash – and the memes. A particularly eye-catching press photo of me on the ground in the finish area looking absolutely wrecked had been captioned numerous times. My favourite was, '*Cycling: more expensive than therapy.*' I also quite liked, '*Rethinking my life decisions.*'

A great shot from my solo breakaway was doing the rounds too, one with the caption, '*Never tell me the odds.*' Knowing as I did that it was a quote from Han Solo, I was tempted to get that one framed. At the beginning of my career, I'd occasionally participated in the online fan spaces, before the pressure got to me and I couldn't take the attention. But I enjoyed scrolling the old subreddits while Chris massaged my poor legs that evening.

Although I hadn't won, the team treated me as though I had and it was so much that I ended up hiding behind my phone at dinner, even though I was only scrolling cat pictures and funny science videos.

Anything to stop me messaging Lori. I couldn't credit her for my performance today. But I wanted to share it with her anyway.

Thinking of memes and Han Solo and Lori, I spent a stupid amount of time creating an edited version of the iconic scene from the old film, where Leia declared her love, except when it was finished, it pinched me much harder than I'd expected. Like Leia, Lori had told me she loved me – in a roundabout way – but the more I thought about it, the more I believed she'd meant it, the conviction blossoming inside me like its own life form.

She'd probably never forgive me for my own, ill-judged, 'I know.' But she *might* take me back, especially if I could show her I understood how wrong I'd been to push her away.

The meme – and the subreddits – gave me an idea. It would be a little embarrassing – very public. But at least she'd have to believe I meant it. I only wished she'd give me a hint about what she was feeling.

My mind full of wild plans, I collapsed onto the bed after my shower. Colin was already snuffling quietly on the other bed, recovering from another day of suffering under the weight of the team's expectations.

Reaching reflexively for my phone, I saw I had a message. From Lori. My heart kicked into gear and I nearly dropped the device in my hurry to unlock it. Huh, it wasn't exactly the hint I'd been looking for, but I'd take it.

My mind was made up: I was mobilising the fans.

20 July 21:48
Folklore: *message deleted*

21 July 19:46
Folklore: *message deleted*

22 July 20:52
Folklore: *message deleted*
LoonieDunes: I know what you want to tell me.
Folklore: Yeah, right.
LoonieDunes: I look hot in bike shorts.
Folklore: Are we seriously pretending nothing happened?
LoonieDunes: It was 37° today. I was hot in my bike shorts.
Folklore: The goats can eat your bike shorts.
LoonieDunes: Ah, so you do want to get me naked.
Folklore: I'm starting to regret letting you break my texting rule.
LoonieDunes: I'm glad you did. How else am I supposed to butter you up for my apology in a non-confrontational manner?

Chapter 38

Lori

Seb's performance was abysmal for the last two competitive stages of the Tour. He'd obviously thrown too much into stage 18. He could barely keep up with the gruppetto in stage 19 and lost a miserable 25 minutes. Back in Colin's service for stage 20, he managed okay for the first half, only to fall back in the second. But Colin made it home in ninth overall in the general classification, a decent performance for his first Tour as leader. Then there was just the ceremonial leg into Paris remaining for the men.

Most of tomorrow's ride would be non-competitive by tradition, with the sprinters contesting the win in the final kilometres. But while the men had an early piss-up with the champagne popped before they even crossed the finish line, the women were actually racing the first day of our Tour. My brain was shooting off in a million directions.

Installed in our hotel in Lyon, trying to chill, I couldn't stop wondering if Seb's words on camera after stage 18 had been a hint. I'd even lost all willpower and actually asked him three nights in a row, before deleting it immediately after: *You love cycling? You want to be involved in the sport?*

When he finally replied, while Leesa and I were watching a cheesy Netflix romcom, the relief, the joy, the utter *frustration* shook me. We had a lot to talk about, problems to iron out — at least I hoped he wanted to iron them out too. But silly text messages were our love language and I felt tears pricking when he reached out in that small, but significant way.

There was a rap at the door and I was so jittery I leaped up and wrenched it open before Leesa could even press 'Pause'.

One of the members of the hotel staff stood there with a small box that made my stomach flip.

'This just arrived for you, mademoiselle. It's from—'

I grabbed for it rather rudely but, as I tugged open the lid, the end of the man's sentence made me freeze.

'… your brother.'

'Merci,' I managed to respond, closing the door after him. Slumping onto my bed, I glanced into the box with a little less enthusiasm.

'Did you think it would be a diamond ring from Seb?' Leesa teased.

'No!' I was pretty sure it would take me several more years to convince Seb we could do *that*. I would probably drag him to Gibraltar for a quickie wedding next week if he'd let me, but I was also only twenty-six and I didn't want to give him even more of a complex. 'I thought it might be another hint.'

'You're more excited about a hint of getting back together with Seb than with a lovely pair of earrings? Although if they're from Colin, maybe they'll shoot water in your eye.'

'Maybe my little brother is finally growing up — a bit.' I studied the gift with a smile. The hoops were thick, but small enough not to get caught on anything. Sending Colin a quick text in thanks, I slipped them in. He was a bit of a dick sometimes, but he was all right. He texted back quickly.

I'm sorry I didn't notice you'd lost one. Lucky someone tipped me off. Looking forward to catching up after you slay the others in the women's Tour.

A grin stretched on my face and lightness expanded in my chest. Everything was going to be all right. Racing was hard. My family a bit fraught. Things were up in the air with Seb, but he'd been wrong and I'd been wrong and I could convince him to give it another go when I saw him.

But it would be a whole lot easier to convince him if I won...

'Leesa, do you have a chain I can borrow? I broke mine, but I want to wear something tomorrow.'

As the men headed for the Champs-Élysées on Sunday for the final sprint and the podium, our Grand Départ was 500 km away in Lyon. Feeling like myself with my earrings in, Saint Francis and Joan of Arc against my chest and a redback drawn on my forearm, I hit the race hard, loving every second of attack and every breather in the peloton.

I spent most of the stage with a grin on my face, not only from the warm air, the surge of adrenaline and the taste of victory, but also because the crowds were large, a real Tour de France moment, although the Tour had been men-only for so many years. It didn't hurt that my old rival, Laura Colombini, moved in and out of my peripheral vision. Loredana 'Folklore' Gallagher was full of fondness and respect as well as the ruthless desire to win and, if I got the chance, I would wrap my arms around her after the finish.

I spotted a little round Cochonou saucisson van with its red-checked paint job. I saw people draped in national flags, raising a hand every time I saw the Australian one and even managing a few high fives: with a group in sumo suits, another in bikinis – the men *and* the women. Someone had even scrawled my name in enormous chalk letters on the road, making my vision blur with tears.

A month ago, I might have panicked about bursting into tears in the middle of a race, but that day I wasn't focusing on what could go wrong – only on what felt right. I would always have the scars, but my skin and muscle had grown over them – and I had grown more emotional soft tissue to protect my fearful heart. I was strangely glad neither Mum nor Dad was there that day. I was racing for the new me, the one who loved a dorky Star Wars fan and occasionally ate waffles and cuddled goats.

When Laura surged out from behind her support riders and went on the attack, I inwardly celebrated, hopping on her wheel and following easily. We took turns in the lead and I apparently freaked her out with my cheerful camaraderie, if her flummoxed looks were anything to go by.

As we hurtled towards Grenoble, through the sun-drenched valley of the Isère river, with rocky outcrops ranging on either side, a spectator shaking a sign up ahead gave a whoop loud enough to draw my attention.

After the supporter who took down half the peloton with a cardboard sign that just said, 'Hi Granny and Grandpa' a few years ago, we all had a healthy fear of unpredictable fans, so I flinched and ignored him, even though he waved the sign more frantically as I passed him.

At the last minute, I caught sight of the writing on the cardboard, messily handwritten, and I almost did a double take. Glancing over my shoulder before I could stop myself, I read the text again, still in disbelief.

'Allez, Lori!' he called out with a grin and I snapped my attention back to the road.

Three kilometres later, approaching Grenoble, I saw another one, then a cluster of three together, held by a group of women who whistled and cheered as I zoomed past. But no one knew I had used the handle Folklore99 – or, only one person knew.

Prickles of anticipation shuddered up my spine as more signs appeared in the crowd the closer we got to the finish at the top of the old fort in Grenoble. The stage ended with a gruelling climb, which gave me ample time to spot more signs as my heart expanded as though filled with helium.

Laura tried to drop me several times, nearly succeeding on the flat, but I was still within reach as we headed for the finish.

'Go, Lori! Colombini looks like she's struggling. Go for the win if you can!' I heard Alf over my radio.

As the lead rider, I was supposed to be saving my strength for the later stages, but I felt so damn good that I went for it, catching and then shooting past Laura 100 m before the finish. Time slowed down as the momentum of my bike hurled me towards the line. My heartbeat echoed in my ears – lavish and powerful. As I stretched to raise my arms above my head in victory, for the first time since I'd crashed and hit bottom, the future opened up in my mind, bright and shiny and new. And I bellowed from the depths of my stomach.

Coming to a stop and leaning heavily on my handlebars, time sped up to its normal pace. The burn in my lungs and shooting pain in my muscles were familiar, but the elation... I wanted the whole world to be as bright as this. I'd just fought my first victory as a woman in love – with a man who'd pulled a stunt that gave me every hope of fixing things between us.

Pushing to the barrier, I beckoned for a fan holding one of the signs to hand it over, stopping to give a couple of autographs, which nearly made me cry again.

The cardboard rectangle tucked under my arm – probably getting sweaty, but I didn't have time to care – I paused for jubilant hugs from the swannies and from Doortje and Leesa and Bonnie when they rolled in a few minutes later.

I briefly wondered if Mum would see my finish, but she'd

have to do a lot more than congratulate me on a good result to be allowed back into my head. Today was for me. Regardless of her feelings and sacrifices, it was *my* career – my life.

'What was the story with all those signs?' Doortje asked, making me laugh all over again.

'I'll tell you later,' I promised, as a race organiser shepherded me behind the barriers for the post-race podium protocol.

Then it hit me: I would wear the yellow jersey. Even if I lost it again over the course of the next week, I'd wear it tomorrow. Every disappointment of the past year fell away and I burst into ugly tears, right in front of the cameras.

The reporters were going to freak out to see 'Top Gun' bawling, but between the pain and uncertainty of the past few months and the wonderful sign under my arm, I was a different rider – a different person. And that was okay.

I only had time to wipe the sweat off my face before someone was zipping me into a yellow jersey over the top of my team kit, slapping a little cyclist's cap with a flat visor over my sweat-soaked hair, and then I was shoved out onto the stage to confront the cheering crowd. Clutching the sign, I dipped my head to receive the stage win medal, sobbing again and swiping at my nose with the back of my hand.

Someone else handed me a floral bouquet and I held it up high, blubbering and grinning. Fumbling with the slightly damp sign, I turned it towards the cameras and hugged it to my chest. I'd have to answer questions later, but I wanted Seb to see me holding it in the pictures – in the yellow jersey.

He was in Paris drinking champagne — as he deserved after three weeks of fighting his own fight. But he must have mobilised the fan groups in his absence to remind me of everything we'd shared, as though I needed any reminders, when everything from those early weeks — his patience, acceptance and even his bad jokes — was still fresh in my memory. I had no idea what he'd told them, but I kind of hoped it was the whole story of how we'd found each other.

I was more than ready for the world to know how I'd struggled after my injury and how that vulnerability had brought me to this moment. No matter what happened during the rest of the Tour, I was the luckiest person in the world.

I held up the sign, decorated with hand-drawn hearts and bearing my new favourite hashtag: #FolkyDunes4ever.

23 July 19:12
LoonieDunes: Congratulations on winning!
Folklore: You pulled a stunt today…
LoonieDunes: I did. Did it work?
Folklore: You'll have to find out.

Chapter 39

Seb

There was no way I could wait a whole week until the end of the women's race. Text messages and cardboard signs had been better than nothing, but I was free now the Tour was over. I probably would have blown it all off after stage 18 if I hadn't known Lori would kill me for that.

Today the women would conquer one of the most iconic climbs of the Tour de France, the Alpe d'Huez, and I would be there to see her do it – holding a #FolkyDunes sign and my heart in my hand. I'd been an idiot for long enough. The instant she'd said her feelings were real, I should have told her I wanted to be together.

It couldn't be too late, not when the image of her wearing a stage winner's medal, holding a bouquet in one hand and a floppy cardboard sign in the other, was seared onto my memory. Posting our story in the subreddit with my silly Leia-Han Solo meme and a plea for help had worked even more swiftly and effectively than I'd hoped.

One of the happiest moments of my life and I hadn't even been there.

I was mostly packed and ready to head straight to Huez to make everything right. I just had to get out of bed first, which was easier said than done, as my legs didn't seem to work – something about cycling 3,500 km across Italy and France over the past three weeks.

As I rolled over, a stab of pain cracked through my vertebrae. My hand shook as I reached for my phone on the bedside table. The veins in my arms stood out and I hated to think of the state of my legs.

Damn, I should have told her what she meant to me before I died.

Hauling myself up, even the heels of my hands hurt and, when I threw off the sheet, the sight of my legs made me flinch. I had a tan line as defined as the North Korean border, a spider-web of thick veins, as well as bruises and scrapes in angry purple and red. My head pounded after the champagne last night. I hadn't hit the celebrating hard after I'd caught sight of that photo of Lori on the podium and decided I had to live today. But three glasses had been enough to throw me to the deck.

'Stop shouting,' Colin snapped from the other bed.

I thought he was dreaming until I realised I'd been groaning and gasping with every movement. 'Sorry,' I said, my voice gravelly.

One of his eyes opened a slit. 'Why are you even awake?'

Leaning forward, I used gravity to help get me up, leaning

on the bedside table so I didn't overbalance. I felt 64 instead of 34 and if I hadn't developed the wild conviction that gorgeous, 26-year-old Lori might actually want me, I would never have moved.

'Going to Huez,' I mumbled, moaning as I leaned down to fetch a shirt out of my suitcase.

Colin's other eye cracked open. 'You still messing with my sister?'

'No,' I contradicted him immediately. 'Look, I know she probably deserves better than a retiring domestique, but...'

'She knows what she wants, Frankie,' Colin rasped. 'And I'm pretty sure it's you. Took you long enough to see it.'

'Hope so,' I said, studying him. Colin was young and he dealt with the pressure he was under in some stupid ways, but he was more perceptive than I'd given him credit for – and protective of Lori in a way I had to admire.

'Fuck, you've got to get out of here before this FolkyDunes shit makes me sick.'

In the breakfast room, hastily inhaling a few croissants and hopefully enough coffee to get me to Grenoble, I called the one person who could enable my mad dash to get the girl.

'What's—? Do you know what time it is, Frankie?'

'Already late. You know we have to get to Huez, right? How quickly can you get a car?'

'I'm joining the women's Tour tomorrow,' he insisted.

Time for the big guns. 'You're going to miss three race days? When she's in yellow?'

'All right, all right. Give me twenty minutes,' he grumbled.

When he arrived in the breakfast room, rumpled and sallow, he eyed me warily. 'I thought it was all over between you two. I thought there was never anything between you to begin with! She's ambitious – and young.'

'I know,' I agreed solemnly. 'And I'm retiring.' Taking a deep breath, I looked Tony in the eye. 'But she's important to me. I need her to see that.'

The sprinkle of emotional blackmail sank in nicely and, five minutes later, we were careening through Paris in a team car, sloshing coffee and risking our lives – or at least a traffic fine.

'I like you, you know, son,' Tony said stiltedly.

'Thank you,' I answered with a huff of a laugh.

'You're much better than the last guy.'

'I'm… glad you think so.' I might not have agreed to the extra season she'd wanted me to fight, but I'd found some self-respect. I was retiring to make us happy and it was the best decision of my life – if I could get her to understand. 'Thanks for making this season the best of my career – you and Lori and Colin.'

He smacked me over the shoulder, sending more muscle pain shuddering through me.

'I could almost say "welcome to the family", mate. If you're crazy enough to join us.'

I was crazy – crazy about Lori. And I was looking forward to the future in a way I never had before, once I'd admitted everything I wanted and let her respond.

'Eh, Tony? One more thing. I'm going to need a lot of cardboard.'

Lori

The crowds on the Alpe d'Huez were legendary and that day they were there for us – for the women's peloton. Our prize money was a fraction of the men's, but the racing was top class.

Doortje had fallen back earlier in the race after protecting me from the headwind, but Leesa stayed with me until she finally cracked before the final 20 km. I'd give her a hardcore hug when we finished, even if she had a genius IQ and a whole stack of gilt-edged qualifications and was moving on at the end of the season.

Laura Colombini had tried to fight alongside us in the breakaway, but she eventually dropped back as well. I probably didn't have quite enough gas to get me over the line in first place, but I might hang onto the yellow jersey.

I'd seen at least ten #FolkyDunes signs and tried to wave to each fan holding one. After my staged kisses after his races – which had been excuses to do what I wanted anyway – it was the true story of us meeting online that had eventually taken off among the fans. I'd found Seb's post last night and had another Folklore bawlfest. He might have even convinced me to watch more *Star Wars*.

Damn, how many days did I have to hold out until I could go and get him?

I shook my thoughts back into the present, thankful the feared distraction had come at a moment that hadn't required all of my concentration.

After the final switchback, the pace stepped up as we pushed for the finish in the little sporting town of Alpe d'Huez. The cheering spectators, the helicopters overhead, were all a blur as I struggled to stay on the wheel of the last rider in the breakaway, but my time should be good enough to keep the yellow jersey at least one more day

The finish line loomed ahead and I sailed across, waving to the crowd and tugging at my jersey with pride.

Glancing forward, I caught sight of my dad, rushing up to enfold me in his arms, and then I wondered if today would be another of those blubbery days and whether my new nickname should be Lori 'Waterworks' Gallagher.

'Did I do it? Can I keep the jersey tomorrow?'

'You did, Moll – third place in style, and plenty left in ya, by the looks.'

I nodded, letting my bike clatter to the ground so I could squeeze him back. 'I'm feeling good again, Dad. Everything's going to be okay.'

Giving me a sharp pat, he said, 'I know. I'm so proud of you – but not only for this bee-autiful colour on your jersey.' His grin was giddy and I couldn't help but return it.

'What do you mean?'

'You mother and I... maybe we didn't give you the best foundations for some parts of life. But it's a... joy seeing you work things out for yourself. You're strong and sharp and insightful and...' He dropped his voice. 'I hope one day your brother grows into half the woman you are.'

I wrapped my arms around his neck for another hug.

'Thanks, Dad. But I didn't think you were coming until tomorrow? The call of the podium, huh?'

'Ah,' he said, throwing a glance over his shoulder. 'It's not that, sweetheart. Someone needed a lift and convinced me you'd be happy to see me, even though you've been keeping me at arm's length these past few months – which is your right. I know it's not always easy having your dad for a coach.'

'Don't worry, Dad. I'm not mad you're here, but what are you talking about?'

At first I thought some zealous fan – or my idiot brother – had made a life-size cardboard cut-out of the figure I most wanted to see in the world and placed it with the support staff milling by the finish line to get a rise out of me. But the cardboard cut-out was holding a sign and since cardboard people didn't hold cardboard signs and he was the figure I most wanted to see, I was probably hallucinating.

The fact that the sign said, 'I Did Something Bad (Taylor's version),' and then I had the song in my head, confirmed it. Oh well, it was a lovely hallucination, even reminding me of the time I'd explained the whole saga about Taylor's songs. I stood there with an idiotic smile, enjoying the way his hair fell over his forehead in a wiry wave, the sharp jut of his jaw, his eyes that made me think of honey and waffles and everything warm and delicious.

The cardboard cut-out blinked.

My smile faded, watching as his hand came up, flipping the sign so it read, 'Back to December'. I took a halting step in his direction, my heart fluttering as he changed the sign again, and I waited to see what song title would appear next.

I could have guessed it: 'We Were Happy'. I didn't notice my feet moving, but he was getting closer, close enough that I could see the lingering sunburn on his cheeks, the dimple moving as he managed half a smile.

He flipped over two in quick succession: 'The Way I Loved You' and then 'The Very First Night'.

My vision blurred as I tasted tears, the rhythm of my heart stuttering and accelerating.

'The Lucky One'. 'I Can See You'.

My chest was heaving and I quickened my steps as he flipped over another one: 'This Is Me Trying', and then 'How You Get the Girl'.

I couldn't take it any more. I rushed at him, podium protocol be damned. Flinging my arms around his neck as the cardboard signs fluttered to the ground, I searched for his mouth and found it, sobbing into the kiss that I'd spent weeks wanting. Fumbling for his cheeks, I opened my mouth and ravished him, screw the censors, and his fingers curled into my back, sliding over my jersey.

Bringing his hands up, he slid off my sunglasses and unclipped the helmet I'd forgotten I was still wearing and held my face up, brushing his thumbs over my cheeks and studying me with all the heat and intensity I could take.

'I love you, Lori. I've loved you for a long time.' His lips thinned to a tense line as he stared at me with all the pain

397

and loss I'd felt myself over the past two weeks. 'I'm sorry it took me a while to trust in it – to be brave like you. You know I'd race until I was eighty if it was the only way to be with you. But I think this will be better. I'm retiring – to be on *your* team – always.'

I was melting on the spot – at least that's what it felt like, with tears burning down my cheeks and my nose running. 'What about your bad luck rubbing off on me?' I prompted with a poke.

His gaze dropped to where the medallions on my necklace were peeking out of my jersey and then back up to my eyes. He looked a little wobbly too, so I grabbed fistfuls of his T-shirt to hold him steady.

'Good luck and bad, we'll deal with it together.' He brushed a hand along my neck, tracing Leesa's chain and dancing his fingertips along my skin, as though he needed to reassure himself that I was real. 'I have two more signs,' he continued and bent down to retrieve them, clearing his throat as he shuffled to find the ones he wanted.

Next came, 'You Are in Love', along with a flash of his eyebrows. Crossing my arms, I gave a thoughtful tilt of my head. The last sign said, 'You Belong with Me', and then he glanced at me, his gaze provoking.

'I'm sorry I tried to end things. Us together… is everything. I've always pushed people away, terrified of the end, but you sneaked through online because I could tell myself you didn't really exist. I started falling in love with you the first time you laughed on the voice channel. You turned out to be even more amazing in real life and I'm still terrified, but I can't run away any more. I'm already so in love with you I don't know what I'm doing.

'I want to keep making you happy. I want to watch you and support you – since I won't have my own race schedule. And when you go and I can't follow, you can come back to me and I'll be there.'

'"Something Human" to come home to?'

'I thought you didn't like Muse.'

'The things we do for love,' I murmured, pressing another soft kiss to his mouth. 'But you obviously needed Taylor in your life.'

'I need *you* in my life. I *want* you in my life. And if that comes with Taylor – and competitiveness and losing socks and banter and amazing sex – then... you know I can do that.' His hands snaked around my waist and dragged me to him. 'Are we good? Are we... back? FolkyDunes?'

'I never let you go. I fell in love with you when you told Colin that Ken means to fuck in French.'

He choked on a laugh.

'Or maybe when I saw how considerate you were to Matilda. You're good for me, Seb, which is lucky, because I love you so much.'

A cheer rose in the crowd and we both froze, finally taking note of the camera trained on us, capturing every word. My forehead fell to his chest.

'Oops.'

His hand slid to the back of my neck as he pressed a kiss

to my forehead. 'Don't worry. You're wearing the yellow jersey. They have to treat you with respect.'

I lifted my head, smiling at him through tears. 'I see you noticed my outfit.'

He grinned, leaning close to whisper in my ear. 'You look hot in yellow.'

Yes, my luck had turned that day in the hills of Girona when I'd met him in person for the first time — the luckiest moment of my life.

Epilogue

r/Peloton · 22 July
Loonie_Dunes678

I have a favour to ask and it's a bit of a long story, so bear with me. I haven't been on here a lot over the past few years, but I know how special this space is to you guys and I hope you'll get behind me. You might have seen a few headlines and social media posts, but here's the full story:

Lori and I faked that stuff for the media – the photos on her feed, the kisses at the finish line. We weren't really together. But I was falling in love with her anyway.

The truth is, I met Lori last year online – on Zpeed. I mean, I met a user called Folklore99 and I was enough of an idiot not to realise that this incredibly special woman was, in actual fact, Lori Gallagher.

Then I joined her team and she knocked me off my bike – literally, but she also knocked me on my arse because I'd never met anyone who made me feel this way. I thought she'd never be interested in me. She's under a huge amount of pressure (which she bears so beautifully). We ended up with this mess.

The worst part is that she was smart enough to suggest we could make the relationship real, but I was too worried about it all falling apart – and then it fell apart anyway and I lost my friend, my online training partner, the brightest part of the past year.

I have to get her back and I need your help. She's racing from Lyon tomorrow. Can someone who's spectating write a sign and make sure she sees it? I think it should say:

FolkyDunes4Ever

Thanks all

Bisous

Seb

u/ProCyclingFan: Aw, how sweet is this? I'll do it! #FolkyDunes4Ever

u/Maison_duVélo_Lyon: Bien sûr, we'll make several signs!

u/CycleChick: I wish I could be there to see it! I'll make a pic and post it online! #FolkyDunes4Ever

6 January 03:22

u/Folklore99: Who is this?

u/Folklore99: He forgot the part where I stole his waffle. And he didn't admit that he *actually* said, 'I know,' when I basically admitted I loved him. The dork.

09:33

u/Loonie_Dunes678: It's too late to edit the post to add the waffle.

09:35

u/Folklore99: Would you believe, I saw one of these signs at the Australian Nationals yesterday – which I WON, in case people hadn't heard.

u/Loonie_Dunes678: I was holding the sign...

u/Folklore99: You finally made it to Australia and survived the snakes and spiders and drop bears.

u/Loonie_Dunes678: I haven't got home safe yet.

uFolklore99: Speaking of home, there's a bit more to this story that people haven't heard. LoonieDunes became a ~~canoe instructor~~ mountain-bike tour guide and the spiritual leader of the Lori Gallagher fan army. After she got her shit together again, Lori decided to move to Belgium for all the chocolate and waffles and beer. She got a lease on a place in the Ardennes with three bedrooms.

u/Loonie_Dunes678: ... (SFW version of WTF, Lori) Why three bedrooms??

u/Folklore: After extensive lessons in internet acronyms, Seb agreed to move his Zpeed kit into one of the bedrooms.

u/Loonie_Dunes678: And the other bedroom?

u/Folklore: That's my training room, of course.

u/Loonie_Dunes678: ARE YOU ASKING ME TO MOVE IN WITH YOU OVER REDDIT?? I'm lying right next to you!

u/Folklore99: This is the way Gen Z does these things, old man.

u/Loonie_Dunes678: I could still say no.

u/Folklore99: But you won't.

u/Loonie_Dunes678: Of course I won't. I love you, Lore – online and offline.

Acknowledgements

I am so very proud of this book and the teamwork that went into shaping it and polishing it and producing the best book it could be. First and foremost, thanks to Rebecca at Bedford Square for pulling this one out of her pile and being inspired by Lori and Seb's story. Thanks also to Carolyn for getting on board with the project and Flora for working with Rebecca on the rockstar structural edits. Thanks also to the copy editor and proof reader for their hard work for quality control. *Head Over Wheels* found an amazing home with the team here. The cover artist also had a part in making this something really special, so thank you also to Shaniya for capturing Seb and Lori and working with us through so many iterations. Special thanks go to my agent Saskia, for seeing something here special enough here to bring me on board. Also to Tatiana for checking the French and so much more — I don't know what I'd do without you. My other beta readers were also indispensable. For this book: Lucy Keeling and Madge Maril. Also thanks to my writing buddies for the support, the rants, the jokes and the cheerleading. There are now too many of you to name, but special mention to Lulu Morris, Camilla Isley, Laura Carter, Olivia Spring, Portia Macintosh and Sandy Barker.

As always, thanks to my family for supporting my hobby-turned-profession, for sharing my excitement and helping me keep on doing this when it's hard.

And lastly, the biggest thanks go to you, dear reader!

About the Author

© Tatiana Gimenez

After leaving Australia 'for a year' in 2006, **Leonie Mack** never went home and now travels across Europe jotting down love stories wherever she goes. She has a degree in languages and is an expert at taking public transport and travelling under her own steam on foot or by bike. 'Home' is now in central Germany, in the vineyards along the Main river, where she spends her time writing happy endings in English and speaking German with bad grammar.

leoniemack.com

Bedford Square Publishers

Bedford Square Publishers is an independent publisher of fiction and non-fiction, founded in 2022 in the historic streets of Bedford Square London and the sea mist shrouded green of Bedford Square Brighton.

Our goal is to discover irresistible stories and voices that illuminate our world.

We are passionate about connecting our authors to readers across the globe and our independence allows us to do this in original and nimble ways.

The team at Bedford Square Publishers has years of experience and we aim to use that knowledge and creative insight, alongside evolving technology, to reach the right readers for our books. From the ones who read a lot, to the ones who don't consider themselves readers, we aim to find those who will love our books and talk about them as much as we do.

We are hunting for vital new voices from all backgrounds – with books that take the reader to new places and transform perceptions of the world we live in.

Follow us on social media for the latest Bedford Square Publishers news.

🐦@bedsqpublishers
facebook.com/bedfordsq.publishers/
@bedfordsq.publishers

https://bedfordsquarepublishers.co.uk/